What Hope Have You!

For Jean
with love,
best wishes
from

Elaine Bunbury

Elaine Bunbury

AmErica House
Baltimore

First printing

WORKS CITED.

Shakespeare, William: The Tempest.
Browning, Robert: Caliban Upon Setebos.
Josh, 9: 21 - 23: The Holy Bible.
Shelly, Percy Bysshe: To A Skylark.
Bunting, Briann: The Rise of the S.African Reich
Shakespeare, William: Sonnet No. 73
Milton, John: Paradise Lost.
Santayana, George: The Life of Reason

ISBN: 1-58851-083-2
PUBLISHED BY AMERICA HOUSE BOOK PUBLISHERS
www.publishamerica.com
Baltimore

Printed in the United States of America

In memory of my daughter, Elizabeth-Anne for her encouragement and enthusiasm, and of my mother, Ethel May, who loved to tell a story.

To my husband, Richard for his patience. To my children Richard and Anne; and Rosalind and Grahame and to my grandchildren: Oliver, Johnathan, Rosalind, D.J. and Stephanie; Roxanne and Nicholas, for their interest and support. Especially Nicholas for his practical help with high-tech.

Acknowledgements

I thank those of my teachers at Durban Girls' High School who first made me aware, many years ago, of the social and political injustices in the country at that time. I have spent almost twenty years writing this story, which stems from the lives of member of my own family and others close to us. It tells of the struggle of women and their families over the last one hundred years, under colonialism and apartheid. The story illustrates the vast differences in the life experiences of the various racial groups in South Africa. It has been said that apartheid is now history, but that does not mean it should be forgotten because "those who cannot remember the past are condemned to repeat it" (George Santayana.).

Prologue

Kate
Vancouver, Canada
Circa 1992

The best holidays we ever had were those spent with our grandparents. They lived in Kimberley in those days, in an old house with wide sash windows and a verandah on three sides, with wooden posts and decorated railings. Overhead hung a corrugated iron roof, and in heavy rain or a hailstorm the noise was deafening.

Grandfather loved animals. He had dogs, cats, a brightly coloured parrot, and a monkey. I remember the day he bought the monkey from a sailor in Durban, much to Grandma's dismay. "Not another animal to care for!" she said. Yet it would not be unusual to see her feeding an abandoned lamb from a baby's bottle, or caring for a lion cub orphaned by a hunter, and she would put the two animals to lie down together in front of the coal-fired range.

The garden at the back stretched up to the *kopje* then joined with the *veld* which extended to the hills on the distant horizon. It was a child's paradise. A place to play cricket. A place to climb trees. There was an old water-tank we swam in on scorching summer days.

We often packed a picnic basket and walked to the Modder River; past the tall iron windmill creaking in protest at each passing gust of wind. We lazed in the shade of the willow trees, their pale green tresses trailing, tranquilly in the slowing flowing stream. When clouds gathered low on the horizon and the sky darkened in a sudden thunder storm, the branches bent and swayed like distressed damsels in a Gothic novel.

My brothers took fishing rods and joined Grandpa on the bank to catch bass for supper while Gran and I had to wash the picnic plates before settling on the rug. I would lie back chewing a piece of long grass, watching strange shapes form in the clouds as they drifted high, while listening to Grandma's tales. She was a wonderful storyteller.

"Kate," she would begin, "Did I ever tell you about the time my sister, Martha and I..." and she told of the journey from Europe in a sailing vessel with her parents, sister and baby brother when she was a small child. She told of the trip by wagon from the Cape of Good Hope to the diamond fields in Kimberley. She described the "Big Hole" where diamonds were dug out of the ground. She talked of life on the diggings in those early days, the laughter and the tears, the hope and despair, the good times and the sad.

One day, just before she died, as I sat at her bedside preparing to read to her, she handed me a small key.

"Take this, my child, and open my bureau. You will find two books. One is my Mother, Anna's diary, and the other my own. I am putting them in your care. Keep them safely and one day write it all down. It is important for a family to know about its beginnings." I was sixteen when Grandma died, and the Second World War was waging in the world.

Now the story is told. The story of our family and how it grew and spread over the land. The story of a friendship begun in tragic and unusual circumstances between my great-grandmother, Anna, and the young black woman, Ruth.

It is also the story of Ruth's family. How the actions of a white man changed forever this black woman's life and the lives of her descendants. My Mother, Meg, told me about her childhood in Kimberley during the Boer War and later how the First World War affected her life and consequently the family.

After the old home in Kimberley was sold when Grandfather died, I came across a small wooden box with the name of my great-grandfather, "Frederick" carved upon it. Inside were letters written to him, all carefully tied together, and a shabby notebook he used as his diary. I also found a bundle of letters in an envelope marked "Sara."

Many years later I was able to put the pieces together when, by a strange coincidence, I met Sara's daughter, Emma, and learnt that Sara was in fact, Ruth's daughter. Emma and Mother renewed their old friendship. How closely our families were bound together and yet so far apart, separated by the gulf of Apartheid.

Chapter 1

The girl turned over, putting out her hand for Tembu, then remembered he wasn't there. He had been gone more than three months. Glancing towards the small narrow opening of the hut, she saw the eastern sky slashed red, stained, as if with the blood of a freshly slaughtered ox. She felt a sense of foreboding and shuddered. A rooster crowed. In the distance a dog barked. She stood, stretching both arms above her head, then leant over and rolled up the straw pallet. Picking up the child, she bent as she went through the low doorway, carrying him on her hip down to the river in the valley which, after the long dry season, was now a narrow stream. Slipping out of her sarong, she stepped into the cold water, splashing it over them both. They shivered, for although the sun shone, a late frost covered the ground and so she quickly returned to her hut that stood among the others, clustered like mushrooms on the hillside.

The girl's large dark eyes were set slantwise above high cheek bones and her full lips filled her face. Her hair was cut close to her head. Beaded bracelets wound around her arms and ankles. Beads hung around her neck and from her ears.

She heard the voices of others in the village as they woke and prepared for the day. Her mother lit the fire under the three-legged cast-iron pot of *putu* and the girl inhaled the smell of the porridge. She put the child down among the grass stalks and swept the dung floor of the hut. The walls were made of sun-hardened clay with painted designs in shades of sepia.

Within the hour she would walk with the other women to the distant farm buildings. They walked in single file, brushing against the long dry grass, most of them balancing pots or jars on their heads and with babies tied to their backs. They wore long cotton-print dresses provided by the farmer's wife.

As the women walked they talked of this and that; how the rains were late and the crops were dying and what must be done about the children. But the girl and two of her cousins lagged behind. She saw the stream winding its way down the hillside, like a sluggish snake, she thought, winding its way between the banks of the *donga*, slithering and sliding, spiked tongue probing between the rocks. She told them that she had heard the farmer's wife complaining to her husband.

9

"We can't have the women working in the kitchen in tribal clothes with their breasts bare, y'know Frikkie, the preacher wouldn't like it," the girl mimicked, pitching her voice high. "And then," she told her cousins, a look of indignation on her face, "the farmer, he wink at me an' he pinch my bottom even as his wife she standing right there beside him reading the recipe in the cook book. Then he say," and her voice deepened, "I reely don' notice what the *kaffirs* wear. And his wife she say, I'm telling you, man Frikkie, you can't be too careful, they mus' cover their heads, they mos' likely got vermin." The cousins giggled as the girl continued her story.

"Oh! I dunno, the farmer, he say to his wife. But the wife, she get cross an' she say. I know what I'm saying, hey! They not clean, they don't wash so much. Anyway, you tell them they mus' wear these *doeks* when they work here." The girl acted out the wife's indignation while her cousins stopped in the pathway, throwing up their arms then bending over, shaking with laughter. Then the girl's tone changed abruptly. She bowed her head and wiped her eyes with the palms of her hands.

"But I am afraid," she said, "the farmer, he watching me all the time. What mus' I do?"

Her companions sensed her change of mood and understood her concerns. Their laughter dissolved as they soberly shook their heads.

"Oew! that farmer, he is bad, all the time he do that," one of her cousins replied while placing an arm around her shoulders.

The farmer, Frikkie, was a lean man, tall and angular with ginger hair, bleached by the sun. Light lashes fringed light blue eyes. His pale skin, where exposed, was freckled and burnt red. His wife, Wilhelmena, was large. Rolls of fat clung under her chin and under her arms, hanging in layers, like lard. It's no wonder he looked elsewhere but white women kept their distance, afraid of his wife whose family had influence in the community, and so he confined his attentions to the black women.

The women continued their walk up the pathway. Their broad feet with pale cream soles were scratched and scarred, toes splayed and heels caloused. Wilhelmena did not provide shoes. The girl now talked about the father of her child.

"Tembu, he say he hear that the white people dig bright stones out of the ground, and that there are many jobs to be had in that place called Kimberley."

"Oew! And they say the money, it is good?"

"Ja, very good." She smiled, then her expression changed, "He say he will send a message, but I am hearing nothing."

The women shook their heads in sympathy as they walked on in silence then one of the cousins remarked, "The *mealie* crop is bad."

"Ja, ja," they replied in unison, "very bad."

"Will there be no rain again this year?" The girl asked. The others clicked their tongues and shook their heads, then the elder cousin said,

"For too long there has been no rain."

Approaching the back door of the farmhouse, the women untied their babies, leaving them in the yard with an older child, before entering the kitchen. The air inside was hot and humid, heavy with the smell of stale food. Fried sausages from breakfast; onion stew cooking for dinner; the wet-fur smell of dogs; the sour stench of sweat. Flies hovered over a bowl of ripe fruit.

The girl carried the bundle of clothes outside then lifted the heavy galvanised iron bathtub from the hook on the wall, filling it with saucepans of water heated on the coal-fired range. She carried out the ridged scrubbing-board and home-made soap and began her task, singing in rhythm with her movements. At last, the clothes, rinsed and wrung, hung on the wash line; long grey underpants, red flannel petticoats, calico bloomers, billowed outwards filled by the wind like barrage balloons bobbing against the blue sky.

She ate some *putu* and boiled spinach for lunch then fed the child from her breast until he fell asleep, when she put him on her back, wrapped in a cloth with the ends tied in front. She rocked to and fro, singing a lullaby, "tula, tula, tula babba," and began work in the laundry off the kitchen. She lifted the flat-irons off the hot plate above the furnace to press the clothes. When the farmer walked in she lowered her eyes.

"When is Tembu coming back?"

"I dunno Master."

"What you mean you don' know?"

"She say she's grandmother she die and she mus' go home. The girl couldn't tell him Tembu had left to find work in the town because he didn't earn enough on the farm.

"You bleddy *kaffirs*, you always lying. Always the same story about a grandmother dying," he said, while reaching to stroke her breast through the unbuttoned opening of her blouse. She jerked aside, knocking the flat-iron to the stone floor and, bending to pick it up she felt his hand groping her leg. He pulled her towards him when a step sounded.

"What you doing in here, Frikkie? I thought you was going to look for them missing animals."

"Oh ja, ja, I'm jus' going," abruptly moving away from the girl and bending over to hide his red face, pretending to look under the table. "But the girl say a button come off my shirt. I'm jus' looking for it hey!"

His wife splayed her legs, awkwardly leaning over next to him while holding on to the table for support.

"Can't see nothing here." She looked up and scowled at the girl, "You mus' take more care when you wash the master's shirts. Let me see which one's lost a button?" she said, reaching towards the pile of clothes on the table.

"*Nie, nie, dit maak nie saak nie*, it doesn't matter." The farmer took his wife by the arm to haul her up and steered her out the door. The girl trembled, covering her face with both hands.

When her work was done at the end of the day, the girl began the long walk back to the kraal across the valley. She was alone because on wash days she finished late. She walked beside the river winding down the hill and noticed clouds gathering on the horizon then heard thunder. Lightning streaked the darkening sky and in the distance funnel-shaped dust clouds coiled upwards. Thunder echoed again from the mountains and then the rain fell, a slanting silver-beaded curtain. She ran under some bushes for shelter, slipping and falling on the dirt pathway that had become muddy. She squatted, holding her child in her arms watching the swollen river. She waited until the storm was over.

The sun broke through the clouds and her thoughts turned to her family in the village where her father and uncles would already be sitting around the fire, smoking pipes and conferring with other elders of the Tribe about serious matters affecting their people. Her father was the Chief and his younger brother was the Induna, or Headman under him. Her mother and aunts, would be grinding corn on hollow smoothed-out stones, preparing the evening meal, while her sisters and cousins and the wives of her brothers, weaving grass mats or braiding beads into each other's hair. She glanced down at her muddied dress and legs and decided to wash in the river, now swollen and surging after the sudden rainstorm. *Now it's like a leopard,* she thought, leaping and lurching over the rocks and boulders, licking the edges of the *donga.* She felt suddenly afraid.

Frikkie had spent the day searching for missing cattle. With the setting sun he turned his horse towards the homestead and galloped across the veld. As he approached the river he noticed the gathering clouds and reigned in his horse. He jumped from the saddle and tethered the animal to a tree stump. Taking a flask of brandy from his pocket, he put it to his dry lips and sat under the trailing branches of the willow trees to shelter from the rain. The storm soon passed and he savoured the wet-earth smell of the *veld*. He heard a movement across the water and, peering through the leaves, saw the girl laying the sleeping child on the bank before slipping out of her long cotton-print dress and wading into the river.

"God-in-Hemel!" He watched the water gleam and glisten, glancing off her shiny skin. Her full breasts were firm as melons, *yurrah man, but soft hey*, he thought, *like ripe peaches.* As she turned away in the diminishing light, he saw her swaying buttocks. She reached the far bank then pulled on her dress and picked up the child, tying him on her back before walking up the pathway. The farmer's eyes followed her until she disappeared over the top of the embankment. He jumped up and ran after her, his breath exploding in short bursts when he bent over and began to creep along the pathway hidden by the long grass.

As she approached the wild fig tree growing next to the path, the girl's thoughts were on Tembu. She remembered walking there with him before he left for the town.

"Please don' go away," she had said.

"Why you go?"

"I mus' go. I not earning enough money on the farm to pay your father the *lobola* so we can be married."

"When you coming back?"

"I can't say. I don' know what job I'm finding. If I'm getting work on the mine, they pay good money, then I'm coming back soon an' we can be married then you can come live in the town."

"But I not want to leave my family an' live in the town. You not ask me if I'm wanting to go."

Noticing her tears he pulled her towards him. "Don' cry, *intombi*. It will be alright, I promise you." He had pushed her down beneath him into the long grass and she smiled to herself, recalling that moment.

She began to sing, but her smile froze and her song died, as a hand closed over her mouth. Letting out a muffled scream, she fell forward on to her knees. The cloth around her waist loosened and the child rolled to the ground, crying loudly on the deserted hillside, under the darkening sky.

"Lis'en here, girl! Don't make a noise or I'll put this in your throat." She recognised the farmer's voice. He held a short knife in front of her face "You do what I say, hey! You'll like it plenty I promise." With his free hand he loosened the belt around his trousers then pulled up his shirt and she felt his hot bare chest and his moist clammy skin. She struggled, kicking and pushing, but he was too strong and her resistance only increased his desire. He straddled her threshing body.

"Please master, please let me go. My child is very afraid. *Asseblief baas*."

"Hou stil!" he said, hitting her across the face.

She stopped struggling, sobbing silently too afraid to scream. He put his face next to hers, and she saw the saliva drooling from his mouth and smelt brandy on his breath. His beard scratched her skin, "That's it girl. You do what I say, you understand? Then you and me, we can have a good time. I can give you plenty things, more than Tembu can give you. Only you don' tell anyone, you hear." He loosened his grip to unbutton his trousers and she attempted to escape but he caught her and beat her with his belt, the sharp, shiny, silver buckle tearing her skin.

After he had finished he rolled off her and stood up, pulling his trousers over his knees. "I can make a place for you in the old barn. Don't worry about Tembu. He won't come back. I'll arrange that." He gave a sly grin. "And don't you tell your father. If you tell him and make trouble, I'll say your father stole my cattle and I'll send your people off my lands." Buckling his belt, he walked away over the hillside to fetch his horse.

Wilhelmena greeted him at the farmhouse door, "Why is you so laat, Frikkie? You're very late, man. I've been waiting for you this past hour. It's the prayer meeting at the Church tonight. Did you forget?"

"Ooh ja! ja! I did forget hey! I'm sorry I'm late, but I couldn't help it man, it's these bleddy *kaffirs*, they're stealing my cattle again. I had to go and look myself because Tembu's left. He sent a message with the girl to say his grandmother died, bleddy liar! I don't believe him. They're all the same y'kow, they don' care a damn about family. Tembu goes off, leaving the girl and his child because I suspect he's got another woman somewhere. He lies to me and then I end up having to do his work." The farmer paused and smirked, "Ja, that's what made me late, doing Tembu's work."

"You too good to them, that's the trouble. They take advantage of you. You got to show the kaffir who's the boss. But we must leave now. Jeremiah's got the cart ready to drive us to the Church. It's time to do the Lord's work."

"Of course, m'dear, time to do the Lord's work," the farmer replied, frowning somberly then, looking at his stained trousers, "but I must jus' change."

"Nie man, Frikkie! I told you, we're late already. The Preacher will be cross, he don't like people coming late to Bible meetings."

"Well then, I'll just wash," he replied, putting both hands out.

"Nie man!" she repeated, voice rising in irritation. "It's too late, hey! You should have thought of it before, and come home early." She advanced on him, finger pointing, mouth open, spewing spittle as she screamed, "I already say we don't have time," then, turning abruptly, she walked out the back door.

He shrugged, rolling down his shirtsleeves and mumbling, "Bleddy woman, thinks 'cause she got all the money she can push me around," but he grinned at the empty kitchen.

Dragging herself up on her knees, the girl crawled to her crying child then, sitting with her legs stretched, pulled him towards her. She picked him up and held him close, rocking back and forth.

"Don' cry, my baby. Tula baba," she comforted, then leant over and threw up in the long grass, gagging from the sour smell of the farmer and the sweet smell of her vomit. She heard the plaintive sound of a gourd and saw the shepherd, strolling over the hill behind the straggling sheep and remembered the red sky that morning.

"Oew! Oew! What can I do if the farmer come again." Rocking on her haunches, and nursing her ache, she looked across the *veld* and saw the Baobab tree silhouetted against the sunset. Its short, bare, entangled branches, stretched upwards and looked like roots, as if it grew upside down.

The child began to cry. She stood and, tying him on her back, limped slowly to the *kraal*. No one saw her in the darkness, as she crept into her hut. She carefully took the sleeping child off her back, put him on the mat then lay down next to him, trying to quiet her fears, when she heard footsteps then her father's voice calling.

"Ja Obaba, I am here Obaba."

She watched her father stoop under the low doorway and step inside. She stood to greet him nervously, noticing his anger. "My brother's child, she telling my brother and my brother, he telling me that you say the farmer he watching you. What you mean? I hope you not encourage the white man because you think he can give you things."

"No, Obaba."

"That can only bring plenty problems," wagging his finger in her face. "The white man can take our lands. You understand?"

"I understand Obaba."

He put both hands on her shoulders and shook her. "Now you lissen to me. I don't want trouble with the white man and I don't want the whiteman's blood in our family. You mus' not let him think..." his voice dropped.

She shook her head, horrified, *How can my father say that*, she thought, *how can he think I encourage the white man?* But she said, "Oew! my father, you think I am bad. It is not so."

"I hope not, my daughter."

She knew her father was fair and just, but she also knew he was powerless against the white farmer and would not sacrifice the family for her. He left her with a warning to be careful and to stay out of the farmer's way. She knew that to be impossible now. She curled up on the mat next to her child, crying silently. *Oew, Tembu, why you not come back; why you not sending a message.* She recalled walks across the *veld* holding his hand as he taught her the names of the birds and the different buck like the springbok that leapt so high with curved back and straight legs. She shook her head, *Tembu, you always help when I have problems, why you not come now?* She lay down, twisting her bead necklaces.

The following day the girl gathered her few belongings, the little money Tembu left her tied in a cloth and, with the child strapped to her back and a bundle of clothing on her head, she slipped away from the huddle of huts. The sun in a cloudless sky beat down as she trudged across the veld; along dusty roads scarred with cattle spoor. She smelt the smeared, splashed dung, where green flies buzzed. One night she stopped at a village where an old woman with wrinkled cheeks and sunken toothless gums, squatted, her head pivotting on her lizard-neck as she offered the girl a calabash of *maas* to cool her parched throat. The girl's stomach rumbled as she savoured the sour smell of the curdled milk. They began to talk. Children gathered, then more women.

16

"Ja, we know that place called Kimberley; it's not so very far from here. All the young men have gone there to work on the mine where they finding the bright stones. There is only us and the old men and the children here now to grow the food and look after the cattle."

"Do they earn good money in this place, Kimberley?"

"Ooh ja! They can earn good money, but sometimes they steal the stones they dig out the ground and sell them to the foreigners. Then the money is very good!" The speaker, a young girl, rolled her eyes.

"How do they steal these stones, surely the white people are watching?"

"Ooh ja! They watch all right, but the men swallow the stones, then they go home and drink the medicine." The women laughed, their bodies shook and the children tumbled in the dirt, joining in the laughter. The old woman put up her hand for silence. "But there is also plenty trouble in that town. This *umfazi*," pointing to a young woman at the edge of the group, "her husband get killed in a fight." The young woman began to wail and the girl shook her head in sympathy.

"Oew! I am very sorry, but I mus' go to the town, I mus' go an' find Tembu."

"Then, if you mus' go," the old woman continued, "my son he driving the cart with vegetables to the market every week, so I'm asking a ride for you, if you like."

The girl accepted gratefully.

The next morning the wagon arrived at the market and the driver delivered his load and then helped the girl begin her search for Tembu.

"Wait, stop here, that man over there," she cried, pointing, "he can be Tembu!" she jumped off the wagon and ran across the street,

"Tembu," she shouted, "Tem..." the man turned around. He was a stranger.

When the sun dropped low behind the far *kopjies* and the child became restless, they returned to the village.

During the following weeks the girl went to the town many times with the wagon and its driver, searching for Tembu. "The farmer," she told the old woman, "he say to me, 'don't worry about Tembu, I will take care of him.' Oew! *Umfazi*, I know I will never see Tembu again and now, I'm very afraid because I think I am having a child - that white man's child. I can never go back to my home now, my father, he is the son of the Chief. He don' want whiteman's blood in our family. But what can my father do against the white man? And my father he can think I encourage the white man. He can be very angry with me; he can beat me for bringing disgrace to our family. What can happen to me? This child will have the look of the white man. Oew! what can happen to this child? What can happen to this child?"

"Are you so sure your father will be angry?" asked the old woman. She sat next to the girl in front of the black three-legged pot, stirring *putu* for the evening meal. They were alone, the other women were still out on the land weeding the rows of corn and the children were playing on the river bank.

"Oh yes, I am very sure." The girl paused as she stripped the *mealie* and dropped it into a pot of water. Then she continued while nodding her head, savouring the smell of the corn as it cooked.

"Ooh ja! I am sure but you know what? That tree," pointing to the Baobab growing in the *veld*, "that tree make me think of my father."

"Why you say that?" asked the old woman.

"Because the grandmother she telling me a story once about why that old tree look like that. She say that God get angry with the Baobab and that he pull it out the ground one day then he throw it back in, upside down, and that is why the branches look like the roots. My father, he can get very angry."

"Oew!" exclaimed the old woman. She stopped stirring, scratched her hair above her forehead then sniffed and wiped her hand across her nose while frowning at the girl.

"Is that what your grandmother telling you?"

"Ja."

"Well, the witchdoctor here in our village he telling a different story."

"Oh! what the witchdoctor saying?"

"He saying that the Big Spirit give all the animals seeds to plant and the hyena he get very angry because he the last one to get the seed of the Baobab tree so he plant it upside down. And THAT is why the tree look like it growing upside down."

The girl shrugged.

"Oh well! If it is God that get angry or it is the hyena that get angry what does it matter? My mother she say that the Baobab is a good tree because it give food and medicine for the people."

"Ja, that is so. The fruit is good to eat and we also can grind the seeds for food," replied the old woman.

"And I remember when I have the pain in my stomach my mother, she grind the leaves for the pain and it go away. And she make the bark into fine powder for my brother that time he has the fever."

There was silence broken by the sound of the cattle lowing and the young boy, shouting their names as he herded them into the enclosure and under the tree. The girl looked up,

"Ja, it is true that tree make me think of my father. He can get very angry but he also is a good man and he look after his family. But what can my father do against the whiteman. No, it is better I do not go back to the *kraal*." She sniffed and wiped her palms across her eyes, then dropped her head and began fidgeting with her bracelets. The old woman put the wooden stick used for stirring the *putu* to one side and leant across to place her arm around the girl's shoulders.

"Don't be sad, *intombi*, you can stay here."

"No, I cannot do that. You have helped me too much already. Now I must find a job. I must go back to the town tomorrow." She sniffed and swallowed then wiped her nose.

The girl took one last ride in the farm cart to the outskirts of the town. She thanked the driver then climbed out the cart and approached the first cottage where she knocked hesitantly on the back door to ask for work. A young woman opened it, her pale face was framed by thick black hair pulled back in a bun at the nape of her neck. Her eyes were large, dark and almond-shaped below arched eyebrows. She wore an apron around her narrow waist and her sleeves were rolled to the elbows. Her expression was sad but she gave a slight smile as she invited the girl inside.

Chapter Two

Anna's Story
Germany
Circa 1875

"We'll have to get the blazes out of this country, Anna. Times are bad here for Jews." Driving rain hammered the window panes. "I have heard that diamonds have been discovered in a place called Kimberley in the southern part of Africa. People are talking about it in my business and say there are lots of opportunities. A man can make a fortune."

Frederick took the handkerchief out of his top pocket and wiped his forehead before returning it, then he placed his hands behind his back under the tails of his coat. He stood in front of the fireplace, looking at Anna where she lay on the sofa. Her large dark almond-shaped eyes were set far apart above high cheek bones and below strongly marked eyebrows. Her face was pale and framed by her thick dark hair, pulled back in a bun at the nape of her neck.

Frederick was a handsome man. Tall with thick dark curly hair that grew low in his neck and over his ears. His dark beard was neatly trimmed, his clothes neatly fitted. He wore a diamond ring on the little finger of his left hand and on his right hand a signet ring embossed with his family crest. His eyes were dark brown set deep and close.

Anna struggled for words but, "No, Frederick," was all she could get out.

"What do you mean 'no'? Are you saying you do not want to go with me?"

"I'm saying I . . I d. .do not want us to go." she stammered.

"But I have already made arrangements and have someone interested in buying my business.

Anna made an effort to compose herself. Her black eyes blinked and her voice shook. Her complexion was pale and her skin flawless. She wore an elegant taffeta gown to her ankles with full puffed sleeves, tapering to her wrists. It was low cut and her bosom swelled and rose with her agitated breathing while her diamond drop earrings trembled.

"Why have you not spoken about it before?" She began to cry, "And what about Pappa and Mamma? We will never see them again. The children will forget their grandparents."

"Nonsense! Your parents can visit."

"Visit!" Her voice rose. "Visit, so far away!"

"You're a grown woman now with a family of your own to consider. It is time you stopped worrying about your Mamma and Pappa," sarcastically. There was silence between them broken by a sob from Anna. Frederick shrugged then said, "I have to go out. I have an appointment and will be late so don't wait up for me."

Anna jumped off the settee and ran to him her eyes pleading. But before she could say anything he put up his hand to quiet her and said, "We cannot stay here in this country."

"We have influential friends," she replied. Then she thought, *he's exaggerating the situation for his own ends; to get his own way.* She put her hand on his arm, "Pappa doesn't appear to be worried."

"Your Pappa is not in business anymore. There is a conspiracy against Jews." He shook her hand off his arm and took out his watch, hanging on a chain from his vest pocket, looked at the time, then tucked it back. "I must go or I will be late for my appointment."

Anna returned to sit on the sofa, twisting her hands in her lap and biting her bottom lip. She felt helpless, as she so often did with Frederick, knowing once he had made up his mind, nothing would change it. She stood up and paced the room for a while, then sat at the piano, her fingers running over the keys, as she tried to calm herself. But her hands felt heavy. She stopped playing and rotated her rings, the diamond's iridescence, reflecting the lamplight. She picked up a delicate Dresden china ornament, looking at it with vacant eyes, then returned it to the table covered with the fringed velvet cloth and put it next to the silver candle-sticks on the tray with silver-framed photographs of her family. Then she stood again and walked to the window and, parting the dark wine-red velvet drapes, she stared outside. The rain had turned to snow which banked in the corners of the window-panes.

The grandfather clock in the hall struck the hour and Anna began to walk up the broad staircase but before entering the bedroom, she went into the nursery where Anton lay sleeping in his crib. Maybe Frederick is right, she thought, perhaps it will be better for the children to grow up in a society without racial hatred. She glanced at the photograph of her parents. Her mother holding the baby. How could she leave them? She looked in on the sleeping five year old Martha, and Lisa who was two years younger.

Kept awake by her troubled thoughts, Anna lay on the big double bed. She felt drowsy as her head filled with the whisperings of her friend, Rachael Fineberg.

"It's about Frederick." Rachael had said, "I thought you should know that people are talking. He has been meeting that Leah Goldstein y'know." Anna sat up in the bed. Perhaps Leah was the real reason Frederick wanted to leave. Maybe she was becoming too serious. He never liked it when a woman became serious. At the time Anna had reported Rachael's remarks to Mamma who had told her not to worry.

"I shouldn't listen to gossip m'dear. The women are jealous of your good-looking husband, besides, Anna y'know, men are different." Anna remembered her sense of alarm but had kept silent while Mamma continued, "Maybe you can be grateful he seeks some of his pleasures elsewhere."

Anna had shaken her head while looking down at her swollen stomach.

Anton cried out and Anna stirred, brought back to the present. She put out her hand for Frederick but he wasn't there. She climbed out of bed, noticing the lateness of the hour, and went into the nursery. Picking up the baby, she rocked him gently while singing a lullaby. In nine years of marriage she recalled many sleepless nights, either submitting to Frederick's needs or the needs of a new baby. She returned to her bedroom and lay awake until she heard Frederick at the door then closed her eyes, feigning sleep, while he fumbled with his clothes before laying on the bed next to her. He smelt of whiskey and a strange perfume.

The following morning Anna sat opposite Frederick at the breakfast table while Trudy, the maid, served coffee. Frederick called after the girl to close the door.

"I do not trust that Trudy. When will Gerda be back?"

"Trudy is very obliging."

"So you haven't noticed her sly looks? I think she does not like working in a Jewish household."

"I don't agree. I think she's very polite. Besides, I couldn't manage without someone to help while Gerda is away."

"I hope Gerda will be back soon. I saw Trudy talking to her young man at the kitchen door last night when I came home. I suspect he is sleeping here but his manner was quite insolent and I did not like the way he looked at me."

Anna burst out, "I do not believe that. You are saying it to frighten me into agreeing with your plans to leave here." Frederick scowled and she put her hand to her mouth, surprised at her own boldness.

He changed his tone. "This diamond field that has been discovered in Kimberley is reported to have great potential. If I can get established over there at the beginning, I can make a lot of money." He rubbed his hands together. "Some have already struck it rich, Soly Joel and Barney Barnato are highly respected in the financial world." He wiped his mouth with his napkin and stood up. "Anyway, I must leave now and I will not be in for dinner," he said as he walked through the door to his waiting carriage.

Anna remained seated at the table. Another dinner engagement! Perhaps he was meeting Leah. Maybe they should leave the country. She heard a carriage in the driveway and ran to the window. Parting the lace curtains, she saw her parents arriving and ran through the hall, across the black and white tiled floor and threw her arms about her mother's neck.

"Mamma, oh Mamma! How pleased I am to see you both." She turned to her father who embraced her.

"Well, well, such a greeting m'dear, and it's been less than a week since we last saw you!" Anna burst into tears.

"What is it?" asked Mamma.

"What's the matter, child?" inquired Pappa.

She put her head on her mother's shoulder and her tale of woe tumbled out. When she finished Mamma led her to the sofa and sat her down; then took the large pin out of her hat in a deliberate manner before taking it off and handing it to the waiting Trudy. Mamma then seated herself on the sofa next to Anna.

"What's this all about? Has Frederick taken leave of his senses?" Her bosom rose. She appealed to her husband.

"You must speak to Frederick. How can he talk of taking our daughter and our grandchildren so far away to another country?"

Pappa paced the room his hands behind his back tucked under his coat-tails. He loved his daughter, but... "What are you asking, Mamma? I cannot come between a man and his wife. A woman must obey her husband." Mamma didn't reply. After all, Pappa was only repeating what she herself had often told Anna.

Chapter Three

Capetown
Circa 1876

Anna looked at the sky in the east, tinted red by the sun rising above the far mountains. She shrugged off her sense of foreboding as she felt a shiver run down her spine. The early morning was chilly. She stood with Frederick and the children at the Capetown terminus of the Diamond Fields Transport Company.

Eight travellers were gathered around. There were two merchants from Capetown and a banker who would be opening a branch office in Kimberley. Nick, a young digger was returning after buying mining supplies and a preacher or Dominee as the Dutch called their ministers stood with a stout tall woman, a farmer's wife by name of Tannie van Rooyen. The other two passengers, a man and woman, were a little apart. Anna recognised the woman as a fellow passenger on the ship on which they had travelled to Capetown, "Die Arendt."

Tannie walked over to Anna while Frederick helped load the luggage on the wagon. The old woman put her hand up to her mouth and spoke in a rather loud whisper, indicating the couple. She raised her eyebrows and jerked her head.

"That's Tommy, that one, he's the brother come down to meet her. The husband stayed behind in Kimberley. What's his name again?" She wrinkled her forehead then added after a moment, "Ooh ja! Now I remember. It's Charlie, that's the husband's name. Got a temper I'm told. What's the wife like? You were with her on the ship."

Anna's expression was blank, she hadn't paid attention to Tannie's gossip. Tannie repeated the question. Anna was embarrassed, hoping they hadn't overheard the old woman.

"I think her name is Donna... or maybe it's Dora. No it is Donna, I'm pretty sure. Someone said she is Irish. I don't remember much about the journey because I was sick most of the time." She hesitated then quickly added, "Seasickness, you know."

Anna held the baby in her arms while Martha and Lisa clung to her long skirt, staring at the wagon which was to be their home for the next weeks, maybe months. Frederick said it was a long journey from the Cape to Kimberley. She felt some misgiving, but it couldn't be worse than those terrible months on the ship where she had hardly moved from the bunk in

25

the small airless cabin filled with the smell of cooking from the galley and the sour smell of her vomit.

Frederick lifted the children into the wagon then jumped up himself and bent over to take the baby from Anna. He lay the sleeping child on a cushion then took Anna's arm to help her climb aboard. The wagon had low wooden sides and a curved canvas roof supported by iron stanchions. The side canvasses were furled and bottles, flasks and strips of dried, raw meat hung down. There were benches along the sides and the space at the rear was reserved for luggage.

The driver cracked the whip over the heads of the oxen and the wagon moved off along the dusty track. Conversation lagged at first but Tannie began fussing over the children and the men started discussing the business of mining and buying and selling diamonds. Waterfalls cascaded down fern-lined gullies and the wagon seemed caught between deep ravines on the one side and high rocky crags on the other. A slip of an animal's foot or a wheel too near the stony edge of the trail, would cause them to crash headlong down the mountain.

"There's baboon and leopard out there. If you look carefully you might see one," Tannie said to Anna who kept her eyes turned away but then her attention was caught by some dirty-legged children, standing at the roadside in ragged clothing. Their arms were lifted up, begging for hand-outs. Anna's eyes widened in horror at the bedraggled children and placed her hand across her swollen stomach.

Once over the mountain pass the scene changed. For miles in all directions the semi-desert stretched to the hills on the horizon. The vast loneliness relieved only by windmills and isolated farmhouses sheltered by tall trees. Sheep grazed on the dry grey scrub of the plains.

"This is the Karroo, Anna." Tannie sniffed the air, "Jurrah man! It's good to be back eh! Give me the Karroo any day. I don' like Capetown, hey! Too many people and it's too blerry wet. Jurrah! but it can rain in Capetown. Hellalula! But the Karroo. It's jus' beautiful."

Anna looked around in dismay at the stark, barren land.

The days dragged. Anna lay in the wagon pretending to sleep to avoid conversation with the talkative Tannie. Most mornings she felt sick. Frederick sometimes borrowed a spare horse from the outrider and rode off across the *veld* with Nick or Tommy or he would walk beside the wagon, easily keeping pace with the oxen. Anna envied him. She was

26

unable to walk on the uneven ground but Donna joined Frederick and Tommy.

Anna noticed the easy familiarity between Donna and Frederick as they sat around the camp fire that first night.

"Remember that snobby English woman on board who told us she was related to lord someone-or-other, eh Freddy?" Anna was surprised to hear her call him Freddy, he had always insisted on Frederick but he didn't seem bothered at all. Donna dropped her voice and bent her head as she put her lips close to Frederick's ear. He clapped his hands on his knees, put his head back and laughed loudly and didn't notice when Anna stood up and walked over to the wagon. Lying in bed under the curved canvas she thought about her Mamma and Pappa and recalled the night she had first met Frederick. He represented his father's diamond-cutting business in those days and Pappa was buying a ring for Mamma for their anniversary. He invited the young man home to dinner and at sixteen Anna came under the spell of his charm and attention. He visited more often but was given no opportunity to be alone with Anna, Mamma made sure of that, so he made his intentions known to Pappa. Mamma felt that Frederick was too charming and persuasive but Pappa saw things differently. "Nonsense, m'dear," he replied when Mamma confided her misgivings. "The young man comes from a well-to-do family with good business connections. Our Anna will be very fortunate to have him for a husband. What more could we ask for our daughter?" Mamma knew better than to argue. Anna recalled how exciting it had all been at first, like playing grown-up.

The baby began to cry, waking Anna from her daydreaming. She sat up and bumped her head on the iron bar of the wagon. Rubbing the sore spot she moved over to lay next to the child and when he fell asleep her thoughts returned once more to recalling how Frederick had changed over the years. It was while celebrating their last wedding anniversary, she remembered, her parents had called with a gift so Frederick invited them to a downtown restaurant for dinner. The evening started off well enough but when Pappa raised his drink in a last toast and indicated to Mamma that they must leave, Frederick shook his head and insisted they stay for more drinks. Pappa put up a restraining hand but Frederick was adamant. Pappa politely agreed.

An hour later Anna put her hand to her mouth to conceal a yawn and noticed the violinist walking towards her. She felt her face flush and looked down. When she looked up he was standing at her side and began playing to her. Frederick looked furious at the interruption. He was deep in conversation with Pappa, who, taking advantage, stood up once again in an attempt to leave. Frederick's face clouded.

"Wha d'yer mean, you muss go? The night is young." His words slurred. He called the waiter to order more drinks but Pappa put his hand on Frederick's arm. Frederick turned in anger and knocked against the waiter who dropped his tray, spilling wine over Frederick's trousers. Frederick retaliated by punching the waiter while shouting insults. It was a while before Pappa was able to sort out the mess, pay for damages and persuade Frederick to leave.

The following day Frederick begged forgiveness. He sent her and Mamma roses and extravagantly worded cards. The event was not mentioned and if Pappa had heard of others, he kept his opinions to himself.

"After all," he told a friend, "Men will be men, y'know. What is a little drunkeness now and then? My daughter has a comfortable home and much prestige, married to such a wealthy man. What else is there for a woman other than marriage?"

There was movement at the front of the wagon. Anna sat up and saw Martha, her eyes dark in her pale, round face. The child hesitated, then crept forward and knelt beside her mother. Anna smiled and Martha, encouraged, put her head on her mother's breast. "I hope you have been helping Pappa with Anton while Mamma's been sick, my child."

"Pappa doesn't need my help. That lady is helping him." Her voice was scornful.

"You mean Tannie?"

"No, not Tannie. That lady who helped him all the time on the ship. The one Pappa calls Donna. I heard her tell Pappa he has the most beauuutiful eyes," she mimicked.

Their voices had woken Lisa who sat up.

"Yes, that't right. I heard her, Mamma. She also told Pappa he has such lovely hair." The child rolled her eyes. Martha scowled, "I don't like her. Do you like her, Mamma?" Lisa interrupted. "I do. I do. And she likes us. She even said so... so there."

A dove call broke the early morning silence. Frederick woke then picked up his rifle and climbed quietly from the wagon.

No one stirred in the tents scattered around the camp site. He walked through the long grass towards the *kopje* which was topped by a thorn tree, then squatted on a dried out ant heap and took his pipe from his pocket, filling it thoughtfully then clenching the stem between his teeth, he prepared to light it. A movement in the bushes alerted him and he reached for his rifle, expecting to see a buck or other wild animal, but it was Donna. She had a shawl drawn closely around her head and shoulders and clutched a letter in her hand.

"Mornin' Freddy, luv." She pulled the shawl off her head and shook out her thick, black curly hair. The skin on her neck and forehead was smooth and white, her cheeks rosy and her eyes deep blue. She told him once that her parents had left Belfast before she was born and she was raised in Liverpool. When she was old enough she went into service on the estate of the local landowner where Tommy was the stable lad and when Charlie paid his young brother a visit that was how she met him.

"I was telling you about the letter from Charlie that came before I left Liverpool. Well, here it is, you can read it for yourself to see what he says about all the money he's making on the diggings." She waved the letter in the air and Frederick took it and began reading but quickly handed it back with an embarrassed grin. Donna laughed.

"Oh Charlie, he alway talk like that. He's very passionate, y'know." She pointed to the lines lower down the page and her laughter rippled as she bent towards Frederick. They both looked up sharply when they heard children's voices. Martha and Lisa ran up the slope towards them.

It was a few nights later. The women and children slept and the two merchants, the banker and the preacher had long since retired to their tents. Frederick, Nick and Tommy sat around the dying embers of the fire under the broad sky.

"I hope I have done the right thing, coming here. Anna is not strong, you know. Too many babies, I expect and now she is having another. But... well... y'know how it is." He shrugged and grinned, then became serious. "It'll be better when we get settled then I can send for her parents, you know what women are like?" Tommy and Nick nodded as Frederick continued. "But there are plenty of opportunities here."

Tommy leaned forward, "That's right, mate. There are opportunities for everyone, a man can make a fortune. My brother Charlie and me, we come here last year. We don' wanna be pushed around no more by rich people. Now we're working two claims and have a right good time I can tell ye, making lots of luvly lolly. You won' be sorry you come." Tommy stopped talking and his eyes roved around the camp site towards where the black drivers and outriders slept. "An' we don' have to do no more heavy

29

work either, do we mate?   There are plenty of *kaffirs* to do that hey man. They work cheap too, cheap as dirt, as the saying goes, An' there's plenty of that too!"

Chapter 4

A hot dry wind blew across the land. It blew down from the distant mountains, eddying swirls of dust that settled in layers on the canvas tops of the wagons, on clothing and on the backs of the oxen where bloated blue ticks sucked hungrily on their hosts. Anna felt her long dresses and underwear imprisoned her body so she discarded the petticoats. What would Mamma have said, she thought ruefully as she wiped her hand across her eyes. Her parents could never imagine this. When they travelled it was in a private railway coach or their own carriage. She couldn't write; where could she mail a letter? But she wrote anyway, every day, in her journal, in detail, describing the unfamiliar scenery and the strange new experiences.

The oxen lumbered slowly on, dragging the heavy wooden wagons over outcrops of rock and loose stones on the bare *veld*. Anna felt every bump a jolt, jarring her body as she swayed from side to side, mile after mile. She glanced down at the stained front of her dress; her once elegant boots caked in dirt, and her grimy hands. She felt the movements of the baby in her belly as she comforted the fretful Anton and placated the quarrelsome Martha and Lisa. *Will this never end?* she thought, confined in the wagon with no escape from the children or Tannie.

Tannie was a tall woman, somewhat stout; her strong body held erect by a tight whalebone corset and her own stiff uncompromising backbone. Her face flat and broad across the eyes was criss-crossed by lines of worry and dry weather. Her cheeks sunken; her only teeth were in front, top and bottom. Her eyes were deep set and kind.

She was a young wife and mother forty years ago when, with husband, children, parents, cousins, aunts and uncles, they trekked away from the Cape and the British. Like all the women, she was beside her man, loading and re-loading his rifle when the circle of wagons was attacked by marauding natives. For the rest of the time she was behind him, attending to his needs, cooking his meals and mending his clothes.

"A woman must know her place, y'know," commenting to Anna when relating her experiences of the Trek.

It was the third week of the journey. The squeaking wagons silent, a fire lit and tents set up for the overnight stop, Anna and Tannie prepared the evening meal. Anton clung to his mother's skirts while she cleaned vegetables bought from a farmer. The strong odour of onions rose in her face causing water to gather in her eyes and spill down her cheeks. Her dress fell open at the neck with sleeves rolled up above the elbows, her face was flushed and expression tense. Tannie saw Donna sitting in the shade outside her tent.

"Donna, my *meisie*, can you help me and Anna here, hey? Can you take care of the baby or something."

Donna looked up then glanced down at her hand. "I'm sorry, luv, but I got a thorn in my thumb, 'aven't I?   It's from that tree over there," pointing to a thorn tree growing by a clump of rocks. Tannie and Anna looked at each other then Anna shrugged and called Frederick for help but Tannie put up her hand to silence her.

"*Ag nie*! Anna, what are you saying? Goodness me, you can't ask a man to do women's work. We'll manage."

Frederick looked gratefully at the old woman.   "Well, you know, I was thinking of fishing - something for supper if I'm lucky! Would you like that?" Tannie smiled but Anna scowled, watching him fetch fishing tackle and setting off across the *veld* towards the river.

Tannie called out to Donna, "You betta come here and let me look at that thumb then.   I'll make a bread poultice to draw out the thorn if its too deep in."

"It's all right really Tannie luv, I got a needle here. I'll get the thorn out myself. Don't you worry about me."

Martha sat in the front of the wagon, watching. She saw Donna stand up after a while and set off in the direction of the river, disappearing over the edge of the *donga*. The child climbed quietly out of the wagon, following through the long grass, creeping slowly and carefully.

Frederick, meanwhile, after scrambling down the embankment to the river bed, had stripped to the waist. Rolling up his trousers and taking off his shoes, he waded into the shallow stream, stepping over sharp stones. There was a drought in the land; the Karroo dry and barren, the river barely deep enough to swim or to fish so he sat on a rock, feet dangling, fishing rod set aside. The fish, if there were any, could wait. Over the centuries the river had eroded the soil, cutting the deep ravine. Making sure he could not be seen by those at the camp, he took off his trousers and sat in the shallow pool, splashing his back and shoulders, a sense of relief from all the heat.

He heard a movement behind and, looking back, saw Donna emerge from a bush downstream. His eyes widened at her nakedness. He stood up as sweat gathered in the palms of his hands and beaded his forehead. His instinct was to grab his trousers and escape but instead, like an animal mesmerised by a snake, he walked towards her with both arms outstretched when a shrill voice pierced the silence.

"Pappa, Pappa. Did you catch a fish?"

He turned. Jumped over the rocks across the stream and retrieved his trousers, quickly pulling them on then clambered up the steep sides of the *donga*, looking towards the sound of Martha's voice but unable to see her, hiding behind a bush.

Drums beat in his ears and his breath came in short gasps while he clambered up the embankment. The sharp stones speared his feet and the dry grass cut his hands as he pulled on it, dragging himself up the crumbling slope. At the top he stumbled forward then saw the child crouched under a bush. He lifted her on to his shoulder and walked quickly towards the camp.

Lisa and Anton were playing beneath the wagon, both squatting in the dirt, watching the ants scurrying too and fro. He put out his hand to pick one up and was bitten sharply on his finger. Shaking his hand, he ran screaming to his mother who, with her face flushed and dust-streaked, bent to pick up the little boy. She looked around, calling for Martha to help her and when she saw Frederick with the child on his shoulder, she shrieked at him. He put Martha down and took the crying baby, guilt in his averted eyes. Tannie shook her head but kept silent. Later, during the evening meal Frederick avoided Donna's searching gaze while Martha watched them closely.

The travellers settled for the night. Frederick, pleading the heat under the canvas of the wagon, took his bedding to a grassy bank and lay alone under the stars, cicadas and a chorus of bull-frogs lulled him into a restless sleep.

Gentle hands caressed him, a soft voice whispered his name, he edged away and made as if to stand but hands held him down... down... The voice in his ear grew louder... louder... beating in his eardrums, bursting in his head in a booming blast and a rumble of thunder reverberating from the surrounding hills. He sat up in alarm, sweat running down his neck; wetness in his groin. The storm broke jarring him awake. Lightning, like cannon fire, lit the sky. Rain, like shiny bullets, spurted and spattered around him.

The travellers awoke in alarm and gathered the bedding while struggling to unroll side canvasses. The camp site was soon swamped and the strong, steamy smell of rain-washed earth rose up from the ground.

Suddenly the storm was over and a strange silence fell over the land. A watery sun broke through in the east and brushed the dome of the sky, painting with pale pink the remaining clouds. Brightly coloured buds burst on bushes, reflecting the rainbow that miraculously appeared but the wagon was stuck fast in thick brown mud. Tommy and Nick, with the native drivers, dug the wheels free while the banker and the merchants clutched their dripping wallets in dismay. With a handkerchief knotted at his throat and a felt hat pushed to the back of his head, Frederick wiped his brow then leant on his shovel, his body drained and strangely weak, gouged and wracked like the *veld* after the storm.

"C'mon man," laughed Nick. "What you got on your mind, hey? No time to take it easy, now."

Frederick dug his shovel back into the mud and glanced towards Donna who with Martha and Lisa were picking the wild flowers that had suddenly appeared after the rain. Anna and Tannie were sorting through the wet clothing.

"Nothing is on my mind. I could not sleep last night, it was, what you say? 'too damn hot'." Nick noticed the direction of his glance and grinned.

"Too hot, hey!" pointing with his thumb over his shoulder.

"I don't know what you mean."

"Course you do. Everyone can see she fancies you."

"Well, if she does," Frederick blustered, "I can't help it."

"C'mon man, what happened on the ship hey?"

"Nothing 'happened.' She helped me with the children while my wife was sick, that is all. It's Anna that's the problem. She does not understand how I feel. She never understands, just cries all the time for her parents and the old life in Germany. It's her fault. It's all her fault."

Nick put back his head and laughed.

"You can laugh, but it is true. But now Donna is getting too damn serious. I don't want trouble with a jealous husband and Tommy says the man has a vile temper. God, but women can be difficult." He picked up his shovel and began digging again. Nick grinned.

The wagons were free but the sun had dropped low in the west, casting long shadows. They would spend another night in this lonely place. Frederick poured water on the fire, stamping on the dying embers with ferocious intensity. Martha ran to him.

"Good night, Pappa," pulling on his sleeve. "Come and tell me a story. Mamma is with Anton. He is sick."

"All right, I'll come. Will you fetch Lisa? Where is she anyway?"

"She's in Aunty Donna's tent."

"Well, call her. Tell her she must come to the wagon, it's late and time for bed." Frederick's voice impatient as the child continued to pull on his arm.

"You call her, Pappa. She won't come for me. She says she likes Aunty Donna." There was a short silence while the child stared up at her father; then she continued, still staring intently, "Do you like Aunty Donna?"

He averted his eyes, "Nonsense child, don't be silly, you ask too many questions. Run along and do as I say. I can't go into a lady's tent. She might be in bed."

"But I saw her by you when you were in bed this morning before the storm."

Frederick lay on his back, head resting on his arms, staring at the freshly-washed sky at the stars sparkling and shimmering. Above the noise of the stream which raged in the donga, he heard the thin cry of Anton, fretful and weak and he heard Anna's voice, soft now and gentle, as she comforted the child. He stood up, wearily walking to the wagon where Anna held the baby to her breast, swaying back and forth and singing a lullaby. He put out his arms to take the boy but the child turned away, his body burning with fever.

Anna was afraid. Her baby was ill. The nearest town many miles away and it was doubtful if even there a doctor would be found. The only sign of life a cluster of thatched mud huts on a nearby hillside and some children playing in long grass; little black children with thin limbs.

Tannie van Rooyen, like all farmer's wives, had remedies for most ailments.

"Anna, my child, I'll peel an apple, let it go brown, then you give it to the baby, hey! Y'know that's a sure cure for stomach cramps. For his sore ears, there's nothing like the juice of garlic or an onion, ja man! There are onions in the bag at the back of the wagon. I've used onion juice many times to cure my childrens' earache." The old woman bustled about preparing her home-made remedies. She sponged the fevered body with cool water from the river. For a time he seemed comforted and Anna was grateful, but then he became restless again; his crying increased. Anna saw farm buildings in the distance, nested in the fold of the hills protected by tall gum trees standing guard behind. She begged Frederick to ride for help.

Anna held the baby close, her eyes searching for Frederick's return. At last, between the hills she saw him, his horse kicking up a cloud of dust. The hoofbeats grew louder and finally stopped at the edge of the campsite. Frederick dismounted, threw the reins over the horse's head and strode towards the wagon. "The farmer's wife says there is a doctor in the next town but it's a long way. We will have to drive all night."

On and on they rode, under the cathedral dome of the sky. The Southern Cross hanging in benediction over them. Anna lay with the baby in her arms. Suddenly he arched his back in a convulsive spasm, rolled his eyes, then lay limp and still. In the deep quiet of the early morning an anguished wail tore into the silence. Anna realised her baby was dead. She sat rocking back and forth, clutching his frail body.

Frederick and Nick prepared a place to bury the child then the travellers gathered around while the Preacher read from the Old Testament. He was told the young couple were of the Jewish faith.

Anna recalled little of the remainder of the journey to Kimberley. She thought of the lonely place where they had buried her child and knew she would never be able to visit his grave, so far away. She would never know him in boyhood or as a man. She shed bitter tears.

"You mus' not grieve so much, my child," said Tannie. "*Alles sal regkom.*" That's an old Dutch saying and it means 'everything will come right.' You must have hope. Two of my babies died y'know, when we trekked up from the Cape. But God gives us the strength to overcome." Anna marvelled at the old woman's courage but found little solace in her words. She looked at the scene around her and saw no beauty in the jagged mountains and the crusted *veld*, nor even the bright wild flowers.

"It's God's Will and not for us to question His ways," Tannie continued. "The Lord giveth and the Lord taketh away. The Scriptures are a great comfort in times of trouble." Anna looked up at the old woman and shook her head. *Comfort!* she thought, she found little comfort in those words. She didn't believe in predestination. *Let twenty pass, and stone the twenty-first,/ Loving not, hating not, just choosing so.* The words of Mr. Browning's poem came to mind. *Tannie believes God's nature is like man's nature,* she thought, *like Caliban as he reflected upon his god, Setebos.* She didn't believe that. But what did she believe? She slowly shook her head as she looked about her and felt trapped in this wilderness place. She recalled the long days and nights when Frederick was away supposedly on a business trip but more likely visiting with his current woman friend. She had spent those lonely nights reading the German philosophers. Then she read Shakespeare, first in German, then, her interest in English literature aroused, she studied the language and re-read his work in English, and many of the great novelists and poets as well. Shelley's ideas interested her, but now her faith was shattered. Could the Rabbi help her? She shook her head. *All people were the same,* she mused, *whatever their religion. They all recited the same trite words.*

Anna and Tannie were alone in the wagon. The evening meal over, Martha and Lisa asleep. Frederick sat around the camp fire with the men, discussing the diamond business and the prospects of success on the new diggings. Donna had retired to her tent. Tannie put her arms around Anna's stooped shoulders.

"Ja man, the Scriptures give a person comfort, hey!"

Anna moved away. She hoped Tannie wasn't starting that all over again. Blurting out, "I don't believe there is a God. If He exists, why has He deserted me, if He's all powerful, why didn't he save my baby, and if He's loving and knows everything, why then He must know that I have not sinned, unless He thinks I am not submissive enough to my husband, Does He only see things from a man's point of view and how does that help me?" Her voice was bitter. "It's Frederick who has sinned, and if God is punishing him by taking our child, why must I suffer as well?" It all came out, her emotion and resentment.

Tannie shook her head. "No, Anna my love. You got it all wrong, hey! God is testing all the time. The stories in the Scriptures teach us that. Think of that story of Joseph now. Jurrah man! He had plenty of troubles that one, one after another they come, hey! He was a good boy and his father love him the best but his brothers, they get jealous and throw him into a pit. Joseph trusts God. He doesn't sit in the pit looking down and feeling sorry for himself. Nie man! Not at all! He looks up and so he sees the caravan going to Egypt and so his brothers take him out the pit and sell him to the people in the caravan. When he gets to Egypt he gets a job with Potiphar but that Potiphar's wife she fancies Joseph and she tries to trick him into sleeping with her but Joseph, he say 'No way!' to the lady and she get very cross and tells Potiphar that Joseph is after her, instead of the other way around.

"Well, to make a long story short, Potiphar is very angry and puts Joseph in gaol. Joseph don't say, 'Hey man! Why has God done this to me?' Not at all! Joseph looks around to see who he can help and he tells the other prisoner's what their dreams mean. Now when Pharoah is having bad dreams he hears about Joseph and he send for Joseph who tells Pharoah that his dreams mean that there will be seven years of plenty and seven years of famine and Pharoah must save the corn in the years of plenty. Pharoah listens to Joseph and does what he says, and when all the people are saved they say, 'this Pharoah is a good king.' Pharoah is so pleased he makes Joseph the big boss and you know what...?"

Anna sat transfixed listening to Tannie's version of the familiar story. Her father had read it many times but it sounded different the way Tannie told it. It sounded believable. As if this man Joseph really had overcome all his problems. He was real, had suffered real human tragedies like herself. Was there comfort in the Scriptures after all? Deep in thought she didn't reply to Tannie's question so the old woman repeated it.

"And you know what?"

Anna shook her head.

"Well Joseph didn't hate his brothers for throwing him into the pit and selling him to the travellers going to Egypt. He made it all turn out for the best. He knew 'alles sal regkom!' You see, my child, Joseph never gave up hope. He never got sorry for himself. If he had of got sorry for himself there in that pit and not looked up he wouldn't have seen the caravan going past. If he had of got sorry for himself there in that gaol and not helped the other prisoners, Pharoah wouldn't have heard of him. If he had of got sorry for himself everytime he got problems where do you think he would have ended up, hey?" Without waiting for Anna to reply Tannie went on, "He would have ended up still at the bottom of that pit!"

All night Anna pondered the story of Joseph which now took on new meaning. She resolved to try and overcome her wretchedness but as the journey dragged on she fell again into depression and sat with downcast head and resentful thoughts.

Frederick tried to comfort her. "I'm sorry, Anna, truly sorry. I don't know what I can do, but I swear I will never touch liquor again."

"You've promised that before."

"I know, but I mean it this time." He put his arm around her, she pushed him away. She knew that hating Frederick was wrong but she couldn't love him. Not now.

Anna and Tannie were tidying the camp site while Frederick and Nick talked around the fire. Tommy, the banker and the two merchants played poker and Donna sat in her tent. Martha and Lisa played with their dolls.

"I don't understand, Tannie," Anna picked up the big saucepan, carrying it to the back of the wagon where it was stored with other utensils.

"What don't you understand, my child?"

"I don't know what is the Truth." She stood deep in thought. Tannie remained silent.

"What is the Truth, Tannie? The Bible says God is all powerful and loving and compassionate. Is He all powerful but not sufficiently loving to care about my baby and allowed him to suffer and die. Or is He loving and compassionate but not all powerful and could not prevent my child from suffering?" Not waiting for her reply Anna continued, "Why did you leave the Cape, Tannie. Did you want to?"

"Well, y'know, I didn't want to, not reely, but my husband, he say we must and so I go with him. A woman mus' do what her man says."

Chapter 5

The long journey was nearly at an end. The travellers' eyes searched the *veld* for the first signs of the diamond fields as the road became busier with carts and wagons lumbering by, loaded with farm produce, household furniture and mining equipment. Tents stood in rows with billowing smoke, spiralling upwards from camp fires. Diggers, sieving through the sand, made little hills of siftings, their faces grimed.

The wagons turned into Kimberley's main street. Wooden buildings with corrugated iron overhangs supported by wooden posts. The market square was surrounded by stalls. The wagons creaked to a halt and the travellers, gathering their bags, prepared to go their different ways, promising to keep in touch.

A short, burly man stepped forward and Tommy turned to Frederick and Anna,

"Meet me brother Charlie." Frederick stretched out his hand while Anna nodded, noticing the family likeness but hardly concealing her surprise. Charlie was considerably older than she expected. A crumpled felt hat squashed on thick black curly hair with a dark curly beard clinging to his face, and a moustache drooping over his wet sensual mouth. Sweat shimmered on the black chest hairs which grew up his neck. His trousers were hitched up with suspenders over a short sleeved, stained spencer. He put his arms around Donna, patting her bottom before shaking Tommy's hand while scowling at the men who had travelled with his wife.

Tommy took Frederick's arm and steered him down the street, leaving Donna and Charlie to follow. "Come with me, guv., I'll take you to the hotel." They walked ahead, Anna lagging behind, shoulders stooped, surveying the shabby town. Lisa skipped beside her, stopping to stroke a cart-horse or stare at a crate of chickens while Martha tightly took hold of her mother's hand.

"What about our luggage? We better take it with us." Frederick protested.

"Don't be daft, guv., you don't have to worry about the luggage. We'll tell the receptionist at the hotel, they'll send a boy to fetch it, won't they?" Tommy pointed towards the stalls in the square. "You can buy all the mining-gear you need, right here. Blokes always leaving, wanting to sell equipment - pick up stuff at a good price."

Donna, Charlie and Tommy lived in the hotel but Anna wanted a place of their own.

"I've heard of a cottage, Anna. Van Schalkwyk, Tommy's friend, told me about it," Frederick told her as he walked into their bedroom in the hotel. Anna looked up and watched him pour water from a china jug into the matching basin on the stand to wash his hands. They had been in Kimberley some weeks, Frederick was already working in partnership with Tommy and Charlie on a new claim.

"Some Englishman's selling up - going back, we can buy his place, with all the furniture. He didn't mention that the man's wife and child had died of fever.

They walked along the dusty road flanked by dwellings, no more than shacks, hastily put together; not warm enough in winter when winds blew across the *veld*, too hot in summer under the unrelenting sun. The cottage was at the end of a row with a wire fence separating it from the open *veld*. A living room with a range in one corner, a bare scrubbed wooden table with four chairs in the centre, a faded settee under the window. In the second room, an iron bedstead with a patchwork quilt thrown over and a child's crib against the wall. Hanging from a nail on the wall, a galvanised iron bath tub. The toilet, a hole in the ground at the end of the garden covered by a tin hut.

Anna leant against the table, pressing her hands against her swollen stomach, remembering the home she had left. The grand-piano covered with a fringed tapestry cloth, chintz sofas and velvet-draped windows. Nausea overcame her as the tears gathered. She wanted to be anywhere but this dismal place, and wished she were dead but then she felt the movement of the new life. Frederick looked at her for approval, "It is only for a short while, until we get established."

She shrugged, walking outside to where the children played with a mother cat and kittens.

Once settled, Anna began scrubbing and cleaning, sewing drapes for the windows and planting marigolds along the fence. Most of the time, keeping to herself, although Bessie next door, brought home-made preserves and fresh vegetables from the farm. She made clothes for the new baby expected in two months. Anticipating its birth, the pain of Anton's death lessened but the sadness stayed. Tannie's story of Joseph came to mind in her search for hope.

A new "rush" was rumoured at Beaconsfield some miles from Kimberley. Tommy and Charlie went to stake new claims while Frederick remained to work the old. The day was hot and dry. Frederick shook the sieve of blue ground, grasping the tray with roughened hands, his throat parched. He took off his felt hat to mop his forehead when he noticed a coloured man who rode up and reigned in his horse.

"*Middag my baas.* Is you the *Meneer* who work with *baas* Charlie?"

"Ja, that's me. What's the matter? Is there a problem?"

"*Nie, niks makeer nie.* Nothings the matter, things are good, but they must stay longer. They won' be back for another week. They send me to tell you, and to tell the *Mevrou.* She stay at the hotel in the Square? Right?"

Frederick nodded. "Ja, at the hotel. That's where you'll find the *Mevrou.*" He stopped the motion with his hands.

"*Tot siens, my baas,*" raising slouched hat and turning his horse in a cloud of dust.

Frederick moved forward. "Hey! *Wag 'n bietjie,* wait a minute, man. I have to go into the town. I'll give the *Mevrou* the message."

The coloured man's face broke into a grin. "*Ag man! Baie dankie.* Thank-you, thank-you my *baas.* That will help. I live on the other side, very far away in the location." Frederick waved him off, packed up and set out for home.

Anna looked up in surprise, she was giving Martha a lesson in numbers.

"You're early, I haven't prepared dinner yet. Anything the matter?"

Frederick lowered his eyes. "No, nothing the matter, just have to see a trader about some stones and meeting him at the hotel. It's so damn hot out there, thought I would pack up early. Don't worry about dinner for me, I'll eat with him."

He stripped to the waist, washed, and put on a clean shirt and carefully brushed his hair and beard, while Anna continued with Martha's lesson. He tweeked Martha's hair and pecked Anna on the cheek. She turned away. He bent to pick up Lisa who ran joyfully into his arms then after hugging her and swinging her around and, without another glance at Anna, he walked through the door.

"What's a man supposed to do," he muttered. Only Lisa stood at the door waving.

The hotel was a long, low building with a *stoep*, stretching across its width. A hallway extended from the front to the rear. The saloon on one side, the dining-room on the other. The guests' bedrooms beyond. Frederick walked almost to the end of the hall and tapped on the brown painted door. It opened a crack and Donna's face peered out, eyes lighting. She opened the door wider. He stepped inside. She had changed out of day clothes. The restricting corset, catching her waist into a fashionable eighteen inches was discarded. She wore a negligee cut low at the neck.

Frederick struggled to breathe. "I have a message from Charlie to say they will be staying in Beaconsfield another week. He said I must tell you," his voice croaked as he lowered his eyes. Her eyebrows raised, in surprise. Moving closer, he smelt her perfume, *crushed ashes of roses or some such thing*, he thought. Desire washed over him, tinged with guilt so he turned to leave but she put up her hand, while leaning across him with the other, firmly closed the door.

Hours later, lying close on the iron bedstead, a thin sheet covering their moist bodies in the airless room, she whispered, "Take me away, Freddy, luv. Me life is a right mess. Charlie is wild. His temper frightens me. He's right mad with jealousy, only left me alone here now because he hopes to make more money on the new claim. That's what he likes more than me!" A wry smile. "When I complain to Tommy he says, 'don't be daft,' and that I must listen to me 'usband and be a good wife."

Frederick looking alarmed, moved to get up but she clung hysterically. He edged away.

"Don't be silly, Donna. I must go. You ask the impossible. How can I leave Anna and the children? Anyway," searching for an excuse, "what if you get pregnant? We better not see each other again."

"You don't have to worry about that, luv, that can't happen I promise you," waving her hand. "I can't have a baby, something the matter inside, the doctor says it's a right mess, but I ain't complainin'."

She began to sob. "Please don't go, luv, I need you," pulling him close. He felt her softness and her passion. Once more his desire was aroused. A few minutes later he fell asleep, head on her breast. The clock in the hallway struck twelve but he didn't hear it.

* * *

A gentle breeze blew, lifting the lace curtains. Anna felt her stomach harden, a sharp swift pain. It passed. She moved her chair to catch the cool draught. The pain again. She clutched her side, it receded, then returned. She was afraid. The baby was only due in two months but these were frightening signs. She heard the clock strike twelve.

Why was he so late? The pains became stronger and more frequent. She crawled to the doorway to call Bessie, then remembered they were away. She looked towards the town for someone walking, but the road was deserted. She returned to lay on the sofa.

A strange cry woke Martha. Climbing out of bed and glancing at the sleeping Lisa, she ran into the other room to see their mother lying on the floor. Something was very wrong. Anna was screaming and clutching the table leg, her body convulsing and shuddering. Martha ran to her side, put her head down, but there was no sign of recognition. The pain eased momentarily and Anna focused, but before she could speak was overcome with another sharp stab. She arched her back and splayed her legs, Martha watched in horror. A wet and slimy object appeared. Another spasm, another scream. The object slid on to the bare linoleum, lying still in a pool of blood which widened and spread. The object moved and Martha realised it was a baby.

Anna roused herself. "Run, Martha, call someone quickly. Look outside, it's dark but don't be afraid. Maybe someone is walking on the road, maybe you can see Pappa coming." Anna gasped out words, glancing at the clock on the dresser. Almost three. Where was Frederick? Not with Charlie and Tommy, they were in Beaconsfield and Donna must be with them. Had he been attacked on the lonely road?

Martha ran to do her mother's bidding. She ran to the wire fence as a cloud scudded across the moon casting frightening shadows, then down the road, her courage spurred by desperation. Tripping on the rough surface, grazing her knees, crawling forward, stumbling up, her breath coming in gasps. A figure appear over the hill. "Pappa," she screamed. He ran towards her, it wasn't her father. But it was a grown-up, someone who could help. Her shoulders heaved, trying to get breath to get out words.

The digger, walking home from a night of poker at the hotel, was a miner recently from Wales. He lived alone, his wife and family left behind in the old country. He had helped deliver his own children and knew what had to be done. He followed the child into the house.

* * *

A sudden gust of wind banged the screen door and rattled the wooden shutters. Frederick opened his eyes in the strange room with a musky perfume. He looked down at Donna's sleeping form, easing his arm from under her shoulder. She stirred. He moved carefully, edging off the bed, casting the sheet aside, revealing her bare thigh but felt no excitement at her nakedness now, only guilt and remorse. Glancing at his watch, he panicked. Five o'clock. He must hurry before Anna and the children woke and, if lucky, could pretend he had been there all night. He dressed quickly and quietly, careful not to disturb Donna, and, holding his boots, he opened the door and slipped through. A shaft of light piercing the dark room. He glanced up and down, no one in sight. Quietly he stepped into the night.

Lamps were lit in the cottage. He began to run, to be met at the door by Martha.

"What is it child? Why are you up so early?" bending to talk to her, but she smelt a strange perfume, and turned away.

Chapter 6

Kimberley
Circa 1878

Anna sat at her sewing machine, her foot pressed down hard on the treddle. She was making clothes for Martha and Lisa. Those sewn for the baby had been carefully packed away with Anton's. Tears spilled down her face as she recalled the night, three months ago when the baby was born dead. *It's all Frederick's fault,* she thought. *I know Mama always said it important to be forgiving, but how can I forgive him? How can I love him? And, if I do, it will mean more babies. Oh dear, what can I do? What can I do?*

After Anton's death she had lost most of her faith. *What was Truth?* she thought. The Bible was full of contradictions "God made man in his image... God made man of the dust of the ground." She took her foot off the treddle and sat deep in thought. Did her negative and depressed thoughts cause her troubles, or were her troubles the cause of her depression? She felt at the bottom of a deep, deep pit.

A pit! She sat upright, her sewing forgotten and remembered the story of Joseph. A pit! What was it Tannie had said about Joseph? She wrinkled her brow as she rubbed her forehead. Now I remember. Tannie said that even in the pit Joseph had never given up hope. If he had, she said, he would have stayed at the bottom of the pit! Each time trouble overwhelmed him, Joseph turned to help someone else. Anna chewed thoughtfully at the nail on her forefinger as she pondered the old woman's words. Was that her answer?

Tannie always said she must recognise the good, that is to see God's likeness in others. To overcome a problem she must be positive and refuse to submit to it. Tannie always said we must look for the good. She said that Joseph never looked into the pit of his own self-pity. With these thoughts filling her head Anna clasped her hands together, stood up and began pacing the room. She must not feel sorry for herself. She must find someone to help. But who? She stared out the open window at the deep blue cloudless sky and the *veld* stretching out to the low *kopjies* on the horizon. The drapes billowed softly in the breeze. She saw Bessie hanging washing on the line. Bessie, so strong and capable. Bessie certainly didn't need help. But there must be someone? She sat back on the chair in front of the sewing machine and bent to thread the needle when she heard a knock at the back door. She pushed her sewing to one

47

side, walked through the kitchen and opened the door. A girl stood in the doorway. She was about Anna's own age and had a baby tied to her back and a bundle on her head. Anna invited her in, helping her with the crying child. She boiled water for tea, cut thick slices of home-made bread and listened to the story told in broken English.

"*Asseblief*, please madam, can you give me work? I can wash and iron and clean your house if I can jus' have enough food for me and the child."

The girl spoke of her missing husband. "He say he must find work in Kimberley with the white people on the mines and then he is sending for me and the child, but I hear nothing."

She spoke of the farmer, van Niekerk. "He rape me," she whispered, dropping her head, "then he say he will come again. But he always talking about the man Jesus. Does this Jesus say the white people is better than blacks?"

She spoke of her terror and her shame.

Anna put her arm around the girl's shoulder. "I can give you work. You can help me clean the house and plant and grow the vegetables. You can stay here." She didn't know where but maybe Frederick could board up part of the back stoep. That night the girl and her child slept in the kitchen. "What is your name?" Anna asked.

"At home they call me Nikwe." Her tongue clicked as she said the foreign sounding word.

Anna shook her head, "I can never pronounce that name," she replied. "I think I will call you Ruth. Do you like that?"

The girl nodded. "And your baby I will name Joseph," Anna continued.

Frederick was persuaded to enclose the back *stoep*, where Anna put a bed and a crib, but he wasn't pleased with the arrangement.

"You can't have a servant sleeping in the house and sitting at our table."

"Nonsense. Gerda slept in our house. She ate at our table." Anna's voice rose.

"Well, yes but she slept in a room in the attic and she ate at the kitchen table."

"We don't have an attic and we only have a kitchen table."

48

"But it's different here. Servants sleep in backyard rooms or else they live in the location," he paused. "And besides," dropping his voice, "Gerda's white. "

One day shortly after Ruth and her baby were settled, Anna was feeding chickens at the bottom of the garden when Bessie called her to the fence, smiling, "I see you got a girl, now Anna."

Anna walked towards the fence, wiping her hands on her apron. "Oh yes, Bessie, indeed I do. You must meet Ruth. "

Bessie's eyebrows rose. "But you don't have a room in your yard for her. Is she staying in the location, then?"

"Well, no, the location's so far away, you know, it's a long walk every day especially with little Joe."

"You mean she got a *picannin* as well?" Bessie's eyebrows rose.

"Yes, that's right. Ruth's come to look for her husband really, but she will stay with us 'til she finds him. Frederick has closed in part of the back *stoep* for her and the boy."

Bessie's eyebrows disappeared into her bangs. "You mean you got that native girl sleeping in your house?"

Anna ignored the remark.   "Shame, Bessie, such a terrible thing happened to her you know, she was raped." Her voice sunk to a whisper.

Bessie stepped closer to the fence. "What did you say?"

Anna repeated.

"Anna, my dear, *jy weet*, black men are always raping their women."

"No, you don't understand. She was raped by a white man, the farmer where she worked."

"I don't believe that. All lies. A white man touching a black girl? She's lying to you, Anna. You mustn't be fooled by these people, hey!" Bessie sniffed, shaking her head.   "As I'm saying, you must be careful of these people, Anna. They lie all the time." Her face was flushed as she drew herself up. "It's lies Anna, all lies. You jus' better be careful. The next thing is she'll be gone and all your nice things gone as well. I know these people." She turned away and walked towards her house.

The following day while once again hanging washing on the line between the apple trees, Anna overheard Bessie talking to her other neighbour.

"What's the matter with these *uitlanders*. Can you believe it, they have a native girl living in their place, eating from their dishes and using their lavatory? They're *dom* man!" she tapped her forehead. "Give the *kaffirs* an inch and they'll take a mile, that's what I told her but these foreigners don't understand that. The *kaffirs* don't appreciate what we do for them. They just keep wanting more."

Anna glanced towards the kitchen, hoping Ruth hadn't overheard. Browning's poem came to mind, *Took pains to make thee speak, taught thee each hour / One thing or other:*
Then she heard Bessie's voice again, "Why doesn't these *uitlanders* go back to their own country?"

Frederick wasn't happy with the arrangement and discussed his problem with Tommy. "It's the neighbours, they're talking. I don't want the damn woman and her child living in our house, but what the hell can I do?"
Tommy scratched his head.
"Anyway at least the black woman's problems take Anna's mind off her own, so my life is easier," Frederick conceded. "That's why I agreed to making the *stoep* into a room for her."
"Talk to Jacobus," Tommy suggested. Jacobus was the coloured man they employed on the claim. "He lives in the location. If this Tembu fellow is in Kimberley, Jacobus might know."

Ruth knew Frederick wanted to be rid of her but she also knew Anna needed her.
"What's the matter, Ruth?"
"It's nothing, madam, except I'm worry I don't find Tembu then where I can live. I cannot go back to the farm, the farmer Van Niekerk, he will find me," she sighed, shaking her head. "My father is the chief, but all his land is taken and now he mus' work for the farmer. My grandmother, she telling me when she a very small child all the land belonged to our people."
Anna listened. The same talk she heard from Bessie. The natives complain the Boers took their land, and the Boers complain the British and the *Uitlanders* have taken their land.

Ruth was pregnant. There was no doubt the father was the farmer, van Niekerk. The young woman was terrified. Who would this child resemble?
"What must I'm doing? My father he not like it if I'm bringing this child to the *kraal*."

The pains began in the early hours, continuing throughout the day and night. Joe's birth had been easy. Squatting on the *veld* with the village midwife, her mother and grandmother, giving encouragement. This child was different. It seemed as if, conceived in a violent act, it knew the trouble it faced and so resisted leaving the shelter of its mother's womb.

The midwife summoned by Anna from the town, refused to attend the delivery.

"*Ag jurrah man*! I'm a white person. You can't expect me to nurse a *kaffir*."

In desperation Frederick fetched old Dr. MacLeod. He found him half drunk in the saloon, but Anna gave him cups of strong black coffee and he sobered enough to help the young woman.

"C'mon, my wee lassie, yer doin' fine the noo, one more push, c'mon I say."

At last, after loud wails from the mother the child came, whimpering weakly.

"It's a wee girlie." The doctor put the baby at its mother's breast but Ruth turned her head away while tears ran down her cheeks. The child had the look of its father.

The doctor understood, but he knew that once the baby suckled the mother's heart would soften, and so it did. Ruth was robust and the milk flowed but she had no name for her child so Anna called her Sara. Ruth gave up her search for Tembu.

Time progressed and Lisa and Sara grew close as sisters, playing and squabbling. Sara resembled her white father. Her skin a pale satin; her hair light-brown and softly curled. Her eyes were deep blue.

Frederick kept away from Donna as he attempted to mend things between himself and Anna who kept herself busy with the children, teaching Ruth to cook German dishes and to sew. She also gave Sara lessons in letters and numbers with Martha and Lisa. She learnt to forgive Frederick but resisted his love-making, fearing more children. He felt her rejection as well as Martha's who hadn't forgiven him. Only Lisa showed affection.

"A man needs more than that," Frederick confided in Tommy.

The evening meal was over and the dishes done.

"I think I must finish showing you how to sew that dress for Sara," Anna said to Ruth.

"Oew! I would like to do that."

Frederick stood up. "Well, looks like it's no place for me around here." He lifted his felt hat off the hook behind the door, pushed it onto his head while taking his watch out of his vest pocket and glancing at the dial. He was a miner now, a prospector and it showed in his clothes. He dug the ground and sifted the dirt, hoping, like all the diggers, to find the one bright stone that would make his fortune.

"I'll be off then. Must go into town and have a look at what's on the market," Anna with her mouth full of pins, nodded.

It was a chance meeting. Turning the corner into the Square, Frederick almost knocked the young woman over. He bent to retrieve her parcels and saw it was Donna. For months he had made very effort to avoid her, although he worked with Charlie and Tommy. They stared at one another, then both spoke at once. They walked a short distance, then began making plans.

"I know a woman who lets rooms. Her place is on the other side of town and she doesn't ask questions," said Donna.

Chapter 7

Nkiwe.

Today I am very sad, I am holding my child in my arms and I see the look of the white man. She is one month old but already I see she can look like the father. What can happen to this child when she look white and the people see she got a black mother? Oew! What can happen to this child?

Today I'm getting the news that Tembu, he is dead. For a long time I'm believing I will never see Tembu again. I remember what the white farmer telling me that Tembu won't come back, that he will 'arrange' that, but today I know for certain because the madam here in Kimberley where I'm working, she asking them at the mine and she asking the police and now, the police they telling her that Tembu, he get stabbed at the beerhall. "Oew! *Inkhosikazi*," I say to my madam, "And now I cannot go back to my home because I have the whiteman's child. My father he get very angry with me if I bring this child home. My father is a proud man. He the son of the Chief. What mus' I do?" The madam, she very good, she say she will help me.

When I first am working for this madam after I come to Kimberley and cannot find Tembu, she asking my name and I say it is Nkiwe but I tell her the farmer and his wife they never calling me by that name they always calling me 'the girl.' She say Nkiwe is a very nice name but she can't say it the proper way so she like to call me Ruth. I think I like that name 'Ruth'.

Today I am thinking about my family; about my mother who is a Zulu and she telling me that after she is married to my father who is a Sotho, she asking to go to her home in Impendhle in Natal so I can be born there but then, after I am born, she mus' go back to her husband who live in Thaba Nchu across the mountains. So she go back. My mother tell me, when I am three years old, the rains don't come for many months and when it is more than two years and there is no rain, nothing can grow and they have no food and my father, he say they mus' leave the district. I can remember my father, he ride his pony with his coloured blanket over his shoulder and his pointed straw hat on his head. We go slow across the *veld* where my father must drive the cows who are very thin because the grass is dry.

At last, my mother say, we come to the town called Kimberley with the Big Hole where they dig for diamonds and my father, he take us to his

53

mother's father, my grandfather, who lives on his land land near that place, Kimberley. My uncles, they all work for the white farmer and he also give my father a job and we live with the other workers in the *kraal* on the farmer's land. Later, my father, he marry his cousin for his Number Two wife and my father has many chil'ren. My mother work in the farm as the cook and my father, he look after the cattle.

Me, I am not very big and look younger than I am. When the farmer asking my age he look at me and he say I am old enough, and that I must work in the kitchen and do the laundry. I always like my cousins to plait my hair with beads but the farmer's wife she say we mus' cut our hair very short and wear *doeks*. She also say we mus' wear long skirts and blouses with sleeves and so I wear these same clothes now at this new job but this madam, she say she don't mind if I plait beads in my hair.

When I have my free weekend I go to my friends in the village not far from Kimberley and we play music. I like to play the gourd. My father he show me how to scoop out the gourd and put animal gut for strings. We also make pipes from the reeds growing by the river. I like to dance, to stamp my feet and clap my hands.

One day, I'm thinking, I like to build a house in this village. My house will have walls of mud and the floor made with dried dung and the roof with thatch. I like to paint designs on the walls. I like to live there with my chil'ren but I don' know when that can happen because I mus' work for the madam. I have no husband now. First I live in the room her husband make for me on the back *stoep* at her house. But now, after I have the baby, her husband he make a room in the back yard for me. It has walls and roof of tin and in summer time it is very hot.

When I thinking of Tembu I thinking of the food he like me to cook for him. Me and him, we like the same food, we like to eat *putu* with spinach. Sometimes we stew the meat to eat with *putu* and spinach.

I remember one day when I'm cooking *putu* in the big black pot over the fire inside the hut, I'm stirring it and the cloth in my hand gets on fire. I get very frightened and throw it down and the grass mat gets on fire. I run to pick up my child who is playing on the floor. I am very afraid for my child. The thatch catches fire and very quickly the whole hut is filled with smoke. I'm holding my child and I'm crawling to the door. Then my father and Tembu they come and they stamp out the fire and the people all run to the river and carry water in pots to throw on the fire and at last it is out.

People think I only care about putting beads in my hair and making necklaces and bracelets to wear, but they make big mistake, I am not like that. I am wishing that time that I can stay at the Mission school, but the farmer, he say I mus' work in the kitchen and my father, he say I must get married and have chil'ren. My father, he say it is arranged for me to marry Tembu. Tembu's father is the Induna and he helps the Chief. At first I am afraid, but when I meet Tembu I can see he is a good man and I know I can love him.

Oew! My father he is very strict, he can get cross very quickly, but he also good to his family. He work hard and make sure when we sick we get the medicine and he make sure we always have plenty food. But, my father, oew! He can get very cross. If I am planting a tree for my father I am planting the Baobab tree. My grandmother, she telling me the story that God, He get very angry with the Baobab tree and He pull it out of the ground and throw it back in headfirst. My grandmother say that is why the tree looks like it is growing upside down. The branches, they look like the roots. But the old woman in the village here, she say the witchdoctor he telling a different story about the Baobab tree. The Baobab tree live for a very long time and it give food and medicine for the people. The fruits of the Baobab tree we eat; the leaves cook like spinach and the seeds we grind and roast. The leaves we can also take for medicine for the stomach and the bark for the fever. This tree I would plant for my father.

Oew! I am the most sorry that Tembu, he leaving the farm to go to the town for work. He say he mus' get a job for the money to pay my father the *lobola* but I am wishing that he never leave the farm then he not getting killed and the farmer, he not rape me. Oew! That make me the most sorry, that Tembu he go away.

But I remember it is Tembu that teaching me to be happy. He teaching me many things. He telling me to listen to the birds and he teaching me their names like the *korhaan*, heavy birds but with big wings so they can fly very high. He teaching me names of the buck like the *lechwe*, and the springbok that leaps high with curved back and straight legs.

On Sundays when we don't have to work, then Tembu and me, we walking across the veld to the river and after the rains come when the river is full, we like to take off our clothes and lie in the water then Tembu, he telling me he love me and he will come back soon. Then we lie in the long grass and Tembu, he lick the water off my breasts. But now, on Sunday morning, I am by myself in my room with this child of the white man suckling at my breast. Now I am thinking all the time about Tembu, who is dead; about my family who are very far away

I am remembering the day when my cousin at the farm, he giving me the leaves to smoke. He grow it in the field between the *mielies* where the farmer can't see it. Oew! it make my head funny and my body it feel like its floating. I only smoke that one time. Tembu, he say it is not good.

My madam, she come from very far across the sea to live in this place with her husband and her two chil'ren. She telling me about where she living before. Today I'm thinking about Tembu and today I am sad for me and for my child. What can happen to this child?

Chapter 8

Kimberley
Circa 1886

Smoke from the camp fire rose and mingled with morning mist, hanging heavy and hollow in the valley. Frederick and Tommy sat on up-turned wooden boxes while Jacobus brewed coffee. He handed each a tin mug and Tommy pushed his slouch hat to the back of his head then, leaning forward, resting both elbows on his knees, sipped the steaming liquid. Dribbles dripping down his beard.

He wiped his mouth with his hand, then turned to face Frederick. "All the blokes is talking about this bleeding gold that's been found in the Transvaal. They say it's in a ridge of hills called the 'Wit...waters.r.a.n.d', and is about thirty miles south of Pretoria."

Frederick drained his mug and nodded, calling to Jacobus for a refill. "Ja, I have heard about it, it means, 'ridge of white waters', or something but there's been rumours of discoveries of gold all over the Transvaal for a few years now, as far east as Barberton even. People don't talk about their crops or the weather any more, y'know, only about finding gold in the Transvaal." He laughed and shook his head.

"Well, this is no rumour, guv. There's been talk for months of a reef of gold-bearing rock and now they believe the're on to it." Tommy handed his mug to Jacobus and took his pipe from his back pocket, putting it into his mouth and sucking on the stem while striking a match and placing it in the bowl packed tight with tobacco. A mingled aroma of pipe-smoke and coffee filled the air. He looked up at Frederick again, and continued talking.

"They say, Freddy, that two blokes, George Harrison and George Walker, has discovered part of this reef in a place called...," he wrinkled his forehead, then snapped his fingers, "Lang..laagte, that's right. Strange names!" Frederick nodded while Tommy spoke, finishing his second mug of coffee then he too, lit his pipe. "Me and Charlie, we has decided to go to the Transvaal and have a shot at prospecting gold."

Frederick, who had been slouched forward, staring into the fire, sat up, surprise on his face. He took his pipe out of his mouth to speak but Tommy continued, "You know that Rhodes and Barnato are buying up every bleeding claim they can get their hands on here, but we'll give you first option on ours, guv', unless you want to join us up there, of course."

57

Frederick thought for a while then shook his head, "No. I'll stay put, but thanks all the same."

Later that evening Frederick told Anna about Tommy's proposition. She was sure that Frederick and Donna still saw each other and yet it was strange, she thought, he didn't seem unduly upset by Tommy's news. She didn't comment.

"I think I'll do better on my own anyway. Tommy's O.K. but I've never trusted Charlie. The fellow's a liar and I suspect he's cheated on me often."

Anna's eyebrows rose.

Frederick's profits increased. He built a bigger and more comfortable house and Anna was proud of her new home, "As a good wife should be," Frederick once confided to Tommy, "but a man needs more than that y'know."

Before they left for the Transvaal Donna again begged Frederick to take her away. "Can't you take me back to the old country? Anna will be O.K. She will return to her parents. She hates this place, anyway." But he feared Charlie more than he desired Charlie's' wife.

"That's not possible, I told you before. Charlie will follow us wherever we go."

Donna reluctantly left with Charlie and Tommy and Frederick found that he missed her more than he had been prepared to admit and he also missed Tommy's easy going friendship. He put in longer hours, working both claims, then one day he received a letter from Tommy.

"You should get yer arse up here, old chum. As I said before, there's plenty of lolly to be made here."

It was early evening. Anna sat on the old wooden rocker on the *stoep*. She could see the Big Hole, where the setting sun caught the mounds of earth at the top in a wide gold band, narrowing and turning dark purple in the shadows. Wires, carrying buckets up to the surface from the diggers working below, criss-crossed the wide pit like a giant cobweb as the desire for diamonds and riches, like a gigantic spider, lured men into this vast black hole. But Anna knew many had left for the goldfields and the promise of even greater riches.

How the town has grown in the nine years since their arrival, she thought.   Houses made of wood with corrugated iron roofs, replaced tents and now the hotel had another story. Frederick and Anna had lived in their new house for almost a year but she was uneasy as she sensed he was restless once again. He kept talking about the gold in the Transvaal. Her thoughts were interrupted by the sight of his tall figure striding up the hill so she hurried into the kitchen to help Ruth prepare a tray for coffee.

A short while later, sitting together on the *stoep* with coffee and *koeksusters* on a table between them, Frederick licked at the sticky, sugary globules clinging to his moustache, then drained his cup and wiped his mouth with a large handkerchief taken from a back pocket. He stood up, pacing the *stoep*, while Anna bent over and picked up the crumbs that fell from his shirt front. She sat thoughtfully for a moment then took a sock from her sewing basket, picked up a cowrie shell to push into the toe, and began darning the hole.

Lisa, playing with a kitten and a ball of wool, noticed the cowrie in her mother's hand. "Mamma, that's the shell Martha found on the beach the first day we were in Capetown, don't you remember? Let me listen," putting out her hand for the shell and placing it to her ear. She listened to waves pounding a distant shore. Held it in front of her, then curiously turned it over.

"Mamma...," she began. Anna smiled.

"Now don't ask me why you can hear the sea from inside that shell."

Undeterred the child turned to her father. "Why...?" beginning again.

Frederick laughed, putting up both hands. "You ask too many questions, Lisa."

Anna looked up at the two of them, alike in so many ways, both demanding and both persistent. "Run along now, my girl. I want to talk to your Mamma." Lisa reluctantly picked up the kitten and went indoors.

Frederick continued pacing the *stoep*. "I'm doing well here now, but Kimberley is not the place for the small man these days. Rhodes and Barnato are going for a monopoly of the diamond business. It won't be long before they have full control. Now's the time to get out and it's also the time to get in on the Witwatersrand. Tommy and Charlie were right, I should have left with them a year ago."

He reached into the inside pocket of his coat. "I have a letter from Tommy inviting me up there. Johannesburg is a growing town, Anna.

Kimberley is nothing but a mining camp." As enthusiastic as a young boy, as always.

She shook her head.

"I'll do well up there and build a big house for you then we can send for your Mamma and Pappa." His voice persuasive.

"You promised to send for Mamma and Pappa before." Her voice bitter.

"It will be different in Johannesburg, Kimberley never was the place for your parents." He continued. "I've made enquiries and can sell my claims with no problem. I intend leaving quite soon. When I find a place for us to live, I'll return and fetch you and the girls."

"What about Ruth and her children?"

Frederick ignored the question, continuing to talk about his plans.

Anna wanted to remind him of what he had said about Charlie cheating; she wanted to ask him why he would resume their partnership? But she kept the thoughts to herself. She suspected it was Charlie's wife who drew him to the Transvaal, equal at any rate to his desire for gold. She kept silent.

"Well, Anna, what have you got to say?"

The idea of moving appalled her but if Frederick had made up his mind she knew he wouldn't change it.

"I have nothing to say. What difference would it make whatever I say? You will do what you will do." Her voice was edged with bitterness and her hands shook as she picked up the tray to return it to the kitchen.

Lisa ran through the open doorway, she had overheard the conversation. "Will Ruth and Joe and Sara come with us, Pappa? Once again Frederick ignored the question. She pirouetted in front of him.

Disappointed by Anna's lack of enthusiasm but encouraged by Lisa's excitement he sat down and pulled her on to his knee. "Come here, my princess. Pappa will buy you new dresses and lace petticoats and ribbons for your hair when I make my fortune in gold."

Lisa clapped her hands and Martha, hearing the laughter, walked outside to join them. "Pappa says we'll live in a big house and he'll buy us lots of lovely things,"

Martha scowled. "I don't believe that. I don't want to leave here," looking for her mother's reaction, before running inside.

Within a few weeks Frederick sold his claims and mining equipment and left for the Transvaal. Months passed with no word. Anna made enquiries. She wrote to the address he left for her, anxiously waiting a reply. Nothing came. The letter was returned. Was the address incorrect? At night her darkest fears took over as she imagined him in Donna's arms.

Ruth reassured her. "Oew! You know it take time to get settled in a new place. Maybe one day soon he will be back."

"Oh Ruth, what would I do without you?"

Ruth smiled. "Well I can say, what I'm doing without you? You help me when I'm got trouble. I'm thinking before that all white people mus' be like the farmer van Niekerk. He say, 'You have to show the *kaffir* who is the boss and then he'll respect you.' That's what van Niekerk always say."

Anna shook her head. "I wish you had known Tannie van Rooyen, she was a farmer's wife but she never spoke like that." Anna put the dirty dishes into the basin on the kitchen table, poured in a saucepan of water, heated on the coal-fired cooker and began to wash up, while Ruth took the broom from behind the door and swept the floor. Privately she feared Anna was right, Master Frederick would not come back. Tembu hadn't returned. Maybe the master was sick. Maybe he'd been murdered. Maybe he was with the woman, Donna. She kept those thoughts to herself.

Chapter 9

Johannesburg
Circa 1887

The line of wagons halted, brakes shrieking, wheels crunching, while cattle grunted and lowed; stamping hooves in the dust and billowing out dirt like yellow banners. Frederick, his bag in his hand, jumped clear. He turned to help a woman passenger, then made his way across the busy street.

Johannesburg bustled. Anticipation and anxiety reflected on the faces of passers-by as they rushed back and forth like ants in an antheap kicked over by a careless boot, scurrying in all directions and covered in a cloud of dust.

The street was wide. A full span of oxen could turn in it. On either side it was bordered by low buildings with corrugated roofs overhanging boardwalks and supported by wooden posts. Frederick entered the saloon through swing doors and strode towards the long bar counter. Pungent cigar smoke, fetid body odours and the powerful aroma of beer rose in a cloud, filling his nostrils.

"'Ow-de-doo, me love. What can I getcha? Nice cold beer and a chaser?" The barmaid, her straw hair piled high, took hold of the tap and released a jet of amber. Frederick's eyes rivetted on her low cut dress. She returned his stare so he hastily shifted his gaze.

"C'mon luv, don't be shy. Stranger in town? Like to come to my place after? I'm going home jus' now."

"Er... er... no thanks, thanks all the same. I'm meeting someone," he stammered, with thumb and forefinger he pulled out his pocket-watch, noting the hour, then slid it back into vest pocket. "Late already."

He threw back his head, swallowing the cool liquid then pushed the glass across the counter for a refill. After the second beer he made his way through the packed saloon. The barmaid called after him, her voice raised above the din, "C'mon luv, come on over, I'll make ye feel at home, that I will," laughing shrilly. He shook his head, hurrying through the crowded room.

He stepped outside and put up his hand to shade his eyes from the bright sunlight then took Tommy's letter from his pocket, reading the address scrawled across the top. A few enquiries led him to a narrow, double-storied building down a side street. He hesitated, wiping his forehead nervously. Excitement and anticipation mingling.

"'Ello guv', so you got me letter." Frederick spun around to see Tommy appearing around the corner. He had noticed the sheet of paper in Frederick's hand, and, putting his arm around his shoulder, led him into the building.

"Ja, ja! I got your letter, and decided to take up your offer."

"Well, I wrote that a long time ago, didn' I, and things have changed." He hesitated then continued, "but anyway pleased to see you, I'm sure. So you decided to come and join us after all. Me and Charlie'll show you the ropes." He led the way up a narrow, dark staircase, turning at the top, and walking down a bare hallway with Frederick following. He stopped in front of a dark painted door and hammered with his fist.

"Hey! Charlie. Donna. Open up. Look who I find outside."

Charlie opened the door. He wore a pair of trousers with suspenders hanging down. His chest was bare. Donna stood behind, buttoning her blouse. The bed was unmade and rumpled. Sheets and clothing were strewn about, striped with sunlight, sifting through the brown wooden shutters, The air was stale with smoke and sweat. Their voices rose in greeting.

A short while later the four sat around a table in the dark-panelled dining-room. A fan whirred, flies buzzed in window panes and the smell of fried food, drifted from the kitchen. The men discussed business.

"Prospecting is too hard at my age, y'know squire, I'm getting out of it. The damn Jews have taken over here anyway," said Charlie, slurping soup between his sentences.

Frederick didn't reply.

Tommy gave an embarrassed grin, quickly interrupting. "'e means the competition's too strong, guv, that's what e's saying. There are financiers here from all over the bleeding place, so we been looking at the hotel business, something with the bar-trade, that's where the money is."

"Ja'betcha! That's what we're going into and Donna here can help us, it's time she did a bit of work, the lazy bitch. She's had too much free time, don' know what she been up to," bending over and planting a kiss on her lips.

"Ow! Get away with you," she remonstrated, turning her head sharply.

64

Frederick laughed nervously, hoping Charlie's remark was a joke. "But you wrote and told me about the great opportunities prospecting for gold, Tommy."

"That was nearly a year ago, guv'. A year is a lifetime up here. Anyway there ARE lots of opportunities. Businesses are growing aren't they? And the new stock-exchange - that's the place to make money, I can tell'ja!" Tommy continued, "Anyway, it's good to see you, fellow me'lad!. It's goin' to be like the old days in Kimberley," shouting above the noise of the pianist, pumping out a popular melody

Frederick avoided Donna's eyes while telling them he needed a place to stay. "Somewhere suitable for Anna and the children. I'm not bringing Ruth, have no intention of starting life in this place with people talking about my wife's friendship with a native girl. People in Kimberley talk you know. Anna doesn't care - but I do." His voice thickened as Donna's soft thigh pressed against his, her hand, under the table, curving over his leg in a gentle stroking motion. He moved away, his shaking hand, flickering the flame, as he leant forward to light his cigar from Charlie's match.

"I know just the place, Freddy luv. A private boarding establishment in a quiet part of the town. Just the ticket! I'll take you there tomorrow." Donna's voice was serious but her eyes were taunting.

"You can't go tomorrow, we're going to van der Merwe's farm, remember?" Donna looked at Charlie, but didn't reply.

The soft glow of the oil lamp cast a circle of light on the table at the bedside. Frederick lay on his back staring at the ceiling, Tommy sat on a chair across the room.

"I wrote to you because the girl's unhappy, guv. Charlie is no bloody good for her. Thought if you came you could take her away. You don't have to stay in Jo'burg, there's gold all over the Transvaal. You could go east to Barberton."

Frederick sat up gesturing wildly. "Goddamit, Tommy What the hell are you saying? What about my family?" He dropped his legs over the side of the bed and, leaning over, propped his forehead on his hands. "I came because I thought I could make a fresh start. I thought I'd got over Donna." He stood up, "Hell no! Tommy. That's a lie. I came because I had to see her again but I can see now it won't work. I thought it could be the same as in Kimberley but Charlie is talking about the hotel business and having Donna working with him."

He paced the room, still talking, rubbing his hands together then scratched his head. "I must get back to Kimberley; made a mistake coming here." Silence for a while then, standing in front of the window, he turned to Tommy. "Ja man, I think I'm better off in Kimberley but I'll not go back into mining either. There's talk of amalgamating all the separate claims to keep the price of diamonds up and costs down. The De Beer's group under Rhodes wants a monopoly." Tommy slowly nodded.

Frederick continued, "You've given me an idea. I think I'll also look into the hotel business. If I bought a place, with the capital I have now, Anna could help me run it and, as I'm stuck with Ruth, she can help as well. Kimberley's booming, we have electric street lights now, y'know."

At breakfast the following morning Frederick told Charlie and Donna his decision to return to Kimberley. Donna frowned and pursed her lips. Charlie shrugged and shook his hand.

"Whatever you say, guv'nor. So it's goodbye then. We better be off now." He stood up, indicating to Donna to stand as well. "Like I told you yesterday, friend of ours, fellow by the name of van der Merwe, has invited us to his farm for some shooting. It's up Pietersburg way." He turned back to Donna who remained seated. "C'mon now, woman! Hurry up. We haven't got all day. It's getting late and you're not ready. I tol' you to pack the food. What you sitting around for? Van der Merwe will be here just now."

She shook her head. "It's no good me going Charlie, luv. I got a splittn' bleedin' headache. Couldn't drive all that way in this heat in a wagon an' all."

Charlie scowled, "Too much wine las' night. I tol' you to cut it out. Anyway you got to come, you can't stay here alone all week and what about cooking our food there, who's goin' to do that, and wash our clothes?"

Van der Merwe arrived in the middle of the discussion.

"Hell man! That's no problem. I got a cook boy on the farm, hey! We can take him. And clean clothes doesn't matter when you're in the bush eh!" he said, laughing, relieved not to have a woman in the party. Charlie opened his mouth to protest but Donna forestalled him.

"Ooh! My stomach's sore as well, luv, feel lousy," Donna moaned, bending over, she clutched her side then leant back on the chair.

Tommy looking grave, put his hand to her forehead.

"Maybe we shouldn't go, what you think Charlie?"

"Not go! What yer mean, not go! Course we're going, everything's organised. If she can't come, she can't come, we'll have to manage with Koos' cook boy. Is he any good?" turning to van der Merwe, who nodded his head.

"Ja man, no problem. Nobody can *braai* meat like ol' Johannes."

"That's settled then," said Charlie, rubbing hands together.

Seeing Tommy's concern Donna straightened up.

"Don't you worry about me,luv. You fellows go and have a good time. I'll be OK. Right as rain in the morning. Jus' need a good night's sleep," winking at Charlie.

Charlie looked her over, "Alright, you don' look that bad, but you stay in the room, you hear? You don't go out no place, there's funny blokes around this town. I'll tell the maid to bring your food to the room. Anyways if you're sick you don' wanna eat?"

Tommy looked closely at Donna. "You sure you're OK, luv?"

She nodded. Charlie picked up bag and rifle, slinging them across his shoulder and turned to Frederick,

"So you leaving today?" His inquiry sounding like a command.

Frederick nodded. "Ja, I'm off just now. Must get my things together." He shook hands with the men, avoiding Donna's eyes.

Half an hour later he sat writing in a notebook at the table in his bedroom, almost ready to leave, his bag packed when he heard a knock at the door and, opening it, saw Donna, her eyes alight, panting and breathless from running up the stairs.

* * *

Frederick rolled over. Bright afternoon sun filtered through the dark, drawn drapes. He looked down at his side. Donna opened sleepy eyes then stretched her arms and pulled him on top of her, her legs tight around him. He sank into her soft flesh. Blood bumped his temple and bounced in his head then... boom - boom, and... blackness.

Donna's scream scratched the silence then stifled as a hand closed over her mouth.

"You bloody bitch, you bleedin' little whore. Jus' what I suspected, eh! Headache my foot!" A familiar voice was loud in her ear. She cowered against the bed. Frederick's body, heavy across her, rolled over and slid to the floor like a sack of dried *mielies*. Her dark eyes, wide with fear, watched Charlie bending over him.

67

* * *

Frederick stirred and groaned, then looked slowly around the strange room, trying to remember. Must have fallen asleep after lunch! Hammers hit his head. He closed his eyes and slowly the blurred vision cleared and the bed came into focus. He saw his packed bag, his notebook open on the table and his memory returned. He rolled over, lifting himself on to his knees, he rested on his hands his head hanging down as he shook it as if to clear a bad dream.

"A bad dream!" he began muttering to himself, "My God. A bloody nightmare!" looking towards the dressing-table where the bevelled edge of the mirror caught the light, he blinked, shaking his head. The door creaked, opening slowly. Part of a man's boot, toe scuffed and dusty appeared. Frederick's eyes moved upwards and saw stained khaki-drill trousers, a creased shirt-front. He tensed his muscles then stared into Tommy's eyes.

Squatting on haunches he rubbed his head, "What the blazes are you doing here? I thought you were in Pietersburg? I just had the most terrible nightmare, dreamt Donna was here and Charlie came in and found us together, phew!" Frederick was shaking his head as he leant forward on the bed then slowly rising to his feet. *Thank God that's over.*

"That was no bloody nightmare, guv? It 'appened for real alright. Can tell you that for sure. Bloody-'ell! Charlie did find you two together. We had trouble with one of the horses, had to turn back. Got to our place. No Donna. Clothes packed and note saying she was leaving with you. Couldn't stop the bastard. Said he was going to find you and kill you. Look here, guv', you'll have to get the hell out of here, and quick too. Charlie is threatening to return 'to finish you off', as he put it. You betta hire a horse and make for Vereeniging right away. You can get wagon transport from there to Kimberley."

Frederick picked up his bag. With Tommy's help, he hired a horse and set off on the dusty track, south, out of Johannesburg, putting the miles as quickly as he could between himself and Charlie. He arrived in the *dorp*, dusty and exhausted, handed his horse to the African groom and entered the saloon. He enquired about transport to Kimberley then found a table in a corner and took out his battered notebook and began writing in the events of the past few days. Charlie wouldn't find him here.

The saloon was quiet after the rush of evening customers. Two miners began an argument. Frederick, concerned with his own problems, paid no attention. The argument developed into a brawl. Some, who had left, returned at the commotion, gathering round the fighting men. Frederick turned to leave, picking up his bags.

The sound of the shot stunned the room to silence and then pandemonium. The gunman seized the opportunity and made his way out by the side door, disappearing into the darkness, taking Frederick's pocket book, diary and bag. He was out of town before dawn. The authorities made inquiries about the stranger who had been shot in the saloon by an unknown gunman, but to no avail. The body buried in a corner of the graveyard, was not identified.

The small town buzzed. Two farmers sat on their stoep discussing the tragedy.

"*Dit is baie sleg*, man, very bad. We only want peace and quiet to farm our land and now the bleddy *Uitlanders* come out of greed to get the gold and diamonds out the ground. I say let it stay there. President Kruger warned this would happen." His companion nodded, pushing tobacco into the bowl of his pipe, "*Ja man, Oom Paul is reg*. The *Uitlanders* must go."

Chapter 10

In time Anna came to believe that Frederick would not be coming home. She wrote to Charlie and Tommy at the address Frederick had left with her, but her letter was returned. It was a few months later that the secretary at De Beers contacted her. They had a letter mailed from Liverpool, addressed to Frederick care of the Company. She opened it.

> *"I am writing to tell you that our Tommy is dead.*
> *We went to Van der Merwe's farm after all and while*
> *hunting, Tommy was attacked by a lioness. The doctor*
> *couldn't do nothing for him he was mauled so bad.*
> *Tommy told me before he died, that he helped you get*
> *away. Charlie wanted to kill me after he found us.*
> *He said he'd kill you as well. I thought you was dead*
> *when he hit you so hard you fell off the bed and you*
> *jus' lay there. I was real scared, but I saw you was*
> *breathing so I reckoned you was alright. I asked*
> *Tommy to help you. I couldn't stay with Charlie, he*
> *beat me so bad. He tol' me he was goin' to get you.*
> *I hope you got back to Kimberley O.K. I met a man*
> *from Liverpool, he brought me back home and we are*
> *getting married."* She sent her love.

Anna folded the letter and put it with the rest of Frederick's papers. She told the children their father had died of fever. Shortly after Frederick's death her parents were killed when their house was fire-bombed. Her uncle had written her with the news and said there was more trouble for Jews and he was planning on leaving the country himself.

* * *

Anna sat at the kitchen table, bills open before her while Ruth dried the dishes.

"I just don't know how to earn enough to keep us."

She chewed on the end of her pencil. "The only jobs I can do are sewing and house-cleaning. Do you think I could get work dress-making?"

Ruth shook her head. "Not here in Kimberley. Lots of people are sewing for themselves. But I'm getting other jobs. *Mevrou* Kruger wants someone to clean her house and I also getting work doing washing and ironing." She shook her head, "but housework don' pay good money."

"What about house-keeping at the hotel? I could do that," Anna continued.

"That's not a job for a lady, not at the hotel where all the diggers go."

"What if I taught piano, then?" Anna's voice rose, then dropped despairingly. "But how many pupils would I get? Not enough to keep us." She thought for a while. "I could teach German. But how many people in Kimberley would want to learn German?"

Ruth packed away the dishes and Anna added figures one more time. "At least the house and all the furniture are paid for, but we need money for food and clothes and all the extras." Gloom descended as they sat in silence which was broken by the sound of a knock at the door. Smoothing her apron, Ruth opened it to see Jacobus standing on the step.

She invited him in and began setting out cups for coffee while Anna cleared away her account books.

"How are you doing Jacobus? Did you get a job after the claim was sold?"

"Ja, Missis. I'm working for De Beers as driver and messenger and that's why I come to see you." A pause. He picked up the mug of coffee in both hands, swallowed it quickly then scooped *melk-tert* into his mouth.

"When I drive I hear them talking and they are saying they got some men coming from London next week but they got no place for them to stay because the hotel it is full. I was thinking, Missis, you got this big house and you an' Ruth you cook so good." He grinned at them both. Ruth put another slice of tart on his plate. They laughed while Jacobus took another bite.

"I'm thinking, why can't Miss Anna take these people who are coming here to work for the Company."

Anna jumped up, clapping her hands in excitement. "Jacobus, that's a brilliant idea. We'll be able to earn money, do the only job we know and still be here for the children."

Jacobus smiled modestly, helping himself to another slice of tart.

Anna had a natural ability for business and boarding-house soon showed a profit. She divided her time between business and the education of Martha, Lisa, Sara and Joe. Ruth took charge of the kitchen and they shared the house-keeping. It was a time of fulfilment for both and, although shunned by most of the townspeople, they were too busy to care.

* * *

The years slipped by. Anna bought the neighbouring property as an annex. The boarding-house became "The Grange" a private hotel. She sent the children to the Convent.

* * *

Anna sat at her desk in the small front parlour, checking accounts when she was interrupted by a knock at the front door.

"*Goeie more*. Is die missis here?" The voice sounded familiar. Anna put away her ledgers. The parlour door opened and Ruth ushered in a woman, tall and stout, dressed in black, a veil over her face. She lifted it and Anna jumped up in surprise.

"Tannie van Rooyen! What are you doing in Kimberley?"

She remembered that Frederick had told her a long time ago that he had heard that diamonds had been discovered on Tannie's husband's farm. She hadn't seen Tannie again because they had sold out and retired to Beaufort West.

"Ooh jurrah man, Anna! It's good to see you, hey! My husband died last year, you know, and now I come to Kimberley with my son to visit my relatives here. It's the first time I've been back in all these years."

Anna led her to the sofa under the window while calling to Ruth to make coffee. They caught up on news of their families until Ruth walked in with the tray of coffee and *rusks*. She placed them on the low table then turned to leave the room.

"Bring another cup for yourself, Ruth. This is Tannie van Rooyen, you remember I have told you about her?" Anna leant forward and squeezed the rough hands of the old woman.

"You were a good friend to me Tannie, and helped me more than you know. Come on Ruth, come and sit down." She made a place next to her on the sofa. Tannie pursed her mouth. Ruth looked embarrassed as she mumbled, "I busy in the kitchen, missus."

Anna looked surprised and insisted but Ruth's face was set like stone so Anna let her go. Ruth could be stubborn.

Tannie told Anna how she had become involved in the Church; about the missionary work she did, spreading the Word to the natives. "We must teach them about Christianity, you know." She smiled as she took Anna's outstretched hand.

"You're very familiar with your girl, Anna my dear. It's a mistake to be too familiar. The Bible says they will always be 'drawers of water and hewers of wood' - you know, servants. They don't have the same brains as us whites, you see, they're not as smart, but we mus' help them to be better."

"But you told me that Jesus said all men are equal in the eyes of God.. Now are you saying God made white people better than blacks?" The old lady shook her head.

"It's a matter of position. We are God's chosen people here in Africa and we mus' teach the natives. They are like chil'ren, you see. They mus' learn their proper place."

The next day Anna discussed the matter with Ruth.

"Tannie believes God made white people smarter than blacks. How do you understand God?"

Ruth considered for a while, her brow wrinkled, then replied, "I believe God is a great Spirit."

Anna smiled, "That's what I believe."

* * *

Anna lay alone on the big double bed. Moonlight silvered the face of the clock and reflected off the candlesticks and silver-backed hairbrushes on the silver tray. She picked up the cowrie shell and put it to her ear, listening to the sound of the sea. A sudden pain broke over her then pulled and receded, like the waves, leaving her limp and weak. She was afraid. The pain was more severe and more frequent, something was wrong. What would happen to the family if she were to die? She knew Ruth would care for them but would the people in the town allow her.

The pains became worse. One day Martha noticed her mother's distress and spoke to Ruth. They called in Dr. MacLeod who chided them for not fetching him sooner. He arranged to send Anna to the hospital but she refused to go. She would die in her own bed, she said. She took up her journal and wrote in it for the last time. Ruth's devotion and loyalty supported her but the disease, like her fears, took root and spread.

One morning, in the early dawn hour before the sun lit up the *veld*, Anna died, quietly and without fuss. Lisa was inconsolable. Martha held back her tears. She would continue her mother's work and manage "The Grange" with Ruth.

Book 2
Chapter 11

Kimberley
Circa 1894

Sunlight filtered through the coloured glass panels on the front door and glanced off the edge of the mirror above the oak hat-stand, forming stripes of purple, green and red that fell across the young girl standing at the desk as she talked earnestly to her sister. Martha was checking figures in an account book.

"Kitty's cousin is visiting from Capetown and she has invited me to a picnic on the Modder River tomorrow. Please Martha, please say I may go. Kitty's Aunt Queenie will be there."

Martha put down her pen and wearily pushed away the strand of hair, fallen loose from her bun. Lisa, her headstrong impulsive sister was a big responsibility. It had been two years since their Mother, Anna had died and Martha, with Ruth's help, continued to run the private hotel.

Martha believed that Kitty Frobisher was an unsuitable companion for Lisa, who was easily influenced. Kitty's father was on the Board of Directors of De Beers, and he left the raising of Kitty to his sister, Queenie, who had come from England to keep house for him after his wife died when Kitty was twelve. Queenie was ineffectual and incapable of controlling her spoilt and wilful niece. She did feel it her duty, however, to lecture Kitty on etiquette and manners.

"It's most important, Kitty dear, never to forget who you are. In all other matters Kitty was left to her own devices.

Queenie had a comfortable routine, spending mornings writing letters to friends and relatives in England and afternoons drinking tea and playing whist with the wives of other prominent businessmen or members of the Colonial Service. "These Boer women have no class, m'dear. Quite common I declare." She commented to Mrs. Paine-Smythe one of her friends from the Women's Institute, run by the Anglican Church. Appearances were all important to Aunt Queenie, an ardent Royalist who believed in the glory of the Empire. "This young man Rhodes has the right idea." She was overheard telling Mrs. Proudfoot, while arranging flowers in the Church.

"We must expand the Empire - northwards through Africa." Mrs. Proudfoot's husband was in De Beers with Kitty's uncle. Queenie, not having a husband, gleaned all her gossip and inside information on the business and political manipulations of Cecil Rhodes from her two friends whose husbands were associates of Rhodes and members of the exclusive Kimberley Club.

Mrs. Proudfoot's husband, however, was more interested in expanding his profits in diamonds than the expansion of the British Empire.

"Well, I don't know about that, m'dear," she replied, repeating her husband's words, "but Rhodes certainly had the right idea when he amalgamated all the claims to form De Beers Consolidated to take control of the diamond industry." Queenie nodded, knowingly.

The eldest of her three brothers had inherited the Baronetcy from their father and as the Estate was entailed, the two younger sons left to make their fortunes in the Colonies. James soon abandoned the Colonial Service for the lure of diamonds. John joined their uncle's law firm in Capetown and later married into the de Villier's family, well connected and descended from the French Huguenots. Queenie, however, never considered them good enough for the Frobishers.

When appealed to by James to help him raise his only child she rallied to the call and left England for Kimberley. "Must do m'duty to dear old James, can't think why he will live in the Colonies, but we all have to make sacrifices to bring civilisation to these backward people, m'dear." Her maid reported these comments to Ruth who told Anna.

"Making them rich in the process," was Anna's response at the time.

The Baronet's wife in England, meanwhile, ignored her sister-in-law's complaints.

"Queenie enjoys being the martyr," she said to her husband. "Besides, she has more prestige as a hostess to her wealthy brother in Kimberley than as the spinster sister here at the Hall." The Baronet grunted from behind his copy of *The Times*, crunching on toast and marmalade.

Martha didn't consider Queenie a responsible chaperone for her young sister. Martha didn't trust men. It had been only a few nights earlier while discussing the problem of Lisa with Ruth that Martha had commented, "Men are domineering and self-centered. I have no desire to submit to their autocracy nor pander to their egotism, and never intend to marry. It was Pappa who caused Mamma's unhappiness. Remember how she blossomed after he left us."

Ruth nodded, not fully understanding the long words.

"I know Lisa feels differently. She is such a romantic and allows her emotions to get the better of her. I fear this will inevitably lead to marriage." She paused, sorrowfully shaking her head, then continued, "Oh dear! Oh dear! Ruth, what shall I do? If only Mamma were here."

"Never you mind, it'll come alright, *'alles sal regkom.'* Don't you remember your Mamma telling us that the old Boer woman, Tannie, always said that?"

"If only I could afford to send her to Europe but we have no one there, now that our grandparents have died. That was another promise Pappa never kept, he told Mamma he would bring them here," Martha continued, ignoring Ruth's attempt to cheer her up.

Martha was recalled to the present by Lisa's persistent nagging voice. "But, Martha..."

She put up her hand for silence as Ruth walked through the Reception area on her way to the kitchen. "What do you think Ruth, should I allow Lisa to go on this picnic with Kitty and her friends?"

Ruth pursed her lips, she didn't much care for Kitty who was often rude to herself and Sara. "I'm sure I'm can't say what Lisa may or may not do."

Martha turned to her sister, "I really need you here, a new guest is arriving shortly."

"Please Martha," Lisa rolled her eyes, "just say yes and I can go and tell Kitty."

"I can't discuss this matter with you right now. We'll talk about it tonight when I have more time. I have to give Ruth a hand in the kitchen. I was rather hoping you'd help Sara sort the laundry and make up a bed for the new guest in the front room." Ruth was in charge of the kitchen and marketing, while Sara and Lisa did the bedrooms and Joe doubled as waiter and porter.

Lisa opened her mouth to continue her protest. She never gave up easily, but stopped when she heard the sound of a carriage drawing up outside and male voices in conversation.

"I say, Jack, old chap, I've booked you in here at this private hotel where I've stayed for the past two years. I'm sure you'll be comfortable, has an excellent table; is owned by a very capable young lady, y'know.

Knew her Mother, splendid little woman." His voice lowered and Martha and Lisa were unable to hear the rest of the sentence.

Jack Patrickson had recently arrived in the country from the north of England where his father owned large Estates in the Lake District. Jack had travelled in Europe and when his friend, Bob, lured him to the diamond mines in Kimberley, he decided to pay him a visit before continuing his travels to North America. Joe appeared from the side of the house to carry the baggage. He followed the two young men up the steps and through the front door. After the noon sun the cool breeze in the hallway soothed their sweating foreheads. As their eyes grew accustomed to the dim light, they saw an oak hat-stand and persian rugs on polished floors.

Jack noticed the young girl standing against the reception desk. Her eyes, large, dark and almond-shaped, were wide apart in her pale oval face; black curls were tied back behind her ears. Now, however, her lips were pouted.

Jack adored women, he would do anything for them and believed they should be cossetted and protected and never burdened with problems of business or politics.

"They haven't the capacity to think rationally, old chap," he once confided to his friend Bob, "but are motivated by impulse and their emotions." He felt sympathy for the young girl and inexplicably drawn to her. When he finally noticed the elder sister he saw a young woman with her hair severely pulled back into a bun at the nape of her neck. Her dress was tight-fitting with a high neckline and a neat white collar. White cuffs finished off the long sleeves. She wore no jewelry. He was later to be confounded by Martha who didn't conform to his ideas of womanhood. She was quick and smart with a good head for business.

The guests' arrival distracted Lisa. She greeted Bob warmly. Tall and thin with a beaked nose and chin sliding back into his long neck while his Adam's apple worked up and down as he spoke. His friend Jack, was of medium height. His eyes were deep blue. His hair and moustache were blonde, tinged with ginger. Jack wore clothes with confidence. Collar winged and stiffly starched, above a white shirt. His jacket was tweed and a gold watch chain hung from his vest pocket. In contrast, Bob's collar wilted and his tie lay loosely around his neck.

"I say, Jack, old chap, meet these two charming young ladies. They keep me in Kimberley, don't y'know." Bob put his arm possessively around Lisa's shoulder while Jack stretched out his hand to clasp hers.

"Well that's just simply not true, Bob, and you know it. It's diamonds that keep you in Kimberley." Martha, protested primly. They all joined in the laughter.

At the first opportunity Lisa spoke privately to Bob, whom she regarded as a benevolent uncle.

"It's Martha, she insists on treating me like a child." He was told about the picnic and promised to discuss it with her elder sister at a suitable moment. Lisa threw her arms around his neck. He felt a constriction in his throat and panic in his heart.

After luncheon Bob spoke to Martha on the subject of the picnic and suggested they all went along. Lisa was ecstatic. Bob smiled indulgently as he sucked on his pipe.

"Splendid, splendid. That's settled then, old thing. The problem is solved, we'll all go, and have a smashing time."

Lisa excused herself and went looking for Sara. As she approached the door of the linen room her steps slowed as she thought about their friendship. They had been inseparable since childhood. She pushed open the door and saw Sara seated on the floor sorting and folding towels. In half lengthwise, then over, and in half again.

"Thank goodness for some company, folding towels is mind-boggling." Sara laughed, then continued, "I was thinking about what Sister Angela said." Sara had only recently completed her schooling at the Convent. Lisa had been out of school for a year.

"She said I should apply to the Normal College and study to become a teacher." Her eyes shone, then her shoulders drooped and she looked down, "But it's hopeless we can't possibly afford College fees."

Lisa knelt on the floor next to her, "Why worry about College, Sara, for goodness sake. You'll meet a nice boy and get married one of these days."

Tears pricked the back of Sara's eyes, "What nice boys do I ever meet? White boys won't invite me out and the coloured boys mostly haven't got very far at school.

"Nonsense, Sara." But Lisa knew her friend spoke the truth.

"It's not nonsense, Kitty only tolerates me because of her friendship with you - you know that."

Lisa was bothered. She was devoted to Sara who had always been a good friend, but Kitty was fun, yet she knew Kitty didn't care for the coloured girl. She sighed, "Oh dear! Why can't everyone just get along?"

She squeezed Sara's hand. "You'll never guess! Bob has arrived with his friend, Jack something-or-other, I forget his last name. He comes from England and is oh, so handsome." She rolled her eyes and a dimple appeared in the corner of her mouth. "Just when I was hoping Kitty's cousin Paul, from Stellenbosch would fall in love with me and carry me off to Capetown." Paul was a law student at the University in Stellenbosch.

"Kimberley is such a dump. Nothing ever happens here and now, when there's a chance for some fun, Martha wants to spoil it all. Anyway, thank goodness for Uncle Bob, who has suggested we all go on the picnic."

She jumped up from the floor where she had sat next to Sara, "Hurry, I'll help you pack away the linen then we must consider what to wear to-morrow. Do you think my flowered muslin suitable?"
Sara tried to share her friend's enthusiasm but shook her head.

"Sorry, I can't go, I have to help Ma clean out the kitchen cupboards, I promised her a long time ago."

Lisa wouldn't accept her excuse. She appealed later to the others and they joined her in persuading Sara, "I'm quite sure that Ruth can manage," Bob insisted.

Ruth could and would manage but she took no part in the discussion. She later confided in Martha, "I'm knowing all about Sara's problems, but what can I do about it? It is very difficult. It's that farmer, van Niekerk, he brought all this trouble upon the child."

Chapter 12

Kimberley
Circa 1894

Joe drove Bob's carriage from the stables to the front of the hotel. No one suggested he join the picnic party but he didn't expect an invitation. Joe was happy with himself. "Why you want to be like the white people anyway?" He once said to Sara.

"Because white people get all the opportunities. You know that."

"I'm proud to be a black man. Hey! my father, Tembu was the son of a chief. What mus' I care about the white man?"

Joe had left school after Grade IV. He told Anna he couldn't manage the work but it was some of the boys at the Christian Brothers' College who made his life miserable.

"Why can't you go to the Mission School in the Township with other black kids?" they taunted him. Joe had no regrets about leaving school. He was naturally optimistic and he enjoyed his job. It was good to have a few pounds in his pocket.

Ruth packed the picnic hamper and Joe loaded it into the back of the carriage with rugs and cushions. Martha climbed in and sat beside Jack with Lisa and Sara opposite, while Bob drove them to Kitty's house. The oxen were already inspanned and the covered wagon loaded with yet more food and cushions and rugs.

Aunt Queenie directed the proceedings with her rolled-up parasol.

"Mrs. Proudfoot and Mrs. Paine-Smythe will drive with me in the scotch-cart, Kitty. It's not very comfortable but we can't take your father's carriage across the *veld*."

"But what about Tessie's Ma, *Mevrou* du Toit, and Lena's Ma is also coming, you know *Mevrou* Viljoen. Remember I told you, Aunt Queenie. Can't they travel with you?"

"No, my dear, I don't think so. The covered wagon has plenty of space and besides there is Martha as well, they can't ALL expect to fit in with us. She will also be travelling in the wagon." Aunt Queenie disapproved of Martha's friendship with a black woman.

Kitty and Queenie were interrupted by a scuffle behind them. Nessie, Lena's six-year old sister ran down the pathway her *kappie* had slipped off her head and fallen across her back, held on by ribbons around her neck. Her braids flew out behind. She was being chased by Frans, Tessie's younger brother who was a few years older than Nessie. Frans held up a dead rat by its tail, "I'm comin' to get you, I'm comin' to get you. You betta watchout." he shouted, terrifying all the girls who ran screaming in all directions. Queenie at once stepped out firmly in front of the boy and poked at him with her parasol.

"Frans!" she bellowed, "stop that this minute and throw that filthy creature on the rubbish heap." Frans stopped in his tracks and walked meekly away, his hands behind his back with the dead rat dangling down. Nessie looked up from the ground where she had fallen, her long skirts bunched up around her knees. She smiled mischievously, feeling brave now that the danger was over.

At that moment *Mevrou* Viljoen and *Mevrou* du Toit came into view down the street, carrying baskets of home-baked bread and preserves.

"*Wat makeer?*" *Mevrou* Viljoen put down her basket and ran forward with her friend following close behind. "What's the matter?" they repeated in unison.

Aunt Queenie affected her most charming voice. "It's nothing at all, my dears, nothing I couldn't handle. Just a childish prank," and she smiled sweetly at Nessie who stood up quickly, when her mother appeared, and began brushing off her dusty skirts.

Aunt Queenie's commanding voice rang out, "I think we are almost loaded and here at last, come Martha, Lisa and Bob and Bob's great friend who is out here visiting from the old country." From behind her hand she whispered, "He's very well connected you know, m'dear," turning to face her friend, Mrs. Proudfoot who had also just arrived. She looked back at the approaching carriage. "Oh dear," muttering under her breath, "they have brought that Sara with them." But she looked up and smiled as Joe reigned in the horse. "Martha, my dear, how nice to see you and Lisa," stretching out her arms to the two sisters. "And Bob," she continued, with a gracious nod of her head, "is this your friend from home?"

Bob looked down with his arm across Jack's shoulder, "Yes indeed, Miss Frobisher, let me introduce you. Jack, old chap, meet the cream of Kimberley society."

Aunt Queenie extended her gloved hand, "So pleased to meet you to be sure. It's simply ages since I was home. How is the old country and from which part do you hail?" But before Jack could reply she chattered on. "We also have a visitor, you know, my nephew from Capetown." She turned towards Kitty. "Go and fetch Paul, Kitty dear." Bob and Jack helped their womenfolk out of the carriage then Queenie moved across and stood next to Jack, her back to Sara and continued her conversation.

At last everyone climbed aboard the wagons and they set off down the dusty street. Paul, Kitty's cousin from the Cape, played the harmonica and everyone joined in the singing. The girls in summer dresses with wide picture hats, the young men in striped blazers, white pants and straw boaters.

Jack sat beside Lisa, their voices rising in harmony as they joined in the singing, while the wagon trundled down the narrow track through the *krantz* to the valley below. The oxen, lumbering over the *veld*, stirred up the dust in the wake of the wagon. Dust filled the air and lay in layers on leaves of thorn trees and bushes. Dust lay in layers on the backs of the oxen. They flicked their tails at huge hovering flies and dust blew upwards. The hills on the horizon shimmered in the haze.
Sara sat next to Paul, her shyness evaporating as she responded to his friendliness. His blonde hair fell forward over his tanned forehead as he put the harmonica down and bent to speak to her. Dark blue eyes, deep-set, looked earnestly into hers. He spoke of life at the university and his future plans to join the family law firm. "I'm lucky, I have a job when I qualify, but many of my people can't find work. The English keep the best jobs for themselves, you know. Although my father is English my mother is a 'de Villiers' and I understand the grievances of the Boers." Sara's eyes widened in surprise at his words. She hadn't thought white people suffered from discrimination.
"Whoa! Whoa! *Hou still Swartbooi! Kom nou, Rooibont!*" The driver shouted at the oxen and the wagon shuddered to a halt in the wide stretch of veld next to the river above the waterfall. Steps were lowered at the back and Paul put up his arms to help Sara down. He held her for a moment and a flush stained her cheeks.
"I've just realised, I've been doing all the talking. You haven't told me anything about yourself," he said, as they began walking through the long grass to the spot chosen for the picnic on the river bank. Sara smiled.

Aunt Queenie's cook and kitchen maid prepared the luncheon. Wood was collected for the fire for the *braaivleis* and the lamb was placed on the spit. There was game biltong, pumpkin fritters, *koeksusters* and watermelon-*konfyt*. Ouma van der Merwe had sent a tin of her homedried *meebos*. The meal was followed by strong coffee brewed over the fire. The unfamiliar smell of *braaied* meat rose in Jack's nostrils.

After lunch Jack and Lisa strolled beside the river. Sitting on an outcrop of rock jutting into the water, Jack took a cigar from his top pocket and prepared to light it.

"I say, Lisa, your friend Sara is a beauty, by jove. Have you known her a long time? What does her father do, is he in the diamond business?"

Lisa was surprised. Obviously Jack hadn't realised that Ruth was Sara's mother and Joe, the porter, was Sara's half-brother. She hesitated, not knowing if she should tell him Ruth's story, then decided he would soon learn it anyway and so she related how it happened that Sara was light complexioned while her mother and half brother were black.

Jack nodded his head gravely, "A tragedy indeed." He puffed on his cigar and wondered if Paul knew, but made no comment as he bent over to dip his hand in the river.

Lisa laying on the sun-warmed rock, stared at the sky. So high above, so deep and blue. She felt part of it, a cloud drifting - a hawk gliding. Oh to be a cloud sailing so effortlessly across the blue-painted sky. *Why is life so full of problems?* she thought, *like the colour of Sara's mother's skin?* Suddenly she heard a splash and, sitting up sharply, saw Jack sinking under water. His head surfaced then disappeared again into the muddy pool. Lisa screamed, "Jack, Jack, my God, somebody help. Please help! Bob, where are you?" Her voice rose. The rest of the party, hearing her screams, rushed to the river bank to see Jack surface again and struggle against the strong undertow. "Help, help," Lisa repeated, "Over here. Come quickly," and bunching her long skirt and petticoats, while holding them with one hand, and without waiting she waded into the river although she knew it was deep with treacherous undercurrents and clinging underwater reeds.

Bob, sitting with the others, had seen Jack lean over and lose his balance before falling into the water. He knew Jack couldn't swim.

"Get back, for God's sake Lisa, get out of the water," he shouted, running to help his friend and reaching the river's edge just as Jack's head appeared one more time. But he was been pulled by the strong current to the rocks on the edge of the waterfall. Bob thrust out a long branch, he had broken off the overhanging willow. Jack reached up his hand to grasp it, and Bob dragged him ashore. He rolled the half-drowned man on his side and pounded his back. Paul, meanwhile, jumped into the river and caught hold of Lisa who, although not far from the bank, was struggling with the current and the weight of her wet clothes. She collapsed on the grass next to Jack, her body shaking. Dry clothes and blankets were brought and the two were made comfortable around the fire.

A stray cloud drifted across the sky. More clouds appeared and blocked out the sun; Jack and Lisa shivered as they drank from the mugs of steaming coffee. A flash of light streaked the sky, which was darkening on the distant horizon, followed by a rumble and more clouds gathered. Her fears forgotten, Lisa felt a spasm as if an electric shock passed between herself and Jack. He put his arm around her shoulder and felt her tremble.

The two *Xhosa* drivers had waded into the water downstream. They looked up in alarm and pointed at the darkening sky. Scanning the veld for the oxen that had strayed, they set off to round up the animals before the storm broke. Meanwhile the picnic party began to gather up blankets, cushions and clothing. Everyone clambered into the wagon and the canvas sides were rolled down. Lightning lit the sky and the booming thunder blasted across the valley. The rain fell. Jack, now dressed and his composure regained, moved closer to Lisa, feeling the warmth of her body.

Paul reached his arm along the back of the wagon bench and encircled Sara's waist. He bent forward and whispered, "I must see you again. May I call on you tomorrow?"

Sara hesitated, "I .. d..d..don't know. I'm not sure. I.. I may be busy." Her head hung down and her shoulders drooped. Paul frowned at her change of mood. Neither noticed two pairs of eyes staring at them from under the lifted canvas cover, nor heard the giggles as young Frans and Nessie raced off, chasing each other in the pounding rain. The storm passed and a late sun lit the landscape while raindrops jewelled every leaf and a rainbow spanned the sky.

Lisa sat at the dressing-table brushing out her long, thick black hair while Sara lay curled at the bottom of the bed. "He obviously thinks I'm an Afrikaner. "I have to agree with him, now I come to think about it, people like Kitty's father and her Aunt Queenie are condescending to anyone who isn't British. They do keep the best of everything in the country for themselves. Paul feels that Afrikaners are denied opportunities. I wanted to ask him about coloured people. What opportunities do we have, and what about women? I didn't of course."

"You're far too serious, my dear. Have fun. Who cares about opportunities for women? He fancies you, that's obvious. Why, he may even ask you to marry him and if you like him well, what better opportunity could you have than marriage into a wealthy family?" Lisa stopped brushing her hair and watched Sara's reaction, reflected in the mirror.

"Don't be silly. It's not as simple as that. He doesn't know my mother is black, at least he didn't know on the picnic but I'm sure he does by now. I bet Aunt Queenie has done her duty!."

"So? What if she has. There's no law to prevent the races intermarrying."

"There may not be a law, but you know what people are like in this town. I can imagine all the whispering going on even now." She paused for a while, staring wistfully into space. "Anyway he did say he wanted to see me again but I don't expect he will now."

Paul said he was in love with Sara. When told her circumstances he said it made no difference. He ignored his relatives' disapproval and asked her to marry him. He did not care that her mother was a *Xhosa*. But Uncle James, Kitty's father cared, and Aunt Queenie cared and they knew that their sister-in-law, Magriet Frobisher, nee de Villiers, would care when she heard that her only son planned to marry a coloured girl from Kimberley.

Chapter 13

"She is only a child, Jack, not ready for marriage. It is useless to even talk to me about it. I won't consider the idea." Martha's usual composure was shaken as she talked to the handsome young Englishman. She had been caught up in the talk about Sara and Paul's engagement and hadn't noticed Lisa and Jack's growing attraction for each other. Her hands trembled on her lap.

"When I think of the tragedy of my parent's marriage, Pappa's weaknesses, causing Mamma's unhappiness, I must protect Lisa." she confided to Ruth later.

Jack, hands clasped behind his back, paced the room. They were in the front parlour. A shaft of sunlight shone through lace-edged shades, onto the polished floor and reflected off the silver candlesticks on the mantel and the silver frames of family photographs on a circular table, covered with a fringed velvet cloth, which stood in front of the bay window. She looked around the room and noted the familiar things belonging to her mother, brought from Europe all those years ago. She stared at her Mama's portrait, painted in oils, hanging over the mantelpiece. *Oh Mama,* she thought, *what should I do. If only you were here.*

"She's not a child, by Jove, she has a natural maturity. Look how she supports Sara in spite of opposition from Kitty and the disapproval of Paul's family over their engagement."

Jack's words brought her back to the present.

"But you are so much older."

"A mere twelve years."

"Well, what about the differences in religion. You know that we are of the Jewish faith. What will your Anglican parents say?"

Jack stopped pacing and stood before her silencing her objections with a wave of his hand. "Balderdash, m'dear! The difference in our religion is unimportant, what is important is that we love each other."

"But you hardly know each other. Go to America as you planned and when you come back after a year renew your friendship. If you both still feel the same, we'll discuss an engagement then. Give Lisa time to learn a little about life."

"No, my dear, I cannot leave her, I might lose her and I have to have her."

Martha looked up in alarm. She wished he wouldn't speak of her sister in this way. As if she were an object he must possess. Lisa ran into the room just then and into Jack's arms. They both turned towards her, Lisa's face alight with happiness.

"Please, Martha. . ." Lisa began.

Martha put up both hands, "All right, all right. I'll give my permission but you have to wait at least a year before you marry."

The rejoicing was interrupted by the sound of the dinner gong. Martha jumped up, "Goodness me, is that the time already?" She disappeared through the door in the direction of the kitchen.

Jack and Lisa sat on the sofa. They were not often alone. He took a small velvet box out of his coat pocket and placed it in her hand. She opened it. Five diamonds sparkling on a gold band. He placed it on her finger.

Lisa sighed and put her head on his shoulder. "You remind me of my Pappa. I feel safe with you."

He reached into his pocket again and brought out a bracelet of diamonds and sapphires and put it on her wrist.

"Pappa always gave me presents," she said as they embraced then walked arm in arm into the dining room.

Martha and Ruth sat at the kitchen table, the coffee pot between them. Dinner was over and calm restored. Martha stretched her arms above her head then put her hand over her mouth to cover a yawn.

"Goodness gracious, but I am tired." She rubbed her eyes. "I have some disturbing news and I honestly don't know what to do." She told Ruth about the engagement. "I like Jack well enough but I have one problem. He reminds me of Pappa. Self assured and, well, maybe a little too charming. He said he had to have Lisa, as if she were an object to be possessed."

Ruth sat silently, remembering Anna and Frederick.

Jack joined Bob in the business of mining and marketing diamonds and they prospered. Paul returned to Stellenbosch to complete his studies while Lisa and Sara prepared for their weddings, learning to sew and to cook as was expected.

* * *

It was Sunday morning. Lisa and Jack sat under the wild fig tree at the end of the garden. Church bells rang and the two spinster school teachers, Miss Harriman and Miss Jennings, appeared on the front porch putting their hats straight and pulling on their gloves.

"A delightful pair, don't you agree, Gertrude," indicating Jack and Lisa. "I can't abide that coloured girl though, that Sara, setting her cap at that nice young man from Capetown. The very idea! The town is talking." Miss Jennings mumbled a reply.

"What's that? What's that? Speak up, you know I'm hard of hearing."

"I just said it's none of our business. If the young man loves her, and she is very pretty, why I think it's very romantic."

"Utter nonsense. Of course it's our business. Can't have intermarriage. What will happen to the white race?"

* * *

Jack and Lisa's wedding day was at hand. Martha sat at her desk totalling figures. The hotel was doing well. A knock at the door interrupted her work, and Bob's head appeared around the corner.

"May I come in?"

"Of course," she replied, closing her account book.

Bob slumped into a chair opposite and crossed his legs. "Just want to say I'm returning to the old country." He reached into his pocket and took out his pipe, preparing to light it.

"Oh dear, we shall miss you. This is unexpected. Is there a problem with your family, your father's health?"

"No, nothing like that. Well, may as well admit it I suppose. It's Lisa. Been in love with the gal for - well ever since I met her in fact. Damn fool, of course she would never look at me. Haven't let on my feelings though. Hope you understand." He clenched his teeth on the stem of his pipe.

"I had no idea....," she began.

He put up his hand. "Just between you and me, m'dear, don't breathe a word, promise?"

She nodded.

It was a few short days to the wedding and Jack held a parcel out to show Lisa.

91

"Have a little gift for Martha, m'dear."   She opened the box and lifted out a gold locket with a picture of their mother inside.

"Oh, Jack. Martha will love this. It's exactly right for her."

"Had hoped she and Bob would make a match but Bob is returning home. Can't think why. Thought he liked it here; thought he was settled," shaking his head.

"Anyway De Beers have made us an offer for our claim and have asked me to join the company."

"But I thought you preferred your independence."

"Well, actually I do, but have no option. It's becoming more expensive because we have to go deeper and sink shafts and excavate tunnels which entails risk and to meet these additional expenses the price of diamonds must be kept high. The only way to do that, by Jove, is to control the diamond market. That has been Rhodes' plan for some time, to have the monopoly."

Lisa gazed in awe and admiration.

"Oh Jack, you are so wise. You know simply everything."

Jack then began discussing the house he was having built in Kenilworth, a new suburb established by Rhodes in his vision of expanding Kimberley, part of his larger vision of expanding the Empire.

"I like the work of that carpenter fellow, what's his name again?" He thought for a while. "Meintjies, that's right. He's a coloured but he does a good job. Seen some of the furniture he has made. Splendid stuff. Thought we should get him to make a dining room suite.

"I've heard of him. He's a friend of Jacobus who says the fellow supports his sick mother."

Jack slapped his knee.   "Splendid, splendid. Will give him the business. Open up opportunities for him. That's what these people need, y'know, more opportunity."

* * *

Lisa looked radiant, walking down the aisle on Bob's arm. He had agreed to give away the bride. Sara was bridesmaid but Kitty declined to stand with her. Paul travelled from Capetown to be best man. His family were still angry over his engagement to Sara and Aunt Queenie was in a dilemma.   She wanted to refuse the invitation to demonstrate her disapproval of her nephew's engagement to Sara but she knew Jack's family were wealthy land owners, neighbours of her brother's country home in the Lake District in England. Jack himself was making a name in the business world in Kimberley. She decided to attend.

Chapter 14

A cool breeze stirred the net drapes and sunlight patched the papered walls. Boxes were piled in the corners of the living room. Lisa and Jack had returned from their honeymoon in the Cape and were settling into their new home. It was mid-morning. Jack had left for his office and Martha was helping Lisa unpack and list wedding presents.

Lisa sat on the floor in front of the white marble-fronted fireplace. She held an ornament in her hand, a delicately featured lady seated in a rocking chair, in fine English Bone China. When touched, the head nodded.

"Isn't this charming, it's from Uncle Bob. Dear old Bob, I do miss him. Jack says he left Kimberley because he was secretly in love with you, Martha, and that you never gave him any encouragement. How could you be so unkind?" She teased her sister.

"Nonsense! Jack is absolutely wrong," Martha retorted, her face red.

Lisa's eyes widened in surprise, "But Jack is never wrong. You're so critical. It would be fun if you married Bob and we could raise our children together." Her eyes had a dreamy expression. "I am so happy to be married to Jack and can't wait to start a family. What can be more rewarding than motherhood? Being a mother is more important than any other job a woman can have, after all, a mother has the responsibility of influencing the future generation."

Martha looked surprised at her sister's outburst, and opened her mouth to reply, but Lisa continued,

"You're always complaining because you never had the opportunity to go to the university to study law. Why would you want to be a lawyer when you could be a mother?"

"My word! You have gotten serious since becoming a wife. Whose philosophy is this? Are these Jack's ideas?"

"That's just where you're wrong. Sara and I have discussed this often."

"Well, let me tell you my girl, becoming educated is very important for a woman because educated mothers are better mothers."

The conversation was interrupted by the sound of footsteps on the gravel path outside. Lisa jumped up and ran to the window. "It's Sara."

Martha glanced down at the watch, pinned to her lace-front blouse, "Goodness me, is that the time already? I must get back, it's Ruth's afternoon off." She stood up, rolling down the sleeves, puffed at the top and narrow at the wrists, then adjusted her long skirt. The two sisters embraced then walked into the front hall. Martha took her hat from the stand, placing it on her head and jabbing in the hat pin while Lisa opened the door as Sara mounted the steps. Greetings were exchanged before Martha set off to walk the short distance home.

Lisa put her arm about her friend and steered her towards the kitchen then noticed tears in Sara's eyes.

"It's Paul's father. He's ill. It's his heart. Our wedding has to be postponed." Sara gulped, speaking in staccato sentences with a shaking voice. "I would go to Capetown to be with Paul. We could be married quietly. I don't want a big wedding anyway. But his Ma won't hear of it. Says a wedding in the family at this time, is out of the question. I'm sorry about his Pa." She twisted a handkerchief in her hands. "He's the only one, besides Paul of course, who has been decent to me. I don't trust Paul's Ma. I know she doesn't want him to marry me because of..." She hiccuped a sob, wiped her eyes and blew her nose.

Lisa broke in. "My dear! I am sorry about Paul's father, but he will recover and then you can go ahead with your plans. Don't be so gloomy. Let's have a cuppa." She removed some boxes from a chair indicating to Sara to be seated then filled a kettle with water and placed it on the coal-fired cooker before setting out the cups.

"I have the feeling that Paul and I will never marry."

"Nonsense! Such dismal thoughts. Paul loves you, he wouldn't allow his mother to come between you." Sara shook her head but their talk was interrupted by a loud knock on the back door.

"Expecting anyone?" Sara wiped her eyes again.

Lisa looked up with a frown "No..." then her expression cleared. "Oh! Yes of course, it'll be Sol with our new dining-room furniture." She threw open the back door to admit a young coloured man.

He stood in the doorway, hands nervously holding a cloth cap. The fingers slender and sensitive, although stained and scarred. He was a lean man, his clothes, baggy trousers and worn jacket, hung loosely on his narrow frame. His hair close-cropped, tight waves in ridges. Eyes, light brown and deep set, burned above prominent cheek bones. Sara felt them boring into her.

"*Goeie middag, merrem.* Your furniture is here." While staring at Sara, he gestured towards a cart standing in the back lane, drawn by an emaciated horse, head drooped, too weary to shake away the flies buzzing around its rheumy eyes.

Lisa looked from Sara to Sol. "This is my friend, Sara and Sara this is Sol Meintjies who has designed and made our dining-room furniture." The young man recovered himself and remembering his place, cast his eyes down, mumbling an acknowlegdement of the introduction.

"I met that girl Sara," he told his mother later. "She is a friend of the people I been making the furniture for. You remember I tol' you about them? He's an Englishman, and they jus' got married, hey!"

His mother nodded her head. "*Ja, ek weet,* her Ma works for the wife's sister who owns The Grange, hotel. Jacobus worked for the same family. People in the township say that girl Sara's stuck-up and only mixes with the whites."

"Well she might be, I dunno about that, but heleleulah *sy is baie pragtig* hey!" He whistled through his teeth. "Ooh ja she pretty. Her skin is like cream and her neck is long and curved like a swan." His expression was wistful. "Jurrah man, I would like to carve her head and neck, hey!" He looked down at his hands and picked up a piece of wood, stroking it gently.

"Jurrah man, you and your carving! You's a strange boy, hey! Is that what you thinks a woman is for?" the old woman cackled, retelling the incident to Jacobus.

"Ol' Ma Meintjies tol' me that her boy Sol, met Sara. The old lady says she thinks he fancies her, hey!" Jacobus chuckled as he related the story to Ruth. "I tell her that our Sara wouldn't look at the likes of her Sol."

Ruth sighed, shaking her head, "I'm not knowing what can happen to that child. I'm not believing that white boy will marry her." Her voice dropped, "an' she don' want no coloured boys."

Chapter 15

Sara was right. The pressures and prejudices overwhelmed Paul. His mother, Magriet, a member of the prominent de Villiers family, had married John Frobisher, brother of Kitty's father, James who were sons of an English baronet. After reading law at Cambridge, John had settled in Capetown where his uncle had a successful law practice.

John Frobisher met Magriet at a party at the British Garrison. Her father wasn't happy, wanting her to marry the son of his cousin and old friend, Etienne-Piet de Villiers. But it wasn't to be.

After her marriage to the Englishman, Magriet settled down as a young matron, taking her social and civil responsibilities seriously.

"The Coloured and black people must know their place," she told her husband. He was astounded at her vehemence, seeing a side of her she hadn't displayed during their courtship.

"The Scriptures say that 'the sons of Ham are to be the hewers of wood and drawers of water,'" she quoted.

He shook his head, "don't know much about that, y'know, 'fraid I didn't pay all that much attention to the Lesson on Sundays. Vicar was inclined to mumble somewhat."

She had many servants to help her run the old Cape Dutch homestead, most of them coloured and when she heard her son, Paul, was in love with a coloured girl from Kimberley, she was devastated.

"What will people say?" she asked her husband and called on him to forbid the match. "Do something about it. Send Paul away to your brother in England. Threaten to dis-inherit him."

Her husband was in poor health and didn't have the strength, or incliniation to argue with his wife or his son. Privately he liked the girl, had met her on his last visit to Kimberley, "She is certainly a good looker," he related to his friend over luncheon at the Kimberley Club. "Lovely piece of flesh. Reminds me of a young filly, has the clean lines of a thoroughbred and been well educated I'm told.
What difference does a black mother make? People in Capetown needn't know about it, the mother can be kept out of sight in Kimberley. It's not as if Paul's likely to inherit the Baronetcy."

Magriet appealed to her brother-in-law, Kitty's father, James, who, unlike his brother John, was high-handed.

"Sorry Paul, old chap. Can't accept a coloured woman into the family, not the thing, don't y'know. Not cricket, if you get what I mean. Reputation of the family and all that. Not done. Simply not done, old boy."

"No one interferes in my life." Paul told Sara. "I'll make my own decisions. If Ma makes it uncomfortable for us in Capetown I'll move to the Transvaal. No one there need know about your family."
Sara's shoulders sagged. Ruth kept her own counsel, knowing all about racial prejudice and hypocrisy.

When his father suffered a heart attack Paul agreed to postpone the wedding.

"Just until my Pa can return to the office, or, if he doesn't improve, until we can re-organise the business." he wrote to Sara. His father didn't recover and when he died Magriet implored her son not to leave her,

"Not now, Paul. Not at this time. I need you to help me make decisions regarding Pa's estate."

Paul sat at the desk in his father's study, the soft glow of the reading lamp cast shadows on the oak panelling. He rubbed his forehead as he bent over the blank page in front of him. This was a difficult letter to write.

"My darling, you will have received by now my
letter telling you of Pa's death. This is a sad time
for us all, especially Ma. It would be unthinkable
for me to leave her now. Pa's death has shaken her and
it is a sorrowful sight to see her on the verge of
collapse. She has always been so strong. I hate doing
this, my dearest, but I must ask you to wait a little
longer, until things settle here and Ma recovers.
Love you forever, your devoted Paul."

He sealed the letter and decided to mail it without delay. As he stepped into the hallway he heard his mother call from the front parlour.

"Come and talk to me for a while my son, I'm feeling so low. I haven't shut my eyes the whole long night." She glanced at the letter in his hand.

100

"I have written to Sara, Ma, and asked her to wait a little longer. I will stay with you until you feel better." She smiled weakly and patted the settee next to her. Paul sat down and she stretched out her hand,

"Give me your letter, Bessie can mail it for you." Paul reluctantly agreed and she put it in the pocket of her gown.

When Paul left the house Magriet took the letter and tore it open, reading it quickly before pushing it back inside her pocket. She went into the study and began her own letter to Sara.

"Paul has asked me to write to you. He finds it difficult to tell you, my dear, but he has confided to me that his feelings towards you have changed. Since his Pa's death he realises the importance of his family name and his responsibilities towards me. He know that the business would suffer if he were to marry you. I can accept you, my dear, but will others? People will talk, you know, it's your mixed blood. If you truly love Paul you will not wish him harm. It will be better for all concerned if you do not reply to this letter, nor try to communicate with Paul in any way. Believe me, I know what is best for both of you."

Magriet had always been forthright. The sooner the girl understood the situation, the better.

A week later she noticed a letter on the hall table. It was addressed to Paul with a Kimberley postmark. She recognised Sara's handwriting. The girl had disobeyed her. Magriet tore open the envelope .

"I received your Ma's letter, she said you asked her to write to me. I understand if your feelings have changed but why didn't you write yourself? I won't, of course, hold you to your promise but, nevertheless, shall always love you."

The months passed. Paul expressed surprise at not hearing from Sara. He couldn't understand her silence.

"Do you think I have offended her Ma, for postponing the wedding?"

"Well, she hasn't much understanding if she is offended. Being a woman she should know how I feel, as a mother and a wife."

Paul wrote again, and Magriet again intercepted his letter.

"I'm going to Kimberley at the weekend, Ma. The office is running smoothly now that Cousin Leonard has arrived from England to take over some of the work. I must see Sara." They sat at either end of the long dining table.

"I really think that Sara is unreasonable, Paul. She is obviously upset because you asked her to wait. Anyway it would be unseemly to celebrate a marriage at this time." She clutched her chest and leant forward across the table.

Paul jumped out of his chair and rushed to his mother's side. "What's the matter? Are you ill?"

"It's nothing, dear, just a little burning pain in my chest, have had it before. It'll go away, please don't give me a thought. I'll be perfectly alright alone here with Bessie while you are in Kimberley." She sat with her head resting on her hand.

"Of course I can't leave you if you are unwell. I wouldn't dream of it, anyway I think I must call Dr. Willem, Ma, he'll know how serious this is."

Magriet looked alarmed. "No, no, that won't be necessary, in any case Willem is away at present and when I saw him about this problem before he left, he advised me to take a holiday. He recommended I go overseas but I told him that was impossible, I couldn't travel so far on my own and he agreed, and suggested you accompany me but of course I told him you were planning on getting married." She hesitated then continued, "But it would be nice to visit your father's family." She spoke wistfully her eyes on Paul. Her brother-in-law, James had recently left Kimberley and returned to England to live, with his sister Queenie and daughter Kitty.

"I would like to see dear Queenie again and young Kitty."

Paul looked surprised. "Didn't know you thought that much of Aunt Queenie," under his breath.

Magriet sighed. "Oh dear, it's not much use thinking about the impossible. But a rest in England would do me the world of good, it's the right time of year now as well, the beginning of summer. How I love England in the summertime," voice trailing. She wiped her eyes and stifled a sob, then once again clutched her chest.

"Oh dear, I think I'll go and lie down upstairs. You go ahead with your arrangements. Don't worry about me."

Paul looked confused and worried. "Nonsense Ma, I can't leave you alone here with Bessie, especially with Dr. Willem away. Think I'll call in his locum anyway."

"No dear, don't do that. I can't stand the man. I'll just take the pills Willem prescribed," wiping her eyes and patting her nose with a delicate lace trimmed handkerchief. "I had better write your Aunt Queenie and tell her we can't come after all. I must admit, Paul dear, I had told them you might possibly accompany me on a trip before your marriage. But they'll understand if I can't go."

Paul stood deep in thought before taking her arm to help her up the staircase.

"I'll write to Sara one more time. Maybe my letters were lost in the mail the service is not that reliable. I know she will understand that I must look after you now that Pa has gone. We should have insisted he took more holidays, and rested more often, you know. I feel guilty about Pa and don't want to neglect you. I'll tell Sara I'm taking you overseas on doctor's orders."

"Oh Paul! You are a wonderful son. I do appreciate your sacrifice and I promise you I will make every effort to ensure that Sara is made welcome by the family. You just write to her now and tell her you will marry her when we return from England after six months. We can even fix a definite date, she will like that. I'll get Bessie to mail the letter, just leave it to me."

Paul accompanied his mother overseas and Sara was to remember her premonition.

Chapter 16

Ruth was dead. She woke with a sore throat one morning but insisted on getting dressed, only to collapse at the kitchen table. Martha called the doctor but Ruth stopped breathing before he arrived. It was diptheria, he said.

The private hotel had to be closed and Martha moved in with Lisa and Jack. Lisa was expecting a baby in the Spring and she needed Martha's help. Jack helped Sara find work as an assistant to the Librarian and she found herself a room in a boarding-house downtown. Joe was employed by De Beers as a driver, also thanks to Jack's recommendation, and he was given accommodation in the compound where they housed their black workers.

Martha decided against re-opening the small hotel after the health authorities gave permission. How could she ever replace Ruth, and besides it held so many memories. The property was sold and she moved in permanently with Lisa and Jack. Sara, however, stood firm in her decision to move out despite persuasive arguments from Martha and Lisa, for she was trying to recover from her disappointment over Paul and felt she needed time away from the family for her private grief.

"By Jove, Ruth served this family well," remarked Jack, trying to comfort Lisa and Martha. "I remember how upset my Mamma and the sisters were when old Nanny died."

"You don't understand, Jack. Ruth wasn't like a nanny to us, she was a surrogate mother. After Mamma died, she was the only family we had in this country."

"Hardly family, my dear. You are inclined to overstatement Martha. I mean to say, Ruth was a servant after all." He put up his hands as Martha opened her mouth to protest. "I know she lived with your family for many years and was as loyal as any friend, but nevertheless..."

Lisa interrupted before Martha and Jack became involved in one of their full-scale arguments. "Does it matter you two? The fact is we all loved Ruth and miss her dearly." She indicated to Jack to keep silent and Martha picked up her embroidery and walked out of the room.

"I wish you were less argumentative, Martha," Lisa complained to her sister later. "Jack means well, after all he thought the world of Ruth and he helped both Sara and Joe get jobs."

Martha looked up from the book she was reading, "I know, but he can be so infuriatingly patronising at times."

Lisa frowned but before she could say anything Martha continued, "I will apologise, however, for my rudeness. Jack is a good man."

A smile lit Lisa's face and she bent to hug her sister. "That is praise indeed, coming from you, my dear!"

Martha looked thoughtful, "Perhaps I shouldn't have sold "The Grange.""

"Don't say that, I'm so glad to have your help and advice raising our children. Jack and I will need your level head to stop us from spoiling them!"

It took a while for Martha to settle in but in time she mellowed and found contentment in her sister's family.

"I have to admit," she said one day, "that I was wrong about Jack, he is not a bit like Pappa."

"Oh but he is! I think he is just like Pappa. I feel he has taken Pappa's place. I know Pappa would have done well for us it wasn't his fault he died of the fever."

Martha shook her head, she had never shared Lisa's view of their father.

Martha sat at the sewing machine which had been one of Anna's treasured possessions. There were other boxes, that had come from the boarding-house attic when the property was sold, still to be unpacked. Some clothes of Anna's and old papers and letters.

Martha was making clothes for the expected baby, her foot moved rhythmically on the treddle. Although the french-doors were open to the wide verandah, the afternoon heat was heavy. A storm was imminent. Clouds gathered and rumblings of thunder could be heard, followed by flashes of lightning. A sudden gust of wind loosened a shutter in the bedroom where Lisa was resting. Martha went to close it then returned to her task.

She heard footsteps on the wooden verandah and jumped when a figure appeared in the doorway. An old man stood there. His clothes shabby. He carried a well-worn carpet bag in one hand and held a Bible in the other. Putting the bag down, he lifted his dusty felt hat, bending his head in greeting.

"Excuse madam, is you Miss Martha? The maid said I'd find you here. It's about your father."

"My father! What are you talking about? My father died years ago." Martha stood up knocking over a tin of pins in her agitation.

"I know that, Miss, that's why I come. I was there when he died."

Lisa woke with the sound of the voices. She walked into Martha's sewing room, overhearing his last remark and ran forward to take his arm.

"Oh, were you really? Poor Pappa. It was the fever wasn't it? Did he suffer very badly?"

The old man shook his head, clutching the Bible close to his chest, "Forgive me madam, it wasn't the fever."

"What was it then, did they call a doctor? Was it pneumonia?"

The old man looked from one sister to the other. "I beg your forgiveness. It was me. I k. . k . . killed him with these very hands." He looked down at his rough, rugged old man's hands, then began a fit of coughing, causing him to bend over, clutching his side. Words spattered from salivated lips. Tears coursed down corrugated cheeks. His jowls shook and perspiration poured off his forehead.

Martha lifted a jug of water off the stand and poured a glass then handed it to him. He took it gratefully, gulping it down. "Lord, forgive me. I done a wicked and evil thing. Lord, I beseech you, forgive me." His eyes were squeezed closed. In the distance thunder rolled.

All colour drained from the faces of Martha and Lisa as they stood staring at him, speechless. The praying and the coughing stopped and silence fell on the room, broken at last by a hoarse whisper from the old man.

"I come to beg your forgiveness. I want to tell you everything what happened." He took a grubby, crumpled handkerchief from his coat pocket and wiped his face before accepting the chair Martha offered.

"It was this 'Pommie man I knew. I met him on the diggings here in Kimberley, then later met him again in Jo'burg. I was down in my luck and he knew that. He also knew I was a good shot. He offered me a job. I didn't know what he meant at first, when I realised what he was saying, I said I wouldn't touch it. But he talked me into it. He showed me the money he would give me, enough to feed my wife and kids for a long time. He told me a man was messing with his wife and said that it was the right thing to do because God told him to. I believed him."

The old man gave a loud sniff then blew his nose before continuing. He put his head up, raising his eyes. "I was weak Lord. Oh Lord! I was weak. Can you forgive me?" He laid the Bible on the table and slid to his knees on the floor, clutching his two hands together in prayer, his body shaking. Thunder thundered overhead.

The story came out in bits and pieces, falteringly at first, then a torrent of words interspersed with cries for forgiveness. He told how he followed Frederick as he made his way from the hotel to hire a horse and then riding southwards towards Vereeniging. When Frederick stopped at the saloon, he watched him through a window and when the argument between the miners developed into a brawl, he seized the opportunity, shooting Frederick in the chest.

In the confusion that followed he grabbed Frederick's bag and notebook he said, to make sure no one would discover his identity. When he returned to Jo'burg the next day for the other half of the money promised by Charlie, he discovered the Pommie had disappeared. They told him at the hotel the man had left in a rage, looking for his wife who had gone off with his brother.

"I had to leave it at that. Had no money to go looking for the fellow. The bloody bastard!" His voice had sunk to a whisper then he put his hands to his mouth as if remembering the company he was in. "Sorry Lord. I didn't mean to swear in front of these ladies."

Martha and Lisa stood with their arms around each other. Neither spoke. The old man continued.

"I carried this sin all these years and then I got sick. Very sick. It's me chest. I coughs so badly I can't hardly work and then there was this Revivalist meeting; an American fellow come to town. My friend took me because he say the Preacher could put his hands on a person and that person would be healed.

"I didn't believe him at first, but what the heck! I decided to go. When the Preacher spoke I had to listen, his voice was so strong. He say we mus' be baptised and take the blood of Christ who died for our sins. He say we mus' beg forgiveness and then we can be healed. He say we mus'beg forgiveness before we die or we will fall into hellfires." The old man stopped speaking to clear his throat then took another gulp of water.

"I felt like something pushed me forward and I run with all the people to where the Preacher is putting them into the river. I feel the hands push me under the water and I sees a bright light that goes straight up to the sky and a voice calls me, telling me I must be born again, and I mus' confess

108

all my sins and give the money I have to Him and He will take me to Heaven when I die." The shaking voice dropped low once again. "I gave the Preacher all the money I had and took my wife to my married daughter and told them I would be away for a while. I find your names in the book in the bag and come here to confess my sins and beg your forgiveness." He leant forward and opened Frederick's bag, taking out a worn notebook and a packet of letters. He made as if to give them to Martha, but she turned away. Lisa took them instead, hands shaking.

Silence descended. The old man began coughing again. He clutched his chest, making a strange gurgling sound before falling forward in a heap on the floor. Martha bent down and turned him over. His eyes stared out in a look of terror. She put her fingers on his wrist then covered his face with a sheet.

It was months later when Martha and Lisa decided to sort through the boxes that came from the boarding house, that they found the letter written to Frederick from Donna and realised their mother must have had suspected how their father met his death. Lisa had not believed the old man's story but Donna's letter seemed to confirm it. Sadly, she packed her father's notebook and letters into a wooden box and with her poker-work pen, carefully carved his name "Frederick" upon it, before putting it at the bottom of an old sea chest.

Martha never mentioned their father's name again.

Chapter 17

Lisa sat on the front stoep in the early evening. She heard the sound of crickets in the long grass... chirrup... chirrup and bullfrogs in the creek. She looked at the sky left scarlet by the sun as it sank behind the *kopjes*. The honeysuckle hung from the verandah posts and she smelt its pungent sweetness, filling her nostrils. She felt a sense of peace as she absorbed the sounds and the smells of the *veld*.

Jack appeared in the doorway and stood with his hands pushed into his trouser pockets, his brow furrowed. Lisa patted the seat next to her.

"Come, sit. It's a beautiful evening; why the worried look? Is there a problem?"

Jack wiped his forehead with his snow-white handkerchief as if to wipe away frown and problems, then smiled, "No. Not exactly. In any case, nothing to worry your pretty head about, by jove!" He sank into the cushions next to her, taking his pipe from his pocket and putting it into his mouth. The frown returned.

"There is something worrying you."

Jack sucked pensively on his pipe. "Well, actually m'dear, there are rumours about Rhodes and this fellow Jameson. They're talking of... no... nothing really," he hesitated, then continued. "Personally I don't think Rhodes should get involved with the chap who is supporting the hotheads in the Transvaal. They do have a point, of course, these "uitlanders" as the Boers call them. Kruger takes their tax money but won't give them any say in the government. But, on the other hand, the Boers also have a point. They never invited the foreigners here in the first place and would like them all to get the blazes out because, as far as the Boers are concerned, the gold can stay in the ground. But Rhodes has other ideas. He would like to annex the Transvaal to the Cape Colony."

Lisa listened intently then asked, "What exactly is the rumour?"
Jack shook his head, "Forget it, m'dear. As I said, it's nothing to worry your pretty head about. Women shouldn't get involved in the dirty work of politics. Think no more of it, shouldn't have said anything." He patted her knee and stood up, "Must get back to those papers I'm working on."

Lisa's adoring eyes followed him then she turned back to the view of the *veld* and noticed darkness had descended. She gave an involuntary shudder, pulling her shawl across her shoulders as she felt the cold rise from the ground. Footsteps on the gravel caught her attention and she saw

Sara walking up the driveway. She ran to greet her friend and they walked back arm in arm and sat on the swing.

"I've decided to marry Sol Meintjies," Sara began abruptly. Lisa's mouth fell open as if to reply but Sara put up her hand as her friend started to remonstrate with her. "No. Don't say anything. I've made my decision. I love Paul but wonder if he cares as much for me. He's never replied to any of my letters." Her voice was defiant.

"But Sara," Lisa interrupted. "Is this fair to Sol? I didn't know you had been seeing him. He's sensitive and you would hurt him if you marry without love. Another thing, is he right for you? You'll need something more."

Sara shook her head. "White people in Kimberley have never accepted me and if I don't marry Sol, what's my alternative? It's not as if I have a career. Meneer Johnson at the library likes me O.K. but when he retires I might not even have a job. His assistant, van der Merwe doesn't like working with a 'coloured' girl. I overheard him telling that to Meneer Johnson. I don't feel secure. With Sol, at least my future will be safe. He is a good man and has a good trade."

Sara and Sol were married quietly a month after Lisa's first baby was born. Sol could hardly believe his good fortune.

"*Ag man*, Ma!" he said to his mother, "the beautiful, proud Sara will be my wife."

His mother shook her head as she confided later in Jacobus. "Nie man, I don' think this marriage is a good idea. I'm scared of that Sara hey, she's too smart for my Sol."

Jacobus had agreed, "Ja, the girl's got problems. She look too much like a white person. Shame hey! Like it's made her mixed up in her head."

"But she mus jus accept her place. You know Sol's father was a white man. An Englishman with blue eyes and red hair. He went back to England and I couldn't do nothing about it, hey! But I never let Sol get ideas above his station. It's that Patrickson family's fault. They given Sara big ideas."

It wasn't long before Sara felt herself trapped. Sol was slow. He lacked her lively imagination. He was good at his work with a keen sense of line, carving out wood but not exactly imaginative.

"He has never learnt to read, you know," Sara confessed to Lisa. "I want to teach him but he refuses. Says what he's doing is man's work and reading isn't important. Anyway he's not having a woman teach him anything."

Sara looked around Lisa's comfortable home and compared it with her drab shanty in the township. *If only*, she thought, as Paul came to mind, but didn't confide in her friend as she recalled the nights lying next to Sol but thinking about Paul.

The months dragged by. Sara leant over the tub, scrubbing Sol's socks with her stomach swollen, carrying his child. She heard footsteps then a tap at the front door. Wearily she brushed the hair from her eyes, hauled herself up and walked down the hall. She opened the door and saw Paul standing there. *I'm dreaming*, she thought, another one of my fantasies, as she shook her head. The room swung around and her legs buckled but a strong arm caught her, helping her to recover her balance as his voice penetrated the mists in her mind.

"Why didn't you wait for me? I wrote and promised I'd come as soon as things settled at home." The voice was accusatory, thick and hoarse. They walked into the living room where faded linoleum only partly covered the scrubbed wooden floor. The chairs sagged.

"Come away with me. Leave this place." He looked around in distaste. "Why didn't you wait for me? I had to settle Pa's estate and wait for Ma to recover from it all. You didn't once reply." He placed his hands on her shoulders and turned her face up towards his.

"I did write. Your Ma replied. She said you asked her to tell me you couldn't go through with the marriage. I wrote again, but you didn't answer." Her voice was bitter.

Paul looked puzzled, then his face clouded. He paced the room while Sara huddled on the sofa. She could smell the curried stew boiling in the kitchen and should turn it off, Sol would be mad if his dinner was spoilt, but her limbs were paralysed.

"Are you saying Ma wrote you and yet you never received any of my letters? That's strange. I gave my letters to Ma for Bessie to mail. I certainly did not ask her to write you on my behalf." His fists were clenched as his thoughts cleared. "I couldn't understand at the time why I never heard from you. Ma said you must be offended when I asked you to wait until the estate was settled. Then when she became ill and asked me to take her overseas, I wrote you again and was sure you would understand... but still no word from you. I allowed Ma to persuade me that you didn't love me enough after all. At least not enough to wait."

Sara explained her despair and then her decision to marry Sol. Paul joined her on the sofa and took both her hands in his.

"Come away with me. It's not too late."

She patted her stomach, "Oh but it is, Paul. It is too late." She jumped up and ran into the kitchen.

When he returned to Capetown Paul confronted his mother. He insisted she give him the letters. Magriet broke down, sobbing, "I did it for the best, my son. I swear I did. You could never have married a coloured girl. Think of what people would say. Think of the children you would have."

Paul sent his letters to Sara. He never forgave his mother.

Later he married an Afrikaans girl, a distant cousin by the name of de Villiers. She bore him a son and called him Etienne Piet after her grandfather. Paul never knew the boy. He was killed shortly before his son was born when his hunting rifle went off while cleaning it. Some believed it was an accident but there was some talk. It was only after the news of Paul's tragic death reached Kimberley that Sara told Lisa about his visit.

She gave Lisa the bundle of letters. "You keep these for me. I can't burn them but have no place to hide them and wouldn't want Sol to find them." Lisa put them in the old chest with her father's papers and her mother's diary.

Sara miscarried the baby that had prevented her from running off with Paul. Two years later she had a daughter, she called Emma. Had Sara known her father, the farmer van Niekerk, she would have seen the child's resemblance to him.

The years ahead were difficult for Sara. Sol had no head for business. He charged too little and laboured too long. Sara realised she needed a job. Sol couldn't give her security after all. She approached the new librarian but he turned her away and she overheard his remarks to his assistant. "That ol' fellow Johnson who gave her a job here before, he was soft in the head, man. Once you start giving coloureds and blacks these jobs where will it end, hey? There's not enough jobs for us whites as it is."

Lisa and Jack had two childrenn. The eldest named for his father and the second a girl, called Margaret but they shortened to Meg. Meg and

Emma were the same age. Lisa suspected she was pregnant again. Life was good to her. Raising Jack's children and being a good wife were her goals and she felt guilty because she gained so much happiness while Sara lost so much hope.

Lisa heard about the library incident and, in her impulsive way, paid the new librarian a visit. The man was unrepentant. Lisa stormed out and took her crusade to Jack in his office.

"We have to help her, Jack, she needs a job."

"Upon my word, m'dear. Of course we'll help the gal, I'll give her a job."

Lisa threw her arms around his neck. "I knew I could rely on you. She's very bright you know, always did better than me at school."

"Should have thought of it before," Jack mumbled under his breath. "Martha has her hands full and you with another baby on the way you'll both need extra help. Splendid, splendid!" He slapped his knees and stood up, putting his arm around Lisa and ushering her out of his office then patting her bottom affectionately.

Lisa stopped. "That's not exactly what I had in mind. I was thinking about a job for her here, in your office. She has a good head for figures and I know she hates housework."

Jack looked up in alarm, "Don't be ridiculous. Of course can't possibly have a woman working here in the office. Not the thing at all. Simply can't be done. An office is no place for a woman."

"But why not? She's got brains and ability."

"Balderdash! Don't even mention it, especially to Sara. Give the gal ideas. Simply not done." He shook his head vigorously. Lisa opened her mouth to continue her argument but Jack put up his hand to silence her so she shrugged and turned away, accepting her defeat.

She called on Sara on the way home. "I have asked Jack and he agrees that Martha needs help with the housekeeping. I know you hoped for something more stimulating but helping in the house will mean you can keep Emma with you, instead of paying someone to care for her." The last thought coming suddenly into her head.

Sara accepted gratefully. "You're right. The library wasn't a good idea now I have a child to consider."

Martha was pleased with the extra help but remarked to Lisa later, "having a child shouldn't prevent Sara from having a career, m'dear."

"What career? Helping them sort books at the library. They'd never give her anything better to do."

"I wish I'd had even that much opportunity for a career," Martha mumbled.

"Well that may be, but for Sara it's much better she and little Emma are not separated."

"I expect you persuaded Jack to employ Sara."

Lisa smiled, "there are ways of winning with men, you know."

Martha frowned.

Lisa had another son later that year and they named him Harry. Meg looked upon Emma as a sister and the two girls grew close.

Chapter 18

Kimberley
Circa 1899

War was brewing although Kimberley was isolated from the troubles in the Transvaal Republic. People of Dutch and French Huguenot descent or Boers, had moved away from the Cape in 1836, from British rule which they found oppressive, particularly when forced to give up their slaves. They trekked north, ignoring the presence of the native tribes already living in the interior, and claimed the land as their own.

They were pastoral people, who desired to be left alone to farm the land. They were religious in the narrow Calvanistic sense, with strict codes of morality, believing they were God's chosen people. Modern-day Children of Israel, convinced that the native people were inferior and claimed Biblical authority for this conviction.

When gold was discovered in their newly declared Republic they resisted changes - it could stay in the ground. But such news could not be concealed and before long thousands of foreigners arrived to make their fortunes. Uitlanders, the Boers called them, and believed them to be self-serving and greedy and Paul Kruger, the Boer leader, did not intend giving them political power. Had his people not already endured terrible hardships during the Great Trek northwards to find freedom and independence? Kruger taxed the foreigners but gave them no representation in the government.

Some of the Uitlanders, under the leadership of Dr. Jameson and supported by Rhodes, planned to take the goldfields by force. The plan failed. Discontent and distrust grew and could be contained no longer. War broke out. Britain supported the Uitlanders which embittered the Boers.

While it appeared as if Kimberley would not be affected by events in the Transvaal, Jack worried about the political situation. He told Lisa and Martha to stock up the larder.

"You never know, Lisa m'dear, these Boers might decide to besiege Kimberley, by Jove, to prevent diamonds from getting out of the country." He sucked thoughtfully on his pipe. "Might be an idea to have a shelter built, these chaps might start shelling, yer'know!" The children were excited and when the shelter was completed they used it as a playhouse. Nobody in the family except Jack, took the situation seriously.

Mr. Rhodes, however, took it seriously. He worried about his De Beers Company and applied to the British for reinforcements. Kimberley became crowded with men in uniform.

Lisa awoke to the sounds of birds building their nests in the nearby wild fig tree and felt a sense of peace. There was a brightness over the *veld* after the spring rains and she didn't believe the quarrels in the north over the gold would affect them. Lying next to the sleeping Jack, her thoughts turned to her childhood, her Mamma, who seemed always sad, and her Pappa's sense of fun. She was too young to understand her mother's frustrations and fears and in her child's mind her father's cheerful optimism was spoilt by her mother's sharpness which made his smile disappear and most often, after a silent meal, he would go out. She often wondered where he went and why Mamma always brought sadness to Pappa's eyes. She knew now of his affair with Donna. Mamma and Lisa had condemned him, but she never did. She believed he craved love and affection.

The soft coo of the doves broke the early morning silence. A *Piet-my-vrou* bird called to its mate. In the distance a rooster heralded the sunrise. The smell of bacon cooking drifted through the house. Jack awoke and put his arms around her and she snuggled into his side.

"I was thinking how happy I am, Jack. Everything is so comfortable and peaceful."

"Hope you're right, m' dear. Maybe Kimberley will be left in peace by the Boers. They'll have their hands full in the Transvaal, after all they haven't a properly organised army, just a bunch of farmer fellows. Not much hope against the mighty power of the Empire, I'd say, but Rhodes isn't taking chances."

A distant rumble echoed. "Sounds like thunder," remarked Lisa. "It's unusual to have a storm this early, late afternoon is the time for thunder storms." She got up and walked across to the window, lifting the lace drapes. "Not a cloud in the sky. Must be blasting at the Big Hole."

The rumbling sounded again.

At the same moment Lisa awoke, savouring the early morning tranquility, a soldier on guard duty climbed the high ladder to the scaffolding on the headgear of Kimberley's main diamond mine. With his telescope he scanned the veld. Below him lines of sandbagged dugouts comprised the perimeter of Kimberley's defences. In the distance he saw the laagers, wagons drawn up in circles, from where the Boers loaded their guns. The bombardment of Kimberley had started. The siege of Kimberley had begun.

The siege was to last one hundred and twenty-four days.

The Boers offered safe passage to Capetown for the women and children but most refused to leave. The war was a desultory affair at first with few casualties. The Boers began shelling at sunrise each day, however, as the months dragged on, problems arose. There were shortages of food and ammunition. People worried. Something must be done.

"I say, Lisa m'dear, there's a fellow here who works for De Beers, an American, name of Labram, quite a remarkable chap y'know." Jack and Lisa sat in the front parlour, the children in bed. Jack was reading some notes and stopped to refill his pipe. Lisa played a game of patience and Sara tidied the kitchen. Martha had retired for the night. Lisa looked up from her cards.

"What's so remarkable about Mr. Labram?"

"Well, he's an engineer with the Company, been here about three years, most resourceful fellow, damned likeable. He cast some shells in the workshop as the ammunition supply is low." Jack leant back in his chair and puffed on his pipe, then continued. "About a month ago the question of cattle in the area of Kimberley was discussed. Far too many for the limited grazing now, since the siege. Decided they would have to be slaughtered and the meat destroyed. Can't be kept fresh in this heat, y'know. But if the siege lasts much longer food will be scarce. The authorities have worried about this for some time. Now, I'll be damned if this fellow Labram hasn't designed and built a refrigeration plant."

Lisa smiled and shuffled her cards, "Well isn't that something?" absently.

Jack shook his head, returning to his papers.

Mr. Labram proved even more resourceful in the months ahead. The Kimberley garrison possessed no guns that could match the Boers and severe damage was being inflicted on the town.

"I say, Lisa, when I was at the Club last evening overheard Rhodes talking to Labram. He asked the fellow if he had ever built a canon. Labram replied that he had but 'only as a boy to shoot firecrackers on the

119

Fourth of July to celebrate the time the Americans licked the British!'" Jack slapped his knees, throwing back his head in laughter.

The family was at the breakfast table and young Jack let out a hoot of mirth, "Can't we make firecrackers, Father, to lick the Boers?"

Jack scowled at his son, disapproving at being interrupted in the middle of a story. "As I was saying, Rhodes then replied, 'Well build one now, old chap, this time to save the British!'"

Some weeks later Mr. Labram's name came up once more.

"The fellow Labram has done it again, by Jove. He built the canon Rhodes asked for from material in De Beers workshop. They're going to call it 'Long Cecil' in Rhodes' honour, and we've been invited to a Reception and Dinner in gratitude to Labram, next week.

Lisa smiled, "Oh good! I'll be able to wear that new taffeta gown Martha made."

Jack shook his head while smiling indulgently at her, "Just like a woman. In the middle of a war and thinking about what to wear!

In preparation for the Reception Jack and Lisa dressed for the occasion. Lisa's gown of lavender moire with a bustle caught up at the back, a deep neckline and the fashionable leg-o' mutton sleeves. Joe drove them in their carriage. As they approached the town square the explosion occurred. The horse shied, front legs pawing the air while Lisa fell against the footboard with Jack on top of her. The sky was illumined with an orange glow. Women screamed. Men shouted and children cried. Joe calmed the horse and Jack helped Lisa to her feet then instructed Joe to drive her home while he went to offer help at the hotel which had taken a direct hit from a Boer shell.

The fire was out and Jack, white shirt a ruin, bow-tie awry, helped attend the survivors. George Labram was not one of them. A shell from a Boer gun, brought to the area in retaliation for 'Long Cecil' had gone through the ceiling of Labram's room, killing him instantly. Kimberley mourned the loss of this resourceful American.

* * *

"Mama, Mama," shouted Harry, running into the living room.

"What is it, child, what is the matter?" Lisa jumped up a look of concern on her face.

"The soldiers are here, the soldiers are here."

120

"What soldiers, do you mean the Boers? In Kimberley?"

"No, the English soldiers. Come quickly and see, all the people are out in the streets with flags. Have we got flags, Mamma?"

Martha, hearing the commotion, appeared out of the kitchen, wiping her hands on her apron, then Sara joined the group and with the other children they ran outside to see people collected in the streets. The British cavalry, under General French, had broken through the Boer lines and word had gone through the town, people gathered to cheer the British troops. Lisa, Martha, Sara and the children joined in the flag waving. The siege of Kimberley was over.

Chapter 19

Kimberley settled after the siege. Life went on in spite of the upheaval in the rest of the country. Lisa and Sara were both pregnant and their sons were born the same day. Lisa's boy, Danny inherited her dark good looks; Sara's baby was also dark, very dark, like his African grandmother Ruth. They named him Jakob.

Jack sat at his desk in shirtsleeves, a jeweller's eyeglass in his right eye, examining diamonds on the table in front of him when the shriek of a siren split the silence, rising to a crescendo, then falling. The mine hooter blared. Jack ran to the window, looking out, he saw people pushing to the minehead. Gathering up the stones, and bundling them into a chamois drawstring bag, he threw it into the safe in the wall.

Outside he followed the crowd then heard his name above the din, looking back saw the manager, Boet du Plessis.

"Jack, man. Jus' the person I've been looking for, hey! Hell man, am I glad to see you. It's a mud rush in one of the drives. An underground spring broke out and the bleddy water is flooding the levels and all the bleddy mud has rushed down one of the tunnels and trapped du Preez and Mostert and their gang - four boys. They tell me it has stopped now, but hell man, it's almost at the top of the tunnel.

"And you got experience with this, man! Remember the last time it happened and you went down? The space between the roof and the mud in the tunnel is so bleddy small a big chap wouldn't make it. That's why I'm asking you if you could get to the men in the chamber while we start clearing the mud in the tunnel? We know they're still alive because we can hear them, but you know there's always the bleddy danger of gas escaping. Hell man, I'm sorry to have to ask you to do this."

"Of course, of course, old chap, by jove! Anything to help." Jack took his arm.

Stripped to only a pair of cotton trousers and a miner's helmet and lamp, a rope tied around his waist and a first-aid kit rolled up and attached to his belt, Jack began the journey, crawling on his stomach over the mud in the tunnel. The light of his lamp lit the darkness, revealing ribbons of water running down the walls like the streams of sweat streaking his forehead mingling with dust, making a mud mask over his face and neck. He crawled slowly, fearing a rockfall or another mud slide.

Martha and Lisa, meanwhile, in their kitchen were making jam and bottling fruit. Baby, Danny slept in his crib; the dog lay under the table, while Jack's pet parrot strutted on his perch.

The siren's wail shattered the quiet morning, like splintering glass. It woke the baby, set the dog barking and startled the shrieking parrot. Pandemonium! Martha clapped her hands to her ears, while Lisa cried out in alarm.

"Something has happened at the mine. What can it be?" Shredding apron strings with shaking hands. "What if Jack is down there?"

"Nonsense, you always imagine the worst." Martha, red faced from rising steam, stood over the saucepan, stirring the boiling jam. "Why should he be? His job is in Administration." Her logic belied her fears.

"But if it's a mud rush he'll go to help, you know he did the last time there were problems underground. Anyway, I'm going to the Big Hole. Give Danny his bottle for me?"

Lisa joined other women running to the minehead. No one knew what had happened except there had been a mudslide and some men were trapped. As she approached the skip Mnr. du Plessis saw her.

"Mevrou Patrickson! Just the person I've been looking for, hey! I was coming to see you." He told her the circumstances. "We've contacted the wives of du Preez and Mostert.

"What about the wives of their men?"

"What do y'mean?"

"Well, have you contacted the wives of the black men working with them?"

"We can't do that, it's impossible."

"Why on earth not?" voice raised above the din.

"You know how it is. They mostly come from far away. du Preez and Mostert have houses here on the mine but their boys live in the compound and sometimes we don't even know where their families are. We can't have all the native women and their children living on the mine, you know, and we sure as hell can't be expected to contact them everytime there's a problem. They come from all over the place, Bechuanaland, Nyasaland, Portuguese East."

But Lisa stopped listening to du Plessis and his excuses. She couldn't worry about the miners' families right now, she had Jack to worry about. She made a decision. When he got out, if he did, she would insist he leave De Beers because she knew that whenever there was trouble he would be

124

involved in rescue work. Her thoughts raced on oblivious of what du Plessis was saying.

"After all they're only *kaffirs*, man and they all have so many wives, we . . ."

We could buy a business of some sort with the capital we have.   A hotel maybe...

"Maybe they aren't like us whites. Maybe they don't feel about their families like we do. They sure as hell spend their wages on kaffir beer in the beerhall. I bet most of them never send a blasted quid home to their wives. I know . . . "

I know something about the work and Martha will help and Sara. Jack is popular, he would do well in this business...

"This business has enough problems without worrying about all the native labourers and their families..."

Family - Jack must think about his family now.

They reached the minehead and Lisa nodded absently to du Plessis, she hadn't heard a word he said.   He patted her shoulder, then made his way to the waiting skip to take him underground.

While Lisa was making decisions about his future, Jack was crawling along the narrow tunnel, losing all sense of time. It seemed he had been all his life in this narrow space. The mud beneath him turned slushy as if more water was flowing down. His heart bombarded his chest like a bomb waiting to explode... if water began flowing again and more mud swept down the tunnel... if there was gas in this area...if the roof caved... he knew his chances of survival were minimal. He stopped moving, hearing a faint sound - more mud, or a rock fall? His body tense, straining to listen. The same noise again. He relaxed, it wasn't what he feared, but rather more a knocking sound. He called out but mud muffled his voice. Inching forward, his fingers felt the edge of a rock face. He swept the lamp around and detected movement, then heard a weak call. Sliding over the edge of the rock, landing on his, feet, knees bent, he staggered, then stood upright. Six men lay there, all alive.

Du Preez told Jack they had heard the sound of rushing water, then mud poured down the tunnel. "Shit! Mr. Patrickson, we had just enough time to get to this chamber," voice croaking. "It's partially sealed by rock and other debris now, swept before the mud. Thank God the bloody mud lost momentum as it was absorbed by the length of the tunnel and the *stopes* from the main drive so this chamber didn't fill completely. It's a bloody miracle we're all alive. Problem is, we're all too bloody big to crawl through the top of the tunnel."

The heat in the chamber was intense. Jack gave the men water from the flask he carried.

"Can you give me a hand with one of my boys here? It's Johannes. I think he hurt his leg bad." du Preez called Jack. With Mostert's help they made the black man as comfortable as possible.

Johannes groaned, "Sorry, old chap - try not to hurt."

"No, that's O.K. that's O.K. baas, it's jus' I'm worried if I'm can't work. I'm got ten chil'ren, you know, and have to send my wife money every month. I'm was sending her some when I'm come off this shift, now I'm having to go to the hospital and she will be looking at the Post Office every day for the money."

"Ten children!"

"*Ja, baas*, well I'm married a long time now. My firstborn is twenty one years already."

"We're you from?" Jack asked, bandaging the leg with de Preez's help.

"Bechuanaland," Johannes winced, "It's not good there. No rain this year. No rain last year. The *mealie* crop is not good. Things are very bad at home. My wife mus' buy food for the family, nothing can grow when there's no rain. I hope they can tell my wife what happened."

"Of course they will, old chap. Don't worry about that." Jack reassured him. "Everything will be taken care of."

Johannes shook his head, unconvinced, then dropped it on his chest, dozing off.

Du Preez leant against the rock wall of the underground chamber and turned to face Jack. "I expect the wife is going to start nagging me again to give up mining and go back to the farm."

Jack laughed, "Women are all the same."

"I make good money underground. Farming is a dicey business, either a drought or a bloody flood."

Jack nodded in agreement. His thoughts far away thinking how to handle Lisa.

"I heard Rhodes likes you." du Preez continued, "they say one day you could get on the Board of Directors."

"I don't know about that," he replied modestly, "but I do know that Rhodes has big plans for the Company to ensure the monopoly of the world diamond market. De Beers has a big future.

The long wait was over; the mud cleared from the tunnel; the men taken to the surface   When Jack was awarded a medal he was embarrassed but gratified by all the fuss, Lisa, however, kept her resolve and Jack left De Beers and the diamond mining business. He bought a hotel. Du Preez also left the Company. He opened a trading store. "*Die vrou* is very happy," he told Jack.

Johannes' leg healed. He returned to his job underground, his wife protested.

"Where must I'm finding other work?" he asked her.

Chapter 20

The hotel Jack bought was situated between the Big Hole and the Market Square. They called it "The Halfway House" and it prospered. The years passed, in time they bought a second property. Martha, in spite of her experience, stayed out of the business. She and Jack could never work together. Lisa, however, found that like Martha, she had a natural aptitude, although Jack always insisted her place was at home raising the children.

At first she helped out when Dora, the housekeeper, was called to her dying mother, then Henderson the bookeeper, suddenly took ill and Lisa began to learn all the aspects of hotel business. When Henderson eventually retired due to his health, Lisa just continued doing his job and a replacement was never found. It wasn't that her ideals about motherhood had changed, but the children had grown, and besides, Martha was always there.

Jack was the perfect genial host.

"Lisa likes to help," he confided to his patrons. "The little woman enjoys having something to do, y'know."

Sara was also on the permanent staff of the hotel, in charge of Reception and helping Lisa with the Accounts. But her health was failing and it worried Lisa.

The scent of mimosa hung heavy on the summer air. Emma gazed through the open window of the schoolroom to the garden beyond. Eyes fixed on a yellow bloom but thoughts on the previous night and the argument she overheard between her parents.

She had woken with voices raised in the next room. The walls were thin. She knew her mother was unhappy. Her once beautiful face, now fine-drawn with lines of worry. Her father, also changed from the gently-spoken man she remembered to an embittered, dis-illusioned stranger forced to give up his carpentry business and take a job in a furniture factory for meagre money and monotonous work.

Emma knew Jack paid the school fees at the Convent for herself and Jakob, a source of resentment with her father and apparently the cause of the argument.

"What good, can you tell me, is it goin' to do Emma to go to that bleddy school, eh! She's jus' goin' to get big ideas, man. What good did it do you to get educatin'? Jus' made you wanna be like the white people. Emma mus' leave school and get a bleddy job. I don' wan' no bleddy charity from Jack Patrickson."

"My education helps me have a better paid job at the hotel." Emma strained to hear her mother's reply.

Another underlying irritation to Sol was the fact that his wife earned more than he.

"I don' want their bleddy money. I tol' you already. If the factory paid me enough, like I was a white man, then I could support my family myself. When I had my own business, I don't even get paid like a white man. They think 'cos I'm jus' a coloured I'll do the jobs cheap. So I can't make enough outta my business. They jus' full of shit, man. One day, I tell you, one day they'll have to pay us more but then they'll be forced to do it because there won't be enough white people to do the bleddy jobs. Look what that fellow van der Merwe in the Libray say when you want a job there. He say they can't let a coloured girl work there. Ja man! They won't give us the opportunities until they are bleddy well forced to. Jack wouldn't have you working in the hotel even thoughs you do the work well, if it wasn't that you's a friend of Lisa's."

Her mother's reply was drowned by a train passing on the tracks outside and Sister Veronica's voice brought her back to the present.

"Emma Meintjies!" She jumped. "I've been watching you sitting there daydreaming. Answer my question." Emma looked blank. Meg scribbled something on a piece of paper, pushing it across the desk towards her, she couldn't read it. She had to confess she hadn't been listening.

The other girls giggled, pleased to see her chastised by Sister. Her mother said they were jealous because she did well at school. She knew they didn't like her. Once she overheard herself referred to as "that coloured kid who hangs around with Meg Patrickson." She was much younger then and didn't understand what being "coloured" meant. She wasn't blue or red! Her skin was creamy-almond and her hair blondish. Jakob looked different, though. His skin was dark brown, almost black. But there were others at school with dark skins like Helen Popadopalis and Maria Andreoli.

She asked her mother what 'coloured' meant. It was then Sara explained about her African grandmother and white grandfather. She was afraid. At first she didn't tell Meg, her best friend, but she couldn't keep such a secret long.

"Ma says that my Grandma was black." She watched Meg's face for a reaction. Meg was sketching in pastels. She shook back a strand of hair that had fallen forward and continued drawing without looking up.

"I know that."

"When did you know?"

"Oh, a long time ago. Danny told Father that the boys at the College called Jakob a *kaffir*. He asked Father if it was true. Didn't Jakob ever tell you?"

"No."

There was silence broken by the scratching of pastels on paper.

Emma continued. "Did you feel differently about me?"

"Of course not, silly. Why should it? Your Ma and my Ma are best friends."

Emma had jumped up and hugged her.

"Look out! You're smudging my drawing." Meg put her work aside, Emma remembered, taking her by the arm, "Come on, I'm starved, let's ask Aunty for *melk-tert*," running together down the hall and into the kitchen.

Emma smiled, recalling this incident as she waited for Meg to finish her piano lesson then her shoulders sagged, hearing her father's voice drumming in her ears.

"Emma mus' leave school and get a bleddy job."

She didn't want to leave school. Sister Veronica said she should go to the Normal College and become a teacher. That wouldn't be possible now. Her father would never agree.

"Why so gloomy? You're not still upset about what Sister Veronica said? She's just a fuss-pot. Why worry?" Meg appeared around the corner, swinging her music case. She took Emma's arm. "We're having a party tonight, can you come? The parents will be out and old Aunty is always in bed early, so Harry has asked some of his pals over. He has a new friend just come to live here, a bit older than Harry also keen on music. They want to form a band. His name is Gerry Miller and is so good looking," holding her forehead and pretending to swoon.

Emma couldn't help laughing, but shook her head. "My Pa won't allow me." She told Meg about the argument she had overheard.

"You're... so... lucky," Meg drawled. "I wish Father would let me get a job. I'm sick of school. I hate arithmetic and grammar. Anyway

131

we've persuaded him to let me just take music and art and Sister Irene will give me private lessons. Meg prattled on but Emma wasn't listening.

Lucky! she thought, *if only you knew, Meg*, but she kept silent not daring to voice her thoughts as once again she relived the nightmare, the nightmare that had gone on for so many years... The stealthy footsteps across the wooden boards of her bedroom... the fumbling as she steeled herself, feeling the hardness at her back... His voice in her ear, telling her they were going to the playground in the park. First the see-saw... up and down... up and down... up and down... and then the swing... higher and higher... higher and higher and finally swooping round and around on the merry-go-round... round and around until she was dizzy and felt herself flying through the air, then losing consciousness and waking up on her bed her bedclothes all awry, her hair wet with perspiration, wetness in her palms and under her armpits and wetness between her legs and the memory of the horror of what she had endured. Had it all been a terrible nightmare?

"Don't look so miserable, what's the matter with you, one minute you're fine and then you're looking miserable and depressed. Come on cheer up, race you to the corner." Meg began to run then remembered Aunty told her it was time she acted like a lady, now that she was sixteen. She stopped in her tracks, giggling.

Emma forced a smile, "You're... so... lucky, she imitated, you don't have to worry about your future. What future do I have? What's going to happen to me?"

132

Chapter 21

Pain gnawed at Sara's chest. Coughing wracked her body. Sleep eluded her. She was afraid. She had no energy and knew she had dropped in weight. Her life, a series of pain and worry. Worry about the unpaid bills, worry that she would be unable to do her job for Jack at the hotel, worry about Jakob and his wild ways and worry about Emma, because Sol threatened to take her away from the Convent and send her to work.

Sol was bitter. He resented white people and particularly Jack, who had prospered while he had failed.

"Shit man, Emma, it's not my fault, hey! It's not fair I don' have the same chances as white people do," he complained. He took to drinking cheap brandy and became morose at times and at other times, aggressive.

Lines of pain etched deep into Sara's face. She hardly thought of Paul and what might have been. Sometimes she did wonder about the wisdom of sending Emma to the Convent, remembering her own disappointed aspirations. Perhaps Sol was right, yet how could she deny the child the opportunity to be educated. Then there was Jakob. Jack wasn't pleased about his influence over Danny.

Her troubles seemed more than she could handle so she confided in Greta, who was the Housekeeper at the hotel. Greta lived near her in the township.

"Why don't you come to the Prayer Meeting with me at my Church tonight? You mus' accept Jesus, you know? You must repent and take His blood because He died for your sins."

"My sins? Where have I sinned?"

"All of us are sinners; we are born in sin."

Sara shook her head, "An innocent baby born a sinner?"

"*Ja, dis reg.* And we must take the blood of Jesus Christ to get saved."

Sara wondered how she was to blame for the white farmer raping her mother, but didn't comment. It might help to listen to what the Preacher had to say.

"O.K., perhaps I'll do that." She began attending services regularly.

Sara crept in the back door of the small wood and iron house beside the railway track that had been her home since her marriage. Walking into the kitchen, she saw Sol standing next to the cooker, he held a *sjambok* in his hand. Jakob stood defiantly against the wall. Emma sat at the table with downcast eyes.

"What's the matter?"

"Matter? Your blerry kid's the matter, that's wots the matter. He givin' me ch..ch..cheek, hey! He jush' full o' sh..shit! An' I tell you wot, I won' sh..stan' f'r it." Sol staggered as he advanced on the boy.

Sara stepped across the room and stood between them.

"Sit down, Sol, leave the boy alone."

He pushed her away, knocking her off balance and she fell, hitting her head against the edge of the table, then blackness as it hit the stone floor.

"Look what you've done, Pa!" Emma screamed at her father. The shock of seeing Sara's ashen face with blood running from the cut in her head, sobered Sol. He bent down, picking up her limp form, and carried her to the iron bedstead in the front room. When she came round the coughing started. It wouldn't stop. Blood gushed from her mouth, staining the sheet and pillow before she lapsed into unconsciousness.

The doctor was called but there was little he could do and they all stood helplessly around the bed as Sara gave up the effort of living.

There were but a handful of people at the graveside. Emma looked up and saw a puff of white cloud crossing the grey sky, a sail boat, setting off on a journey, she thought, while the trees lifted bare branches in supplication and a stray leaf drifted down, settling in benediction on the coffin. The Preacher read from the Bible. "Dust to dust... ashes to ...

Emma dropped her head and stared at the Preacher, pondering his words. *What had religion brought to Ma's life?* she thought. *It's not fair.* The white man who raped her grandma was surely the sinner, not her Ma, the result of that sin. *I won't struggle like Ma. I'll find a way. I'll show them.* She clenched her fists. Tears squeezed from her tightly shut eyes as her nightmare returned. Now things could only get worse at home. She shook herself and once again blocked the thoughts.

Martha too, stared at the Preacher, not hearing his words, recalling instead the day Ruth arrived at their house with Joe on her back. What a long time ago that was. She remembered listening behind the door while the black woman told Mamma about the farmer and what he did to her.

Not understanding at the time, except that it was something bad - a terrible thing, they said. She remembered the night Sara was born. She hadn't understood it all then.

Lisa stared at the Preacher, not listening to his words, thinking instead about the picnic on the Modder River when Sara had met Paul and she had fallen in love with Jack. How differently things had turned out for the two of them. Sara and she were raised together and were friends but their lives, as they grew older, had grown apart, separated through no fault of theirs.

Joe stared at the Preacher, not comprehending his words about a God he couldn't understand, recalling instead those far off happy days when he was a small child, living in the kraal, way up on the hillside, close to the land and the sky to be suddenly changed, as he searched his memory and recalled the bad thing that happened to his mother that night on the veld.

The service was over. The mourners walked slowly towards the waiting carriages. Martha turned to Joe.
"Poor Sara."
Joe stood fingering his cloth cap. He scratched his head. "That white farmer, he make too much trouble for my mother and for my sister. If my sister is looking like me it be better for her."
"Yes," murmured Martha under her breath, "the sins of the fathers..."

Lisa begged Sol to allow Sara to remain at the Convent. "She is doing so well at school, and would make a good teacher."
He shook his head. "No ways, educatin in no good for these kids. Look at Sara's problems, all through gettin' educatin. Emma mus' leave school and find work. Anyways we need the money. It's time she did some work for her living. And Jakob don't need no posh school neither. It done him no good. I was already working when I was his age."
Lisa was disappointed. "If she can't finish her schooling, at least let us give her a job at the hotel."
"No. I don' think so. I got a friend who work for Madisons in the Despatch Department. He tell me they want a girl. He's goin' to speak to his Supervisor."
"But what sort of future is that for Emma, working in despatch in a department store?"

135

"Better than getting fancy ideas about more educatin'. Wot future she got anyways?"

"She could teach. The government schools need good teachers."

"No. I'm sorry but she must get a job now. We need the money now."

Lisa dropped the subject, resolving to pursue it at a more appropriate time. She never gave in easily and retreated to re-think her tactics. One day she spoke to Emma.

"Would you like to continue with your schooling, Emma?"

"Oh yes, more than anything." The girl's eyes lit up and she smiled joyfully.

"There is one thing though, my dear, I was talking to Sister Veronica and she mentioned you have been absent so often since your mother died, does your father know you are missing so much school?"

Emma's expression changed, as if a curtain had descended in front of her eyes. She jumped up, pushing away the chair, "Of course Pa knows," she shouted, then slumped back on to it.

"Well, I'm sure there's good reason for your missing school dear, because I know you enjoy learning, not like our Meg, who openly admits she hates school. You can tell me what is troubling you."

Emma shook her head and ran out of the room.

Sol met a woman in a bar by the name of Lena. They started seeing each other regularly then he took her home to meet his kids. Emma sat at the kitchen table, darning a pair of Jakob's trousers. She heard her father and Lena in the front room. Lena shrieked and giggled as she teased and encouraged him in his love-making. Tears welled in Emma's eyes, thinking of her mother.

"Hey! Emma! Bring me and Lena shome coffee." Emma pretended she hadn't heard.

Sol repeated his call with a threat. "Lissen here, Emma, do you want me to come out there and shlap you or are you going to do wot I shay? Bring me and Lena shome coffee."

She put two cups on a wooden tray then poured in the coffee from the pot standing on the cooker, carrying it into the front room. She turned her eyes away at the sight of the two of them lying together in her mother's bed. Her father looked up with a grin. "I jush' wanna tell you Emma, that me and Lena here, are gettin' married. Come and kissh your new Ma."

136

"She'll never be my Ma," hissed Emma and turned to walk out of the room but at the same time felt a sense of relief.

Sol jumped up and caught her by the arm as she tried to squeeze past him and through the doorway. She smelt brandy. "You'll reshpect Lena, my girl, or I'll give you a bleddy good hiding, hey!" He snatched the *sjambok* hanging behind the door and brought it down across her back. Her eyes filled with horror, then disbelief, fear and pain.

After her father married Lena, home life was even more intolerable for Emma. She had had some respite for the first few weeks but then her nightmares returned when Lena was on nightshift at the factory. Emma saw less of Meg, mainly because of her long working hours but also because Sol objected to their friendship. With two brothers near her in age Meg had plenty of escorts and she confided in Emma that she was in love with Gerry. Emma smiled, thinking it would be someone else in a month or two. Meg was a flirt.

Meg was bored with her social life and envied Emma having a job so she approached her father.

"Isn't there any job I can do at the hotel, Father?"

Jack didn't answer so she repeated her question.

"What do you mean, 'any job?'" his terse response.

"I mean a job. Couldn't I help with the book-keeping?" Then she remembered her dislike for figures, "W..ell, perhaps not that exactly. But what about playing the piano in the Palm Court in the afternoons while High Tea is served? I should like that and I do play the piano rather well. Or I could help the Receptionist in the front office. That would be fun."

Jack's face turned red as he blustered, "Balderdash! Out of the question. No daughter of mine has to work for a living."

Meg ignored his testiness. "But I'd like to have something to do."

"I am sure Martha can give you plenty to do, by jove! Sox to darn. Buttons to sew on shirts for your brothers." Meg pulled a face and opened her mouth to protest, but Jack stood his ground.

Book III
Chapter 22

Capetown
Circa 1913

The loud noise was repeated. The clang of metal against metal. Emma half opened her eyes and a round cheese-face, eye-sockets set in shadow, topped by hair rolled into fat brown sausages, peered down at her. A scream rose in Emma's throat.

"Go away, go away Lena." She pulled the blanket over her head thinking she should never have told her step-mother that she knew about her connection with the diamond dealer.

It had happened during an argument with Lena the day after two strange men come to the house, while her father was at work. Emma told Lena she had overheard the conversation when they were discussing prices they would give her for diamonds she bought from the native mine workers, who had ways of smuggling out stones.

Lena started an argument with Emma over a trivial matter and Emma, to get even with her step-mother, threatened to tell her father what she overheard. As soon as she spoke, seeing the look of fear and hatred on Lena's face, Emma realised her mistake.

"I'll get you." The words hissing out of Lena's mouth between her sharp viper's tongue, shooting back and forth.

Emma had cringed, backing against the wall, her hand to her mouth. She knew this was no idle threat. Lena had gotten her in trouble in the past with her Pa, by telling lies about her. Pa always took his new wife's word against hers, and now Lena had come to get her as before, dragging her out of bed and telling Pa a story. He would beat her with the *sjambok*. She began to shake.

A shaft of light pierced the darkness and Emma's breath escaped with relief as she recognised her travelling companion's face, striped by the station lights, shining through the shutters. She was safely on the train bound for Capetown and her new life.

"Oh! I'm sorry eh! Excuse *asseblief.* I didn't mean to wake you, man, jus' wanted to get my handbag off the rack up there. I have a splitting

139

headache and left the pills in my bag." She indicated the luggage shelf above Emma's head. Emma smiled and dozed off.

After the argument with Lena, Emma had thought hard about her situation and decided to leave Kimberley. Mr. Jones, the Assistant Manager where she worked, liked her so she approached him with her problem. He was due to retire and had nothing to lose by helping her.
"Excuse me, sir, I was wondering if I could get a transfer to the Capetown Branch of Maddisons?" She explained that her step-mother was difficult. Mr. Jones understood. He arranged a transfer and did better than that. He recommended the girl be given a position in sales, never mentioning that she was "coloured." She was bright and a hard worker and in his opinion that was all that mattered. He also promised to keep her transfer a secret from the other employees in Kimberley, and from her father, should he enquire.

Emma was brought back to her surroundings with the sound of voices and shoes crunching on gravel. Her companion, face shiny with night cream, pushed up the shutter and the station lights filled the compartment. The guard loaded milk cans. "Here" - in big letters painted on a wooden board and next to it - "Gentlemen." Underneath hand-printed on a piece of cardboard - "*Blankes Alleen* - Whites Only." On the other side of the station building "Dames" and then "Ladies" beside it, and scratched on the painted door "*Blankes Alleen* - Whites only." Finally, on the edge of the platform, a long white signboard, the word "*Suikerbosfontein*" in black, and the miles to Capetown printed underneath. They were somewhere in the Karroo with another day's journey ahead.

Emma sat with her face pressed against the window pane, breath misting the glass as her eyes followed the railway lines, opening out and widening, then narrowing into the distance. Rain drops raced each other off shining steel. High above was Table Mountain shrouded in a grey cloth of cloud. On either side the two mountains, "Lion's Head" and the "Devil's Peak." As the train approached the station the sun broke through and Emma's spirits lifted thinking of her prospects of a new life with new opportunities. She took her suitcase off the rack and smiled as she helped her companion, promising to contact her, but knowing she never would. From now on she would be "white."

140

She had a slip of paper in her purse with the address of a girls' hostel written in Mr. Jones' shaky hand. He assured her it was for white girls only. She asked directions of a porter then set off to walk.

Approaching the area she noted the run-down neighbourhood and the predominance of black and coloured people. Was Mr. Jones mistaken or had he not kept his promise?

"What's yer name?" An old woman sat behind a desk at the hostel. Emma told her.

"Ooh ja! They tole' me there was a new girl coming. So yer goin' to work at "Maddisons" eh! Where is you from?"

"Yes, I'm hoping to start there tomorrow," she replied, ignoring the last part of the question.

According to the sign the hostel was for "whites only," Mr. Jones had kept his promise while considering her financial limitations. The neighbourhood was poor, poor whites and poor coloureds. Gloom descended upon her, sitting on the narrow iron bedstead staring out of the dirty window. Rain drops ran off window panes, sliding off dusty sills, while the wind blew branches into a wild dance. A gong announced dinner.

"Hi! Who are you?" Emma looked up from her bowl of soup, then stood, ready to move away, knocking the chair over backwards in her confusion.

"You don't have to go. It's OK if you sit here. Are you the new girl?"

Emma nodded as she bent to pick up her chair. The girl was fat. Her eyes disappeared into her cheeks as she laughed at Emma's confusion, making her body wobble. She bent to help Emma restore the overturned chair and her friendliness eased Emma's depression.

The shrill ring of the alarm clock woke Emma with a jolt. Unfamiliar surroundings confusing her, until she remembered - the first day of her new life! She dressed hurriedly to be in time for the appointment arranged by Mr. Jones with the manager of the Capetown Branch and, after a hasty breakfast, set off in the rain and driving wind.

"Cape Times, *koop die Cape Times, merrem.*" She shook her head at the newspaper vendor, looking up at Table Mountain, still partially concealed by cloud as she struggled with her umbrella

"What's your name, girl? Speak up! Speak up! Can't hear you if you mumble." Miss Latimer in "Ladies Gloves," tall and intimidating, hair swept into a chignon, blouse high necked and finely tucked with leg-o-mutton sleeves. She wore rimless spectacles on a dangling chain and inspected Emma as if she were an item of merchandise. Emma nervously repeated her name.

The months slipped by. Letty, Emma's new friend was cheerful but they had little in common and Emma was homesick for Kimberley and Meg's companionship. There were times when she was tempted to end her self-imposed exile. Until she remembered Lena!

Once again Emma woke to the drum beat of rain on corrugated roofing. Would the rain never stop? Dressing by candlelight she made her way down the corridor to the dining room. Ate the porridge, lukewarm and lumpy. Drank the coffee, sweet and strong. It was early, time to sit in the Gardens of the Government Buildings and watch the squirrels at play, before her work day began and, finding a bench under an old oak protected from the rain, she sat pondering her situation. She felt trapped. Her dream of continuing her schooling and finding accommodation in a better neighbourhood was just that - a dream, on the money she earned - a hopeless dream.

The rain fell in big drops, while the sun appeared, shining on glistening leaves, on pools of rainwater and on the mountainside. Fresh air and sunshine revived her spirits. It was a "monkey's wedding" that's what it was. Ma always called it "a monkey's wedding" when the sun shone in the rain. She began to laugh and jumped up, lifting her arms above her head, rain running through her hair and over her face, splashing her legs as she danced, stamping in the puddles. She was free, free of being labelled a "coloured," free of Lena. She saw a rainbow arching the sky and felt optimistic and hopeful. A rainbow meant hope, her Ma used to say. She clapped her hands, sending a squirrel, scurrying into the bushes. Today and all the days ahead would be good.

Emma tidied a drawer of gloves, humming under her breath, heart full of gratitude. At least she had a job and it was better than the one she had had in Kimberley. Here she was accepted as "white."

"Show me some gloves, size nine. Hurry girl."

Emma jumped at the voice invading her thoughts, then turning, saw a middle-aged woman, fashionably dressed accompanied by a young man, standing on the other side of the counter. She attended to her customer's demands. After insisting Emma unpack most of her stock the woman, complaining about the poor selection and inferior quality, walked away, hardly glancing at Emma during the exchange. The young man hesitated then coughed behind his hand. Emma looked up.

"Apologies for Ma's manner. She doesn't mean to be rude. But she has an appointment with..." His voice trailed, realising the lameness of his excuse.

Emma smiled, "Please don't worry. She wasn't rude at all."

The young man hesitated, looking directly at her. "I say, could you join me for luncheon? Ma will be on her appointment for the best part of an hour."

Emma glanced at the fob watch on her blouse front. Almost lunch time and the invitation was tempting, but she didn't know the young man. They had never been formally introduced. Could she accept a luncheon invitation? She began to shake her head.

He put up his hand, forestalling her refusal. "By the way the name is Etienne Frobisher and my mother knows Miss Latimer. Ma has been a customer here for years."

Miss. Latimer returned from her lunch break at that moment and seeing the young man, made quite a fuss of him. When she heard of the invitation she approved heartily, to Emma's amazement, allowing her to leave ten minutes early.

The young couple walked away and Miss Latimer turned to the assistant behind the Jewellery counter.

"That will give his Mother a headache, her precious son having lunch with a shop girl. Serve her right for all the times she has been rude to me. I'd like to see her face when she finds out!"

Maisie, dusting the glass cabinet, grinned. "Ja man! You're telling me. Wait till Edie in "Corsets" hears, jurrah man, she'll have a good larf. The old cow insulted her last week."

Miss Latimer raised her hands, remembering she was supposed to be in charge. "Now, now, Maisie, no need to talk like that."

Maisie, undaunted, ignored the rebuff. It wasn't often Miss Latimer stooped to gossip. "Edie was cross hey, but she couldn't say nothing of course. That old woman thinks she's somebody because she's a de Villiers married into the wealthy Frobisher family. They say her mother-in-law arranged the match and her husband committed suicide because he was in love with someone else, some girl in Kimberley."

143

Miss Latimer's nose twitched, smelling scandal but would not encourage gossip with a junior member of the staff. She pursed her lips. "One shouldn't believe all one hears, my dear." Dropping her voice to a whisper, "Who told you?"

Etienne took Emma's arm, steering her down the street towards a fashionable restaurant where he was obviously well known. They were seated at a table in a secluded corner. Emma studied her escort. Dark blue eyes set deep in a tanned face, topped by blonde hair, falling forward across his forehead. Somehow familiar! She tried to recall her few friends and aquaintances. Was it someone she had worked with, or a customer in Kimberley perhaps? A friend of one of Meg's brothers? A photograph of someone? Who could it be?

He saw a slim young girl. Pale blue eyes in a heart-shaped face with high cheek bones. Her golden-blonde hair, softly curled, and lips full and sensual.

He told her he lived in Rondebosch, on the slopes of Table Moutain. She had walked through the elegant suburb one Saturday afternoon and was impressed. She didn't tell him she lived in District Six. He told her his father was the head of a prominent law firm and had been killed in a shooting accident before he was born. She didn't tell him her father was a coloured carpenter and she had run away from home. He told her his grandmother was an Afrikaner who had married into the Frobisher family and therefore he was partly Afrikaans. She didn't tell him her grandmother was a black woman who had been raped by an Afrikaans farmer and therefore she was also partly Afrikaans. She did tell him, however, that her mother had died and she had left home after the sad event.

A year passed. Emma hadn't contacted her father apart from the letter she left at his bedside telling him she wouldn't be returning home. She guessed he was probably relieved. She and Lena had quarrelled constantly. She hadn't written to Meg either. That bothered her but it was for the best. Meg might tell someone and it would get to her father and Lena. Besides, she didn't want anyone in Capetown knowing she wasn't in fact "white." She would keep her secret and not spoil her relationship with Etienne. One day, perhaps, when the time was right, she would confide in him. She was sure he would understand.

144

Emma and Etienne were in love but he didn't tell his mother. He found Emma a job in the library at the University, cataloguing. She was quick and soon learnt the work. He also found her lodgings in a suitable neighbourhood. After that he took her to meet his mother. His mother had forgotten the incident with the little shop girl, whom she wouldn't have recognised anyway.

Etienne bought a Model T. They motored to Cape Point and stood on that remote spot, on the southernmost tip of the great continent of Africa where two oceans meet with surging energy, thrusting white spray landward, up on to the black rocks. The wild wind whipped the frail trees into submission, flattening the long grass. It blew her hair loose, sweeping it across her face. Her long skirt billowed outwards. They stood holding hands, then Etienne turned and put his arms around her and held her close.

"Marry me, Emma." War clouds were gathering in Europe but that was far away. He wasn't going to spoil this magical moment. With the wind and his words, she caught her breath. Her heart bumping her chest. Was this the time to tell him about her family? Happiness is a fragile thing for it hangs on a slender thread. She put aside all troubling thoughts and savoured the moment. She would tell him some other time.

When Etienne's mother heard the news she was annoyed. "You hardly know the girl. And she hasn't been very forthcoming about her family. Meintjies? I don't know of them. Are they prominent in Kimberley? You did say she was from Kimberley didn't you? Is her father with De Beers? Can't be with the Foreign Service, not with a name like that.

"I don't know Ma! But what does it matter?"

"Of course it matters, Etienne. I think I shall write to your father's cousin Kitty. She was raised in Kimberley until her father took them all back to England. It's a pity Great Aunt Queenie isn't alive, she would know if the family is of any consequence. That's what I'll do," she continued, "I'll write to cousin Kitty."

Etienne shrugged and walked out of the room. He hoped his Ma wasn't going to give Emma the third degree when he brought her to tea on Saturday. He had better warn Emma. But that wasn't necessary. His Ma took ill that very night. She had a stroke, losing the power of speech before she died a week later.

Etienne and Emma were married quietly then drove to Hermanus for their honeymoon. The first night, as they lay together in bed, Etienne noticed her stiffness when he folded his arms about her, but put it down to her innocence. He was inexperienced himself. For Emma the nightmare was returning, the one she had blocked from her memory since leaving Kimberley. She froze at Etienne's touch, remembering the horrors of those nights when she was a child. She wanted to tell him all about it but was afraid, feeling shame and guilt, yes guilt, as if she somehow bore some of the responsibility, and would Etienne understand? They moved into the family homestead and Emma began to feel secure and happy for the first time in her life but war in Europe was imminent and within months their lives would change.

Chapter 23

Kimberley
Circa 1914

The Modder River flows slowly after the dry season and Meg and Gerry sat on the bank watching the sluggish stream meandering between rocks and reeds, their thoughts on the future. War had been declared and Gerry and Harry had volunteered for the army.

"To defend the Empire, m'dear," laughed Harry, thinking it a bit of a lark and an opportunity for adventure. His unit was posted to German East Africa and Gerry's to the German territory in South West. Their departure was imminent and they decided to return to their favourite haunt on the Modder River, recalling shared memories of happier times of picnics and parties. Harry and girl friend, Molly played records on the phonograph while Meg and Gerry strolled downstream, finding a secluded spot to sit.

"Will things ever be the same again?" Meg leant against Gerry's shoulder.

"Oh, I think so, old thing. This will all be over by Christmas," he assured her, smiling and patting her knee. They watched the muddy water. A broken twig floated past in mid-stream then, blocked by jutting rocks, drifted towards the bank, becoming wedged in a bundle of dead leaves. *Was that how Emma thought of her life here in Kimberley?* Meg thought.

They heard Harry's voice uttering endearments and Molly's high-pitched giggles. Gerry put his arm around her, but Meg wasn't to be distracted. She was in a somber mood. She talked about Emma. "I can't understand her. She left without telling anyone, not even me, her best friend. I wonder where she is now, I can't imagine life will be any better for her than here. I understand she'd want to keep her whereabouts a secret from her father and Lena, but she knows she can trust me. Lena was involved in I.D.B. you know. Meg did tell me that and, stupidly, let her step-mother know she overheard her discussing the matter with some strange men who called at the house."

Gerry wasn't paying attention, his thoughts on other things. He put his arm around Meg's waist, pulling her towards him. She squeezed his hand, absently while a frown furrowed her brow. Gerry dropped his arm.

The strains of a popular song drifted towards them. 'There's a long, long trail a-winding to the land of my dreams...'

"Perhaps you'll still hear from her."

"No, I don't think so, it's been more than a year." They sat silently for a while, watching the muddy water.

"Poor Emma and Jakob, and Sara and Joe as well, for that matter. Nothing worked out for them. Mother told me Sara was in love with an Afrikaans boy once, but his family prevented the marriage. Emma didn't know because Sara never spoke of it."

Meg shook her head sorrowfully. "I remember once Emma and I were playing dress-up and looked in her mother's chest of drawers for some ear-rings. I found a picture of a young man under the paper lining. He had a smiling face with deep-set eyes and a shock of hair fell forward over his forehead. I showed it to Emma and she asked her Ma who it was but Sara didn't reply, just snatched the picture away, telling us to go outside and play.

"I told my Mum about the incident and she said the picture must have been of Paul, the man Sara was engaged to marry. He was visiting from Capetown when they met, and was a cousin of Mother's friend Kitty, who used to live in Kimberley but the family went back to England. Mother said Sara was heartbroken and only married Sol because she felt she had no other option when her job in the library was threatened. That was a mistake because they had nothing in common, except their mixed race. They were always so poor. Sol couldn't earn enough so Sara had to work, leaving Jakob to his own devices in the Township where he got into bad company. He and Danny were good friends but Father saw Jakob was a bad influence so arranged a job for him on the farm.

"Father really bought the farm for Harry, you know. Harry always wanted to farm and now he has to go to this horrid war and old van der Westhuyzen with the help of Lucas, the boss-boy and Jakob will run things until he gets back."

Gerry nodded his head. "I think Harry will make a good farmer. But don't be so gloomy. You can't worry your pretty head about all the poor people in the world, you know. I'm sure Emma will be O.K. she's smart enough to look after herself and as for Jakob, he's just lucky your Father sent him to the farm before he got into real trouble."

"It's not just about poverty, it's about opportunity. Emma and Jakob don't have the same opportunities as we do just because they aren't white. Our future is secure. We have everything to look forward to. In spite of her words, she felt a sense of foreboding.

"I wonder if the young woman, Ruth, wouldn't have been better off if your grandmother hadn't befriended her and she had returned to the *kraal* and her own people."

Meg's voice rose in indignation. "To be abused again and again by the farmer? Oh for sure, her people would have been better off if the white people hadn't taken their land in the first instance. Now we have to be responsible for the mess that was created."

"But the natives have benefited from civilisation and Christianity, taught by the missionaries."

"They have their own moral code and a high regard for family life. It may not conform to our ideas but who are we to say what is right." Her brow wrinkled, then she quoted:

"'You taught me language; and my profit on't / Is, I know how to curse. The red plague rid you / For learning me your language.'"

Gerry look astonished. "Who put these ideas in your head?"

"Sister Veronica. We were studying "The Tempest."

Gerry put his hand under her chin, lifting her face to his. "You're being too serious. Let's talk about us. Start planning our wedding. That should make you happy. It does me."

"Oh Gerry, I am happy," she managed a smile and put her arms around his neck. Why did this horrid war have to happen? I just hope things never change."

' There's a long long. . t...r. a . .i . .l.....a. .w. . i ..n. d..i..n...g.' The record wound down. Molly otherwise occupied. Tears spilled down Meg's cheeks.

But a single incident in faraway Sarajevo would change many things.

* * *

In Capetown, Etienne and Emma sat on the wide stoep of the old homestead in Rondebosch a phonograph on the table in front of them. Emma thinking of Meg and Kimberley. One day she would write to her but first she must tell Etienne about her family. Perhaps this was the right time.

Etienne put his arms around her and drew her close. She would tell him now, it was as good a time as any. She smiled up at him.

"Etienne I have something to tell you ."

"Have you? Because I have something to tell you." They were interrupted by the sound of footsteps on the gravel driveway. It was the mailman. Etienne greeted him as he handed over an official envelope and Emma leant over his shoulder as he opened it and began reading. Her smile froze.

"You didn't tell me you had joined-up."

"That's what I was about to tell you. I didn't want to worry you, but we've all been talking about it you know, Koos and Piet and my English cousins Johnny and Jim, We decided the sooner we all get involved the sooner this thing will be over."

Suddenly the future looked gloomy. The moment had passed she couldn't tell him now about her black grandmother.

"I've given you my news, now what were you going to tell me."

"Oh, nothing much. It's not important."

The record wound down. 'Theres . .a. .lo.n. g l..o..n..g t..r.a..i..l   a w i n..d..ing, to the l . .a. .n..d of. . m . y   d..r...e....a....m....ss.'

Emma wiped her eyes.

After some months' training, Etienne was posted with his unit to the campaign in South West Africa.

Time passed slowly. Christmas came and went but the campaign seemed bogged down. Two men sat outside their tent talking while the sun dropped behind the sand dunes, streaking low clouds in bands of orange and crimson. Night came on suddenly with the points of the Southern Cross gleaming like crystal in the crisp, clear sky.

The two soldiers drew closer to the fire. Gerry discussed the progress of the war with the officer from Capetown who had come to relieve him before he went on furlogh. Their talk turned to personal matters.

"I understand you're from Kimberley. That's my wife's hometown, you know. Her parents are both dead. She doesn't talk much about Kimberley and I don't press her." Etienne took a crumpled packet of cigarettes out of his tunic pocket and shook out two, offering one to his companion before putting the other in his mouth.

Gerry struck a match and held it to Etienne's cigarette then bent his head to light his own.   "What was her name before you married. Kimberley's a small place, and my fiancee might even know her. Meg knows everybody. We're getting married when I return on leave."   He gazed into the distance and smiled.

The sound of hoofbeats interrupted the conversation. Both officers stood up as the rider halted in front of them.

"Lieutenant Gerald Miller? Orders to report to the Colonel at once, sir."

Gerry stood up, dropped his cigarette in the sand and tramped on it before stepping forward.   "Will do."   Then, turning towards his companion, held out his hand. "Must continue this conversation another time, old chap. 'Till then, cheers. All the best. Have to see what the Colonel wants." He saluted and walked away.

Within half an hour, Gerry, mounted on his horse leading a platoon of engineers, rode into the desert night on a mission. Shortly after they left Headquarters a message was received informing the battalion that the Germans had surrounded in South West Africa.

But Gerry and his men, riding through the desert, were unaware of this development. Neither was the German sniper out behind the ridge. He saw the enemy within his sights and fired a shot. Gerry fell from his horse as it shied in fright.

Chapter 24

The long weeks of waiting turned into days. Gerry's homecoming was at hand. Martha had pedalled her mother's sewing machine for weeks. Fine hand-made lace stitched to camisoles and petticoats. Blouses, narrow tucked with high collars. Finely hemmed sheets and a combined effort with Meg on a patchwork quilt.

Martha's stern features, grey hair pulled sharply back into a bun, belied her gentleness. But she did have a strong stubborn streak. She had proved herself a good business woman and, in fact, in different times her life might have taken a different course, but she was content, caring for her sister's family.

Lisa had changed little over the years. Her figure plumper but her smooth skin unlined. Jack bought her fashionable clothes made of the finest silks and taffettas. He was proud of her and considered her his most treasured possession.

Meg resembled her father, Jack, and the bond between them was strong. She stood at the table in the breakfast-room, unpacking wedding presents and looked up when she heard the sound of her father's voice, seeing him through the window approaching the house with Gerry's father. Jack's face and figure had rounded over the years; his watch-chain stretched across his ample waist.

Meg ran to the front door, threw it open and embraced her father in her usual impulsive way. "You're far too early for lunch," She laughed but her laughter died, seeing her father's face.
"Something's wrong!" She looked at Gerry's father, he too looked troubled. "What's the matter? Is it Gerry? Has he been wounded? Is he ill? Please somebody, tell me."

Jack stretched out his arms towards her. "I'm afraid it's bad news, my child. Mr. Miller has a telegram from Gerry's commanding officer."
"Has Gerry been wounded?" Meg repeated. She looked from one to the other. "Is he..." her voice trailed off.

"It's the worst possible news, m'dear," said Gerry's father. "Gerald was shot by a sniper and killed."

"But the war is over in South West," interrupted Lisa. She and Martha had entered the hallway at the sound of voices. "The Germans surrendered there."

Gerry's father told what he knew of the circumstances. "It seems Gerald was instructed to go with a platoon of engineers to Swakopmund only hours before the news of the surrender reached the outpost where his Headquarters were located. The German who shot him was probably also unaware of the surrender. Lines of communication were stretched to their utmost, you see." The old man's back was stiff, his head erect. "He died for King and country," he said but his voice shook.

Meg trembled. "King and country," she repeated. "What about me?" then regained her composure, assuring them she was alright while praying silently to be left alone.

The wedding dress was folded, packed in tissue and put away; the gifts returned. All gaiety went out of Meg. She neither cried nor complained, holding everyone at a distance, even her beloved father. She wouldn't talk about Gerry.

She could have talked to Emma. But Emma had gone away.

She could have talked to Harry, but he was with his regiment in East Africa. Christmas was a dismal affair that year.

Durban was hot in January. Lisa and Meg sat on the balcony of the beach-front hotel watching the colourful pagaent passing by.

Zulu men, painted faces with feathered head-dresses, pulling decorated *rickshas*. Stamping, whistling and leaping. These warriors of past days of glory, holding out two hands, humbly begging coins.

East Indian men white turbaned, patiently waiting on impatient patrons. Indian women, their ears and nostrils pierced with jewels, hinting of palanquins and pagodas, and wearing exotic saris in purple, orange and yellow, carried baskets of fruit in matching colours.

African women with beaded hair and naked breasts, oiled and necklaced, carried clay pots on their heads, selling their wares for pennies.

Meg saw none of it.

A waiter brought tall glasses of lemonade. She stared with vacant eyes at the surf, charging and surging, plumes of spray shooting upwards.

The waves breaking, then unfurling and flattening before spreading outwards.

Meg saw none of it.

Lisa tried to interest her. "How about a morning shopping? Or a visit to the Indian Market?" She waved a fan in front of her face. The humid sea air was unbearable. Her corsets pinched and her head ached. "Meg dear, you aren't listening. I said..." She stopped, following Meg's gaze. The girl's eyes were riveted on a soldier making his way slowly away from them, through the crowd of people at the hotel entrance.

She only saw the back of his head, but the set of his shoulders - the way he walked - the colouring! It was Gerry! She knew they had been wrong. It was all a mistake. Gerry wasn't dead! He had gone to Kimberley, as arranged, for their wedding, and Father had sent him on here to fetch her home. What a wonderful surprise. They would be married after all.

Wild thoughts raced through her head. She stood up, knocking her chair backwards, calling Gerry's name. She darted forward, colliding with a waiter, sending tray and glasses flying. Heads turned. People stared. The orchestra stopped. Unheeding, she ran on, reached out and pulled the soldier's arm. He turned. She stopped. Her arm fell to her side, dropping his, staring into the eyes of a stranger. It wasn't Gerry. Gerry was dead - dead - dead, lying somewhere beneath the desert. There was only the picture they sent of his grave. A lonely cross in the sand.

The orchestra leader raised his baton. The band picked up the tune. "There's a long, long trail a-winding to the land of my dreams..."

Chapter 25

The sun dropped behind the mountains in the west but twilight lingered. Shadows from the oak, growing against the wall, dappled the gables of the old Cape Dutch homestead and a delicate breeze danced the leaves of the vine, clinging to the brick pillars supporting the beamed pergola.

Etienne had returned from the campaign in South West Africa and was ready to embark for France where war still waged. He sat next to Emma on the swing seat, looking over the garden.

"The officer I was sent to replace was a damned decent fellow, you know Emma. I'm sorry we didn't get better acquainted. I liked him. Said he was from Kimberley. Damn shame he was killed but that's war. His name was Gerry Miller."

Emma looked up in alarm, but Etienne, stroking Ruff, their airdaile puppy, didn't notice. He continued, "Poor fellow, sent off on a mission and shot the night before the end of his term of duty, man it was a shame, eh! He told me he was engaged to be married."

Emma clutched the side of the swing, waiting to hear if Etienne would say he'd been in touch with Meg? *And what about Meg?* Emma thought, closing her eyes. Poor Meg, having to face such a tragedy and here she was only concerned with her own fears, she hadn't thought of her friend's loss. Should she take the risk and write to her? She considered a moment. Perhaps not. At least not until she speaks to Etienne. *Meg would be alright,* Emma reassured herself, she had her family for support. Emma returned to her surroundings with the sound of Etienne's voice.

"I don't think you've been listening," he accused. "I was telling you about this chap I met who was killed. As I said, he told me he came from Kimberley and was getting married but he didn't get to telling me his fiance's name, because we were interrupted right then by a messenger calling him to an urgent briefing with the colonel. I intended writing to his family, could have got the address but things happened so quickly after that and before we knew it everything was over up there." He shook his head. Perhaps I should still write, I could find out his parents' address."

Emma held her breath. Should she confide in Etienne now? He might understand, then this great burden would be lifted forever. But, what if he didn't understand? What if he was angry at her deceitfulness?

What if he changed towards her; hated her for her black blood? She wavered, then resolved to tell him anyway.

"Etienne..." she began.

He turned towards her. "*Wat makeer my liefde,* don't look so upset. I know you're worrying I might get killed like poor old Gerry, but I'll be OK." He wrapped his arms around her as she opened her mouth to speak, stopping it with a kiss.

She broke free, putting her head against his chest. "I..." she began again, fingering the collar of his shirt.

"Don't worry your pretty little head, I won't get killed, I promise you," caressing her; but a commotion at the end of the driveway caused them to look up. Koos, in his open Ford tourer packed with friends from their student days, drove through the gate. There was shouting and cheering. They were all leaving for France the following day. A party was on. The moment for confession passed. Etienne never did write that letter to Gerry's family.

* * *

In Kimberley, meanwhile, Meg spent more time with Martha, listening to her reminisce about growing up in the rough mining town when diamonds were first discovered. She never spoke about her Jewish, and her German background, however, they were best forgotten in these times. Lisa and Jack were busy with business.

Harry arrived on a week's leave before departing for battlefields in France. He worried about Meg who seemed to have lost purpose. He knew she would like to get a job.

"What can I do, Harry? I haven't been trained for anything. I thought of nursing, but haven't the stomach for it. I would like to teach, but Father doesn't approve of higher education for women and won't allow me to enrol in college. I enjoy drawing and painting but there's no opportunity for a career in art, especially for a woman and particularly here, and can you imagine Father allowing me to leave Kimberley? I thought of Madisons. Father was furious."

"Why, in heaven's name, does the gel want a job?" Jack complained to Lisa. "Can't understand her. Plenty to do around the house, giving Martha a hand. What's this talk about a career? Fiddlesticks! Next thing she'll join this protest for women wanting the vote."

Lisa kept silent. It was a waste of time arguing with Jack and besides, she usually got what she really wanted.

Harry met a friend with whom he had worked in the government department before Jack bought the farm. He brought him home to meet Meg.

"This is Tom Reid, friend of mine. Used to work in the same office in Vereeniging. The army turned him down because of bad eyesight."

Meg saw a shy, self-effacing young man, wearing rimless glasses, dark hair growing back from a high domed forehead. His manner serious. Meg was pleased he wasn't a soldier; memories of Gerry were too raw.

From then on Tom spent every weekend in Kimberley. The friendship ripened and one day he proposed to Meg.

"Don't give me an answer right now. Think about it. I can wait," noticing her look of alarm.

Meg thought about it. She lay in bed at night and thought about it. She sat on a secluded bench in a park and thought about it. She was twenty-one, almost an old maid by current standards. She had no training and most of her friends were engaged or married. What would happen to her? Would she spend her life in her parents' home or, worse, like Martha, in the home of one of her married brothers? The thought alarmed her. Maybe marriage to Tom wasn't a bad idea after all. She wasn't likely to meet any other young men, they were all at the front.

She would have her own home and maybe children one day, she wasn't sure how that would happen, no one had told her, the subject was taboo and she and Gerry were seldom unchaperoned. A tear slipped down her cheek, thinking of Gerry. No one could ever replace Gerry but Tom was kind. What options did she have? She made her decision alone. There was no one in whom she could confide, her mother too busy, her best friend gone away and what did Aunt Martha know about marriage anyway?

Meg and Tom were married quietly. She wore a simple dress and a wide hat. The year was 1917. Jack wasn't happy about the match. He didn't think much of the quiet young man.

Meg lay in the big brass bed, her body rigid, glancing at Tom lying next to her, head thrown back, breathing loudly. Was this what marriage was about? She might have become aroused but Tom couldn't wait. It was all over so quickly.

159

She began to tremble. Would it have been different with Gerry? A tear slid slowly down her cheek. She stopped shaking and fell asleep. Gerry leant over her, she felt his caresses and looked up, then moved over, careful not to waken the sleeping Tom. Her heart raced as she travelled new and breath-taking paths, ending in pure ecstacy. Tom woke and turned over, noting her smiling face. He felt good. He had satisfied her after all.

Their life fell into a routine of sorts. Tom left every morning for his job in the government office, having transferred from the country town. Jack hadn't thought it advisable for Meg to move so far from home.

"But your home is with me now," Tom protested at first.

"Oh, don't let's leave the family."

"But I'm your family now," he argued. However he relented in the end. What did it matter where he worked he had Meg. Having a wife was a damned good idea.

Harry, after being gassed by the enemy in the trenches in France, returned to Kimberley. He was restless, spending his evenings in the bar at The Halfway House talking to soldiers on leave and others like himself, who were wounded and boarded out.

He wasn't ready to return to the farm. Lisa understood but Jack was impatient. "Urged me to buy a farm, said that was all he wanted to do. Can't understand the boy. Can't loaf around forever."

"Be patient, Jack. He's had a bad time. He needs company, the farm's too isolated."

Meg cleaned the new house, a wedding present from Jack. Martha sewed drapes. Clothes and linen for her marriage to Gerry were not unpacked. The war, and all its upheaval was worlds away.

Lisa dropped in often after shopping, "Was in the market and got an extra bird for you." On another occassion, "Madison's have a sale, thought you might like this blouse."

Meg was delighted and showed her gifts to Tom who scowled. "They think I can't provide for you? Your father doesn't think much of me because I work for the government."

"Nonsense. Father thinks the world of you," she assured him, but she knew that wasn't true.

160

Tom couldn't understand her family. He confided in a co-worker.

"They're a strange bunch. Always together and yet never at a loss for conversation. They only seem to go to Church at Christmas and Easter. I have to admit they are good people, though, and I've never heard them speak ill of others."

Tom's family were different. Tight lipped and tight fisted. Chapel three times a day on the Sabbath and Bible readings every evening. Meg recalled meeting them on her honeymoon and had found the experience stifling.

"I understand your father is in business." Tom's father had enquired, shaking out his napkin having just said "grace." The family sat around the dinner table

"Oh yes, he owns two hotels in Kimberley."

"Really!" Mr. Reid's eyebrows rose. "Not public houses I trust."

Tom nudged her leg under the table and, looking uncomfortable, interrupted, "Of course not father, they are private hotels." Meg looked surprised.

"And your mother? Does she keep good health?"

"Very good health thank you, in fact she is in business with my father."

This was too much for the old man, choking over roast chicken, he glared at his five giggling daughters. They stopped immediately.

Tom's mother ventured a remark Small, thin and prematurely old with greying hair pulled back in a bun in the nape of her neck. Her face was lined and careworn. "D..does she do the cooking for the residents?" Her eyes widening in wonder while frail hands broke a slice of bread into her soup.

"Not exactly." Meg smiled, imagining her elegant mother in cap and apron behind the big range at The Halfway House. "She looks after the accounts and the expenditures for the business."

The eyes of the five daughters were on Meg. Their mother opened her mouth to reply but her husband glowered, barking her name, "Abigail!"

She dropped her head.

He put his hand up to his mouth to cough and muttered, "A woman in business! Indeed! What's the world coming to?"

Later, when Meg and her mother-in-law had a few moments alone the old lady confided she would be terrified of working with her husband, who knew simply everything. She was always making mistakes, she confessed, and was relieved when he left for his office each morning and when he locked himself in his study with his prayer books in the evenings. Besides working in a government office, he was lay preacher in the Methodist Church.

Tom said his mother had had twelve children, six of whom died in infancy, but Meg met five daughters and Tom's elder brother. She asked about it in bed that night. They whispered because walls were thin.

He explained the youngest girl was actually the child of his eldest sister. "It's a bit of a mystery how she became pregnant. She is not very bright and never allowed out alone but my cousin says our uncle was the father and my father, showing true Christian forgiveness and charity, adopted the baby, bringing it up as one of his own. But we are all sworn to secrecy so please Meg, never mention it."

Meg was relieved when the visit was over.

"Why on earth did you lie to your father, he'll find out about my parents' business."

"He won't. He never travels. If I'd let you to tell him he would have ranted on about the evils of strong drink and the necessity to be "saved."

Meg was appalled at the lie but later found herself doing the same with Tom. To avoid his anger and a scene, she kept things from him, like the bill she had run up at Madison's which her father paid.

Chapter 26

A ticking clock broke the pressing silence.   Danny opened his bedroom door, peering down the dark corridor to the hall where moonlight glowed through coloured glass. He stepped quietly on the polished floor then slowly turned the key in the lock, gently pushing the front door open and slipping outside. Bending down, he eased his feet into the shoes he carried. A few strides took him across the stoep and down the steps. He crept around the side of the house to his motorcycle, leaning against the wall then wheeled it carefully down the driveway and opened the front gate. Only after passing the next street block did he breathe easily as he jumped on the saddle and started the motor. With a sputter and a roar he was off, hair blowing behind.

What a lark! What a joke! His father would never know. A few hours' fun with Jakob and some girls. Jakob was in town for the week-end. Danny chuckled to himself. He had been offered an introduction to a smasher, a good sport, he was told. The night looked promising. *Good old Aunty!* He grinned, thinking of Martha. She had given him the motor-cycle for his last birthday, his sixteenth, against Jack and Lisa's better judgement.

"Poor boy must have a bit of fun. You and Jack are far too strict with the child." Age had mellowed Martha. She didn't see Danny as almost a grown man. He was her baby; the child she never had. If he went to a party after Jack and Lisa retired for the night, she listened for his tap on her window and let him in, in the early hours.

Whistling to himself, Danny rode towards the run-down area of town. Approaching a shabby building he heard the notes of a Scott Joplin tune exploding into the night, and felt the rag-time music pound his head.

Jakob met him at the door and as they made their way through the smoke-hazed room a friend called, "Hey man Danny! I got a *mooi meisie* wants to meet you." Danny waved a greeting, his smile broadening. The pianist, in shirt sleeves and suspenders, a cigarette between his lips, bent over the keyboard, eyes half-closed against the rising smoke, while a girl in a low-necked sequined dress, hanging loosely below her waist, stood next to him, tapping her foot and bobbing her head to the tune of *The Entertainer*. Her drop earrings jingled and the rows of artificial pearls hanging around her neck reached below her waist.

Danny and Jakob settled at a table and were introduced to three girls. Danny paid particular attention to the one called Winnie. A narrow sharp-featured face topped by reddish-brown curly hair cut in a bob with a band across her forehead. Her low neck dress hung loosely on her thin, flat-chested frame. She appeared somewhat older than the others. Leaning towards Danny, her long rows of beads fell forward and her cheap perfume filled his nostrils as she whispered in his ear.

He stood up, "I say Jakob, I'm taking Winnie here for a ride on my motor-cycle. See you later." The other girls chorused. "Hey Danny man! Can we have a ride too?"

"You'll all get a turn." He laughed, his brown eyes crinkling. He was popular with the girls this good-looking boy who resembled his grandfather, Frederick. However, it wasn't only his good looks and charm that attracted, they knew he was the son of the wealthy Jack Patrickson who owned hotels in the town. Danny's pockets were always filled with gold sovereigns.

Danny took Winnie's hand and the two of them threaded their way through the crowded room. Outside he sprang to the saddle of his bike with Winnie behind on the pillion, her thin arms clasped around his waist. They drove through deserted streets, hair streaming, singing loudly. Soon her arms, cold and goose-pimpled, were numb.

She called out against the wind. "Hey Danny man! I'm freezing. How about calling at my place. I'll make some nice hot cocoa." Danny turned his head sideways and shouted back,

"OK, where's your place?"

"Down the next street," she replied quickly. "But don't make too much noise, *jong*, my landlady's funny about visitors in the bedrooms. We'll have to creep in the back way. They tell me she's involved in I.D.B. but I never ask questions. Her place is cheap; that suits me."

They turned the corner and parked in a back lane. Winnie quietly opened the rusty gate and unlocked the door with a key hanging on a string around her neck. The old wood-and-iron house stood next to the railway track.

"Isn't this Jakob's Pa's old house?" enquired Danny. Sol had died shortly after Emma left Kimberley.

"Ja, right. Lena's my landlady. D'ya know her?"

Danny nodded, "Sort of."

164

Suppressing giggles, they crept down the dark hallway. The walls cracked and grimy, faded linoleum covered the floor and Sara's old worn sofa stood under the window. Everything looked the same, only shabbier. Midway down the hall Winnie stopped and unlocked her bedroom door then entered with Danny close behind. She lit the lamp beside the narrow bed, indicating to him to sit down. A primus stove stood on an upturned box. She took two cups from the dresser and put them on another upturned box which served as a table.

"Wait a bit. Don't light that yet, we can have cocoa later." Danny pulled her on to the bed. His hand went under her short skirt. She giggled, protesting feebly, while pulling off garters and rolling down silk stockings. Danny leant over, fumbling in boyish eagerness, but Winnie had experience and Danny proved an eager pupil.

A pale light shone through the tattered window shades. Danny raised himself on his elbow, squinting at his watch.

"Five a.m.!" he muttered, whistling through his teeth. He had never been this late. It would be risky getting in before Father woke, he rolled over the sleeping Winnie who stirred and stretched and opened her eyes.

"Danny! What yer' doin'? Don't leave me." She attempted to hold him down, but he pulled away.

"Don't be crazy, Winnie. Of course I have to go."

"Will I see you again? How about tonight?" Her voice anxious as she sat up in bed, letting the sheet fall away to expose her nakedness. But Danny was too worried and too agitated to notice.

"Maybe. First I must get out of this place without old Ma Lena seeing me and then get home and into my room without Father seeing me." He dressed quickly and let himself out.

Some months had elapsed since Danny's first night out with Winnie. He liked her well enough, she gave him a good time but she was becoming a bit too serious, dropping hints about marriage.

"Just like a woman!" he confided in Jakob. "I'll have to cool off because I don't plan to settle down. Not yet anyway!" Jakob grinned.

Danny and Winnie sat on the bed in her dismal room. Lena was away for the weekend. Winnie's eyes were red-rimmed and swollen from crying.

"I tell you, Danny man, I'm goin' to have a kid," sobbing silently, sniffing and scraping her nose with the back of her hand.

"How do I know it's mine?

She became hysterical, clutching his arm. "How can you say that? I haven't been with anyone else for months. Only you Danny. I love you." Her sobs grew louder.

She had had a wretched life, brought up in an orphanage and Danny meant escape from poverty. Besides, she did love the boy. "I'm goin' to marry Danny," she confided to her friend, Lottie. "I can make him, if he puts up excuses. What'll happen to me otherwise, spending the rest of my days altering clothes for fancy ladies? No fear. I'm goin' to be a fancy lady!" She was tired, too of satisfying leacherous old men to augment her meagre wages. Danny was her only means of escape.

"Are you sure you're going to have a kid?"

Head nodded, eyes cast demurely down.

He uttered a curse. He had a few pounds saved and could borrow more from Aunty. "You must find someone to help you get rid of it? I'll give you the money."

Winnie looked shocked. "I couldn't do that, Danny. That would be like murder. Maybe your father would help me." She looked up through her long lashes.

Danny shuddered and finally relented. He had no choice. He began making plans.

"We can go to Rhodesia." The more he thought of it the more the idea appealed. It would be an adventure. "I think that would be the best thing. At least I won't have to return to College." He grinned, that was a decided advantage. "If things don't work out up there we can always come back with the kid. Father will get used to it and could hardly turn us away."

Winnie wasn't certain she agreed. It wasn't exactly what she had planned, hoping to be accepted by the family. Danny knew that wasn't likely, not right away anyhow.

"I'll have to sell my motor-bike," he said regretfully. "That money and what I have in the bank, will get us to Rhodesia and keep us until I can find work. I can ask Aunty for some cash." For the moment running away was the best solution. Ever the optimist, Danny began warming to the plan. He told Jakob about the arrangement.

Chapter 27

"Meg, may I come in? Oh my dear, something terrible has happened." Lisa's voice sounded hysterical. "It's Danny," after settling on the sofa with a cup of tea she continued, "Your Father is furious. The wicked boy has run off with some woman from the town, at least six years older than he, so Father has been told."

Meg froze, her cup halfway to her mouth. "I don't believe it," she exclaimed. "My baby brother! "Danny! He's just a kid."

"That's just the trouble," Lisa cried, "We've all thought of him as the baby in the family, forgetting he's been growing up. Your father blames Martha for buying him that motor-cycle, but I don't think we can blame her altogether. I know she has spoilt Danny but Father and I have been so busy these last few years, we have pretty well left the boy to his own devices. I just don't know what to do," she wailed. She set her cup down then twisted the charms on her bracelet.

Meg reassured her. "Harry will be in town later to-day. He'll know what to do."

After questioning Jakob, Harry discovered Danny's plan to travel to Rhodesia with Winnie. The young couple were found and brought back to Kimberley, but the marriage had already taken place. Winnie wasn't taking any chances. It was only later she told Danny she wasn't pregnant after all.

Winnie was full of her new status and discouraged Danny's friendship with Jakob.

"He's a coloured boy, you know, Danny. People will talk. I'm surprised your father allows him hanging round you." She pursed her lips.

Danny ignored the reference to his father. "Jakob and I have been friends for years, since we were little kids. His Ma and my Ma were friends and his sister, Emma and Meg were good friends. His Ma worked for Father."

"Worked for, well that's different. But not mixing with socially, surely? I mean, after all, as I was saying, the family's coloured."

"But you lived in Jakob's Ma's boarding house."

"That's different." He didn't understand why but was basically easy-going, except when drunk when he became abusive, and it was simpler not to argue with Winnie.

Jack though it best that Danny make a fresh start far removed from Jakob's influence. He arranged a job for him in Durban. The friendship with Jakob ended but Danny's drinking did not, and Winnie bore the brunt. She never complained about his abuse, however, what was the use? She had no desire to return to her miserable existence, a seamstress at Madison's? At least Danny had an allowance and, if she handled him carefully, she would have no money problems.

Jakob settled on the farm. Without Danny's distraction he found he enjoyed working the land and attending the animals. He felt close to his roots, riding alone on the open veld. Memories flowed of visits to Joe and stories told of his grandmother, Ruth, the African woman, and her family in the *kraal*. He felt a deep sense of contentment.

He met Mtonya, a Sotho girl, whose father was headman in a distant village. She had attended the Mission School. Jakob was embraced by Mtonya's family, he felt he had come home. No mention of a white grandfather, but talk was about Ruth and old Joe. Neither did he speak of his sister, Emma.

Tom, on the other hand, felt excluded by Meg's family. She expected a baby in the spring and after that event he secretly planned to leave Kimberley and his parent's-in-law and move to Durban as well.

The child was born and they named him David. Meg was happy. She had her baby and her parents and Martha and Harry to share her joy. Tom felt his son hardly belonged to him. He made final arrangements for transferring to the coastal town and then told Meg. She pleaded. She cajoled. She argued. But Tom stood firm. He would be master in his own house, he said. Meg felt alone. She was the outsider now. Tom's father frowned on what he considered her extravagant ways. Four years passed; she had another boy and named him John.

One day she found a picture of Gerry. A proud soldier standing in tunic, Sam-Browne and riding breeches; polished knee-boots and peaked cap, holding a riding crop. She held the silver frame close and memories crowded her thoughts.

"Why are you crying, Mamma?"

She picked up Davey and snuggled him close. "It's nothing. Just a speck of dust flew into Mamma's eye."

"Who's that soldier?" He pointed to the picture.

"Oh, just someone I knew a long time ago."

"Did Daddy know him?"

"You ask too many questions," putting her finger to her lips. She stood the silver frame on the sideboard in an act of defiance against Tom. He made no comment, so she left it there with a smaller picture of a cross, planted in desert sand.

Her only family in this town were Danny and Winnie and the two women became friends. The great depression was upon them. To add to Meg's burdens she suspected she was pregnant again. The year was 1928.

At times Meg thought of Emma. She had little opportunity to read the newspapers, least of all the "Social Column" of *The Cape Times*, where she might have seen an announcement that a certain Mr. and Mrs. Etienne Frobisher, formerly of Rondebosch, and their infant son, Jan, had recently made their home in Waterkloof in Pretoria. Mr. Frobisher would establish a branch of his family law firm in that city in the Transvaal. Meg would have been more than a little surprised to learn that the elegant Mrs. Frobisher was her dear friend Emma, daughter of her mother's close friend Sara and the coloured carpenter Sol Meintjies, and sister of Jakob who worked as herdsman on her brother, Harry's farm. She would have read that Mr. Frobisher was an important figure in the Nationalist Party and would have known this to be an almost exclusive Afrikaans political party with ambitions to rid the country of hated British influence. She would not have read, however, that Mr. Frobisher was also a member of the Broederbond, which was a secret society, dedicated to furthering the Afrikaans language and culture and to finally gaining political power for the Nationalist Party.

Emma sat at her stinkwood dining table in her elegant Waterkloof home. Jan, her ten year old, had been taken to school by Elsie, his black nanny. Ada, the cook, stood at the kitchen sink washing breakfast dishes while Freddy, shook out the Persian rugs whilst carrying on a loud conversation with his cousin, the gardener.

Emma was free to devote herself to social work and her appearance, she had reneged on her principles in exchange for a comfortable lifestyle. At the beginning she fully intended confiding in Etienne, and disclosing the secret of her black grandmother, but she never quite found the right moment and then, upon moving to Pretoria, she noticed his change in views and political affiliations, and learnt that he was a member of the Broederbond. That frightened her. She could never tell him now. But she did have other news, she was expecting a baby in the spring. The year was 1928.

Unlike Meg, Emma was happy to be pregnant. Another child would strengthen her bond with Etienne. The depression had not affected her life unduly. Etienne was a competent attorney with contacts in high places. He had invested in the land and not in stocks.

Emma was an excellent hostess and knew her place as a loyal Afrikaner wife. She didn't agree with Etienne's new political opinions, but remembering her past, kept her views to herself. The months went by. Etienne and Emma awaited the baby's arrival with joyful anticipation. When the little girl was born Emma felt dismayed at the dark complexioned child, bearing, she thought, a strong resemblance to her brother, Jakob. Etienne wasn't at all suspicious of his dark skinned daughter, why should he be? The de Villiers family, on his mother's side, went back to the French Huguenots and many of his relatives were dark with black curly hair.

"She looks just like Ouma," he pronounced proudly. The baby clenched her fists tightly over his forefinger. "She is going to be strong like her too, a strong Boer woman." Etienne never spoke of his English relatives and although he wouldn't be aware of it, the child strongly resembled his great aunt Queenie.

"I think I'll call her Harriet-Magriet, after Ma and Ouma." Etienne had made up his mind. Emma would have called the child Sara. Harriet-Magriet was shortened to Hetty and the child grew strong willed and difficult.

Chapter 28

Durban
Circa 1928.

Meg lay on the bed, the air in the small bedroom stuffy and humid. February could be unbearably hot. Her thick hair, spread on the pillow was damp and her forehead was also beaded with moisture. Nausea overcame her, confirming her suspicions. Tom stirred next to her. They had argued again the previous night when he found the department store account. Today she knew he wouldn't speak to her and the atmosphere would be sour.

Winnie's friendship sustained her. Winnie, light-hearted and funny in spite of problems with Danny. She had learnt to drive an automobile and the two of them would sneak out in Danny's second-hand Ford while the children were at school. Winnie earned a little extra at dress-making, but Meg's only spare cash was a few pounds Jack sometimes sent her, usually secretly so as not to anger Tom. She was in trouble for opening a charge account at the downtown department store.

Meg felt her stomach heave, jumping out of the bed she ran to the bathroom, waking Tom. When she didn't return he followed her. It was early, the children asleep, Davey ten and John a sturdy six year old. Tom pushed open the bathroom door, seeing Meg's head over the basin, shoulders shaking.

"What's the matter. Are you ill? I expect it's something you ate yesterday when you were out with Winnie. She's a bad influence on you."

"It's nothing I've eaten," Meg mumbled, vomit rising in her throat again. Tom continued to block the doorway. Standing up, she wiped her mouth not looking at him. "I think I'm going to have a baby."

His face paled. "Don't tell me that. Where the hell will the money come from? I can hardly afford to raise the two kids we have."

Meg rinsed her mouth and leant against the wall. "Of course you had nothing to do with it." Her voice scratched from throwing up.

She prepared breakfast for Tom and the two boys and after their departure returned to bed, tense and trembling then heard a movement in the doorway and, looking up she saw Winnie.

"What's this, lying in bed at nine in the morning. Come on girl. You forgot about us going to Madisons' "After Christmas Sale."

Meg opened her mouth to speak, Winnie forestalled her. "No excuses now, don't worry about Tom. I expect he has been moaning about money again. Don't give a fig for that, didn't Father send you money for your birthday? But even if we don't buy anything we can try on some of the smashing new styles. That'll give those snooty shop-girls something to do. We'll let them think we've got wealthy husbands."

Meg started to cry, Winnie ran to her side. "Come on old girl, things aren't as bad as all that."

"Oh but they are. Worse than you can ever imagine, in fact. I think I am going to have a baby. What can I do?" she wailed. "You'll have to help me. I'm more than two weeks late."

"You're telling me I'll have to help you old sport, and it'll have to be pretty soon." Winnie had aborted many babies, having overcome her strong distaste when Danny had suggested it before their marriage. Abortion was the only birth control Winnie knew, apart from abstention and Danny wasn't going along with that. Danny, in drunken state, forcing himself upon her, cared nothing for the consequences of his lust and afterwards? Well, it was up to her to do something about it because they couldn't afford a lot of kids. She knew an old woman in Greyville and visited her when necessary. When the pills didn't work, she resorted to a coat-hanger.

Meg continued crying. "I don't know what to do. We haven't any money and things are so bad Tom might lose his job. They are laying people off in the government. Father can't help us. I wouldn't ask him anyway because I had a letter from Harry, saying he must sell some land to help them out. Father lost almost everything in the crash. I don't know if you and Danny know that. Harry says all their life's savings are gone. Oh dear, what can I do?" her voice rising in anguish. "Tom blames me for getting pregnant."

"Typical." Winnie snapped her mouth.

"What if he gets laid off? We can hardly manage now. If only I could get a job but I'm not trained for anything. I wish I could do dress-making like you, but Martha has always done all my sewing. I can't cook very well either. I expect I could take in a boarder." The torrent of words stopped as she thought for a moment, "But we only have the two bedrooms. I expect Davey and Johnny could be with us but now there will be a baby as well," sobbing hysterically.

"Come on, now. Winnie reassured her. Get up, get dressed while I make this bed then I'll put the kettle on for a cup of tea and we can talk."

172

They sat at the kitchen table. Winnie put a cigarette to her mouth, inhaled then threw back her head, blowing rings of smoke. She tapped ash into her saucer, and Meg made a note to wash it before Tom came home. Winnie's smoking in his house one of his pet grievances.

"Don't worry, '*alles sal regkom!*' as the saying goes. I'll take you to old Ma de Klerk. She'll fix you up."

Meg looked alarmed, she knew of Ma de Klerk having once been with Winnie to collect a supply of pills.

"Oh no! Not that. I couldn't do that, it would be like murdering my baby." She gulped, fighting back sobs and raising her face, streaked with tears, to look at Winnie.

"Fiddlesticks! It's not even a baby yet. Just a collection of cells. Ma will give you some pills to take and it will be just like you're having a period. You'll bleed a little more than usual but if you stay in bed you'll be OK. Ma does this all the time, she knows what she's doing. "The churches and the government say it's murder but they do damn all to help us support the kids once we have them. If Tom gets laid off he hasn't got insurance for his wages and he won't have insurance for a doctor. So what will you do, hey! What does the government do? Nothing, I tell you, except make rotten laws, calling it murdering unborn children but they do bugger all for the poor kids that are born, and are starving. They reckon the fathers must support their kids but some fathers disappear and the women are left. Heaven knows where I'd be now if I'd had a baby every time Danny got me pregnant." She stood up, carrying the cups to the sink. "Come on, my girl, no time to lose."

Winnie parked the automobile in the narrow alleyway. A few dull-eyed children in ragged clothes with dirty, matted hair, gathered and gazed in awe at the vehicle. Meg followed Winnie to the door recessed in a brick wall topped with broken glass. The door opened slightly and a face appeared. The old woman recognised Winnie and moved to allow the two girls into the enclosed yard. She wore a dirty black dress, and a double string of immitation pearls circled her scrawny neck. Drop earrings swung with every movement, while two broken combs partially held up greasy, frizzed hair.

As they walked through the door a sour-stale smell of sweat and fried onions rose to meet them. An old man, wearing trousers held up by suspenders over a sleeveless spencer, sat on a chair next to the cooker. Meg held a handkerchief to her mouth and gagged. The old man, a cigarette dangling loosely from his puffy lips, stood up and shambled out of the room in response to a signal from his wife.

Meg swayed, the room swung, she put up her hands, clutching the table, the old woman took her arm and led her to the chair vacated by her husband and pushed Meg into it.

"Put your head down, deary, there you go. Don't you worry eh! Old Annie'll give you something an' you'll be right as rain." She took some pills from a bottle standing on the sink and filled a cracked cup with water. "Take these for now an' I'll give you some more to take home. How many months?" She pointed to Meg's stomach.

Meg closed her mouth and waved the proffered cup away, shaking her head vigorously.

"C'mon now, I tol' you it'll be OK. You'll bleed a little but jus' stay in bed. If the pills don' work I got a friend who will do an operation cheap, and no questions asked." The old woman looked up at Winnie as Meg continued to shake her head, refusing the pills. "What's the matter with your friend, man? Do she or don' she want help?"

Winnie squatted next to Meg but Meg was looking through the doorway into the adjoining room. A young girl, deathly pale, lay quite still on a bed. She couldn't tell if the still figure was alive or dead but the sight of her shocked Meg into realising what she was doing.

What would happen to Davey and Johnny if she died? She really had no choice. This was too dangerous. She should be allowed a choice, the government had no business making decisions about her body. If she had money, of course, it wouldn't be a problem. She could travel to another country where it was allowed. Money. Always money. But then, if they had money she wouldn't be aborting the baby.

She pushed the old woman's hand away. "P..please, I'd rather not. I don't think I want anything after all." Her voice trailed off. She pulled herself out of the chair and before Winnie or the old woman could stop her, ran through the door. Winnie following with the old crone behind shouting abuses at them. "You betta keep quiet, you hear, don' you tell no one you been here. You fancy lady, *wat makeer*? Why you come here anyway?"

Later that year Meg had her baby. A little girl with brown curls falling over her low forehead. Meg held her close, feeling a moment of remorse at what she had nearly done. They called the baby Kate.

Book IV
Chapter 29

Durban
Circa 1935.

I was bored. I had enough toys to entertain me but nevertheless, I was bored. I had ridden my tricycle around and around in circles; had brushed my doll's hair until it seemed certain it would end up spiked to the hairbrush, and had kicked a stone in a desultory fashion across squares drawn in red dirt in a game of hop-scotch, sending showers of soil exploding in sunlight. What else could I do?

I leant over the handlebars of my shiny, new, red-painted tricycle, hot sun bearing down on my exposed neck as the braids fell apart over my shoulders. The full gathered skirt of my floral cotton dress was bunched above my knees. A scuffle and muffled giggles captured my attention. I sat up and looked down to the end of the long garden, the forbidden area, and caught a glimpse of two small round black faces; cut across by rows of white teeth and pierced by glistening white eyeballs. Then they disappeared behind the banana trees.

The banana trees were planted to hide the "eye-sore", I once heard my father call the old wood and iron shack in the backyard where Violet, our black maid, ate and slept. I remember the time I once ventured down to this forbidden area. I had pushed open the door and looked into a round hole at my feet. A shower was suspended from the ceiling directly above with a faucet high on the wall. I quickly ran off, holding my nose, with vomit rising in my throat as the smell rose about me in a vapour, curling up into the mango tree. *How could Violet eat and sleep here?* It was then I realised that this was Violet's bathroom. I had often wondered why she never seemed to have to go to the lavatory, at least I'd never seen her use ours and concluded that black people didn't go.

"Silly child," was my father's comment when I asked him, "Of course Violet goes to the lavatory but she's black, so of course she can't use ours. Black people aren't all that clean you know."

"But..." I replied, then fell silent as I saw Violet through the open door, rolling pastry at the kitchen table. My father had already walked outside. I ran to her and put my arms around her waist, hoping she hadn't overheard his words.

"Oew! Katie, what's the matter, my child? I can't pick you up my hands are full of flour," holding them out for me to see. I looked at her black hands with the pink palms turned upwards, caked white with flour. She returned to her task, cutting the piece of meat then she began to chop the onion and I saw tears spilling from her eyes. She pressed the pastry into the dish, filling it with the meat and onions then covered it with a layer of pastry.

"This is your Daddy's favourite dinner, y'know. He jus' loves my meat pie," she commented as she bent over to open the oven door then placed the dish carefully inside.

She returned to the table and began wiping the surface. I leant against her, feeling comfort in her presence. I had known Violet all my life. I remembered her feeding me porridge when I was little and I remembered lying against her ample breast as she sang a Zulu lullaby when she put me to bed at night. I loved Violet, what a shame she couldn't use our lavatory and must use that awful smelly place.

I rode my tricycle behind the banana trees and stared at the two children of about my own age, but much smaller. They had fat, bulging tummies and thin spindly arms and legs. I recognised dresses I had outgrown which hung below their knees and were caught at the shoulders with safety pins. Holes in the skirts and armpits were neatly darned.

It was school vacation and Violet had asked permission to have her children visit from the farm where they were cared for by their very old grandmother.

"Of course," I overheard my father explaining to Violet. "I am taking a risk, you know, allowing your *picannins* here on the property. If the police raid you mustn't expect me to pay the fine and I won't be able to stop them taking you to *gaol*."

"*Ja baas*, I'm knowing that, but what must I'm doing?" She twisted her apron in her hands. "My old mother is very sick and my sisters is all working in the town. Only my grandmother is still on the farm with the small chil'ren. They are too many for her. I'm promising you they will be very good. I'm making them stay in the backyard behind the banana trees." She sniffed then wiped the palms of her hands across her eyes.

My father pondered her words then, his brow furrowed by a deep frown, said, "All right, but they better not turn the backyard into a location, no mess and no noise, you understand?"

Violet put her two hands together, bent her knees and cried, "*Ja baas,* thank-you *baas*, thank-you *baas*. Oh! I'm so happy to see my chil'ren," clapping her hands and swaying from side to side.

The children's father was never mentioned. Violet was not permitted to have him living with her in our backyard room. He may have left her by necessity to look for work in another area where his labour was needed while his own family's needs were ignored, or he may have left her for another woman. Strange, Violet was so closely tied to our family, but we knew so little of hers. We didn't even know her proper African name!

The children and I stared at each other for a while. The elder put her thumb in her mouth and dropped her eyes. She seemed overcome by shyness. The younger poked her forefinger up her nose and wiggled it around while staring straight at me.
"What's your name?" I asked, but she didn't understand my question. They couldn't speak my language, nor I theirs. Then the gap began to close as we recognised each other's childish thoughts and sense of fun. We began a game of tag, chasing in and out under the long fronds of the banana trees, squelching in the over-ripe mulberries that had fallen on the ground, scuffing them up with the dirt then rolling on the grass exhausted and laughing, the sour sweet smell of mulberries in our nostrils. I ran and fetched my skipping rope from the back porch and showed them how to hold the ends and turn it while I jumped through. We took turns. Then I drew squares in the dirt and showed them how to hop in and out while kicking a stone. After a while I took the apple from my skirt pocket and offered them each a bite. We squatted on the ground, passing it around, grinning at each other between mouthfuls and then the thread of magic we had woven snapped.
"Kate. . . Katie. . .come inside now, lunch is ready." My Mom's voice calling me. Then to my father, "Is Kate with you, Tom? I can't see her in the garden."
"No, nowhere here," a muffled reply from under the hood of his '28 Chevy.
"Davey, Johnny, is Kate with you?"

Slinking through the trees, hoping they wouldn't notice I'd been in the forbidden place, I crept into the kitchen. Violet was at the sink, I went up to her, whispering, "I've been playing with your kids. What're their names?"

"Oeh! Katie. The big one she's name is Beauty."

"Beauty!" my voice rose, "That's not a proper name."

"Well her Zulu name is Mahlodi."

"I like that name... Mahhloodi..." struggling with the pronounciation. "And her sister, what's her sister's name," I persisted.

"My baby?" she asked pausing while she lifted a dish and placed it to one side, water running down her arms and off her elbows, then she continued, "We call her Darling."

"No not that, what's her Zulu name?"

She said a word, her tongue clicking noisily while shaking her head and laughing.

"Oew! Katie that name is too difficult, you can never say that name. You jus' call her Darling."

"OK," I replied, conceding I would never be able to pronounce the tongue-twister, "I'll tell the other children at school their names are Beauty and Darling. They will be starting school with me tomorrow won't they Violet?" It was to be my very first day in the first grade of school and I would welcome some familiar faces.

Violet slowly and sorrowfully shook her head as she picked up the towel and began drying the dishes.

"No, Katie, they cannot go to your school, that's not allowed. They mus' go to the mission school on the farm with other black chil'ren. It's very far away from here."

"Why..." I began, but my Mom walked in just then.

"There you are Kate. Goodness me, but I've been calling you for ages. Where've you been?"

"I've been playing with Violet's children," looking over her shoulder to be sure my father wasn't following. Mother smiled and patted my head, then she took a tin of cookies off the shelf,

"Here, take some biscuits to them. They're too thin, Violet." She shook her head. But what could she do.

Chapter 30

I remember the day Grandfather and I brought Monty home. My Grandparents were visiting from Kimberley, and I had gone with Grandad to the dockside to watch the departure from Durban, of the Union Castle Liner for Southampton.

I loved setting off with Grandad holding my hand tightly as we crossed the street to board the tram-car, then rattling and swaying on iron rails through town and down Point Road to where the big liners docked. I wore my best white shoes with rounded toes and white bobby socks; my best blue dress, the skirt to my knees and gathered at the waist with a broad sash tied in a bow at the back. My hair, in two plaits bound with blue ribbons, fell forward over my shoulders.

Grandfather was a short man with a tendency to portliness ill-befitting his height. A gold chain strained across his vest front with Hunter watch tucked in pocket. He wore a cream alpaca suit, silk shirt with cut-away collar and a bow tie. A white handkerchief peeped from the top pocket of his jacket and white spats covered his shoes. He always courteously raised his panama when greeting acquaintances and he also always kept a supply of peppermints and would hand me some from time to time, blue eyes conspiratorial as we shared our secret indulgence. "Ready for another mint, Kate?"

I watched the swarming streets through the window of the tramcar. East Indian women in saris, yellow, red and green reflected in papayas, bananas and mangoes stacked high in pyramids. African women with brightly beaded hair and bracelets, balancing clay pots on their heads or squatting on grass mats trading their craft; and Zulu "boys" remembering those other wild wars with war cries and painted faces; heads crowned now with chicken feathers while whistling, surging and leaping, pulling rickshaws, wheels wound with paper flowers - tamed, toting tourists who scream at the thrill of the ride, not the thrust of a warrior's spear.

On we rode, past white beaches where wild waves broke, surging and leaping before they unfurled and flattened like lace trimmed tutus - tamed, moving forward and then retreating, leaving crabs that scrabbled for shelter in their holes.

The tram-car came to the end of the line and Grandfather and I pushed through throngs of people making for the wharf. The ship's hooter burped and the funnels belched black smoke, staining the blue sky. A breeze billowed balloons and swayed streamers, while a band played popular tunes Grandad hummed as he swung his ebony cane in time with the beat, smiling behind his bushy moustache.

"Ow about a nice pet for the little lady, sir?" I looked up at the sound of the strange voice. A sailor with a monkey on his shoulder, leant against the railing. I stood on my toes to view the little animal, holding my thumbs in anticipation. Grandfather could never resist animals but he already owned three dogs, two cats, a pair of rabbits as well as a brightly coloured parrot. He once brought home a baby ostrich, in spite of my Grandma's vehement objections. The ostrich had a habit of eating anything that fitted its beak. It was the cricket ball that finally ended its tenure. We all watched with horror, mouths hanging open in dismay, as the round ball travelled down the long narrow neck.

I watched the two men discussing price until finally the sailor handed the monkey to Grandfather who slipped him some folded notes, while taking the animal in his arms. The little fellow stared at me from Grandfather's shoulder with eyes like luminous black beads set close together above a black velvet nose. A wide smile broke across his face as he curled his long tail behind him. I called him Monty and stroked his back. Grandad and I abandoned watching the liner's departure that day and took a cab home.

My Grandma was furious. "You're not bringing that creature here, Jack. For one thing, how would we get it to Kimberley, and don't tell me it's tame; no one ever yet tamed a wild animal. Mark my words one day it'll revert to its wild ways," she warned. I anxiously watched them as I listened to the argument. Grandma's lips were tightly pursed, her hair scraped back in a bun not a single strand daring to escape. Her ample bosom strained against her starched white embroidered blouse with the high collar and leg o' mutton sleeves.

"But Gran," I interjected.

"Now child, don't interrupt while grown-ups are talking. I have told you that many times." I knew my Grandma, she held strong opinions but Grandad could be persuasive and this time he prevailed. He argued that he had perhaps saved the little animal from ending in the circus. Grandma disliked the circus, so Monty stayed. A special box was made for him and he travelled in the carriage with my grandparents with Grandma muttering and complaining.

180

I looked forward to the next visit to my grandparents. Christmas came and time to pack and take the train to Kimberley. Monty was well established in the back garden, happily climbing trees and swinging on branches. I was sure he remembered me. I fed him bananas I knew he favoured and we became friends.

"C'mon Monty, catch me," I ran under the overhanging branches of the willow trees, in and out with Monty close behind, then I turned and chased him. Up he swung into the branches of an apple tree out of reach and then he jumped on my back, his arms around my neck and legs around my waist. I taught him to throw and catch a ball and he was never once mean to me.

We had good times until one terrible day when Toby, the boy next door, came to visit. I could tell Monty didn't like Toby by the way he refused to join in the games he and I usually played together, but I had seen Toby tease him, calling him to the fence and then poking him with a long stick. I always protested but to no avail. Toby was bigger and older than I.

The day I recall was hot. Monty sat in his favourite tree stubbornly refusing to play. Fleas were bothersome and he constantly scratched himself, his tail hanging down. Toby tweaked it, running past. Monty stopped scratching and stared at the boy. Toby, undaunted, pulled again, harder this time. That was enough for Monty. He leapt from the branch on to Toby's back, clawing at the boy's head. Cheeky laughter turned to cries of fear, bringing my grandparents running out of the house. Monty jumped off Toby's back and into Grandfather's arms.

"Bloody little swine. I didn' do nuffin, 'onest to God Mister, nuffin." Toby cried, sniffing and clutching his head. "Jus' walkin' under the bleeding tree over there and the li'll bugger jumps out on me an' scares me 'arf to death."

"How can you say that," I interrupted, "you were teasing him."

"No I weren't."

"Yes, you were."

That's when Grandma intervened. "Enough argument," she said, "the fact is, I was right. You cannot tame a wild animal, they will always revert to their wild ways."

"But Toby was hurting Monty," I protested. Grandma wasn't listening to me she was examining Toby's head for bites or scratches.

"Thank goodness Toby doesn't seem to have been injured."

"Oooh! but I 'ave, I 'ave. Me 'ead 'urts somefin terrible," Toby whined.

"Well now, my boy, how about a piece of chocolate cake?" Grandad winked at me. Toby was instantly placated, but Grandma wasn't.

"You will have to send that monkey to the Zoo, Jack. It cannot be trusted."

"You can't do that," I protested, "Toby was poking Monty with a stick." Grandma scowled.

"Don't interrupt while Grandfather and I are talking."

It never helped to argue with Grandma so I changed my tone. "Please don't send Monty away."

But Monty had to go. Grandad had no choice as he carefully explained to me later, Toby's parents were threatening.

"I say, my dear, can't put Monty back in the bush, by jove, wouldn't be right don't y'know. Poor little fellow wouldn't be able to care for himself, been in captivity most of his life. Shouldn't have taken him out of the wild in the first place, I expect." said Grandad, then he dropped his voice, speaking as if to himself.

"But that's what's happening in Africa. Take them out of the wild, teach them our ways, exploit them and then surprised when they retaliate."

Chapter 31

Mother was troubled. The war which had threatened for so long, finally broke out. "That man Hitler, has gone too far." I heard her say to my father. He had fetched the Sunday papers from the store and the big black headlines stared out angrily.

I saw Mother glance across to the picture of the soldier in the silver frame, standing on the oak sideboard. She brushed the back of her hand across her eyes, and groped in her apron pocket for a handkerchief. She had told me about Gerry, killed in that other war.

"It seems like a lifetime ago, Kate," she had said. In fact it was a little over twenty years. "Gerry was so different from your father."

I watched my parents, sitting at the breakfast table that sunny Sunday in September with the war shadows chilling the world, and remembered Mother's sad experience in that other war.

She and my father seemed more comfortable together. The arguments had ceased and their marriage had survived. Davey spoke of joining-up. Johnny, four years younger, would follow if the war lasted long enough. The war was lasting long enough and going badly in those early days. Davey was somewhere in the desert in North Africa.

Father met the mailman at the front gate. We watched him open the telegram. Mother ran to the door, "It's about Davey! I know it's about Davey! Oh God!" she exclaimed, "please don't let him be dead." But it wasn't about Davey. The telegram in father's hand was from Grandfather. Uncle Danny had taken his own life.

Mother had received a letter from Uncle Harry only the previous week, saying that Danny and Jakob had renewed their friendship.

"Uncle Danny and Jakob old friends?" I remarked. Mother replied absently, reading the letter over to herself.

"Mmm....?"

My curiosity was aroused. "Tell me about it," I persisted, sensing a story. Mother loved to talk about those far off days. About the Boer War and a childhood under shellfire. About life in the "Nineties" and a girlhood that was sheltered. About evenings at the pianoforte, parties and picnics. About the Great War and death, disappointment and despair. I settled down to listen.

Danny's suicide was too much for Great Aunt Martha. When she didn't appear one morning at the breakfast table Grandma went looking for her. She had died in her sleep. The doctor said it was her heart. But we all knew that. It was Danny's death that broke her heart.

It was a few days after Great Aunt Martha died that the Reverend visited my parents. Davey was missing in action. The visitor with the back-to-front collar whom I didn't recognise, spoke glowingly of Davey, whom he had never met. I stood transfixed, listening to the words of praise, trying to match the hero he spoke of, with the teasing big brother.

It seemed as if all the bad things were happening at once. Davey had been taken prisoner by the Germans. The Battle of Britain was waging. It was a dismal time but everyone did their bit for the war effort. Grandma taught me to knit socks.

At last, the war news improved and the end of the campaign in Europe in sight. Finally, the fight with Japan was also over and the free world celebrated.

* * *

The scent of honeysuckle sprayed the summer air. A bee flew in the open window, buzzing lazily over the bowl of flowers on the teacher's table. The lesson, on history, on times past. My thoughts on the future and a possible career. My school days were coming to an end. The voice droned. The bee buzzed.

The droning voice and the buzzing bee lulled me. My head fell forward. Revolution, unrest and anarchy far from my mind. Suddenly the voice rose in crescendo.

"The lesson we learn from history is that a minority will never suppress a majority indefinitely. People must be given the opportunity to better themselves and develop democratically."

My head jerked.

"Black people in this country outnumber the whites by four to one and that will increase over the decades ahead. Christian charity and common sense tells us we must ensure that these masses are satisfied politically and economically. It is important they be better educated because they will demand the vote one day and when they do they must understand how democracy works, because the uneducated can be manipulated by politicians. We must open our schools to all people."

184

The silence was tangible. The words penetrating. A hand rose and waved in the air. Mimi Malan stood up.

"My Pa says if we let black kids in our schools they will want to mix with us socially and that will lead to inter-marriage and the end of the white race."

A murmur of voices. Some heads nodding.

"Black people are just as concerned about preserving their nationality and culture as we are. But we have seen the ugly results of nationalism taken to extreme, and have just fought a war against racism." The teacher paused, looking around the classroom. "As for mixing socially, so what? People with the same interests and intellectual level can mix socially, and what better way to learn of other cultures, in a peaceful manner? Skin colour shouldn't matter. But, if we continue as we are, there will eventually be unrest and uncertainty which can develop into anarchy. We must change now and improve the education of the black people, not only in the school-room but also in training for skilled work, instead of barring them from learning labour skills." She paused for breath.

"My Pa says there are so many blacks if we let them do the skilled work there won't be any jobs for whites."

Mimi again.

"That's just not true. By becoming better educated and able to do skilled work, they will earn more and have more spending power, creating a need for more goods to be manufactured and so making more jobs."

Susan Howard-Jones raised her hand.

"Yes Susan?"

"My father says if we pay higher wages to the black labour then our cost of living will increase because they are unproductive, and if we have to educate them to be more productive then taxes will go up and our standard of living will drop," thinking of their elegant home and garden with swimming pool.

"It will mean sacrifices at the beginning to educate all these people, but the alternative is unthinkable." She leant forward on her elbows, looking intently at all of us.

Silence, while the class pondered these ideas.

"My Pa says..." the bell rang, clanging loudly, drowning Mimi's voice and ending the discussion. But the debate would go on.

The teacher's words made sense. We must learn from history. To know the past helps us to understand the present and avoid mistakes in the future. That's what I would be - a teacher. If all these people were to be educated, there would be a need for teachers. I must continue my schooling.

I approached my father.

"Why do you want to go to university? In my days a girl was trained to cook and keep house to make a good wife for a man. You'll end up getting married and all the money spent on education will be wasted."

I said I wanted to study to become a teacher or maybe a lawyer and then to travel the world and find out about other cultures.

Mother was shocked. "Kate dear, women don't do all those things. Just get a nice job for a few years then settle down with a nice young man and start a family. I'm looking forward to becoming a grandmother," forgetting her own frustrations through lack of opportunity.

"You don't understand," I replied. "I believe motherhood is an important career too, but there are things to do before that and besides, a better educated woman is a better mother. After all, children are the most valuable resource a nation has." Face flushed and fists clenched.

"Fiddlesticks!" Father's hands waving in the air. "So, who's going to pay for all this higher education for women? The next thing you'll be saying we must pay more taxes to educate all the natives as well. You have too many fancy ideas, Kate. Those women teachers have filled your head with rubbish. You should have left school two years ago when I said so, you'd be earning good money now, helping your mother and me. The boys have only been on army pay, and besides, we couldn't afford to send either of them to university so why, in heaven's name, should we send you. After all, you're only a girl."

He sat down at the table, looking expectantly at Mother to serve his porridge and support his point of view. She kept her eyes averted. He carefully spooned thick oatmeal into his mouth, wiped his face with the napkin, then turned to face me.

"I think I'll speak to van Schalkwyk at the office about you, young lady. He might have a vacancy for a typist. It's always good for a girl to know how to type." He stood up, put on his jacket and left for the office. The matter was closed.

I remained seated at the table. Food stuck in my throat. Tears stung my eyes. I looked at Mother. She shrugged her shoulders.

"It's a question of money, Kate."

I escaped to my room and gave in to bitter tears of frustration and disappointment. It had never been any use arguing with Father. I had no hope in me.

Chapter 32

Kimberley
Circa 1946

I went to the farm that year at Michaelmas. It was a relief to get away. Father wasn't about to change his mind and allow me to enrol at university. Our battle had ended in a truce.

"Higher education isn't for girls," he said, "you can go to business college and learn shorthand and typing and then when you meet a nice boy you can get married and be a good wife."

Arguing with Father never helped and so I caught the train to Kimberley. Uncle Harry met me at the station then took me to to my grandparent's house because Grandma Lisa was ailing. She seemed tired but pleased to see me and when we left for the farm I promised to visit with her before returning home.

* * *

Thunder rumbled. I looked up. Clouds mustered above the sun, leaving red streaks on the western horizon like blood-stained fingerprints, dripping on the serrated mountains that were silhouetted against the skyline like sentinels guarding the Karoo. Close by a thorn tree cast a skeletal shadow. In the distance funnel-shaped clouds of dust spiralled. Dust filled the air and lay heavily on thorny aloe leaves. The rains were late, N'tabu's father, Jakob, had said. Jakob was Uncle Harry's head herdsman.

A dove cooed, then thunder drowned out the soft cry. As rain began to fall N'tabu clutched his blanket around his thin frame and slapped his pony across the rump, shouting to me above the noise of the storm,

"Come with me, Miss Kate, I know a place we can find shelter." He and I were the same age and had been playmates during my holidays on Uncle Harry's farm.

I had ridden out with him to bring in some stray animals that had wandered through a broken fence. He lived with his parents and their extended family in the thatched mud huts we could see clustered on the side of the hill and toward which we now rode. When we reached the huts we dismounted, hobbled the ponies, and left them to forage while we ran through the long grass, smelling the richness of the wet earth, our clothes clinging, my long hair flapping.

N'tabu's grandmother's hut had a dung floor and a thatched roof. As soon as we entered she handed us a calabash of *maas* then squatted on a grass mat and stirred the *putu* cooking in the black cast-iron pot. The bead bracelets encircling her arms jingled with her movements. As she talked her tortoise-tongue clicked, flicking in and out over dry lips drawn inwards. She smiled at us with toothless gums. Her tufted hair grew grey above a deeply furrowed brow and her flattened breasts hung limply below the rows of coloured beads around her neck. Bracelets encircled her ankles and her flattened feet spread bare toes. She wore a long length of dark cloth tied around her waist.

We watched the rain through the low narrow doorway, as it swept down the hillside towards the river bed which, until a short time ago, had been a dry *donga*. The raging river, gorged and swollen, swirled by, leaping and lunging, licking at rocks and swallowing up shrubs. I squatted beside N'tabu. "I'm liking very much to be a lawyer, Miss Kate, or a school teacher. I'm not wanting to stay on the farm where there's not even enough jobs for my father and my uncles, and all my brothers. Already my two brothers are working on the mines in Egoli. But my father, she don' wan' me to go. She say I'm too young to do the job in the mines." He grinned, then his expression became serious again. "But if I'm can go to Egoli and am getting a job there, then I'm can go to school at night and then maybe can be a teacher one day. I'm too old now for the school here on the farm." He scratched his head thoughtfully.

"What does Jakob say about that, N'tabu, about you going to Jo'burg to work and continue your schooling?"

"My father, he say it best to stay away from the town. He say when she live in the township near Kimberley when he a boy he get in too much trouble. He say it OK for my brothers because they older now, but I'm too young." He paused. "Although I'm thinking he like me to go to school and learn to be a teacher. Maybe you speak to my father, Miss Kate?"

I nodded my head, promising to discuss it with Jakob even though I hadn't been successful in pleading my own case for further education with my own father.

The rain stopped suddenly. Flowers opened all around on shrubs that had appeared dead. Yellow and pink, purple and orange. The *veld* came to life. The sun inflamed the western sky one last time, rainbows in each drop, dripping from each trembling leaf and a rainbow curved against the sky.

188

I left the farm early to spend a week with Grandma in Kimberley. I could see that she was unwell. She seemed so small and fragile as she lay on the big brass bed with the snow white cover fringed on each side.

"And besides, Kate," she confided in me after my grandfather had once again suggested selling the homestead and moving to Durban, "can you imagine moving all this stuff?" Her arm swept around the room. The light blue painted walls with white window and door frames were filled with family photographs and paintings. Hand-made crocheted doileys covered the dressing table with silver hair brushes on a silver tray. Silver candlesticks stood on the carved stinkwood bureau.

I nodded while choosing a book of poetry from the shelf on the wall then settled down to read. Before I started Grandma handed me her bureau key.

"Take this, Kate, and open the top drawer where you will find my Mamma's diary and my own. I want you to read them when you have time. You're always scribbling, so write something down about our family. It's good for a family to know about its beginnings."

I took the two leather-bound notebooks out of her bureau and put them aside to read later.

The light from the lamp glowed softly, Grandma lay with eyes closed, a smile on her pale lips as I began reading. "Hail to thee blithe spirit!" She opened her eyes. I read on.

"Higher still and higher / From the earth thou springest."

I saw her gazing out the tall sash windows. The lace edged blinds were up and she could see out to the deep sky. Her expression was full of wonder, as if her body's pains were left behind as she soared upwards with Shelly's Skylark.

Grandfather came into the room as I finished reading and she reached out her hand to his, then picked up the cowrie shell which stood on her bedside table. She held it to her ear and heard the sound of waves on the shore. Her voice shook. "Did I ever tell you about the time my sister, Martha found this very cowrie shell on the beach? It was shortly after we arrived with our parents at the Cape of Good Hope. We had travelled all the way from Europe in a sailing vessel, you know Kate. It was a German ship and called 'Die Arendt', The Eagle, I remember." I sat silently, as she continued

"I'll never forget that first day on the beach running across the white sand after Martha..." Grandma's voice fell and she closed her eyes, whispering her sister's name.

"Martha, wait for me... Martha..." Her voice faded, then she sat up suddenly and, reaching out her arms, called to her father as if he were in the room.

"Pappa! Oh Pappa! You have been away so long." She sank back against the pillows, a gentle smile on her face. "But I knew you would come home again." And then, with a sigh, her breath went out of her.

Grandfather put his arms about us both and we knelt at her bedside and cried.

Mother arrived in Kimberley a few days later when the family gathered for Grandma's funeral. Afterwards we helped Grandfather pack up in preparation for selling the house. I showed Mother the diaries but we had no time to read them then. It was whilst we were clearing out the attic one morning that I came across a wooden box with the name "Frederick" carved upon it.

"Who was 'Frederick'?" I called out.

"Frederick? He was my grandfather. Why do you ask?"

"Well, look what I've found in this old chest." I held up the box for her to see. As I picked it up, a bundle of letters fell down. They were loosely tied together with a faded ribbon and the name, 'Sara' had been scribbled across the packet they were in.

"Did you know someone called 'Sara?'" I cried out in excitement.

Mother crept towards me under the slope of the roof, "Sara was Ruth's daughter," she said. "Ruth was an African girl who had been raped by a white man and my grandmother took her in and helped her. When the child was born she was light skinned and resembled the father and Ruth believed she could never return to her family. She worked for my grandmother and they became friends. The trouble really began years later when Sara's daughter, Emma was born, because she also resembled the white farmer, unlike Jakob."

"Do you mean that Jakob has a sister? Where is she now?"

Mother nodded, "Yes, Emma is Jakob's sister. Jakob looked African and is proud of his African heritage and kept from his wife and her family the fact that he had a white grandfather. Emma, on the other hand, looked white and resented her mixed race because society rejected her, so she ran away and it was rumoured that she lived as a white woman and married an Afrikaner. She never ever contacted either Jakob or I."

Kneeling over the dim light of a candle, I began reading but Mother put her hand out and took the bundle of letters from me.

"I'm sorry Kate, but once you get your nose into those letters it will be the end of your help and we have to get this job done as soon as possible. Grandfather has someone interested in buying the house."

Reluctantly, I put the box and the letters aside. I would keep them with the diaries Grandma had given me and one day sort through them.

"Poor Emma," mother said, shaking her head, "there was nothing I was able to do for her. I always felt so hopeless."

We sat silently for a while. I understood what she was saying. I felt the same about N'tabu.

Chapter 33

Pretoria
Circa 1948

For Emma and Etienne, the years of their marriage passed uneventfully. The branch of the family's law firm he established in Pretoria, prospered. Afrikaners in the Transvaal are more radical than those in the Cape. The climate more severe and extreme; their forefathers endured more hardships, and hatred of the British more intense.

When trouble brewed again in Europe Etienne didn't support his country going to war this time, to defend the Empire, convinced that communism was the real enemy. He considered General Smuts a traitor to the Afrikaner cause, and discouraged his son, Jan from joining the army, sending him to the university at Stellenbosch instead.

Etienne believed that men are the providers and head the family and a woman's place is in the home, supporting her husband in all he does but she must not to be concerned with business or politics.

"Life is good, hey Emma!" Etienne held up a glass of frothy-topped Lion Lager after a game of rugger at Loftus. "This makes a man feel good, hey!" throwing out his arm indicating the elegant room and smacking his lips together as he handed the empty glass to Freddy.

Emma quietly nodded. She had chosen to flow with the tide. She had escaped the struggles of her people and raised no argument over politics.

Through Etienne she had gained her passage to freedom and would not challenge his beliefs. There were times when, recalling her childhood, she thought about Meg, whom she expected had married well after recovering from Gerry's death.

The year was 1948 and the country preparing for a general election. Emma's life seemed unchanged. Jan, a junior partner in the family firm and Hetty a student at the university. But things had changed. Etienne was now deeply involved in politics, working to elect the National Party to power with Hetty sharing his views.

Etienne suggested Emma join the *Vroue Federasie* with other political wives. She resisted, not wanting to become involved with the political movement even if it was only baking cookies and *koeksusters* for political meetings. But he continued to press her and so she agreed.

It was summer time in Pretoria. Doves called contentedly and mists hung low in the valley. Above the mist the far off mountains of the Magaliesberg were bathed in sunlight. Like herself, she thought, risen out of the murky secrets of her past, basking in the security of her life now. She was safe. In the middle distance she saw the Voortrekker Monument dominating the skyline. It was a symbol, Etienne said, of the courage of their forefathers.

They were invited to meet the new physician in the town, Dr. Carl Roussouw and his wife, Lavinia. He was a "Smut's man," Etienne explained, "and his wife English." But Etienne was prepared to overlook these shortcomings, Dr. Roussouw being a prospective client. A meeting was arranged to clinch the deal. It was to be a social occasion, wives included.

"Carl's a good *kerel* man, but for his politics. He believes in Smuts, who sold out to the English after fighting for the Boers, then got us into their war in Europe and now the General plans to bring more immigrants from England. We don't need any more *Rooineks* here, I say, because we'll be swamped. Our culture lost and the Afrikaans language will disappear."

Emma recalled these comments made after Etienne's first meeting with the doctor, who had done his training in England where he met and married his English wife. Etienne, ignored the fact that his own grandfather was an Englishman. He broke with his English relatives in Capetown when they supported the coalition government's decision to declare war on Germany in 1939. He never queried Emma's loyalty to Afrikanerdom, however, the name Meintjies proved where her roots were.

The car swung into the driveway between heavy wrought-iron gates, drawing to a halt under the Jacaranda tree growing against the side wall. Emma walked ahead up the short flight of stone steps to the stoep, stretching across the front of the Cape Dutch house. Bougainvillea, like splashed blood, spilling down white pillars, supporting the wooden pagoda. The oak front door stood open and a stream of late afternoon sun painted the polished floor and brushed the brass vase on the marble-topped chiffonier. Early summer flowers reflected in the gilt-framed mirror on the wall behind. A staircase curved upwards. A black man in a white jacket and white gloves walked through a door at the back of the hallway with a tray of glasses in his hand; voices from the next room against a background of soft music.

The hostess, wife of Etienne's accountant and fellow supporter of the Nationalist Party, came forward to greet Emma and Etienne.

"How are you both, it's so nice to see you, man. The boys have been waiting for you Etienne, Koos said you were at the game this afternoon, hey," leading them into the sitting room. The group of men at the bar counter stood up.

Emma looked into deep-set grey eyes in a tanned face topped by thick black hair, turning grey at the sides, and felt the firmness of a fine-boned hand clasping hers.

"Emma Frobisher, meet Dr. Carl Roussouw." Her shrill hostess, stopped briefly in front of the men then led Emma through an archway towards the women sitting around a stinkwood coffee table in front of open french doors.

The men's voices rose in unison. "*Middag* Etienne, old chap," slaps on the back. "What the hell's the matter with the new fly-half playing for Northerns, man?"

The host took up from there, "Where the devil did they get him, hey? No bloody good as far as I'm concerned."

Growls of agreement.

As Emma and her hostess approached the group of women snatches of the conversation could be heard:

"Actually, the new girl I have now is quite useless, you know," the words spoken in cultured tones. The speaker looked up.

"Lavinia, you must meet Emma Frobisher." Emma saw a short, plump, blonde with hair set and sprayed in a balooned, bouffant. A soft, white, plump hand with diamonds on three fingers, was extended. Emma felt the softness and the plumpness and the hard scrape of the diamonds.

"Pleased to meet you, m'dear," the owner of the hand briefly turned, nodded her head then looked back at her audience of women.

"As I was saying, this new girl is quite useless. Raw, you know. Straight from the kraal, doesn't understand a word of English. At least she makes out she doesn't but one never knows with them, does one? Sometimes it suits them to act dumb. Dropped the tea tray yesterday, breaking three of my best Spode cups. I've told her I'll take the money out of her wages. It's the only way, let them know right at the beginning that one won't stand for carelessness."

Heads nodded.

"Ja, you're quite right, Lavinia. You jus' have to show these people hey," rose a comment from Darnie van der Westhuizen's wife.

A black maid in pink linen overall, starched white cap and apron handed around *melktert* and chocolate cake.

"You're lucky with yours, Marie." The speaker tilted her head indicating her subject, well within earshot but passive faced. "The one I've got pinches tea and sugar. You have to watch them all the time, hey!" helping herself to a hefty slice of chocolate cake from the tray held by the maid.

Heads nodded again.

The subject of servants exhausted, Lavinia turned towards Emma. "Did you say the name was Frobisher?"

"That's right." Emma placed her teacup in the saucer.

"Any relation to the Frobisher's of Shropshire? Gravely Hall the name of their seat."

"I believe they are cousins. The English side of my husband's family live in Capetown and they keep in contact with the cousins in England."

"Etienne doesn't get on with them, does he, Emma?" commented the hostess. "His mother was a de Villiers you know," to the other women, explaining everything.

"Really! Doesn't get on with them!" Lavinia cried in surprise.

A voice boomed behind her. "Nonsense. Of course I get on with my English cousins. Do you know them?" Etienne joined the group. Emma looked up in disbelief. Lavinia suitably impressed.

"They're the biggest landowners in the district, don't you know! I have worked on committees with Victoria, a very dear friend, and wonderful hostess, entertains lavishly I can tell you, even royalty."

"Really! Cousin Vicky entertaining royalty?" from Etienne whom Emma recalled complaining about his social-climbing English cousins.

Emma choked. She regained her composure and placed the cup on the table. Etienne ignored her, deep in conversation with his prospective client's wife.

Chapter 34

Emma rolled over in bed, pain pulling at her, tearing at her. She clutched her stomach, drawing up her legs. Sleep impossible. It was more than a month since she met Carl Roussouw and during many sleepless nights, lying in pain, he came to her thoughts, adding to her distress. "Pure foolishness," she argued with herself, "must get him out of my mind." After all she was past middle-age, with a grown family.

Etienne stirred next to her and sat up, switching on the bedside light. "What's the matter? You look ill. Is it that pain again?"

She nodded.

"You can't go on like this. I think I must talk to Carl Roussouw, he's a Specialist you know."

She shook her head. "I'll be all right, probably something I eat disagrees with me."

"Nonsense! It's gone on too long. I'll phone Carl in the morning," settling the matter and turning over to resume his sleep.

Emma took a pill and the pain eased. She drifted into a restless sleep.

Carl was sitting at her bedside and she was confiding her closely held secrets. Her childhood in the township; running away from Kimberley and how she met and married Etienne. It was a relief to talk to Carl, telling him about the burden she had carried all these years. She knew she could trust him, the fears fell away; a sense of relief overcame her. She sighed and stirred, opening her eyes and saw Etienne sleeping there. Her fears and her guilt rushed back.

She felt distanced from Etienne. He was a good provider but he had changed, becoming so political and politics with which she could never agree. Nothing was ever said, of course, just doing all the things expected of a political wife. On the other hand she felt close to Carl and believed he felt as she did.

It was late afternoon and Etienne walked through the front door, dropped his briefcase and threw his jacket over a nearby chair then turned to greet Emma.

"How have you been today?" Then, not waiting for her reply, he continued, "I called Carl. He will see you tomorrow. He's actually booked up for months but will see you after 6:30."

Emma opened her mouth in protest but Etienne put up his hand

"No, no. I won't have an argument now. It's all settled." She closed her mouth. Part of her sensed she shouldn't see Carl, part of her wanted to - so badly.

There were only a few cars parked in the basement garage as Emma made her way to the elevator. The pain was there, gripping and stabbing. She clutched her handbag then pulled her earlobe in a nervous gesture, fearful of what Carl might find, yet excited in anticipation of seeing him.

The elevator door slid open and she walked across the carpeted hallway and saw his name on the brass plate. Chairs were set against the wall but the room empty and the receptionist's desk vacant. Late afternoon sun striped the wall through the horizontal blinds. She took a seat next to a "delicious monster," picking up an out-of-date magazine when the inter-leading door opened and Carl walked towards her.

The examination was over. Emma sat on the edge of the chair opposite Carl. "I'm pretty sure it's a duodenal ulcer causing your pain, but we'll confirm that with an X-Ray. It can be treated with diet and medication, so don't worry." He emphasised the last two words. "Worry will only aggravate it, in fact can cause an ulcer." He smiled at her. "However, I'm sure you haven't any serious worries, a beautiful woman like you, an adoring and wealthy husband and two bright and charming children." Emma quietly smiled. "Yet I suspect you have something on your mind. Am I right?"

He walked around the desk and stood in front of her. "Now tell me about this problem that causes your worry." His tone serious.

She looked up in alarm. Was he reading her thoughts? Then noticing his smile, thought he must be teasing. For one terrible moment she thought he could tell. Did he have ways of knowing? She heard once that there was something tell-tale about fingernails, instinctively clasping her two hands together and pushing them into her lap.

Carl noted her look of alarm and nervous reaction and believed something deep-rooted disturbed her. "You know the human mind can be a cause of some illnesses. Tension and fear disrupts bodily functions so, for me to help you, you must be frank with me." He paused but she didn't reply and so he continued, "some people can't help themselves and worry for nothing, but stress can be a killer, you know. It could be something deep-rooted in your childhood of which you are not even aware. I'm not

198

trained in psychoanalysis, however, but sometimes just talking, helps to unburden and I'm a patient listener."

He smiled encouragingly and she replied, "I honestly have nothing to worry about," while thinking, *It's deep-rooted alright, so deep it goes back to my grandmother, but it must never be uncovered.*

Carl wrote out a prescription which he handed her then escorted her to the elevator but felt convinced she hadn't been entirely truthful.

Carl was right about worry because her worries had intensified in recent months since politics had become the main topic at home. Etienne was working on a party platform designed to preserve Afrikanerdom and protect the white man.

"We will do this by strict legislation separating the races, Emma," he explained to her. "I'm working on drafting laws we intend introducing as soon as possible after assuming power. Laws forbidding inter-marriage between the races and laws determining where people live. We don't want coloureds and blacks living in white areas, they always bring a neighbourhood down."

The blood drained from her face but Etienne, was too engrossed in his plans for the country's future to notice.

"We will also have to bring in legislation to protect skilled workers because we can't have blacks and coloureds taking all the jobs, so we will have to reserve skilled labour for white people only." He didn't wait for Emma to comment. "Ja man, if we give these people equal opportunities to go to the universities with whites, or become skilled labourers and get the well-paid jobs that means their kids will be in school with our kids, and then they'll be moving next door and the next step will be inter-marriage. Ag nie man! We can't have that. It's unthinkable. We have to make sure that can never happen. It will be the end of the white race."

Emma placed the cup of coffee on the table, shaking hands spilling the liquid into the saucer. This would usually irritate him but he was too intent on his subject. She sat down resting her shaking legs while he continued talking, staring through her into this future he envisioned.

"Ja, I can see it all. Afrikaners in control, the government, the banks, the businesses. We must preserve our heritage and to do that we must have an official policy, separating the white and black races, you know. We'll be swamped otherwise. There's too many of them." Silence was heavy between them. He spoke again, "They'll have their own areas, of course, 'Homelands' where they can vote and govern themselves. That

WHAT HOPE HAVE YOU!

should stop criticism from the rest of the world. We'll have to divide up the land, there's no other way. We will need some of them for a labour force in urban areas but that will have to be controlled as well. There will have to be a 'pass system.' They must all carry passes to work in the towns. What do you think of that, my dear. Isn't it a brilliant concept, to separate the races, don't you agree? This is our vision of a new South Africa and we're going to be vigilant in enforcing these new laws."

Silence.

"Come on, you must have an opinion."

She gathered her courage. "What about the black family. It will be broken up. How will black women manage?"

"These people don't feel about families as we do, my dear. They have umpteen wives, you know that," laughing derisively.

"That may be, that is their culture, but they have a strong family based social structure. It's the women who will suffer. If they have to live alone, men will take advantage of them, they will end up with babies anyway but no help in supporting them."

"Rubbish!" he shouted, banging his fist on the table. "The men will be put in compounds. Those who work on the mines and big industries."

Emma twisted the wedding ring on her finger. "They'll still need women."

"We will impose a curfew in the towns. But it's more important to ensure there is no intermarriage between the races. We don't need any more bastards of mixed race."

Blood drained from her head. She made an excuse to escape and ran upstairs to the bathroom where she threw up, flushing the toilet so Etienne couldn't hear her. Sitting on the seat with her head in her hands, her whole body shaking. *What would be the next step,* she wondered, *would it be digging up the past?*

Chapter 35

Two years had passed since Emma and Carl first met. In that period the government had made radical changes. Radical changes had also been made in Emma's life. She and Carl had become lovers. Emma felt safe with Carl, safe enough to discuss the new government's policies towards black and coloured people, but not safe enough to tell him she was coloured.

"Last year they passed the "Prohibition of Mixed Marriages Act" making marriage between white and black people illegal. Now they have gone further and the "Immorality Amendment Act" forbids whites and coloureds to marry or have any sexual contact. This is going to affect a lot of families who are coloured but pass as whites."

Emma's fists clenched tightly. "I didn't know. Etienne is hardly ever home. He said he was working on legislation but I had no idea, not paying much attention when he talks politics and I never bother reading the newspaper."

"Frankly, I can't see Smuts and the United Party ever returning to power," Carl commented, taking his pipe from one pocket and tobacco pouch from the other. "I'm interested in more progressive views. I've heard talk about a new party." He filled the bowl with tobacco then struck a match to light it. "Blacks will have the vote one day and we should start preparing now," biting on the stem between sentences. "We should be improving their education and hospital and living conditions," leaning back, puffing.

She lay her head on his chest and drew her fingers across his face, feeling the hairs of his beard as he held her close. If only she could get away from it all.

"Take me away," she said. "Let's make a new life somewhere, away from all these problems. We could go to America."

They sat on the sofa in front of the fire in Carl's living room. Lavinia was in England on a six month visit to her relatives and Etienne was in Durban, attending a Party meeting.

"We must increase the support of the Party in Natal," he had confided to Emma, before he left. "We intend staying in power for a long time and so we'll have to pack the constituencies with Afrikaners to out-vote the '*rooineks*'."

"I can't imagine that ever happening. Natal is so very British." She accentuated the last three words and raised her eyebrows in a mocking gesture. "They'll never take kindly to '*skaaps*' from the Free State and Transvaal."

"You'll see," was all he said. "You won't change your mind and come with me? The van Rooyen's are going and the du Toits."

"I really can't, I have a meeting with the ladies of the sewing club at the Church. We're trying to get things ready for the Bazaar next week-end. And besides, I don't care for Elsie du Toit, she's always quizzing me about my family. She goes on about how wonderful her son Frans is, and says he will be an M.P. one day. 'Is your Jan interested in politics?' she asked me, knowing full well he isn't."

Jan had his own apartment downtown. He wasn't the son Etienne had hoped for. Apart from working together in the partnership, they had little in common. Hetty was also away, visiting the Game Reserve with a party of students. Carl had no children and with the servants off for the week-end, he and Emma had three full days to themselves.

Carl shook his head, replying to her question. "No, I could never leave my country that is out of the question, but apart from that, surrendering our responsibilities would destroy us both. We can't take our happiness at the expense of others."

"But by meeting secretly we are cheating Etienne and Lavinia."

"If they don't know, it can't hurt them? I would never consider a divorce because I'd lose many of my patients. You know what people are like in this town? They expect their doctor to set an example. If we're careful we can preserve our social standing and my career and still see each other."

"I don't care about social standing." She sat up and moved away to the corner of the sofa.

Carl pulled her back folding her in his arm while placing his fingers on her lips. "That may be, but you wouldn't want your children to be embarrassed if you sought a divorce. Things would come out."

Emma resisted at first then slumped against him, "I suppose you're right."

"Of course I'm right. It's hard for you to understand because you have always had things easy. But I've had a hard struggle to get where I am."

The shabby house beside the railway track flashed across Emma's mind. "Oh but I haven't..." the words were nearly out but her hand flew to her mouth.

"What were you going to say?"

"Nothing." He felt her body stiffen.

"There is something worrying you, Emma. Why don't you tell me? Medication has healed your ulcer but it could return if you continue to worry."

She regained her composure. "There's nothing worrying me. My life has been very unexciting and quite trouble-free. But tell me about your struggles."

He lay back against the sofa, staring into the fire. His mother's face appeared in the flames. Stray strands of greying hair loose from her bun. A flat-iron in one hand and starched shirt in the other. The laundry she did for the residents of Ma Vermeulen's boarding house across the street. She had to do this to keep him at the university, in spite of the scholarship.

"You jus' keep working, my son. One day you is going to be a famous doctor, mark my words. Never let anything stop you." The voice so loud in his head he turned to Emma expecting she had heard. Then he began speaking, very quietly.

"My father was a railway worker. Poor whites we were called. The English taking the best jobs and exploiting us Afrikaners. But Ma was determined things would be different for me. Pa wanted me to join the Railways as a shunter. His Pa and grandpa had worked on the old Cape Railway. But Ma was adamant.

"'Nie Willem,' she would say to my Pa, 'no son of mine is going to work on the S.A.R. Over my dead body!' She was small and wiry but strong as an ox, like her grandmother who left the Cape in the Great Trek." Carl stopped talking, looking down at his fine-boned manicured hands, so important in his work, remembering their roughness when he was a boy.

"I helped Pa with odd jobs. When I became a student he got me work in the holidays with the Railways, stacking wood in the shed at the Siding, ready to load into steam locomotives on cold, frosty, *Karroo* winter mornings."

He stared into the fire and Emma sat silently. The quiet was broken by the sound of crackling logs and the puff-puff of his pipe. He turned back to face her, taking out his pipe, "You see, my darling, I made a covenant with my Ma. I promised her I would succeed. When I returned from England as a qualified Specialist Physician with an English lady for a wife, Ma was so happy. She never hated the English in the same way as my Pa did, but didn't ever think they were better than us Afrikaners. Now, through me, she proved we were as good as them; us 'poor white' Afrikaners, could make it. She died happy. I couldn't betray her now."

Emma stared into the shadows. She had suffered and pulled herself up, yet was prepared to sacrifice for love of him. Why didn't he feel the same? Is he no different from Pa, who rejected her for Lena, or Etienne, who neglected her for politics?

"Your Ma would understand. Surely she..."

He didn't let her finish, his hands began exploring her body.

Emma fell asleep at last and dreamt of her childhood. Meg and the Convent, her brother Jakob. Her mother's death and the woman, Lena. The same dream recurring, always ending with Lena bending over her, screaming, "You mind your own bleddy business, you hear? You tell anyone I deal in I.D.B. and I'll get you. I tell all the people you jus' a bleddy coloured girl with fancy ideas now you is married to a Party member," grabbing with claw hands. Emma wrenching free, trying to run away but tripping and stumbling.

She sat up confused and shaking, looking around the strange room. Carl pulled her close and she leant against him. She could shelter in the shadow of his sloping shoulder. He was a craggy mountain. Etienne was a deep, dark ravine.

204

Chapter 36

Pretoria / Durban
Circa 1950.

Hetty stirred her coffee and smiled at her father.

"This plan to separate the races, it'll be called Apartheid, right Pa?" she said.

"Ja, my girl, ja, *di's reg*."

"Don't you agree with separate development, Ma?"

Emma dropped her napkin then bent to pick it up, strands of her dark blonde softly waved hair pulled back in an elegant chignon, fell forward over her ears. Her almond-shaped eyes set slantwise above high cheek-bones, blinked nervously. Her face was red as she emerged. "I... I haven't paid attention." She hesitated, glancing at Etienne, twisting the ring on her little finger. "Will you be in for lunch, or are you playing golf all day?"

Etienne nodded, moving the lump of *mealie-meal* porridge to the side of his mouth, then with his forefinger, pushed the black-framed glasses back on his nose.

"Ja, we're playing thirty-six holes in a competition, so I'll be late. Must do something about this, y'know!" laughing and patting his bulging stomach.

Hetty interrupted, turning to face her mother,

"Everyone will soon be classified in their own racial group, Ma. They'll live in their own areas." She hesitated, looking at her father who nodded. "In these Homelands blacks and coloureds will be able to vote and the world can't accuse us of not giving them the franchise because, you see, they will be electing their own leaders and governments."

Emma started to reply then looked at Etienne and took a sip of coffee. Anticipating what she thought her Ma was about to say, Hetty continued, "I know some say the blacks have been allocated the poorer parts of the country but, after all, us whites put our hard work and our brains to develop this land so why should we hand over the richest areas? Anyway," she paused, chewing her thumb nail, "they'd never be able to manage them, that's for sure."

"Ja, *dis reg, dis reg*. We are in the minority. We are chosen people and must lead, however, remember," he shook his forefinger, "We should also help blacks and teach them morality."

Hetty had recently graduated and was in her first year teaching at a local elementary school.

"You know what," she looked from one parent to the other, "one day I'd like to stand for parliament." Etienne glanced up, frowning, spoon halfway to his mouth.

"Women shouldn't be concerned in politics. You must find a good Afrikaans boy and settle down and raise a family. Sometimes I think you're a little too outspoken and aggressive. It's not becoming in a woman."

"Jurrah man, Pa! You're so old fashioned," shaking her head in exasperation. "I have lots of ideas. I'm jolly glad the government is taking steps to make sure the universities are kept white because, in time, blacks will outnumber white students. They intend creating 'blacks only' colleges you know, Ma, where there will be lower standards so black people can cope. That's what Dr. Verwoerd says. In fact it was reported in the newspaper the other day when he explained the Bantu Education Act." She rummaged in her duffle bag and pulled out a crumpled piece of newsprint.

"Ja, *di's reg*," Etienne interjected. "We took them out of their own environment, y'know."

"Exactly! That's just what Verwoerd goes on to say. Take note of this, Ma.

'until now he (that is the Bantu of course) has been
subject to a school system which drew him away from his
own community and misled him by showing him the green
pastures of European society in which he is not allowed
to graze.' And then Verwoerd argues, 'what is the use
of teaching a Bantu child mathematics when it cannot use
it in practice? That is absurd.'"

"Ja," Etienne nodded, "d'is so. It's all in the Bible, y'know. 'The sons and daughters of Ham must remain forever the drawers of water and hewers of wood.' Anyway," looking at his wrist watch. "I must be off, am meeting Koos on the first tee at nine. *Tot-siens* hey! And don't forget the Party rally to-night in city hall." He smiled, pecking Emma on the cheek and patting Hetty on the head before walking out the room and calling Freddy to fetch his golf clubs and put them in his car.

"Did you clean my shoes, Freddy?"

"Ja, *Baas*."

"Well, now you can shut the gates after me."

"Ja, *Baas*."

Hetty looked across the table, "You havn't said much Ma."

Emma shrugged.

"Marriages between whites and non-whites will now be illegal. That'll keep the white race pure."

Emma frowned.

"And now that will include coloureds as well. It won't be so easy for coloured people to pretend they're white."

"What do you mean?" Emma's voice was sharp.

"I mean that from now on all people will be classified into the four main racial groups. Records will be kept so the authorities can investigate if they are suspicious about a person. In time everyone will have to carry identification documents."

Emma looked out the window, fingers drumming on the table while she watched Etienne get into the car and drive down the long curved driveway edged with Jacaranda trees, each standing on a mat of purple blooms. As he drove out the wrought-iron gates, she saw Freddy close them, then she replied,

"I hope you're not teaching racism to your pupils." Her hands shook. Hetty had never seen her mother so disturbed nor heard her express such an opinion before.

"What are you saying?"

"Nno..n..nnothing. Forget it."

"You've no idea what it's like because you've never been threatened. It's scary, I'm telling you, there are so many more black students now."

It was the end of a class during her last year of university that she had stayed behind to read over an essay. Looking through the window, she noticed that it was dark outside and that the campus was deserted. She heard a movement at the back of the room and saw one of the black students from her class walk through the door which swung shut behind him.

"Hi, Hetty, you got a problem?" he said.

"No."

"That's a nice top you got on."

She detected a familiarity she didn't like.

Stay calm, she thought, stifling a scream as he walked around the desk and stood next to her. A page of her essay fell out of her trembling hands on to the floor and before she could move, he bent to pick it up, his hand inches from her bare leg. Her body shook as she rubbed her moist palms together. He picked up the page and grinned as he handed it to her then moved to the table and dropped his essay on to the pile.

"Oh man! What d'y' know hey! I left this behind," picking up a book from one of the desks.

"Be seeing you, Hetty. Bye for now, hey!"

She remembered collapsing into the nearest chair, feeling shaken, but foolish.

"How would you feel if I met a black or coloured guy at college and wanted to marry him?" She stabbed her knife into the cheese. "You wouldn't like that, would you Ma?" Then it would affect you personally and if there is no segregation that could happen. But you don't have to worry because I could never be attracted to a black man, however, not everyone feels that way and eventually the white race could disappear altogether. The number of black students in our classes is growing, it scares me. It's all very well for other countries to preach to us, they don't have the millions of native people to deal with as we do here. You can call it racism if you like, but I call it realism."

Emma pursed her lips and walked out of the room.

It was later that evening and Hetty was dressing for the Party Rally. She bent to fasten her ankle-strap shoes then pirouetted in front of the mirror in her pink and white bedroom, her calf-length skirt billowing over layers of stiff petticoats; her brown eyes sparkling and shoulder-length dark, curly hair, flying. She was the only member of her family with tight curls, and curls weren't fashionable. She moved closer to the mirror and pouted her full lips, head on one side as she studied her features. *Strange,* she thought, *I don't resemble either of my parents. Except perhaps my eyes are set and shaped liked Ma's and I do have her high cheek-bones, but my colouring is so different. I wonder where I got my olive skin? Maybe a 17th Century Spanish pirate, ship-wrecked off the Cape of Good Hope, ravaged one of my ancestors.* She gave a little giggle as she pinned a rosette in 'party' colours on to her blouse, before running downstairs to where her parents stood talking in the hall.

"My, my, what is this? Another new outfit?" said Etienne.

208

"Ja, they call it the 'New Look'. Do you like it?" She flashed a smile then noticed Emma's startled expression.

"What's the matter, Ma? You look as if you've seen a ghost."

"It's nothing."

"It must be something. Tell..."

But Etienne put up his hand, "No time for talk. We must be going or we'll be late."

The cheering, the stamping and clapping died as the speakers left the platform and joined with the audience, making their way to the back of the hall. Cigarette smoke spiralled, rasping throats and the stale smell mingled with the smell of coffee and *koeksusters* which Emma and Hetty and other wives and daughters, were preparing to serve.

Hetty noticed a young man in close conversation with her father. He was tall with an athletic body, his chest muscles bulging under his jacket. Blonde hair fell forward over his high forehead half-concealing his deep-set blue eyes. He was clean shaven. She recognised him from her first year at university when he was in his final year, studying law. He was a rugby hero and favourite with the girls. She also remembered he was very interested in politics back then. Etienne beckoned to her.

"Hetty, come and meet Herman Kruger. He's playing for Northern's this season. He's also just become a junior partner in our firm." The young man put out his hand and gripped Hetty's and her face flushed as their eyes locked.

Just then Etienne was called away and Hetty stood, biting her thumbnail.

"Your Pa has a brilliant legal mind, Hetty. I admire his work."

She swallowed and nodded, uncharacteristically at a loss of words.

"Apartheid - separating the races. It is a clever concept, *jy weet*, and will solve all our problems." There was silence while he offered her a piece of gum before taking one himself. He continued speaking, running his hand through his hair. "You know the birthrate of *kaffirs* is growing fast because they don't give a damn about limiting their families to what they can afford. In fact, they don't give a damn about their families - period." He chewed hard on the gum. "They come to the towns, leaving their wives and kids behind and seduce any woman who is willing - or even if she isn't!"

"I agree," Hetty found her voice.

He smiled.

"Their numbers ter..terrify me," she stammered.

He leant over and patted her on the shoulder.

Hetty was attracted to Herman but she knew he didn't approve of "*daardie slim meisies* - those clever modern girls who think they are smart with new ideas about womanhood," he once said to her. And so she acted dumb and learnt not to oppose him. He was cool and controlled, except when discussing politics or religion. She was falling in love and longed for some sign that he was in love with her.

Etienne gave Hetty a party to celebrate her twenty-first birthday, an occasion she would never forget. Some members of the cabinet attended and Etienne was praised for his work in government. Herman's look of adoration was for her father. Hetty felt neglected and frustrated.

They sat alone on the settee after the last guest had departed and her parents retired for the night, she leant towards him, offering another glass of champagne, thinking he would surely kiss her. She inhaled the heady aroma of Youth Dew dabbed lavishly behind her ears and ran her tongue seductively over Passionate Pink lips then laid her head on his chest and noticed his hand holding the glass, was shaking. She smelt brandy. He drained the glass, placed it on the coffee table then put his arm around her.
    "Hetty, I want to marry you," he blurted. "I will speak to your Pa tomorrow and get it settled." Not waiting for her reply but taking acceptance for granted, he pressed his lips on hers and she felt his drooling saliva as his tongue explored her mouth. His hand slipped under her long skirt and up her thighs between her legs. Suddenly he was on top of her, pulling impatiently at her panties. She felt the probing then, almost before she could draw breath, felt his explosion. She was dazed and disillusioned, expecting ecstacy but experiencing dismay. She moved and he rolled off her and slid to the floor with a grunt then turned over and fell asleep. As she crept upstairs to shower and change into her nightclothes, she wondered if he would remember in the morning, that he had proposed to her. She could hardly believe it herself.

Their wedding took place a few months later. Herman's father, a minister in the Dutch Reformed Church, presided and many notables attended. It was predicted that a brilliant future in politics lay ahead for the bridegroom. No one would have predicted the bride was pregnant. In due course the child was born, prematurely Herman insisted. The baby was blonde, resembling Herman and they called her Susie.

"Ooh ja! But it makes a man feel good to hold his grandchild in his arms. Family is important Hetty, and I'm glad you came to your senses. Politics is not for a woman. Her duty is to be loyal to her husband, bear his children and keep his home comfortable like your Ma did for me." Herman nodded his agreement as Etienne carefully handed the baby to her new nanny, Miriam, standing respectfully to one side. "You agree, don't you Miriam? How many children do you have?"

"I have four master. My last one is three months."

"You didn't tell me you had children, Miriam." Hetty handed the black woman a bottle of formula. "So, who looks after them?"

"I'm leaving them with my mother in Rustenburg."

"And your husband?"

"He work on the mine in the Free State."

"Why doesn't he get a job here?"

"He not got a pass to work here. I'm writing long time to tell him the baby is born but I not hearing from him. I don' know if he getting my letter."

"Shame," Hetty said, shaking her head. "Anyway," she pointed to the baby, "take her for a walk and when you come back you must wash the diapers. Oh! And that reminds me," frowning at her, "I must tell you, Miriam, you have to be more careful with Baby's clothes. I noticed one of her nighties has been scorched with the iron. If you don't take more care you'll have to go. There are plenty of girls looking for work. We can't take the chance that you might leave the iron on and burn down the house."

Miriam bowed her head, cupped her hands together and bent her knees. "Oew! Ma'am, I'm very sorry ma'am."

"The girl made me mad," Hetty told Emma later. "She should be more grateful that she has a good job and is able to support her children in spite of her husband's neglect. I expect he got her letter but doesn't want the responsibility of kids. That's if she is telling the truth and IS married. She probably had four different men for each of the kid's fathers." She was silent for a while then continued, "Pa is quite right. We must teach them morality but we must make sure that us whites are protected by laws."

"Oh! I don't th..." Emma began, then changed her mind and started folding diapers.

The following year Hetty and Herman's second child was born. He was plump and adorable with dark tightly curled hair and they called him Pieter. Both Herman and Etienne were delighted to have an heir.

"He'll make a good Springbok one day. Look at those strong legs," said Etienne.

"You're right," Hetty laughed, "he always kicked hard inside me." Etienne, who once worried Hetty was too interested in politics and too aggressive, felt assured that Herman and motherhood had tamed her. After five years they had another daughter, Katrina, with the dark brown, almond-shaped eyes of her maternal great-grandmother and the blonde hair of her father's family.

Herman became one of Etienne's senior partners then left the firm to work for a Cabinet Minister. Hetty recalled her father's disappointment at the time. He had hoped, he told her privately, to retire and hand the business to his son-in-law. Herman said his reason for leaving was that others in the office were mean and jealous of his success. Hetty, however, knew he had political aspirations but wasn't to know of the consequences of those ambitions.

* * *

Unlike Emma's daughter, Hetty, my life was uneventful. My father had arranged a typing job for me in a government office in Durban. The job was dull and depressing and when the Nationalist Party won the election the following year in 1948, the future looked even more dull and depressing. When I met Arthur, a friend of my brother, Davey, and he asked me to marry him, I readily agreed. Higher education and travels abroad were a dead dream. Arthur and I shared the same ideals and values.

It was about a year after our wedding that Arthur's Company transfered him to the Transvaal. We settled in our new home and had our first baby, Robert, affectionately called Bobby. Shortly afterwards my father took ill.

"A heavy feeling in my chest, Meg," he complained to Mother. "Must be something I have eaten." Mother reported this in a letter to me. "But then," she wrote, "he slumped forward in his chair." It wasn't his digestion.

212

My father never understood me. He never liked change and new ideas disturbed him. After the funeral Uncle Harry offered Mother a home on the farm where Davey, now married, farmed with him. The years had slipped by and I still had not fulfilled my promise to Grandma.

WHAT HOPE HAVE YOU!

Chapter 37

We went to the farm to visit mother and of course, we saw Jakob and Mtonya.

"Is N'tabu married yet?" I asked.

"No, Miss Kate, but he's got a girl friend on the farm, he talking of going to Jo'burg to earn more money so he can pay lobola and get married. He say he can make good money there. There's not enough work here on the farm and in the Homeland there is no work for a man either."

"What about school?"

Jakob shrugged.

"If he comes to Jo'burg he must come and see me. Maybe Arthur can get him a job in his office." N'tabu had done well in the Mission school.

* * *

The train sped northwards across the bare brown *veld*. N'tabu, huddled on the hard wood seat, cracked cardboard case across his knees, staring through smeared windows at the bitter night. He turned up the collar of his coat, cuffs frayed and elbows worn. A fat woman sat opposite, hips splayed out taking up two seats. She opened a shopping bag and took out thickly sliced bread and a cocoa-cola bottle filled with strong tea.

N'tabu turned his head, his empty stomach rumbling. He had waited two days at the junction for the connection to Kimberley and then another day in Kimberley for the train to the Transvaal.

"I was so hungry, Miss Kate," he told me afterwards. "But I'm too scared to spend money before I get to Egoli. In Kimberley I'm sleeping in the waiting room in the station then the porter he see me there and he chase me so I'm going to the lavatories. Wow! But it smelling!" Holding his nose.

"But that old woman she say to me, 'you look hungry, my son, have some of this food, there is plenty here for both of us. My child, she pack this for me this morning when I leave to catch the train, she think I'm hungry but I've lots of meat on this ol' body." She laugh so hard I'm thinking she must fall off the seat.

"Are you going to work in Egoli, my son?"

"Ja," mumbled N'tabu, moving a lump of bread to the side of his mouth and picking his teeth with his forefinger. The woman handed him the bottle of tea. He drank thirstily.

A young man of about his age, on the next seat, joined the conversation.

"Have you got a job in Egoli?"

"Well, not exactly. But my friend, she say I mus' talk to her husband and maybe she can get me a job." N'tabu wiped the drips of tea off his chin with his hand.

"Hey man! What her husband do he can offer you a job?"

The young man looked sceptical.

"Well, they white people and her husband got a big job with this company."

"You say you have white people for friends?"

"Ja man, I'm knowing them for a very long time, from when I'm a small child. The farmer where we live, he is the brother of the mother of my friend. My father, she work for the family for a long time now."

The young man looked impressed but doubtful.

"Ow! Well maybe you get lucky. Maybe she can get you a pass to work in Egoli. But if you not born there you can't get a pass to work and you can't get a job without a pass and you can't get a pass unless you have a job."

"Oew!" N'tabu was overcome.

They sat in silence, the wheels of the train drumming out a rhythmical beat.

"What I'm wanting is work on the mines. They says the money it is good," scratching his head.

"Man, it's difficult to get work on the mines. They mostly take people from Rhodesia and Nyasaland. Anyways you have to be strong to work down the gold mine. It's very hard work," looking at N'tabu's small frame then noticing his crestfallen expression. "Don' worry man, if your white friends can help you get a job I know someone who can fix a pass. He work in the pass office and got all the stamps. You jus' have to give him some money and he'll do it for you. But you mus' forget about working in the mines."

N'tabu slowly nodded his head, glancing at the old woman who had fallen asleep and was swaying from side to side.

"Maybe I can get you a job." The voice of his companion broke into his thoughts. "The place I work, they give me a new job." A grin spread

216

across his face, "I'm going to drive the *makulu* boss in the motor car. I got my licence now, so they want someone to do my old job."

N'tabu leant forward, interested. "What job?" The voice continued, "Cleaning, making tea and doing messages."

"Oooh!" His shoulders sagged. "And the money?"

"Well," he replied, right hand gesturing, "so - so. But you can't be fussy there's many people looking for jobs, hey! The madam at the office she find someone for my job, but then she catch him pinching the tea and the sugar. She shout and scream and give him the sack and now he got no money for food and he got five chil'ren. The missis say she don' care and she get the p'lice anyway. She ask me to find someone I know for the job because she say she won't take *tsotsies* off the street now, she don't want a *skelm* again who is pinching the tea and sugar. If you can come I can start my new job. They give me a uniform with a cap," pulling his shoulders back.

N'tabu nodded his head and the matter appeared settled.

They talked about life in the big city.

"The new government make it very difficult for our people. They make a curfew at night so you can't walk in the streets without your papers. All the time they want to see your passbooks and now they say the women must also carry passes."

"Are you married... You didn't say your name."

"Joshua. Ja I'm married but my wife can't live with me so she stay with the chil'ren in the Homeland and Im living in the township with my parents. My father has a house there." The sky darkened and the moisture on the window-panes crystalised into frost. The two young men wrapped blankets around themselves and fell asleep.

A weak early-morning sun shone softly through smog and smoke as the train approached the outskirts of Johannesburg.

Spirals of smoke from chimney stacks rose straight up, hanging sinister and still, over the city, like a grey mantle washed with the soft dawn hues of a Turner painting, blurring the harsh edges of a high-veld winter and a polluted landscape. The train slowed, jerked, jolted and finally stopped. N'tabu, clutched his coloured blanket with one hand and his suitcase with the other. "Go carefully," he said to the fat woman. She responded, telling him the same.

Trucks and tramcars roared past like lions in pursuit of each other. Scraps of paper and cigarette cartons, orange peel and apple cores cannoned down sidewalks by sudden gusts of wind and huddled in gutters, while frost lay all over the ground, on metal door handles and iron gratings like a coat of mail. N'tabu shivered.

"You betta come to my place tonight and I can take you to this fellow I know can fix your papers, but today jus' lie low and keep out the way of policemen. I go to my job now and talk to the madam and meet you here at the bus station tonight at six o'clock. We catch the bus to Sophiatown."

N'tabu nodded, taking note of his whereabouts. Then picked up his suitcase but Joshua took his arm.

"Hey man! Better I take your bag to my work. The p'lice might get suspicious if they see you carrying a big suitcase. They'll say you stole something and then they ask for your pass." N'tabu handed his case over with some misgiving, but keeping it might mean trouble.

N'tabu walked all morning. He noticed a sign, "FISH & CHIPS" painted in black letters across a plate-glass window. His last meal was with the fat woman on the train. Cautiously he looked inside the crowded shop then moved over to stand in line at the greasy, glass counter, watching a big white man in front of drums of boiling oil, immersing lumps of fish and bundles of cut potatoes in frying baskets. The man was in shirt sleeves, a grimy apron pulled across his bulging stomach. The apron traced with dirty finger marks, flies buzzed in the corners of the glass counter, settling on cheese pieces, gherkins and fried fish displayed for sale. The smell of stale fat rose in a cloud of steam.

"Boy! Hey you there! How much fish and chips you want? Quick man, I haven't got all day."

N'tabu turned his head and looked nervously behind.

"You, *jou bobbejaan*. I'm talking to you, you fathead. How much fish and chips you want?"

N'tabu, realising he was the object of attention, clutched a grubby pound note in his hand, folded into a small square, looking about him for a clue as to how much he should order? He stammered.

"Er.... er... sis... sispense fish and chips please, my *baas*." The other customers laughed. The white face turned red.

"What yer mean sixpence fish and chips? You been funny or sumthin?"

A young girl standing next to N'tabu bent over and whispered. He looked at the shopkeeper, "I mean two shilling," carefully opening the folded pound note, holding it out.

The shopkeeper tipped the frying basket on to the sheet of newspaper on the counter, globules of fat spread, spotting newsprint. Chasing off flies with one hand, while sprinkling salt and vinegar with the other, then folding over the parcel he pushed it towards N'tabu, taking the offered money. He rang it up on the till and handed N'tabu four two-shilling pieces.

"Pl ... pl... please, my *baas*.."

"Yes, what's the matter boy? You don' like the service or sumpthin?" laughing loudly, belly shaking.

"Nn..no..my *baas*. NNnothing like that. I.. er..er. I gave the master a one pound note." Sweat on N'tabu's forehead.

"No, you didn't, you bloody *kaffir*. You gave me a ten shilling note. Don't try that trick on me, hey!" his laugh changing to a scowl. "You betta get outa my shop quick, pronto like, before I call the police. I know people like you. You try to be clever."

N'tabu knew he had given a one pound note. He had no other money. He also knew the young girl next to him had seen the note in his hand. He looked at her for corroboration. She turned her face away, keeping silent. No one spoke.

Resenting the injustice, N'tabu opened his mouth to continue his protest but saw the fear in the eyes of the other customers and realised the hopelessness. The police would not take his word against a white man's and he had no papers. He picked up the parcel and left the shop.

He walked a few blocks then, noticing a vacant bench in a nearby park, crossed the road and sat down, preparing to eat when he heard a shout behind.

"Hey! you there! Get off that seat. Can't you read? BLANKES ALLEEN. This bench is for white persons only." Two policemen bore down. N'tabu jumped up, dropping his parcel and fish and chips scattered in all directions. He abandoned his lunch and ran for the nearest corner, disappearing into the crowd.

Although the sun shone and the sky a clear blue, N'tabu felt a sense of gloom. He walked all day. All the washrooms had the same sign as the bench and yet black people filled the streets. They dug up tramlines while their white masters sat under tents drinking tea. They drove trucks, worked on building sites and rode bicycles delivering parcels. He spoke to one worker and the man leant on his pick, sweat running down his face while he shrugged and shook his head.

"No, the stores don't have washrooms for us nor do the offices. But if you walk up that iron staircase outside that building over there," pointing down the street, "and climb to the roof where the cleaners live, you will find a lavatory you can use."

N'tabu thanked him.

The afternoon wore on with the streets becoming busier as office workers poured out of buildings opening umbrellas in a sudden thunderstorm.

"Hey man! Where you goin'? I been watching you, you walk right past me, man. How was your day?" N'tabu looked up at Joshua's voice.

"Oew! I didn't see you, Joshua man. But I'm truly glad to see you now, hey!" They walked together to the bus station, rain swirling down the gutters while N'tabu related his day's experiences. Joshua heard him out.

"Oew! You take big chance hey! To talk back to a white man an' then sit on the whiteman's bench. Hallelulia! You asking for big trouble." Joshua was serious. He put his hand on N'tabu's shoulder. "I spoke to the madam at my work and she say she will see you tomorrow. Tonight we mus' get your papers fixed. How much money you got?"

They approached the bus station and could see the line-up of commuters coiling around the corner of the street like a brightly striped snake. N'tabu was dismayed.

"Don' you worry man, It's like this every day. You mus' jus' wait."

A bus pulled up and the snake-like line undulated forward in a surge of rippling muscle, but a harmless, good tempered snake. A push there, a shove here, laughter flowing through it while the motor of the bus chugged like a pulsing heartbeat as the driver took the fares.

The driver put up his hand. "No more. I'm full up. No more space. Sorry, but you must take the next bus." With a shudder the bus pulled away from the curb, hissing and rattling down the street. Passengers swayed from side to side, clutching straps swinging above. Some stood on the iron steps clinging to the rail and swirling out perilously at every corner. Big cars driven by white commuters on their way to the northern suburbs, speeding swiftly by the sidewalks.

"We must move soon," Joshua turned to N'tabu. They had left the bus and were walking along the dusty street of the township, past wood and iron lean-to shanties with narrow chimney pipes, puffing smoke. N'tabu nodded, pointing to the billboard and slowly read.

220

"'Feed your baby *N u t r i n e.*' What's that?"

"It's a baby food from the factory. But most of the mothers can't pay for it, it cost too much money so they give the chil'ren condensed milk.

"Oew! Why don't they give them from their own breasts?" he asked, tapping his chest, thinking about the women at the *kraal* and their full breasts.

"Well you see, they mus' work and they have to leave their chil'ren in the townships. My sister she got a job as a nanny and she leave her child with my mother. But now they making Sophiatown a 'white area' and are calling it 'Triomf' so we must all move to the new township the government make, Meadowlands. But it is very far and the people must get up very early to catch the train. My sister's madam she say my sister must live in her backyard but she can't take the baby there. The people don't want to move to Meadowlands or Soweto those places are too far. But my mother, she say, what's the use, they will bring the bulldozers anyway."

Chapter 38

He stood at the back door, cap in hand. A slow smile spreading across his face. "I'm getting married. I'm having the money now for *lobola* for Hanna's father and tomorrow I'm leaving for my home."

It was a year since N'tabu's arrival in the 'City of Gold'. "That is good news," I exclaimed. "Will Hanna come back to Jo'burg with you?" I knew it was a foolish question as soon as it was out. Hanna had not been born in the area and therefore could not qualify for a pass to live and work there. They could live together in their homeland but N'tabu had no work there. He sold his labour where the white man needed it.

* * *

The young man in new city suit jumped off the country bus, watching it gather speed for its climb up the long hill. The sun set behind distant hills and mist lay in the valley. He saw the cluster of huts where his family lived. Hanna would be there waiting. She would be disappointed to learn she could not return with him to the city after the wedding ceremony. She wouldn't understand about passes and about a wife not being allowed to live with her husband.

He heard a shout from the valley and looked towards the sound as the voice echoed back from the rocky *krantz*. He saw the girl waving. Her hair braided with beads, beads around her neck, falling between the valley of her firm bare breasts. Bead bracelets covered her arms and ankles and large, heavy bead earrings swung with every movement of her head. Her skin shone with oil as she stretched out her arms, and his eyes shone with pride as he gazed upon her.

They ran towards each other and met in the long grass, then she hesitated, overcome by shyness at the sight of the handsome young man in unfamiliar clothes.

"N'tabu. At last you are here. I'm worry that there is trouble and that you cannot come. Have you the money for *lobola*?" She asked, voice shaking.

"I have the money."

"That is good."

"Are arrangements made for the marriage?"

"Everything is arranged."

The wedding celebrations were over, they had lasted all week and the time had come for N'tabu to return to the city and tell Hanna she couldn't accompany him. They stood next to an outcrop of rock; he felt her breasts, smooth and soft, like the swathes of chiffon mist that swirled around them. But his mood was as low as the cloud hanging over the valley. He must leave her, and it would be twelve months before he came again. He held her close. She felt his hardness and the hardness of the coarse grass, burnt black by wild *veld* fires, tipped white with frost.

"Please take me with you. I'm promising I'm not doing nothing to give you trouble."

"It is not that you can do som'thing to bring trouble, jus' being there you will bring trouble. They won't allow it. If they find you, you go to *gaol*." His voice bitter.

"But if I'm not talking to anyone and if I'm staying inside the house?" she persisted.

"It's no good," shaking his head.

"If the p'lice come I hide under the bed."

"Hiding under the bed!" scornful laughter. "Don't you think they can find you under the bed? They bring their dogs and the dogs sniff, sniff and they find you very quickly."

The argument continued. Another day passed.

They walked up the winding path to the road. Small brothers and sisters following, their feet grey from dirt and the wind whipped their thin bare legs. A swirl of dust spiralled, spraying stones from the big black wheels of the bus. They climbed aboard, turning to wave to the children until they were specks on the *veld*, like fleas on the back of a dog. The bus turned at the bend and the children were out of sight.

"You will have to get other clothes and a *doek* for your head." The girl nodded as they entered the Trading Store.

She was proud of her beaded hair and would be sad to cover it, but a small price to pay to be with her husband.

N'tabu had relented. She would live in Egoli with him and he said the women in Egoli wore *doeks* on their heads.

The air in the shop was thick with the reek of pungent oils mingling with body sweat. Brightly coloured candy filled glass jars on the counters. Sheepskins, hung on hooks on the wall and lay in piles on the floor. Bolts of cotton print, layered the shelves. Blue, purple, red.

The storekeeper in checked woollen shirt and suspenders pointed out the long blue cotton-print dresses then left them to their decision making. He knew it would be long and drawn-out, entailing deep discussion. At last a leather pouch was taken out and N'tabu carefully counted folded notes. Hanna emerged from behind a curtain and stood before him, head bent. The transformation complete. Long blue floral frock, buttoned to the neck and a doek of spotted silk covered her beaded head.

The train journey to Johannesburg was over and Hanna followed N'tabu nervously along the busy sidewalk to catch the bus to the township. She stared in disbelief - so much noise, so many people. She was afraid. In the township Joshua's mother, Matilda, greeted them. N'tabu explained Hanna's presence. "I'm knowing this house is very small and many people already live here but Hanna can help with the cooking and the cleaning and can help minding the chil'ren." He looked hopefully at Matilda, then added, "Also we bring some mealie seeds, Hanna can plant them in the yard." He put a brown paper packet containing the seeds on the wooden kitchen table.

Hanna clutched her skirt and hung her head, overcome by shyness.
"What if the p'lice raid? What if the neighbours talk?" Matilda said then she saw the girl's downcast expression and relented, shrugging her shoulders.
"Oh well, I can see you like to be with N'tabu, so you can stay an' help me with my gran'chilren. You know we have to leave this place, but it is lucky me and Sam we put our names down such a long time ago for a house in Soweto and so now we don't have to move so very far away to Meadowlands with all the others. Some people are saying they won't go but Im saying what can we do against the bulldozers." N'tabu listened respectfully to Matilda's ramblings, nodding his head, then sighed with relief.

Hanna lay close to N'tabu on the narrow iron bedstead set up high on wooden blocks. It was three months since her arrival. They had moved with the family to Soweto after the tin shanties were flattened and removed. Sophiatown became "Triomph" for white families with neat rows of houses surrounded by high security fences. She whispered because Joshua and his brother were sleeping on the other side of the curtain.

"N'tabu," her mouth close to his ear. "I thinking I'm going to have a child."

N'tabu's body stiffened. "What you saying, Hanna? We haven't got the money for a child. You mus' go back to the farm." Without papers Hanna had not been able to look for work.

She cried quietly.

N'tabu was dismayed but he also felt proud. He would write to his father and all the village would know. His father had wanted him to pay the *lobola* and then only get married after she was with child but N'tabu was educated at the Mission School and the priest said it was not good to sleep with a woman before marriage.

The months passed, Hanna's pregnancy began to show. Her rounded belly stretched the seams of her cotton dress. Her rounded breasts bulged like ripe melons. N'tabu brought her to visit me and I learnt how she had refused to stay behind on the farm and how Matilda had helped them. When next I saw N'tabu he told me it was shortly after they'd seen me that the trouble started.

* * *

It was the quiet time before dawn, he said. No sign of a rising sun although a hopeful rooster crowed, taken up by another in Matilda's yard. A car screeched to a halt, a stray dog barked. Hanna stirred, feeling hot in the narrow bed, squeezed between the sleeping N'tabu and the rough wall. Loud knocking on the front door.

"*Maak oop, maak oop. Haastig man!*" N'tabu sat up in alarm.

Joshua's father, Sam, shuffled down the hallway to unlock the door, voice shaking "*Wat makeer?* What's the matter?"

Hanna caught her breath in a sob. N'tabu put his hand over her mouth.

"Ssh, lie still." They moved closer to each other.

The others in the family, clutching blankets, walked into the kitchen.

"Come on, hey! Hurry up *jong*. How many people living here. Give us your pass books, man. *Maak gou!* We haven't got all day."

The family complied.

One policeman looked them over, comparing the number of heads against passbooks in his hand, the other walked through the house. N'tabu heard footsteps approaching and considered pushing Hanna through the window but it was too small. She slid off the bed as the door hurled open. A flashlight beamed across the bare boards, lighting on the two crouching figures. N'tabu reached for his passbook. "Ja *baas*, I'm got my papers here."

The policeman took the book, waving the flashlight.

"What about this girl? Have she got papers to stay here?"

"She jus' visiting, *baas*. She going home tomorrow."

"Ja, I heard that one before," a sniff and a sneer then a punch to N'tabu's head. He ducked.

"Hey *Boet, kom hierso*, I got one here without a *passboek* hey! Better we put her in the van."

Sam followed into the bedroom.

"Please master, don't take this girl to *gaol*. She will go back to the farm. I promise." They ignored his plea.

"What she doing here, anyway? You people jus' make trouble all the time. You know she not allowed here without a pass."

"But she my wife..." N'tabu protested, then ducked to avoid a hit across his head.

"Ja, your wife! I don't believe that, hey! Then next week when we come you have another girl here. I know you people. Since when do you get married? I'm telling you, we don't want no more people in the towns." He pushed the terrified Hanna ahead through the front door and down the pathway, slipping and sliding on the black frost and into the black van. N'tabu watched in despair.

The quiet night was broken by Hanna's sobs. Even the dog was silent, cringing against the wall. It knew the force of a policeman's boot. Faces peered through windows. The black van, with spurt of power, sped down the street, spewing exhaust in a grey cloud that hung in the still air like a shadowy ghost.

Chapter 39

Johannesburg
Circa 1954.

It was Saturday in Soweto. The township streets were noisy. Cabs careened around corners, spraying stones and sand. The vile smell of rotting rubbish rose with the wind that tugged bare branches, blew vegetable peelings and lifted papers and cardboard boxes across the sidewalks. A stray dog with corrugated ribs snuffled for scraps while children played outside corner stores, kicking soccer balls or old tin cans.

N'tabu walked down the street, eyes downcast, hands deep in pockets, viciously kicking a stone, thinking of Hanna and the boy, of the empty days and lonely nights. He had Hanna's letter saying she was pregnant again and recalled the night she was arrested for being in the area without proper papers. They were legally married, and he had a job, and was entitled to live in Johannesburg, but she was NOT, the arresting policeman had said, vapour rising with his voice as he pushed her out of the house, down the pathway slipping and sliding on the black frost and into the black van.

He remembered watching, his stomach feeling hollow like a scooped out *sponspek*, he said when he came to see me to tell me about Hanna's arrest and ask for help in tracing her. We found out where she was being held. N'tabu paid the fine and she was released on condition she returned to the Homeland immediately. The months passed and now N'tabu was back in the township again, after visiting Hanna for his annual fortnight leave.

He felt a hand on his shoulder and swung around, defensively patting pockets for passbook, muscles taut, like a *gemsbok* ready to take off; then relaxed, fear turning to relief when he recognised his friend Joshua. The two of them shared a room in Joshua's mother, Matilda's, house. A young woman stood next to Joshua.

"Hey man! You give me big fright. I'm thinking you was the p'lice, and I'm looking for my passbook."

"Well, you got your pass in your pocket and I'm not a p'liceman so why worry hey?" Joshua bent over, laughing, "C'mon N'tabu man, you look sick hey! What's the problem?"

N'tabu shrugged.

"Come down to the beerhall with me an' Nellie here," turning towards the young woman. "Nellie's my mother's sister's child."

N'tabu noted the comely figure in smart city clothes. A smooth black wig covered her head, her lips painted a defiant red. Then he averted his eyes, disapproving of the wig and afraid of appearing interested.

"Oew! I dunno man. I haven't got money for the beerhall."

"No problem about money, I got my wages yesterday an' Nellie don't come to Soweto so very much, she work in Northcliff." He took N'tabu by the arm and with Nellie on his other side, the three made their way down the dusty street against the sunset sky, slashed scarlet above the smog of smokestacks. A group of musicians stood on the corner playing a mouth-organ, a guitar and a penny-whistle. Nellie began clapping her hands and wiggling her bottom and Joshua, bent his elbow into hers, swinging her around, dust lifting about their feet. N'tabu stood to one side, smiling with his mouth.

Nellie visited her aunt Matilda, the following month on her free week-end, this time she left off lipstick and wig, hoping to see N'tabu. She felt attracted to this young man with the sad expression and sought his approval. They sat together at the kitchen table while Nellie related amusing stories of overheard conversations between her employers. She lifted N'tabu out of his gloom and he found he enjoyed her company.

"You like our Nellie, hey man?" Joshua grinned at N'tabu in the candle light of their shared bedroom.

"She O.K."

Joshua winked.

N'tabu became defensive. "She funny, she make me laugh and anyway, Hanna, she far away and she got the boy and now she tell me she expecting another baby." His voice rose querulously, then dropped... "and I'm here by myself."

"O.K., O.K., I'm only joking."

The months went by and Nellie and N'tabu spent more time together, visiting the beerhall or watching the local soccer teams. It was Nellie he imagined in bed with him, memories of Hanna receding. It would be another six months before his leave was due and he could visit Hanna and the child. He recalled the reason for coming to Egoli was to find work to enable him to save the money to pay *lobola* to Hanna's father so they could be married because his wages as a herdsman on the farm was insufficient. After the wedding ceremony he had given in to Hanna's pleading, taking her with him to the city, knowing it would be illegal for her to live there without the proper papers. He remembered when

Matilda's house in Soweto was raided and the terrified, pregnant Hanna was arrested and returned to the Homeland.

Nellie was lonely, her latest boyfriend had deserted her. She had had one relationship after another, finding it difficult to establish anything permanent because she always needed permission from her employers for a man to stay with her, and now she was falling in love with N'tabu, although she knew he had a wife and child in the Homeland.

"I can't help it if the government don't allow his wife to live here because she not born here," she complained to a friend. "The government make this place for white people only, except when they need us blacks to work for them." She had plans for herself and N'tabu.

Nellie licked grease off her fingers and rolled up the newspaper that wrapped the fish and chips N'tabu had bought on their way from the railway station. They were alone in the house, Matilda visiting friends and Joshua working. She walked around the table and stood next to him, then leant over and, putting her face next to his, brushed his cheek with her lips. At first he pushed away from her, but felt his arousal as she began to caress him. She took his hand and lead him into the bedroom then lay down on his narrow bed, pulling him on top of her. He felt as if he was sliding into the swamp by the river at home; sucked in deeper and deeper until he was out of his depth, panting for air.

"Why don' you come and stay with me in my room there in Northcliff? I got a nice room. The madam and master they good to me, they give me half-a-crown to sit with the chil'ren when they go to the bioscope and the madam, she selling me her old clothes very cheap?" N'tabu didn't reply. He turned over and climbed out of the bed, pulling up his trousers and stuffing in his shirt, a worried frown on his face.

"We better get up because Matilda be coming home soon."

Nellie rolled off the bed and pulled up her skirt, "The master, she say you can stay in the room with me for doing the garden one day a week an' cleaning the swimming pool," she said, looking earnestly at N'tabu, disclosing she had taken some action on her plan. N'tabu remained silent as he fastened his belt around his waist.

"It won't be so far for you to go to work in Egoli from Northcliff, not like from here in Soweto," strengthening her argument.

N'tabu pursed his lips, ruminating, then finally answered.

"I don' know, Nellie. We done a bad thing to Hanna today."

"Who going to tell Hanna, she live very far away." She pushed her full breasts into her blouse then fastened the buttons.

231

N'tabu turned away but she put out her arms and pulled him towards her. Once again he felt as if he was sinking out of his depth and took her arms from around his neck.

"I don' know," he repeated.

"Why you say you don' know. Hanna can't be here so what mus' you do?"

He still hesitated, silent, as if considering what she had said, then he answered, "Anyways, are you sure they let me stay, Nellie. The p'lice make big fine for the white people if they don' have a permit for me to live on the premises."

Nellie worked as a 'live-in' maid in one of the exclusive northern suburbs. Her room was at the end of the long pathway in the backyard, out of sight, hidden in summer behind the mauve curtain of Jacaranda trees, before they dropped their blooms and made a mauve carpet outside her door. Her room was attached to the double garage but was barely big enough for a table, two wooden chairs and a narrow bed raised on bricks so the witchdoctor couldn't hide the *tokoloshe* there. Her clothes hung on hooks, on the wall. She spent her free time on Thursdays, her day off, doing embroidery with coloured thread on white cotton squares. Lazy-daisy-stitched sunflowers in yellow with black centres and green satin-stitched leaves. Samples of her work, neatly starched and ironed, covered the table, bed and a cardboard box on which stood a half-burnt candle and some matches. The window was high on the wall with a green plastic curtain. She did have a shower and toilet next door but in winter she carried hot water from the kitchen.

Nellie smiled at N'tabu's query, he was becoming interested in her suggestion.

"Ooh ja! I ask the madam already and she say you mus' go there next Sunday and talk to the master. She say if you help the master in the garden and with the swimming-pool, you can stay in the room with me for FREE."

N'tabu still hesitated, "Well let me think about it and I telling you next week."

"Please," she cajoled

"I think about it," he repeated, frowning and scratching his head as he walked out of the bedroom into the kitchen. "I worry about Hanna. It not her fault she can't come and live here. Maybe it better I don't see you any more." Nellie began to cry.

"No, no, you mustn't cry. I promise you I think about it."

232

"OK. You think about it, then you come and see my place next Sunday and if you like it, then you telling the master when you are there." She paused, wiped her eyes, then continued to persuade as she took cups off the shelf and put a pot of water on the coal-fired stove. "You know it's very easy to get the bus to your work from my place; much better than catching the train from Soweto. You having to get up very early now, and walking such a long way to the railway station. Where I live you jus' get the bus by the shops at the corner. The *Putco* buses go all the time into the city."

N'tabu slowly nodded his head. "I think about it," he repeated.

That evening Nellie spoke to Matilda. "I'm asking N'tabu to come and live with me in Northcliff." Matilda carefully placed the plate she was drying on the table, then turned to face Nellie.

"That is not good, Nellie. N'tabu has a wife and child. Why you do that?"

"But his wife and child are far away in the Homeland, and if he doesn't sleep with me he sleep with someone else. Maybe one of the bad girls in the city and that will not be good for him or for Hanna. How can you think that he's never going to go with a woman jus' because he's married, when his wife live so very far away and he can only see her once a year?" Matilda shook her head in dismay, her face bleak as she pulled out a chair and sat down arms around her stomach as if to protect all the children yet to be born. Rocking back and forth, she wailed,

"What is going to happen? How can we keep our families together? I don' know what can happen to our people. The wives don't see the husbands and the mother's mus' leave their chil'ren and many chil'ren don't even know their fathers." She felt helpless, like a string of seaweed stranded on the shore, waiting for the oncoming tide.

The following Sunday N'tabu visited Nellie and was interviewed by her employers.

"Nellie tells me you want to stay with her in the room." N'tabu held his hands in front of him, tightly clutching his knitted cap.

"Yes, missis."

"He does look clean, you know Basil," turning towards her husband, "and it will be an advantage to have him. You know you hate gardening at weekends. You'd much rather play golf. I told Nellie he must work in the garden and clean the pool and the cars and, of course, he must polish all the shoes. The children can put theirs with yours in the kitchen after dinner." The wife, her bouffant hair gleaming, panted with excitement, her tongue sliding over thin lips and her eyes darting, searching for more jobs. N'tabu watched her silently, then his attention was caught by an iguana on the window-ledge its brilliant blue head shining as it rocked back and forth, neck pulsating, tongue darting and protruding eyes pivoting, searching for prey. N'tabu knew it spat venom. He should tell them it was there but had no opportunity. The voices continued.

"What about the fine if the police raid?" interjected the husband.

"Just tell him you can't be responsible and he'll have to pay any fine if the police raid," she replied, firmly.

The husband took over the interview. "You'll have to pay the fine if the police raid, y'know. Remember, I don't know anything about your living here. Right? What's your name?"

N'tabu told him, turning his head as he spoke then pointed to the window-ledge, "Master look... over there."

But the husband interrupted, "Oh that name's far too difficult to pronounce, by jove; can't be expected to remember that, hey! I'll call you Jim. So Jim, you can stay here with Nellie in her room but for that you must work in the garden one day a week, on Sundays, clean the pool and wash the cars."

"What about the shoes?" squeaked the wife.

N'tabu nodded his head then looked back at the window ledge but the iguana had disappeared. Stretching behind him he saw the lawn sloping to the boundary with a high bougainvillaea hedge for privacy and high wrought-iron gates for security. Jacaranda trees bordered either side of the long driveway. A poinsettia and a syringa bush grew against one wall and azaleas were planted at intervals in the lawn. Near the patio the kidney-shaped swimming pool sparkled, partly shaded by a thatched summer house.

Nellie finished washing dishes and cleaning the kitchen, then took the leftover vegetables for her and N'tabu's dinner, glancing at the clock, noting it was almost nine and saw N'tabu walking up the driveway. It was three months since he had moved in with her. He travelled by bus to his job in the city but it usually meant a long wait in a long line-up after cleaning the office where he worked, once the staff left at 5 o'clock. They sat on the bed and talked then Nellie lay back and pulled him on top of her.

"C'mon," she said, laughing and pushing her hand down his pants, "show me what you got here."

234

N'tabu stirred and felt Nellie's closeness then opened his eyes and put his arm around her. The sun's rays sprayed through the window, splashing the wall next to the bed. He heard the dog bark at the milk delivery. Nellie woke, stretched her arms above her head, then cuddled up and stroked his cheek.

"N'tabu I have something I mus' tell you."

"O.K., what is it? You want to tell me I must come with you to Soweto today. But you know I can't the master here, he say I must work in the garden Sundays."

"No, not that, I mus' tell you....," she paused.

"Well, come on, tell me," N'tabu pulled her towards him, laughing. "you got no money for bus fare? Is that what you want to tell me?"

"No, wait, I mus' tell you that I am going to have a child."

N'tabu shot up off the bed and paced across the width of the narrow room, the smile wiped from his face.

"What are you saying Nellie?"

"I saying I going to have a child."

"But what about your job here? Where can we live if you have to leave your job?"

"Don' worry, I can still work a long time. The madam won't know." N'tabu shook his head, unconvinced.

Nellie cooked *putu* over the primus stove she used in their room on Sunday mornings then scooped it on to the plate on the table in front of N'tabu. It was a month since she had told him of the expected child. He began eating, a frown on his face, recalling his recent conversation with Joshua.

"I don' know how I can find the money to support so many," he had confided, "It's not my fault the government won' allow Hanna to live with me in Egoli. What mus' I do? I mus' never tell Hanna she can be sad," he hesitated, "and she can be very angry with me. What mus' I do? Next week it is the time for me to visit her and I will take her presents." He shook his head as Nellie's voice broke into his thoughts.

"The madam, she speaking to me today, N'tabu. She say, 'am I expecting a baby?"

"So? What you say to her?" N'tabu looked up from his plate of putu.

"I tell her I'm not."

"What you mean you tell her you not having a child? You told me that you was." N'tabu stopped chewing, the food pushing out the side of his cheek, a look of relief on his face.

"Well, it's not true."

"What's not true. That you are having a child or that you're not having a child?" he asked, losing patience.

Nellie fiddled with a knife and a spoon, her fingers agitated. "It's not true that I'm not having a child."

N'tabu stood up, knocking over his chair. "So why you tell the madam a lie?" He picked up the chair then sat down on it again, looking intently at Nellie.

Nellie lowered her eyes. "If I'm telling her I'm having a baby, she give me the sack." Standing up, she began scraping the leftovers on her plate on to a piece of newspaper.

N'tabu shook his head. "But Nellie, she will very soon see that you are expecting, and what will you tell her then?"

"I'm telling her I'm getting too fat because I'm eating too much *putu*," bursting into laughter, her natural high spirits bubbling, as she stamped out some dance steps, arms waving and fingers snapping before flopping on to a chair. "Then I'm asking for my two weeks leave and bringing my cousin Miriam to do my job while I'm having the baby in Rustenburg."

"And then, after two weeks. What you do with the baby?"

She was silent for a moment, then lowered her head, looking down at her hands now lying limply in her lap. "Then I mus' leave my child with my mother on the farm." Her voice dropped to a whisper, then she wiped her eyes with the palms of her hands.

"I asked the girl if she was pregnant and she denied it. As if I can't tell," scornfully. "It's one thing Basil, to have the husband, but we can't be expected to have the *picannins* as well."

N'tabu overheard the conversation while cleaning shoes at the back door.

Basil agreed. "Damned nuisance, m'dear. He's been a damned good garden-boy, best we've had, by jove, never seen the roses looking so good. It'll mean missing my four-ball now on Sundays, until we can find someone else of course. Damn shame. But there's no question about it, they'll have to go."

Nellie went home to Rustenburg to await the birth of her child and N'tabu, returned to his shared room with Joshua in Soweto. In due course the baby was born, a boy, they named him Petrus. Nellie left him with her mother on the farm and returned to the town, once again looking for a job and a place for N'tabu to live with her. N'tabu, meanwhile, put his name on

ELAINE BUNBURY

the waiting list for a house in Soweto but was told it would be at least five years before it would come up.

"The government can't afford to build more houses, *jy weet*," he was told by the official at the Department of Bantu Housing. "I'm jus' lucky I still got a job an' they haven't closed down the Department. You people make so much trouble you can't control your kids and the government has to buy guns and armoured cars with us white people's tax money so the army can keep the school children in order." He swatted a mosquito settling on his forearm, then took a handkerchief out of the pocket of his safari suit and blew his nose, sniffed, then waved it at the flying ants fluttering around his head attracted to the light on his desk. They fell on his papers as their wings dropped off, their brown bodies struggling and squirming. He brushed them impatiently aside. "You people, you come to Jo'burg to the bright lights and think you can bring your wives and kids as well, hey! It doesn't matter if you don't have houses man, you jus' squat anywhere."

N'tabu remained silent. He knew he couldn't bring Hanna to live with him if he was allocated a house, because she wasn't permitted to live in the Johannesburg area, and officially Nellie wouldn't be able to move in with him either because they weren't legally married. He put his name on the list anyway.

237

Chapter 40

Pretoria:

"Emma, m'dear, I've decided to join the Progressive Party because I think they have the answer to the problems we face in this country. I have a lot of faith in Helen Suzmann, y'know and enormous admiration for her."

Emma nodded as Carl paused while he wiped his mouth with the napkin.

"They advocate improving education for blacks. Of course it's inevitable that the majority will eventually get the vote and so it's important they are educated."

Emma leant forward with her elbows on the table, listening intently to Carl's words. "I hope enough people will support this new Party to enable it to become at least the Official Opposition," he continued, "but it will be a long hard struggle. Most whites prefer to keep the status quo."

Carl and Emma were lunching at a remote country inn. They had grown into a comfortable relationship, their passion now more controlled and replaced by a deep-rooted friendship. Carl was no risk-taker. He only agreed to meet alone in secluded places that were far from the city where they were both well known.

"It's better to avoid scandal, m'dear." At first Emma was hurt, proclaiming she didn't care about people or what they thought. She would leave Etienne, she said, so she and Carl could be together. It wasn't as if Lavinia and he were happy anyway. But eventually she had come to agree with Carl, realising how it would affect her family if she left them or if her and Carl's affair was discovered. Hetty's husband, Herman, had political aspirations and besides, Emma would never want to harm her three grandchildren, Susie, Pieter and Katrina. Jan wasn't married but he and Rupert would have understood.

Carl glanced at his wrist-watch, shaking his head.

"Time flies when I'm with you, m'dear. But I really must be going; have an important appointment this afternoon then must take Lavinia to the airport. She's off to the Cape again. He signalled the waiter and paid the bill with cash then pushed his chair back from the table and stood up. As Emma reached for her jacket he helped her slip it on then held her close for a moment in the empty dining room. He heard the waiter

239

returning and stepped away as they walked out to the car. They drove back to the city in comfortable silence.

"Any possibility of you getting away tonight? I have given Maggie some time off."

"If only I could," Emma shook her head sadly. "But Etienne has invited people for dinner. Some government official and his wife," she grumbled, pulling a face. "Sorry about that."

"Well, how about the following evening? Didn't you say Etienne was also going away."

"'Fraid not. He's got some Party officials for dinner on Thursday. Bit of a nuisance as it's Philomena's day off. Anyway I'll manage. But perhaps the night after that. I'm sure he said something about a meeting in Jo'burg and he will stay at the Rand Club for the night."

"That'll be great. Shall look forward to it."

It was a balmy morning the following day as Emma sat in her garden, looking towards the distant Magaliesberg. The view was uplifting and she needed uplifting thinking of the boring dinner party with Jannie, Etienne's friend and co-worker, and his dull wife the previous evening. She thought of how she might have spent the night. Philomena brought a tray set with her lunch and she remembered the other dinner party tonight that Etienne had arranged.

"Thank you Philomena. I know it's your day off and you want to get away but could you do me a favour and set the table for six and leave everything ready on the hot tray before you go?"

"Yes ma'am. I'll do that."

"Thank you Philomena. What would I do without you?"

They both smiled.

The phone rang and she ran inside to answer before Philomena could, expecting Carl. He often called at this time.

"Is that you Emma?" Her face fell.

"'Fraid I have to cancel the dinner party this evening. Some important government business come up. Have had to call an urgent meeting here. We can't spare a whole evening so the chaps and I will eat at the Club."

"What about the wives?" She asked, thinking *I hope he doesn't expect me to entertain them.*

"Oh, they've been told. They understand when it's Party business."

"Well, that's fine." Emma replied thinking she would be able to see Carl after all. Etienne continued but she wasn't paying attention, planning how to get a message to Carl. He didn't like calls when his secretary was on duty.

Then she heard Etienne mention Carl's name.

"What did you say?"

"You haven't been listening. I was talking about Carl."

"What about Carl?" Had Etienne heard some gossip?" Had someone seen her and Carl together?

"Ja, well as I was saying, it's a shame Lavinia is away."

"She often goes away. Why is it a shame?"

"I've just told you."

"I didn't hear. What did you say?"

"I told you it's bad news."

"What's bad news?" She began chewing the sides of her thumb nail.

"I'm trying to tell you if you'll just give me a chance."

"Well, go ahead. I'm listening. What's the bad news? Has he taken his business elsewhere?"

"Ja, I suppose he has, in a manner of speaking."

"What on earth happened for him to do that? Did the two of you have an argument." They often did, over politics.

"Nie man! Nothing like that hey!"

"Well then. What's the problem?" she asked, feeling exasperated.

Silence. Then Etienne cleared his throat.

"Carl died last night."

Emma groped for a chair. There wasn't one. She leant against the wall and sank slowly to the floor, her face ashen, her body trembling as she heard Etienne's voice from the dangling receiver, far away and faint as if coming from the distant mountains.

"He apparently had a heart attack in bed last night. He was alone as I said, because Lavinia is away and the servants off duty. Poor chap." He shook the receiver. The line appeared dead. "Emma, are you there? Did you hear what I said or aren't you listening? Aren't you interested in the Roussouws? I know you don't like Lavinia much and of course neither you or I like Carl's politics. But he was my client and he was your doctor."

Silence.

"I said Carl Roussouw died last night. In his bed. I got the call first thing this morning. Would have told you earlier but was busy. Got caught up in important matters here."

Silence.

241

Etienne shook the phone at his end. "Emma. Are you there? Think the woman has hung up on me. Oh well, what the heck! Didn't realise she disliked Roussouw that much." he murmured, in an undertone.

Emma shook herself. "In his bed! What a shame." Her voice faint. "I'll send Lavinia some flowers and write a little note."

"I'd appreciate it if you'd do that. Well, anyway, must go now. Wasted enough time on this matter. See you later tonight. Oh! By the way. Don't forget it's the big rugby game tomorrow. Western Province playing Northerns. Looking forward to that hey. Ol' Carl would have enjoyed that game he went to Varsity in the Cape, y'know. Anyway, don't plan an early dinner." He laughed as he replaced the receiver.

Emma remained sitting on the floor. She heard the buzz of the phone as it dangled so reached up and set the receiver back on its cradle on the half moon marble table with curved brass legs while she thought of what she would say in the note to Lavinia. *I'll tell her how sorry I am her husband died last night. All alone. He might have died in my arms if my husband had been more considerate and not arranged a dinner party on the very night you're out of town! But it might have been awkward! Waking up with a dead lover in my arms.* Her thoughts raced on. She recalled the years with Carl and how much she had loved him. She began to cry hysterically and uncontrollably while looking out at the garden. A lazy bee buzzed around the jasmine but she smelt Carl's pipe. The sun was warm and bright but she felt cold and bleak.

Chapter 41

The telephone rang, picking up the receiver I heard coins dropping, some disturbance and then,

"This is N'tabu speaking. I have some very bad news." The line went dead. Not the police, I hoped. I put the receiver back on its cradle, waiting impatiently for it to ring again, with no way of contacting N'tabu. If he had called from his place of work I couldn't get back to him, he wasn't allowed incoming calls. There was no phone in Joshua's parent's house; I couldn't call there. In 1960 there was no electricity nor often running water in Soweto homes, let alone telephones. Besides, it had been a pay-phone. I would have to wait for him to call again.

At the first ring the second time I hurriedly picked up the receiver and again heard N'tabu's voice.

"It's Hanna," he said quickly before the line could be cut off again. "My father, she telephone from the police station at home and give the message to the madam at my work; she tell me that Hanna and the baby is dead."

I knew Hanna was expecting again. In their seven years of marriage, of the five children she had, only two survived and now she had died giving birth to a stilborn child.

"What will you do, N'tabu?" I felt wretched for him and the young girl who started married life with such hope.

"Hanna's mother will look after Samuel and Elsie, but she is very old amd my mother, she's not so very well." I knew Mtonya had chest trouble. Mother wrote from the farm telling me they had taken her to the hospital, suspecting T.B.

"I'm wanting to bring the chil'ren to town to live with me and Nellie but we have no house. They telling me I must be married before I can get a house. I think I mus' get married to Nellie now."

After the birth of Petrus, her firstborn, Nellie left the child in Rustenburg with her mother and managed to get another live-in job in Johannesburg. Once again, making an arrangement with her employer to

243

allow N'tabu to live on the premises for the price of his labour in the garden.

N'tabu and Nellie were married but it would be another five years before they were they allocated a house in Soweto however, by which time they had another boy, Philemon and two girls, Lettie and Lizzie. Hanna's children, Samuel and Elsie were sent from the farm and Nellie's four children brought from Rustenburg. Nellie gave up her live-in job, doing daily work instead, travelling every morning to the white suburbs to clean house, do laundry and care for the white women's children, leaving her own children during the long days, but at least they were together as a family at night.

It was about this time, when N'tabu and Nellie moved to Soweto, that we moved to Pretoria. We weren't to know then of the significance of this move; of the events that would unfold to complete the story of the three families. We settled in our new home. Bobby, Alexa and Victoria all attending new schools and making new friends.

Apartheid not only separated whites from blacks, it separated English from Afrikaners. According to the law white children were to be educated in their home language. Hetty's husband, Herman, an influential member of the ruling Nationalist Party, realising the limitations of education in the Afrikaans medium in the world scene, used his influence to circumvent the law and so his children were sent to English schools, and that is how Emma's grandson, Pieter, met Meg's grandson, Bobby. The boys became good friends, playing rugby together in winter and cricket in the summer.

"School... Sch o o o l!" The triumphant cry went up with supporters throwing straw-boaters in the air. Pieter, oblong ball tucked tightly under arm, dodging and diving past the opposition, threw himself across the line, scoring a try for the School.

A cathedral hush over the crowded field. Bobby placed the ball in preparation for the conversion. The school clock slowly chiming as he stepped slowly backwards. Pulling up slipped socks, wiping sweaty palms then running forward to kick. It lifted and rose in the clear air, high against the azure sky, the school dome silhouetted behind; then began its descent. Time suspended as it fell. The clock finished chiming, the silence palpable before the roar as the ball hit the ground, bouncing behind and between the two tall posts. Once again the cry of "School, Sch o o o

244

I," deafening, almost obliterating the shriek of the final whistle. The supporters running on the field carrying off their victorious team.

I met Pieter's mother, Hetty, but confess I didn't care for her but now we were on the same team, the School P.T.A. Now we would get to know each other better, so much better. I also met Hetty's Ma, Ouma Frobisher as she was affectionately called. I knew Pieter's father was a prominent member of the National Party.

The decade of the Sixties came to an end. A turbulent time. Oppression of black people intensified and their resistance solidified. Langa and Sharpeville happened. The Rivonia Treason Trial took place and Nelson Mandela imprisoned, to remain there for twenty-seven long years. Dr. Verwoerd, the Prime Minister who entrenched the Apartheid Doctrine, was shot, not by a black assassin as everyone assumed, but, we were told, by a deranged white man.

Chapter 42

It was Petrus, Nellie's eldest, who was the restless one and the brightest of all N'tabu's children. He spoke of better times to come and changes that must be made. His generation were not prepared to accept the continued denial of their rights, they were better informed than their parents and knew of the changes in American Civil Rights.

N'tabu and Nellie discouraged revolutionary talk. It worried them. Petrus was only sixteen. They didn't want trouble with the authorities because life was difficult enough, rising before dawn on windswept winter mornings with a long walk to the railway station then riding into the city with all the other commuters who provided cheap labour for whites. N'tabu and Nellie didn't question the social order. Samuel, Hanna's boy, was in the top grade at the Secondary School, working hard to become a teacher. He never concerned himself with politics or student protests.

"Our school choir has been invited to sing for the Secondary Schools in Pretoria," Samuel announced proudly, walking into the kitchen. N'tabu, eating his evening meal, shifted a lump of meat to the side of his mouth to reply, smiling encouragingly.

"That is good. You must look for Master Bobby. He go to that big school in Pretoria. Do you remember Master Bobby? It's a long time since you been to the farm, Samuel."

"Ja, I remember Master Bobby. We always fish in the dam when he come to the farm." Nellie served Samuel his dinner of stewed meat, spinach and *mielie pap*. He pulled out the wooden ladder-back chair and sat opposite his father.

"They asking the students at the school to answer questions about our education."

Nellie looked up from the cooker, alarm on her face. "You be careful, my son, don' you write nothing. You don' say nothing. You hear me? You can't trust these people. Who is asking anyway?" She stood with *mielie-pap* dripping from the wooden spoon.

"It'll be alright, it's quite in order, really. It's the social worker asking the questions, not the police." Samuel assured her, swallowing food hurriedly in his eagerness to explain. "The social worker, he say he wanna help us."

247

Nellie scraped the spoon against the side of the saucepan and moved it off the heat. "They say they wanting to help us, but what can they feel? They still got their nice houses and their big motor cars and their swimming pools. They can't feel for us blacks. It's best you say nothing."

Samuel shrugged at Nellie's outburst. They heard footsteps outside and Nellie put her finger to tightly closed lips while shaking her head, indicating to Samuel to keep quiet when Petrus walked in. She didn't want argument.

The Social Worker was interested in the Soweto school children's opinion of their education system, but the Government was not. The study was ignored by the authorities, in spite of the warning it gave of discontent amongst students. Protests were to come later. For the present Soweto appeared calm.

Samuel's school choir sang for privileged white children who, after the performance, as a gesture, served tea and doughnuts to the black visitors. Bobby and Samuel greeted each other. Samuel was reserved at first. Although proud of knowing a white boy he didn't want to appear forward. Bobby introduced Pieter. They talked of holidays on the farm.

"We were there last December for the holidays, Pieter and me. When are you going again, Samuel. What about the end of this year after the matric exams. We can all go down and have a jolly good time. What about it, hey!" he said, slapping Samuel on the shoulder.

Samuel grinned but shook his head. "I dunno, Master Bobby. I mus' get a job."

"Well that's OK, you can get a job after Christmas, but don't worry about it now, man, we'll work something out. It's a long time away and we still have exams to pass. And, by the way, you can cut out calling me 'master.'"

They shook hands, promising to keep in touch.

248

Chapter 43

"MR. ETIENNE FROBISHER AND SON, JAN, KILLED IN CAR ACCIDENT, DRIVING TO THEIR FARM IN NORTHERN TRANSVAAL." Headlines in the local newspaper. The car went over a bridge in a rainstorm, the report said. I visited Emma Frobisher.

She sat in her drawing-room on a straight-backed chair, head held high. Her shaking hands clenched a tightly rolled up lace-edged handkerchief. We spoke briefly of the accident then silence.

"He was always different, you know, my Jannie. He never joined the cricket game with the cousins when we gathered at Christmas on the farm, nor played touch-rugby at the cottage on the beach. Etienne so badly wanted him to excel at sport and would seek him out in some secluded spot where he escaped with a book.

She sighed, then continued. "He met Rupert at University. They were in the same Literature class. After graduating they took a flat together and have been together ever since. I suspected long ago their friendship was deep and emotional." She paused, her voice dropped to a whisper. I didn't reply. I think she almost forgot I was there.

"Once Etienne saw them holding hands and embracing, they thought they were alone. He never spoke directly to Jan about the matter, but raged at me and said it was my fault. 'You turned him into a sissy,' he accused, 'always fussing over him.' Or he blamed the university. 'Should never have sent him to that liberal English institution, he should have gone to Stellenbosch as I arranged before he changed his mind, or here in Pretoria, and learnt to be a man. His sin will be punished by God.'"

She turned to look straight at me. "I don't believe that, Kate. I told Etienne he was making God like a man. People do, you know, to make God easier to understand. I think mankind should aspire to being more God-like, don't you?"

She didn't seem to expect a reply but continued with her train of thought. I believe God is spiritual and not aware of man's sexuality and the material body that binds us. The Bible says God is Spirit and that He made man in His likeness. This body could not be His likeness." Etienne always quoted the Scriptures, you know." She sat quietly for a while then continued, speaking out her thoughts, "I believe spiritual love is shown in human kindness, consideration and compassion and Jan and Rupert expressed all of that." Neither of us spoke, then she whispered.

"Of course Etienne never agreed with me. We always argued over Jan and yet he never spoke directly to the boy and Jan never discussed with us his relationship with Rupert. I wished sometimes we could have talked about it." A tear rolled down her sunken cheek. She wiped it with her handkerchief.

"I always hoped Etienne would become more tolerant and when Rupert's annual visit to his mother in the Cape coincided with a trip Etienne had to make to the farm, I suggested that Jan go along with him. Jannie always loved the farm from when he was a small boy." She smiled softly.

"Jan agreed to go, albeit reluctantly. 'Pa will want me to shoot guinea-fowl or hunt buck with him and du Preez.' Du Preez is our manager on the farm," she explained. "'Try and understand your Pa a little,' I said to him. 'It would make me so happy if you two got along.' Well, he did what I asked and look what happened," shaking her head sadly.

She dried her eyes and composed herself as the maid brought in the tea on a silver tray.

She told me she would keep up the big house because her husband would have wanted that. His favourite pipe stood on the rack next to his arm chair. The books he was reading on the table at his side of the big double bed. Nothing was changed, as if she expected him to walk in, rub his hands together and call Freddy to bring him a cold lager.

And yet there was a subtle change. After the initial shock she seemed more at ease. She discontinued attending the morning coffee parties with the ladies from the Vroue Federasie.

"Ma, you really should continue working for the Party," Hetty admonished.

"I think I have done my bit," was her terse reply.

Because of Bobby and Pieter's friendship I made an effort with Hetty. We avoided political issues but had a common interest in the school. I called on her in connection with a committee project. Sophie swept the kitchen. She stopped her work, leaning on the broomstick as I called out a greeting through the open door.

"How are the children?" Sophie is a relative of Nellie's, her home also in Rustenburg.

Her usual cheerful face was downcast. "The baby is sick, ma'am."
She turned to Hetty. "Excuus ma'am, can I ask the madam a favour? Will
the madam let me have this week-end off instead of the end of the month?
I mus' take my child to the doctor. Las' night my brother, she bringing me
a message from home, she saying my mother, she is worried about the
child." Sophie sniffed and patted her nose with the edge of her white
starched apron. Her cap fallen awry in her agitation. She scratched her
hair then pulled her cap straight, wiping her open palm across her eyes.

Hetty looked up in alarm and placed her cup on the saucer, shaking
her head in agitation. "Sophie, that's impossible. How can you ask me for
time off when you know I have people for dinner on Saturday night and
the children have invited friends for a sleep-over and besides this Sunday
is our turn for tennis." Hetty and Herman played tennis with their
neighbours every Sunday afternoon. When their turn to host the tennis
party, Hetty made sure both Sophie and Moses were on duty. Sophie did
the teas and Moses helped Herman serve drinks and braai steaks. Herman
recently bought white gloves for the black hands.

Hetty argued. Sophie stood her ground, explaining her mother was
too old to manage the long walk and bus ride into Rustenburg to the
hospital.

"She has my other child, as well, Madam."

We knew Sophie didn't have a husband to call on because when she
became pregnant Hetty asked her about the father but Sophie admitted she
had no idea who he might be. It wasn't that Sophie was bad. She needed
the money, and the men needed the comfort.

Sophie returned to the kitchen and Hetty said, "Herman's not going to
be happy about Sophie taking time off. We had to let Miriam go, you
know. She began taking advantage. Herman is so busy with this
nomination and everything. He even forgot our wedding anniversary last
month. Can you believe it? I prepared a special meal you know, put the
sparkling Cape wine on the table, silver all nicely polished and lit candles
just before Herman got in from golf.

"What's this," he said, "some sort of celebration?"

"Did you forget?" I said.

"Forget what?" he said.

But before I could remind him the bally phone rang.

"Hello," says Herman. *"Ooh Jannie hoe gaan dit my vriend?* Ja
man the golf was good hey. We must have a game sometime..." They go
on and on talking about golf and my special dinner spoiling. Men! I tell

you. Anyway Jan says he has some news which can't wait and I hear Herman say, "OK, I better come over right away. Then he says to me, 'Sorry Babe, I must go. Someone heard he has the nomination and he can't talk on the phone, so he says! Did you ever! He says he's got political enemies. I can't believe that. I told him he doesn't have to worry, we don't have any dark secrets in our family. But who would want to hurt Herman?"

I shook my head in disbelief.

"Anyway, you best forget I told you about this nomination. It's supposed to be a big secret."

The telephone rang and Hetty left the dining room to answer it, her voice clearly audible.

"Ag, I'm so glad you called, hey Millie. I really am sorry, but I must postpone the dinner party on Saturday. Sophie has just told me she wants the weekend off, some story about the baby being sick. Most inconsiderate of her, but you can't expect consideration from them, I suppose. You do understand, don't you? I couldn't possibly manage a dinner-party without the girl. And Sunday is our turn for tennis as well," she wailed her voice rising. "Jurrah man, I don't know what Herman will say."

There was silence while Hetty's head nodded, listening to her friend commiserating. "Yes, I agree, they are getting cheeky. Someone told me her maid asked for a coffee-break mid-morning, if you don't mind. I can tell this one gets fed up if we are late finishing dinner. But I can't help it. Herman only gets in after seven most evenings." Once again silence then Hetty continued. "Ja, you're right, sometimes it's good to have a change, there are plenty of them looking for work."

Herman was doing well in politics as was predicted. An articulate public speaker who could sway his audience with fiery eloquence. I heard his name had been put forward for the nomination for the Hoerkrantz Constituency in a forthcoming By-election. Although popular there were some who considered him an upstart and were jealous of his success. There were those who didn't approve his outspoken, aggressive wife.

"A woman shouldn't have so much to say," they said.

Hetty replaced the receiver, returning to the tea table. Sophie continued sweeping the kitchen. We finished our discussion and I excused myself. Driving home I thought about Sophie's problems and I thought about the possibility of Herman becoming our Member of Parliament.

Chapter 44

Pretoria
Circa 1970

Hetty was not invited by Marta du Toit to the morning coffee party held after the Vroue Federasie meeting and that was where the trouble started. She had offended Marta when she had remarked at the previous committee meeting, that Herman had heard he had a good chance of being offered the nomination for the Hoerkrantz seat for the Nationalist Party in Parliament, knowing that Frans du Toit was also lobbying for it.

* * *

Old Ouma du Toit was up from Kimberley.

"She's a character that one, you wouldn't believe she was eighty-six last birthday," Marta said. "Jurrah man! but Ouma knows everybody, hey! A person just has to say a name and that will remind Ouma of someone she knew in Kimberley in 'the good old days', as she always says. I bet they weren't so good though."

Ouma was small and spry. Her thinning grey hair, parted in the middle was tightly pulled back into a bun at the nape of her neck. Her small face was etched with wrinkles from a lifetime spent in the Karroo. Her small fine-boned hands, brown spotted were knotted with blue veins. Her back was bent but her walk was nimble.

"Who'se this Hetty you was talking about?" Ouma asked Marta. The ladies from the Federasie had left, there were just Marta and Ouma and Marta's good friend Millie van der Merwe sitting around the table.

"Don't you remember Ouma? I told you before. Her Ma is Emma Frobisher and her Pa and boet were killed in a car accident about six months ago."

"No, my girl, you never told me before. I'd have remembered if you had because I know that name - Frobisher, it rings a bell, hey?"

"Well I'm sure I did tell you, because Hetty once said, when I told her that Frans' Ouma lived in Kimberley, that the Frobishers had relatives there, but anyway, it doesn't matter. Hetty's Ma and Pa, that's Emma and Etienne Frobisher, Ouma," she continued, turning to face Ouma making sure the old lady understood who she was talking about this time. "Well they came here from the Cape a long time ago, actually from Rondebosch

I believe. They had a family law business in Capetown. They say Emma is a gracious lady but I say she's a snob and Hetty takes after her. They look down on us Transvalers. Jy weet, the people from the Cape always think they're better than us."

Ouma stopped stirring her coffee and looked up,

"I thought the name Frobisher was familiar," she repeated. "The Frobishers of Rondebosch? Yurrah man, I knew them years ago, hey! They had cousins in Kimberley." Ouma picked up her cup and put it to her lips, blowing on the hot liquid and shaking her head in disbelief at the same time. "Fancy that! If they are the same family that is, but they must be, it's not such a common name, especially in Kimberley."

She swallowed a mouthful of coffee, returning the cup to the saucer while dribbles of liquid ran down her chin. Marta leant over and patted the old lady's face with a napkin, but she impatiently pushed her grand-daughter's hand away, her mind clearly on the past.

"Kitty Frobisher! That was the name. Her father was a big wheel in de Beers and his sister kept house for him and looked after Kitty. What was his sister's name now, man my memory is not so good hey! I can't remember nothing no more." She wrinkled her brow, turning her head to the side, trying to think. "Was it Connie? No, that wasn't it. But something like that. She was very English, hey! Hoity-toity, thought she was royalty... that's it! Queenie... That's what her name was," looking at Marta in triumph. "Us kids was scared to death of her you know. We wasn't allowed to use the front door, always had to go to the back like the kaffirs, but when our Ma's were there, well then she would be sweet as watermelon *konfyt*, hey!" She smiled as she shook her head.

"But then they left Kimberley." Ouma continued, "Kitty's dad took her and Queenie back to England after his brother in Capetown, died. People said he didn't like that Dr. Jameson and thought the country was heading for war, and he was right, as it turned out. Those bally Englishmen, Rhodes and his pal Jameson and the rest of the Uitlanders, them it was that caused the war, not President Kruger or the Boers. Rhodes wanted the gold and the diamonds for the Empire." Ouma shook her head sadly. "If only..."

Marta interrupted. "Ouma, you were telling us about the Frobishers of Rondebosch."

"Ooh ja! That's right, so I was, so I was. Well that Frobisher boy, Kitty's cousin, came up to Kimberley from Capetown on a holiday, and what a good looking fellow he was hey! Jurrah! All the girls fancied him I can tell you."

Millie wagged her finger, "Now Ouma Nessie, did you also fancy him?"

"Me? Of course not, *domkop*, I was only about six years old at the time. Too young to think of boys."

"Nie Millie," Marta interrupted, "don't you know, Ouma only had eyes for Oupa du Toit. They were always together. Oupa told me himself before he died."

Ouma sat with fingers drumming the table, gazing through the open window on to the garden a distant look in her eyes.

"Ja, Oupa Frans and I was always together but we was just good pals in those days," she said, smiling wistfully, then continued after another prodding from Marta.

"Shame hey! I remember now, Kitty's cousin took a shine to that coloured girl who was a friend of Lisa Patrickson. What was her name again - that coloured girl? I remember her mother's name though, it was from the Bible, Ruth she was called. Funny hey! Some things I remember and some I forget. Ruth was a servant rreelly of Lisa's mother in the early days on the diggings and her daughter, man what was her name again, anyway she and Lisa grew up together. People didn't like the idea of a coloured girl mixing with us, but Lisa always insisted. Man I wish I could think of her name, hey! Anyway, it doesn't rreelly matter," she added, scratching her head. "But what did they call her?" She sucked in her cheeks and wrinkled her forehead trying to recall then suddenly smiled and said, "Sara! That's right, now I remember. It was Sara. She was pretty hey, I must admit, even though she was a coloured. But Ruth, was black, black as the ace of spades, as the saying goes! And her brother! Jurrah man! He was a reel *kaffir*. But Sara had light skin and blue eyes. She took after her father who, some said, was a farmer but I don't believe that. Most probably he was a missionary or an uitlander, they like the black women."

They sat in silence for a while then the old woman continued.

"You wouldn't have known that Sara was half black if you hadn't seen her mother and brother. And that was the trouble you see. This cousin of Kitty's, he fancied Sara on the picnic, couldn't take his eyes off her, talked to her all day. Then what a storm there was. Jurrah man! It rained that day, cat's and dogs, as the saying goes. We all had to get in the covered wagon. But it was good fun eh! Ja man, those were the good old days." The old lady began mumbling to herself.

"Ja, Ouma, we know those were the good old days." Marta winked at Millie as they listened to Ouma reminisce.

"But what were you saying about the coloured girl, Sara? Did she marry your friend Kitty Frobisher's cousin from Capetown?" Marta's interest aroused.

"What?" shouted Ouma. Marta repeated her question.

"Oh ja, I was telling you about that handsome boy. No, they didn't marry. He wanted to, mind you, even after he found out she was a coloured. But his mother objected, and prevented the marriage in the end. His mother was a 'de Villiers' and had married the Englishman, Frobisher who came out to Capetown from England to work with his uncle in the family's law business. Plenty of money; they had big estates in England. Old man Frobisher didn't care, they said, if his son wanted to marry a coloured girl from Kimberley, but shame hey, he died suddenly, it was his heart they said, and his wife, Magriet, I remember her name, it's funny, isn't it, sometimes I can remember names and other times I forget." She shook her head then smiled. "Ja, I remember that picnic on the Modder River as if it was yesterday. They roasted a lamb on a spit and we had a *braaivleis* and *koeksusters* and then..."

"And then what, Ouma?" Marta prodded. The old lady frowned at her grand-daughter so Marta patted her hand encouragingly. "Come on, finish the story. How did Magriet prevent the marriage?"

"Ooh ja, I was telling you about Magriet. She took her son off to England on a long holiday to visit the family there." There was a deep silence in the room broken by the sound of the doves in the poplar trees, then Ouma continued. "Shame hey! I heard after the war that Kitty and Queenie both died in the 'flu epidemic in England.

The two younger women refilled their coffee cups and settled the old lady in a rocking chair, encouraging her gossip.

"What happened then, Ouma? What happened to the coloured girl? Did she and Kitty's cousin get together again after he came back from England?"

"No, there was a big misunderstanding hey! He asked her to wait for him but his Ma wrote to the girl and told her to get out of his life, or something like that, so she went and married Sol Meintjies, you know that coloured fellow who used to fix my Pa's furniture?" Marta shook her head. Ouma was getting mixed up, how could she possibly remember Ouma's father or the coloured man who fixed his furniture? But she didn't say anything to interrupt the story and the old lady continued.

"Ja, she married Sol and I did hear that Kitty's cousin, the Frobisher boy, married some girl from Capetown, also a de Villiers, a distant cousin on his mother's side. Magriet, arranged the match but he wasn't happy,

258

they said. Then he was killed in a shooting accident something about his gun going off while he was cleaning it but people talked and some said it wasn't an accident. They had a child, a boy I was told, born after he was killed and raised by the mother and Magriet but we lost touch with the Frobishers in the Cape." She sat in silence for a while, then spoke as if thinking aloud. "I wonder what happened to the family and where that boy is now, shame hey! brought up without his Pa." She shook her head thoughtfully then continued, "My word I expect he would be quite an old man now, if he's still alive that is. How the years go by." The old woman's head dropped forward and she dozed off in the rocker

Molly, in the laundry room off the kitchen, leant over the ironing board, listening intently. She was from Rustenburg and a cousin of Sophie and Nellie.

Marta's curiosity was aroused. The Frobisher family sounded interesting, turning to her friend, speaking softly not to disturb Ouma. "What if the coloured girl had a child by this fellow Frobisher, Millie? There could be a connection with Hetty, serve her right, if we discovered coloured blood in the family the stuck up bitch."

"But Frans' Ouma said the Frobisher cousin hadn't married the coloured girl."

"I know that, but Ouma has a rotten memory, she may have forgotten, or mixed it all up."

Millie raised her eyebrows, opening her mouth to reply when the phone rang, waking Ouma. That was the end of the conversation.

But Marta remembered her Ma had an aunt who had lived in Rondebosch all her life, she might know of the Frobisher family. She wrote to Great Aunt Bessie in Capetown.

A reply came two weeks later. Marta dialed Millie's number and read the letter over the phone. Molly stopped sweeping to listen.

"Yes, my dear," Marta, reading from the letter, "the Frobisher family were well-known in Rondebosch. I remember my Ma talking about the scandal when Magriet's son, Paul, wanted to marry a coloured girl from Kimberley. But no, that match was definitely broken up. I do recall hearing the coloured girl married some coloured fellow in Kimberley, never did hear his name, or hers for that matter. Leastways, if I did, I don't remember.

259

"Paul came back to Capetown after the holiday abroad with his Ma and went straight to Kimberley to find she had married someone else and already expecting a baby. It couldn't have been his child because he had been away more than six months, and she only about three months pregnant. Magriet was so relieved I can tell you. I remember overhearing her telling my Ma all about it, and then later we heard the baby died anyway." Marta paused to turn the page, then continued.

"Ja, Frans' Ouma is quite correct, Magriet did introduce Paul to a second cousin on the de Villiers' side of the family and they married and had a boy, but Paul was killed in a shooting accident. Some said he took his own life because he was unhappy in his marriage. He never knew that his wife was pregnant, the baby was born after his death so Magriet moved in with his wife and helped raise the child. They called him Etienne. He was devoted to his Ouma and broken hearted when she..."

Millie interrupted. "What did she say the child's name was?"

Marta ran her eyes back over the page, then repeated, "'They called him Etienne.' That was the name of Emma Frobisher's husband, Etienne Frobisher." Marta stopped reading, lips pursed, head nodding thoughtfully.

"Don't stop, what else does she say?" said Millie.

Marta returned to the letter in her hand and continued, "'He was at school with one of my brothers, your great uncle Hendrick, and we were all friends growing up. I remember when Etienne married Emma Meintjies. There was a big wedding arranged but they had to cancel it because his mother took ill suddenly. Emma came from Kimberley but never talked about her family. We all lost touch after that because the War broke out in Europe and after the war I heard that Emma and Etienne moved to the Transvaal.'"

Marta dropped the letter.

"Halleluhia! What about that hey?" Think of it - Kitty's cousin, Paul, who fancied the coloured girl, had a son named Etienne who married a girl from Kimberley - Emma Meintjies. Ouma said the coloured girl, prevented from marrying Kitty's cousin, married a coloured man whose name was Sol Meintjies. Maybe... she frowned and tapped her forehead with the envelope. "Maybe Sara the coloured girl, who married Sol Meintjies, had a daughter who went to live in Capetown and met and married Paul's son Etienne. It can't be coincidence that Hetty's parents have those same names - Etienne and Emma!"

"Jurrah man, Marta. What are you saying?"

260

"I'm saying that it's possible that Hetty's Ma, Emma Frobisher, is coloured."

"Nie man, she doesn't look coloured."

"That's so, but remember they said the girl Sara didn't look coloured. Her father was white and she resembled him and if Emma Meintjies is Sara's daughter, then it's possible she took after Sara and Sara's white father.   Ouma said no one would have guessed Sara had black blood if they hadn't known her mother, the kaffir woman and her black brother. It can happen like that.   Anyway, come to think of it Hetty
is dark complexioned and has that frizzy hair."

"Ja, you're right and what about Pieter, Hetty's boy, look how dark he
is.

Marta's face flushed, hardly pausing for breath she said, "Look Millie, come over for coffee. Ouma is having her afternoon rest. We better not tell her our suspicions you know what she's like she'll talk." She put the phone back on the hook. Molly slipped quietly out the back door.

"Molly, where are you?   Where is that girl," she complained, mumbling impatiently under her breath. "They are never there when you want them."

Molly walked back into the kitchen.

"You called ma'am?"

"Yes, I did. *Mevrou* Millie is coming over for coffee, set the tray and we will have it outside on the stoep."

The two women sat on the garden swing. Molly served coffee and rusks on a tray then took out the silver polish, removing all the silver plate to the lawn at the side of the house, shaded from the hot afternoon sun and hidden from the front stoep by the angle of the wall, listening intently to the conversation of the two white women, while polishing the family silver.

The two women discussed the letter again then Marta said, "We'd better not tell anyone."

Millie's head shook, vigourously.   "Of course not," she agreed, refraining from mentioning she had already spoken to her sister about Marta's suspicions. Millie eventually stood up to leave and Marta called Molly to take the tray.

"I don't know why she has to clean the silver this afternoon, she was supposed to clean the upstairs windows.

Marta brooded over the letter then confided in her husband.

They were having drinks before dinner. Frans lifted the cut-glass decanter, filling two glasses with wine and listening attentively, but cautioned her as he handed her the drink.

"We will have to be very careful. This could be slanderous, but hell man, I would like to be able to discredit that Herman Kruger, the bloody upstart. He's full of himself since he married Hetty Frobisher, using her family's money to further his political aims. And you say Hetty says he has already been offered the nomination for the Hoerkrantz seat? We'll see about that!" He held up his glass and swallowed a mouthful of the golden liquid.

"Anyway, Marta. Remember what I say. Don't tell anyone, you hear? Not even your best friend, Millie van der Merwe, in fact especially not her, she's got a big mouth."

Marta was saved from replying by the sound of the dinner bell. She stood up and they walked together into the dining-room. Molly carried in the leg of lamb and put it in front of Frans, then moved aside, ready to pass the dinner plates. Frans began sharpening the knife.

"Where's Ouma?"

"She wasn't well today so I sent dinner to her room but Molly says she's sleeping now."

"And where are the kids?"

"They're at a party. So it's just the two of us," she said, smiling coyly at her husband in the flickering candle light.

Frans clearly wasn't in romantic mood, he put the steel down and picked up the bone-handled fork, jabbing it into the joint, ready to carve. "Sneaky little upstart!" he muttered under his breath, thoughts on his political rival. Then looking up at Marta, "We'll have to be careful but just leave this to me. I know who to contact."

Molly returned to the kitchen.

After dinner Frans retired to his study, closed the door and began making phone calls. Marta walked into the kitchen. She dialed Millie's number on the other line while Molly scoured the roasting pan at the sink.

"Millie. I'm so glad you're there," whispering breathlessly. "Frans says we must be careful and not tell a soul about - you know what." Head nodding.

* * *

Frans did have considerable influence in the Party and had his loyal supporters. Using the resources he had, he set about making enquiries in Kimberley. Lena was interviewed. She was an old woman by now.

"Of course I remember that Emma. Little bitch! She never wanted her father and me to marry, was always jealous. Then she runs away and gives her father all that trouble. She was no bleddy good, I'm telling you." holding out some pictures.

"Jurrah! Is this the brother?" The Special Branch man said, snatching up the photograph. "Where's he now?"

Lena leant against the doorpost, her once fizzed out hair so thick and coarse, was now sparse and pulled back from her furrowed brow. Her nose quivered like an iguana scenting prey and her eyes swooped from side to side, sunk deep in her skull which pivoted on her creased and wrinkled neck. Her long, narrow tongue darted out to lick dry lips from which a cigarette bobbled.

"Ja, that's Jakob. He got into bad company in the township and the Patrickson family sent him to their son Harry's farm. I heard he married a Xhosa woman." She screwed up her eyes against the rising smoke of the cigarette, squinting at the newspaper clipping handed to her. A picture of Emma taken at a Party rally shortly before Etienne died.

"Ja, that's her alright. Stuck-up bitch. Caused me a lot of trouble. Jy weet, groot geraas. Run away and never told her old Pa. So she married a white boy hey? An Afrikaner with the name Frobisher? That's a good one." Derisive laughter. "English snob I bet. She always thought herself too good for the likes of us." She sniffed and wiped her nose with her hand then took more family photographs out of the pocket of her floral wrap-around overall and handed them to the member of the Special Branch in exchange for an envelope he passed her.

"Ooh ja, that's Emma Frobisher." The policeman agreed as he compared the picture of the young girl, smiling into the camera, her arms around both parents and a black youth kneeling in front of the group, with the recent newspaper cutting of an older woman. There was a wood and iron house next to the railway tracks, in the background.

After the man from the Special Branch left Lena looked up and saw her neighbour Edie sitting on her front *stoep*.

Edie called out.

263

"You got visitors, hey? Someone from the city?"

Lena laughed. "You won't believe what I jus' heard."

Edie pulled her old body out of the basket chair and waddled to the railings, her curiosity aroused.

"Com' on over for coffee and tell me about it."

Lena pushed the envelope into her overall pocket with the squashed packet of cigarettes and box of matches and shuffled down the pathway in down-at-heel bedroom slippers, through Edie's front gate and up the front steps. She saw Edie's son's old Ford parked at the side of the house with the hood up, but didn't notice Lucas' head in the engine.

Lena and Edie had been neighbours for years and Edie knew all the trouble she had with Emma. She sat on the other basket chair, taking out the packet of cigarettes and offered Edie one. She lit it, with one for herself then, inhaling deeply, put her head back and blew a smoke ring into the air, while passing Edie the newspaper cutting of Emma in Pretoria. Edie's mouth fell open, nearly dropping her cigarette. Lena proceeded to relate the whole story, everything the Special Branch man had told her, with some added embellishments of her own.

Lucas heard excitement in the women's voices and walked to the side of the house standing next to the wall but discreetly out of sight. He mumbled to himself,

"Heleluliah! Jakob's long-lost sister, living as a white woman! I mus' get out to the farm and tell ol' Jakob." He walked back to his automobile and wiped oil off his hands with a grubby cloth while shaking his head in amazement.

In Pretoria someone leaked the story to the press.

Chapter 45

Hetty

Pretoria
Circa 1970.

"Ma! Ma!" I shout, my voice rises shrilly and echoes through the house.

"The madam she gone to the shops, Miss Hetty, she take Bruno, for a walk. Oew! But she spoil that puppy hey!" Philomena laughs loudly her body shaking as she walks from the kitchen, wiping her hands on her apron. "But, she say she won't be so long. If you like to wait in the Master's study I can bring you some tea." She puts both arms out to me. "Oew! It is so nice to see you." I glance at my watch while chewing my thumb nail then accept the offer.

Philomena began working for Ma and Pa before I was born. Over the years Ma remained elegant and slender, anxious and alert - a *gemsbok*, while Philomena grew plumper; her cheeks round and soft, her bosom ample. It was she who had comforted me when I fell and grazed my knees or in whom I confided when my best friend, Bessie, was mean.

I pace the hallway between the staircase and front door then follow Philomena into the study and watch as she carefully places the tray, set with the Royal Albert teacups and silver teapot, on the *imbuia* coffee table, with carved ball and claw feet. I sit on Pa's reclining chair next to the window, squeezing my hands. The spicy aroma of cinnamon rises from Philomena's freshly baked *melktert* but I have no appetite.

"Oew! Miss Hetty, you are crying. Is there some trouble with the chil'ren?"

"Ag no! Philomena, it is nothing," I wipe my eyes and push the folded newspaper down behind the cushion. I have always confided in Philomena but THIS I cannot tell her. Philomena senses I want to be alone and returns to the kitchen. Through the open door I hear the swish-swish of Freddy's movements and smell the pungent paraffin as he polishes the parquet on hands and knees. From the garden, scented stocks and a wooing wood pigeon. Ming, the cat, her lithe body throbbing, jumps up and settles on my lap.

I pour the tea, my hand shaking as I think about what my friend Velma has told me and what I have read in the morning papers. Velma heard all about it from Millie van der Merwe, she said, a good friend of Marta du Toit. What will happen now? Pa is no longer here to protect us. Since his death so much has changed. Especially Ma.

"Ooh God! help me!" I whisper, recalling what Herman told me the night of our wedding anniversary.

* * *

I had let Miriam off early and prepared a special meal myself feeling excitement as I placed the bottle of sparkling Cape wine wrapped in a white damask napkin, in the silver bucket on the centre of the polished walnut table. I had put a single rose in a silver vase and everything glowed in the soft candlelight as I waited for Herman to come home. He was playing golf and had left early that morning, before I was even awake. I heard his car and went to the front door to greet him, taking his hand and leading him to the dining room. I remember Herman's look of surprise and his words,

"What's this? Some sort of celebration?"

"Did you forget?" I ask, my voice shaking.

"Forget what?"

"It's our..." but before I got the words out the telephone rang and Herman answered it.

"Hello. Ooh! *Jannie, hoe gaan dit, my vriend*?... Ja man, the golf was good, hey. We must have a game sometime. What's that?... You got some news?... O.K. I better come over right away?" He replaced the receiver and turned to me.

"Sorry, Babe, but I must go. That was Jan van der Merwe from my office. He says someone has heard that I've been offered the nomination for Hoerkrantz but he says he can't talk on the phone because you never know who's listening. I've got political enemies, you know. There were others after this seat and they'd stab me in the back, given the opportunity. Sorry about the party. Save it for another time, O.K?"

"But it's our wedding ann..."

Herman was already out the door.

* * *

The cat springs off my knee and jumps on to the window sill, then begins licking her fur the way cats do. I glance at the grandfather clock as it strikes the hour and wonder when Ma will be coming home. I think about my children, Pieter in Grade Twelve at one of the most prestigious schools in the country, Katrina a year younger at a well-known girls' school and Susie attending my old university. *What will happen now?* I wonder then quietly chide myself, *No, I mustn't worry, Herman will know what to do.* Just then I hear footsteps on the back porch and Ma's voice speaking to Philomena in the kitchen. The puppy bounds in, sending Ming scuttling out the open french door. I notice, as Ma enters the room, how vulnerable she looks, and yet she has a spring in her step, almost as if a burden has been lifted.

"I hope you haven't been waiting long, I walked to the shops instead of driving, it's such a lovely day." Ma bends to pick up Bruno and fondles him as she takes a seat behind Pa's desk.

"Have you seen the morning papers?" I thrust the newspaper into her hands.

"No, I haven't actually. I stopped taking the papers after Pa died, the news is so depressing, you know. I heard on the radio this morning that there were more riots in Soweto yesterday. School children marching in protest against their inferior school system and the police fired on them, even as they ran away. I turned it off, can't bear to listen. There is so much violence, so much hatred." She puts Bruno on the floor and shakes her head as she adjusts her reading glasses hanging on a gold chain and reaches out to take the newspaper.

She reads the large black headlines and sees the pictures on the front page of our family at a reception shortly before Pa was killed. There is another, beneath it, of herself years ago but clearly recognisable, standing with her arms around two people, a dark skinned young man next to them.

"Sol and Sara Meintjies," says the caption, "with their son and their daughter Emma, taken outside their house in the coloured township near Kimberley many years ago. Emma, of course, is the widow of the well-known lawyer, Etienne Frobisher. Their daughter, Hetty is married to Herman Kruger who has been nominated for..." The story elaborates the family history but Emma stops reading and looks at me, despair on her face.

"I thought after your Pa died I didn't have to worry anymore." she whispers. "That my past wouldn't interest anyone now," she continued, dropping her voice still lower. She stretches out her arms to me. But I turn away. I run out of the house to my car and drive to Herman's office in the Union Buildings.

"Herman will know what to do. Herman will know what to do," I sob hysterically.

I park the car then run into the gloomy interior and up the stairs and am about to enter his office when I hear voices and see, through the crack in the door, that Herman is slumped back in his chair, talking to Jannie, newspapers strewn across his desk.

"What the hell am I going to do? My career is in ruins, man. I got the nomination for the Hoerkrantz seat, which I'm bloody sure I would have won, and now my future as a member of Parliament is finished. Bloody hell! The disgrace. What can I do?" He runs his hands through his hair.

"There's only one bleddy thing you can do, you must divorce Hetty as quickly as possible and salvage your career. Call a press conference and come clean right away. Tell them you were deceived by that old woman, Emma Frobisher, Hetty's Ma. That you had no idea her grandmother was a black woman."

"But... but what about my kids?"

Just like Herman, I whisper to myself, *putting his kids first. 'He's always been a good father, never sparing himself nor any expense for them. Ja, Herman will know what to do.* I chew frantically on my thumbnail.

"You can't worry about your family. You will have to sacrifice them. The Cause and your career are more important, *jy weet.* You must do this for the sake of the Party. You have to distance yourself from this scandal at once."

I see Herman stand and pace the floor, chin jutted, his right arm punching the air, punctuating his words.

"What can I bloody well DO? Power almost within my grasp. Power to further separate development. Separating the races, it's the right thing to do. Power to entrench our superiority and ensure the purity of our race and..."

He stops in mid-sentence, then thrusts up both arms,

"My God. What have I bloody well DONE? My own children tainted with the blackman's inferiority. Susie so bright and strong Pieter and my beautiful, my darling - Katrina." He runs his hands through his hair, his head hangs down. "I'd hoped he'd become a Springbok one day. He plays for the school's First Team, y'know. But now..." His voice drops. And I remember how we had both campaigned so vigorously against integrated sport in spite of the temptation of international recognition.

With both hands pushed deep into his pockets, he paces the floor again while I listen.

"Hetty and the children will now be classified as coloured under the Population Registration Act. They'll have to leave my house," his voice shakes in an unusual display of emotion, "because Hetty and the children will not be allowed to live in a 'white' area under the Group Areas Act. In fact," he pauses, taking in the reality of what he is saying, "Hetty and I may no longer live together under the Immorality Act." He hesitates... "nor even remain married under the Prohibition of Mixed Marriages Act." He stops pacing. There is silence and then he continues quietly, his voice trailing to a whisper, while I strain to hear.

"Maybe we should emigrate to another country," and walking around his desk, he sits down.

I softly clap my hands, whispering, "Oh thank God, thank you God. I knew it. I knew Herman would know what to do."

Jannie looks up, frowning and I hold my breath. There is silence then Herman's composure returns and he strikes his fist on the desk, "Nie, by God, I cannot leave my fatherland and in any case it wouldn't bloody well work," his voice shakes, "making love to a coloured woman! Hell no! I can NEVER make love to that woman - to Hetty, never EVER again!"

I turn and run. I run down the staircase, out the building and across the manicured lawns bordered by brilliant beds of bright flowers. I run until, out of breath, I stop under a Flamboyant tree aflame with scarlet blossom like drops of blood, blowing about with the wind. They fell all around me as I stand panting, gasping for air, feeling the pain piercing my chest. I walk slowly to my car and drive away from the Government buildings and all they stand for; all I had believed in. I drive to a quiet spot at the top of the ridge to think about what I must do. Herman has unwittingly given me an idea. I will take Ma and the kids and emigrate - get away from this place.

Poor Ma, I was mad with her when I read the newspapers this morning. I recall times Miriam annoyed me when she asked permission to have her children to stay in school holidays, and now I understand why. It was the guilt I felt about apartheid. I didn't allow myself then to think about the break-up of Miriam's family, but I am forced now to think about the break-up of my own.

Clouds bank, blocking the sun while lightning jags the sky followed by threatening thunder. The rain falls. It splatters the windscreen then runs down the glass. I wipe my hand across my face. The storm passes as suddenly as it began, and I look over the tops of the trees to the veld, stretching to the Magaliesberg on the far horizon, deep rocky crags purple shadowed, serrate the sky. In the middle distance, the Monument to the Voortrekkers, those Boer men and women who trekked away from the Cape nearly one hundred and forty years ago - away from the hated British rule into the interior, to face hardships and hostile natives and to build a nation. The great granite monument reaching upwards, penetrates the sky and dominates the landscape. I once believed it a symbol of the aspirations of my people but now I see it as a different symbol as Herman's words penetrate my mind and dominate my thoughts.

I drive up the driveway of Ma's house and look up at the sky and this time I see a cloud tipped by sunlight reflected in a trailing multi-coloured band dissolving into the mist in the valley and for a wonderful moment I feel a sense of optimism and uplift and a promise of hope for the future.

Chapter 46

Hetty and the children left Herman's house and moved in with Emma, but Emma was also preparing to move. She was also now officially classified as "coloured", a second-class citizen and could not live in a "white" area. These were the laws Etienne helped draft. Her beautiful home was to be sold.

There was the problem of the children's education. They must leave the government schools which were for white children only. Katrina transferred to the Convent and Hetty consulted with Pieter's Headmaster who explained that the present laws of the land must be obeyed.

"One day, I hope, these repressive laws will be repealed. I believe change will come but it will take time. We must work for peaceful change. It does seem, sometimes, change will never happen but right will win."

He arranged for Pieter to be tutored separately and to write the public exam separated from other white boys.

In the midst of the drama unfolding in Emma and Hetty's lives into which we had been drawn because of Pieter and Bobby's friendship, Uncle Harry died on the farm.

"We're going to miss the old man," Davey wrote, "especially Ma, but she is not well either. She would like to move Pretoria and live with you."

Mother arrived and settled in. I told her about the scandal that had rocked Pretoria. She shrugged, not particularly interested.

"I don't read newspapers, my eyesight is too bad."

"But this is about Bobby's good friend, Pieter's family." I explained, "And the news has caused such a stir because Pieter's father is a prominent Nationalist. 'It has been revealed that the mother-in-law of Mnr. Herman Kruger' is a coloured woman who has lived as a white person, concealing that her grandmother was actually black!'" I quoted.

Mother nodded absently.

"You must meet Pieter's Ouma, I'm sure you will like her. You do remember Pieter don't you? He spent the last school holidays on the farm with us." Mother looked vague.

"I'm not sure dear. The children have so many friends, I get mixed up."

"Well anyway," I continued, "they have been pals since starting High school together. Bobby is really upset. It's so unjust. He asked me to

271

invite Pieter's Mum and Ouma for tea this afternoon. He wants you to meet them." I had to shout, Mother being a little deaf.

"I'm not very sociable, you know Kate, since living on the farm. Bobby's friend's Ouma sounds rather posh, mixing with Cabinet Ministers and the like. Too posh for me, I think,"

"Nonsense, she is not at all like that."

But Mother wasn't listening. She sat staring into the middle distance, then said, "Speaking of injustices, I had a very dear friend once who was coloured. She went to the Convent with me, in fact our mother's were also friends and, although no apartheid laws in those days, people were prejudiced and could be cruel. Although my friend did well at school she couldn't get a decent job and then she had family problems so she ran away from Kimberley. I heard, years later, she went to Capetown but I never heard from her again. That was a long time ago." Shaking her head pensively, she went on, "anything could have happened to her. but I expect she married and probably lives in a coloured township somewhere, like District Six. I believe they are talking about making District Six into a white area. Fancy that, after all these years. What about the families living there? Shame, they don't consider people, just bulldoze their houses and move them out." Shaking her head again. "I remember once when my friend..." Like so many of Mother's stories I'd probably heard this one many times, I usually encouraged her but Hetty's car turned into our driveway.

I put up my hand, "Sorry Mother, visitors arriving, you'll have to tell me about your friend some other time. As a matter of fact I have been thinking that while you are here we should go through those diaries Grandma gave me and the letters and papers we found in Grandfather's house. I always meant to read them but know it will consume me once I start and quite honestly I never seem to have time," hurriedly folding the newspaper and pushing it out of sight under a cushion. I walked across the lawn to greet the visitors.

There was a change in Pieter's Ouma. She looked frail and thin like, *yellow leaves, or none, or few, do hang / Upon those boughs which shake against the cold,* I thought. Hetty - was also changed, appearing crushed, as if the problems of the last few weeks weighed her down.

I took Ouma Emma's arm and we walked towards the chairs and the table set for tea. I helped her to a seat next to Mother, who turned to face her. As I began introductions I noticed the expression on Mother's face change, from polite friendliness to amazement and disbelief. I turned to

272

Pieter's Ouma and saw a similiar expression. A joint intake of breath, then Mother stood, stretching out her arms and they embraced. Hetty and I shook our heads, staring. The two boys, mouths full of *koeksusters*, gaped.

Talk, tears and laughter. Mother and Emma, caught up on the lost years.

"Well, at least something good has come out of this," from Hetty. Quite a concession, I thought.

Emma was the friend who had run away from Kimberley. Emma was Jakob's sister, and therefore N'tabu's aunt. I was overwhelmed.

"I should have considered Jakob," Emma sighed.

Mother disagreed, "you don't have to worry about Jakob, he has been happy all these years."

Emma wiped her eyes, "Jakob accepted who he was, I didn't."

There was one thing the government couldn't take from Emma, her inheritance from Etienne and Jan, which was considerable. She was a wealthy woman. Hetty, on the other hand, had very little after her divorce, being considered the guilty party, and as the law favoured the husband, and Herman owned all the assets and felt no obligation towards her, her settlement was small.

Emma began to tell her story. She told of the argument with Lena and leaving Kimberley. She told of her meeting with Etienne.

"I always felt his face familiar, as if I'd met him before. I realise now it was that photo of Paul, the likeness to his father was startling. Do you remember that day, Meg, when we found that photo in Ma's drawer? She was so angry and snatched the picture away."

She told how she heard of Gerry's death from Etienne who met him briefly in South West. "I was terrified Etienne would contact you Meg, and it would all come out. I intended telling Etienne everything, but at the right moment." A pause, then she continued, "there never seemed to be a right moment." After we left Capetown and moved to the Transvaal, he was so involved in politics and apartheid, I was too afraid to tell him the truth."

Emma's revelations drew Hetty closer to her mother. "I never understood Ma, you know. She was so brittle and distant. Never letting herself go. Everything she said sounding carefully scripted. So perfect, I couldn't live up to her. A barrier between us. I understand now.

"In a strange way," Emma confided to Mother, "of course I regret the pain I've caused the family but it is a relief to have this burden taken from me. I never understood Hetty, she always seemed more Etienne's child than mine. So passionate about politics - apartheid the only way. On paper it looked reasonable, dividing the country into ethnic societies, allowing people to vote in their own states. It was never intended to be fairly divided, the homelands were never viable. White people made sure they kept the riches."

They sat quietly. Then Emma continued, "I was afraid to talk to Hetty about my convictions in case I gave myself away. I did the wrong thing, of course. I thought I could run away from my problems and that everything would come right. I didn't want to suffer like Ma, but of course, you don't escape by running away, life doesn't work like that. I have just imposed more suffering on my family."

"You did what you thought was right at the time. Why shouldn't you have tried to better yourself? No one can blame you for that my dear." Mother leant over, taking Emma's hand. "Don't torture yourself."

"I would like to see Jakob but I don't suppose he wants to see me." Hetty and I walked into the room, hearing the last part of the conversation.

"As a matter of fact I was waiting for an opportunity to speak to you about Jakob," Mother continued, "Davey phoned to say Jakob had heard the news from an old friend living next door to Lena in Kimberley. He told Jakob that Lena had had a visit from a stranger with pictures of Emma taken at a diplomatic reception in Pretoria. Anyway, it appears that Jakob would like to see you." I watched Emma and Hetty's faces for reaction to this news. Emma's showed consternation but, hearing Jakob wished to see her, she smiled. Hetty's face was stiff.

"Davey also said that if you want to go down they can accommodate you all." Mother walked over and put her arms about Emma.

"I think we should go, don't you Hetty?" Emma glanced at her daughter.

"No, Ma." Her expression like stone.

I told them about my many holidays on the farm and of my friendship with N'tabu, not realising quite how closely our families were connected, going back to our great-grandmothers. Mother and Emma talked about their mothers, Lisa and Sara and their grandmothers, Anna and Ruth. Hetty heard about the rape.

"Alright, Ma, if it's what you want. I'll go to the farm and we'll take the children."

274

That would be a true test for Hetty, I thought.

"Why don't we all go together," suggested Emma. She was looking at Mother, looking for support when she faced Jakob.

Mother shook her head, "No, Emma. I think you should go alone with your family. But, I tell you what," she paused and we all waited for her to finish, "we could follow later."

Chapter 47

We visited the farm and found Emma and Jakob had healed their hurt. Hetty accepted her new relatives but, I think she was relieved they would soon be leaving the country for ever. It was the day before the end of our stay, and after breakfast we decided to walk to the stables to see the new-born foal with Jakob and N'tabu. After admiring the animal we joined Hetty under the willow trees on the bank of the stream, wandering through the garden. Mother, Emma and I sat on a bench. Jakob and N'tabu squatted nearby.

"There is something that puzzles me. How did this whole thing come out? Do you have any idea, Emma?"

She shook her head, "I can't think who would want to get at an old woman like me."

Hetty looked up from the sweater she was knitting, "I have my suspicions," then glancing back at her work, "Bother... I've dropped a stitch." We all waited while she struggled to pick it up, but it unravelled further. "What shall I do?" she wailed, "it's gone all the way down." Her voice on the verge of hysteria, "it's so complicated."

Emma nodded, "I know dear, it is complicated, you'll just have to start again."

"It's not as easy as you think, Ma."

"Here, let me help you," she offered, putting out her hand.

Hetty handed it over, "What was I saying? Oh! I remember, about my suspicions. Herman and I believed it was the du Toit's, Marta and Frans. He was jealous when Herman was nominated for the Hoerkrantz seat and I know he dislikes me, but I've no idea how they connected with that awful old woman in Kimberley."

"You're right about the people du Toit." We all looked up in surprise at N'tabu's voice. "Molly, she works for *Mevrou* du Toit, she is Nellie's cousin. Last Thursday, on her day off, she come to see Nellie in Soweto and she tell Nellie about all this trouble people are talking about, that's in all the newspapers. She tol' Nellie about the Ouma from Kimberley who was visiting and who talk about the Frobisher family. Molly say that *Mevrou* du Toit and *Mevrou* van der Merwe are talking, talking, all the time about this, and then *Mevrou* du Toit write to her aunty in Capetown and she write back and tell her more things, and *Mevrou* du Toit she ring the other madam on the telephone and she read her the letter. Then she

277

tell the master." N'tabu proceeded to give a detailed account of Ouma du Toit's reminiscences as Molly told Nellie.

When he finished Emma said quietly, "And then it wouldn't be difficult for them to trace Lena in Kimberley." Her hands shaking.

"Ja," Jakob nodded his head, taking up the story. "My friend Lucas, he living next door to Lena, he telling me, he hear Lena and his Ma talking. Everyone in the township was talking about Emma, he said, and so I tell Mtonya, my grandfather was a white man and my father a coloured." He stopped speaking, sitting thoughtfully for a while, "Mtonya, she say she don't care but she glad her father is dead now. He won't like to have white blood in the family."

When Jakob finished Emma quietly said, "I remember Edie, she never liked me. In fact I'm almost sure that it was she who introduced my father to Lena." She stared ahead to the homestead nestled under the kopje, shaded by tall gum trees. "It has all come back to Kimberley and Lena and the township."

We returned to Pretoria. It would be more than a year before Emma and Hetty finalised their arrangements for leaving. I helped pack their belongings to be shipped to Canada.

"It's not easy for me to say this, Kate." I looked over at Hetty, wrapping a precious ornament in tissue. "But I do want to tell you I am grateful for your friendship and what it has meant to me. I know I was always abrasive and dogmatic and I can't think why you bothered with me when others deserted me. I know now, how wrong I was about everything. I only thought of our own prosperity and never cared about the people who were affected by the laws I supported."

I knew how difficult it was for the proud Hetty to admit she had been wrong and I respected her for acknowledging her mistakes. "Well, I have to confess it wasn't my idea to invite you and Ouma over that afternoon; it was Bobby who persuaded me. I wasn't all that sympathetic towards you, you know, in fact I felt you deserved it. I was too hasty making judgement. Now that's all in the past," firmly sealing a box with masking tape. You can start a new life in a new country. In some ways I envy you, leaving this place, and yet we must try and change things here. It seems an impossible task, the problems insurmountable." I paused, then continued, "at least all your troubles are over."

Emma and mother walked into the room. "That's right," said Emma, "all our troubles are over." Or so she thought.

A few days later her name appeared again on the back pages of the Sunday papers.

"It appears that *Mevrou* Frobisher not only lied to her husband about being white but she had seduced his friend and client." Hetty read aloud from the newspaper report.

Lavinia, it appeared, found out many years ago, about Carl's association with Emma and agreed to keep silent if Carl made it worth her while. She had a young lover in Capetown, and it suited her to have Carl preoccupied with Emma in Pretoria. "Dr. Roussouw was obviously unwilling to inflict pain on Etienne Frobisher, a prominent politician, and paid his wife to keep silent." Hetty continued reading from the newspaper Editorial, shaking her head in disbelief.

"Who wrote the report?" I asked.

"Some guy called van der Merwe," she answered then returned to the story. "After Dr. Carl Roussouw's death and his wife, Lavinia, inherited all his wealth, she grew tired of her young man and took another."

Hetty paused, looking at her mother. "It appears that the former boyfriend, realising the connection with the now notorious Emma Frobisher could be lucrative, sold his story to the press."

She paused again as if trying to take it all in, then said, "This has to be lies, Ma." But her mother's expression told otherwise.

Emma had handled the disclosure of her mixed race with decorum and dignity, but her lover's betrayal was almost too much.

"He always said we could never take our happiness at the expense of others; that Lavinia would be devastated if she knew." She sobbed silently. "He stood for everything that was good and upright, at least that was what I thought. His passion so great for the things he believed in. He was so warm and kind, compared to Etienne, and was everything I believed Etienne had once been. I felt neglected. I felt I could never be myself with Etienne whereas with Carl I could relax and be at ease. We believed in the same things." Her voice dropped to a whisper, her hands twisting, "or so I thought.

"I sometimes suspected he knew I was concealing something but he never put undue pressure on me, so I kept quiet, knowing the consequences, if the truth were revealed. Too many people would be hurt by then... as we have since learnt," her voice trailed off.

Emma told us with trembling lips, of her last meeting with Carl, how he had wanted her to spend the night.

Hetty sat stunned with disbelief. "I remember Dr. Roussouw, Oom Carl we called him. I liked him." Then sarcastically, "Fancy Ma, you and he lovers and no one suspected. My straight mother!" Looking into her mother's eyes then she ran across the room, throwing the newspaper aside, "I'm sorry Ma, I didn't mean that. Men can be bastards!"

"No, Hetty, don't say that. I was as much at fault. I knew I was doing wrong. In a way I understood why he wanted to preserve all he had worked so hard to achieve, after all, I was doing the same thing. When I was younger I was reckless and prepared to abandon my family for him, but later I appreciated his point of view. Of course I didn't know of his arrangement with Lavinia."

It was a few days before Emma, Hetty and family were due to leave South Africa for good. We had a farewell dinner. Arthur left early for a meeting and the young people played records, promising to keep in touch. Katrina and Bobby held hands, their promises more than casual.

Mother, Emma, Hetty and I sat around the dinner table, discussing the past, the diaries Grandma had given me and the letters with Sara's name we had found in Grandfather's house.

"I will give you those letters, Emma," I said, and I told them about the diaries. "One day I intend reading all the material and telling the story. May I include your part in it?"

She thought for a moment and then replied. "Why not? After all, they have heard Carl's side, why not hear mine?" She leant forward, placing her elbows on the table, "I would like to read Ma's letters, perhaps they will help me understand why she was always so sad, then I'll return them all to you." She smiled softly, putting her hand around the stem of her wine glass, then raising it in front of her said, "Here's to your story, Kate."

Chapter 48

Pretoria
Circa 1975

It was almost two years since Emma and her family had left to live in Canada. Mother had settled in well with us and it appeared that Emma too, had adapted to her new environment but not Hetty. "The weather too cold. It rains too much. People are different. The culture strange." she wrote.

We had news that Jakob had died, quite unexpectedly.
"Oh dear," Mother said, "I feel so sad, poor Jakob separated from his sister by apartheid and half a world."
"At least he got to see her before he died."

N'tabu paid me a visit. We talked of the family in Canada and we talked of the family in Soweto. He told me that Samuel was teaching in a local school.
"It's Nellie's boys that give all the trouble," he confided. Samuel, he with his mother when he a small boy but Nellie have to leave her chil'ren when they still too small when she have to go every day to her job. Every day those boys got some problem. They mixing with the *tsotsies*." N'tabu shook his head. "Petrus say he won't go back to school, he say the school no good anyway. Most times we don' know where he is. Now he talking about going north to join the A.N.C. I tell him that organization is banned and he get in plenty trouble with the Security P'lice, but he don' wanna lissen to me. He also talking about Steve Biko and that is more trouble because the police are after Biko as well." N'tabu's forehead wrinkling like a corrugated, country road. I understood his concern. Bobby, while at University had also been involved in protests. The police were brutal.
"Now Philemon, he also joining the protests. They protest because they don' wanna be taught in Afrikaan. Philemon is in the top grade now and Samuel tell him to keep off the streets and stay at school but he won' lissen."
"Davey says Petrus has gone to Port Elizabeth.
N'tabu nodded.
"Davey says the workers on the farm are talking about Steve Biko."
N'tabu closed his mouth tightly.

"They say that Biko has a strong following and the authorities are afraid of his growing popularity and are determined to get him."

No answer.

He leant against the kitchen cupboard, stirring the coffee I handed him.

"Come on, N'tabu, you can tell me. What do you think of Steve Biko and the Black Consciousness movement?"

He swallowed a mouthful of steaming coffee then took a bite of a thick bread spread with apricot jam. He looked straight at me. "I think he's a good man with a lot of influence with the young people and I think the authorities should be speaking with him and listening to what he say. He say he don't want violence. But the Security Police they only know violence." N'tabu's voice was bitter.

I tried to find out more. But Steve Biko was banned, discussing him was illegal. N'tabu wasn't talking.

Chapter 49

I opened my eyes, yawned, and then remembered I was alone in the house. As I lay deep in thought my eye caught the silver moonbeam dusting the bedcover and followed it up through the open window to where the Southern Cross shone, like a diamond brooch, pinned high on the dark-blue velvet sky. The horizon slowly began to lighten while a breeze danced the drapes as a pale ray of sunlight lapped at the corner of the window-frame, reflecting off my grandmother's silver hairbrushes on the stinkwood bureau with the ball-and-claw feet. A *piet-my-vrou* started its early morning gossip and, above the chorus of the cicadas nesting in the grass, a contented dove called to its mate. Promises of spring, I thought, as the scent of the golden honeysuckle, creeping up the trellis outside, wafted in the window. I felt October's optimism, after September rains had washed away the dust of windy August, in spite of the trouble in the land.

My day-dreaming was interrupted by a faint knocking. I thought it a bird on the windowsill but then realised it came from downstairs as Butch, our bulldog began barking. I also realised how scared I was. *Oh my God! someone's trying to break in,* I thought. It had all seemed so different in the clear light of day when Arthur had called from his office.

"Another problem at the Sight, I'm afraid Kate, have to fly down immediately. Can you pack a bag and I'll pick it up on the way to the airport." Arthur is a civil engineer and involved in an irrigation project in the mountains of Natal.

"But," he hesitated before continuing, "I'm worried about leaving you alone. I was hoping I could delay this until Bobby gets back from the Game Reserve, but that's not possible." Bobby, our son, was on a field trip with the university.

"I'll be fine," I assured him.

"What about asking one of your friends to stay."

"Absolutely not, I have a committee meeting this week at the Party office, and must prepare Minutes - no time to entertain." Arthur and I were active in the Opposition Political Party. He still hesitated.

"I don't want to worry you, but remember what happened to Hester."

His words brought my neighbour's recent bad experience to mind.

* * *

"God in Hemel but it was jus' terrible hey!" sniffing, while wiping wet cheeks with her open palms. "You have no idea... those big BLACK hands... ugh!... grabbing me an' touching me all over." Shivering, while spilling words punctuated by sobs. "An' then, when he pull down his trousers and I see that big BLACK thing! Oeh yik!" She was crying, while clutching my hand. "I jus' wanted to vomit, hey! Jus' wish I could have died right then. I tried to scream but he put his hand over my mouth and was pulling at my skirt and then I must of passed out... when I come to, there's old Lucas with the garden fork in his hand. Jurrah man! Was I glad to see him, but I was scared hey! Lucas chased the swine but not before he took my purse and car keys," She burst into hysterical sobs, "Jurrah man! But Koos is gonna be so mad, hey! He jus' bought that BMW."

"She probably exaggerated," I replied, trying to reassure myself. "Koos didn't seem all that concerned, remember what he said to you afterwards?"

"Brand new BMW! Three hundred k's on the bleddy clock, but thank the Lord it's insured, hey! Those bleddy *kaffirs*, they not interested in looking for jobs. They don' wanna work, *jy weet*, they jus' wanna take what us white people work for. The bastards have no respect for a persons property; leave the wife for a couple of hours in the middle of the day to go to the rugby game and look what happens, hey!" Pausing and shaking his head dolefully, then his expression slowly changed and a wide grin appeared on his broad face, "But talking of rugby - jurrah man! what a game hey! You should have been there man, Arthur. Transvaal beat the hell out of Natal. We won all the scrums, y'know. That new hooker they got - what's his name again? Ooh ja... Van der Merwe, he can hook the bleddy ball alright. I'm telling you man, we're going to win the Currie Cup this year. You jus' mark my words hey!"

* * *

The noise from downstairs sounded again and with my turmoiled thoughts tumbling, I ran to the window, thinking I would climb out but realised the trellis would never hold my weight. I decided if someone was trying to break in I should get to the phone in the hall and call the police as quickly as possible. I took my gown from the closet and wrapped it around myself then grabbed the knobkerrie from behind the door and crept

284

down the stairs, back pressed against the wall. The knocking became louder and more persistent. *It MUST be a caller,* I thought, *a burglar trying to break in would hardly make all that racket and it couldn't be Bobby and his student friends, as they were due back tomorrow.* That sent my thoughts in another direction and my palms began to sweat. I suspected Bobby was involved with the banned African National Congress and now I was afraid it WAS the police - the Security Police after Bobby. As I entered the kitchen the knocking began again, much louder from down here and definitely the back door. Butch barked belligerently, leaping from door to window, then back to the door, running his nose along the bottom, sniffing and snorting the way he does, picking up a strange scent. Above the noise I called out, my voice sounding stronger than I felt, "Who is it?" I asked, holding my breath.

"It's me - Petrus." My breath escaped like a released bird as I exhaled and licked my dry lips. Unlocking the door and cautiously opening it, I saw the young man standing in the early morning cold, clutching a coloured blanket around his shoulders; a cracked cardboard suitcase at his feet; a cap on his head.

"Come in, for goodness sake. What on earth are you doing here so early in the morning? Why have you left the farm, you're supposed to be working there. Have you been to Soweto? Your parents are worried about you, you know. Your father was here not long ago and he said he hadn't heard from you. Are you in trouble with the police?"

When at last I paused he answered quietly, "No, nothing like that," his breath curling in a cloud in front of his face. "No trouble. Just that I wanting Bobby, is he here?" He stepped across the doorway as I moved aside.

"My God, Petrus, I was scared half to death I thought someone was trying to break in." I leant the *knobkerrie* against the wall. "You're the last person I expected to see at this time of the morning but it's a relief to know you aren't in any trouble. As for Bobby, he isn't here. He's camping in the Game Reserve with some 'varsity friends. Sit down while I make coffee and we'll talk."

Petrus resembles his father, N'tabu, with whom I spent school vacations, when we were both teenagers, on my grandfather's farm. N'tabu was a herdboy in those days and gave me my first horse-riding lessons. He and I spent many hours riding across the veld rounding up stray cattle. He lived with his family on the farm before he left to find work in the city to earn the money to pay Hanna's father *lobola* so they could marry. I remember Bobby once asking about Hanna. We were on vacation on the farm.

"She was N'tabu's wife and he took her to Johannesburg after they were married but she didn't have a permit to live there so was arrested and returned to the Homeland," I told him.

"And then what happened?" asked the ever curious Bobby.

"Well, it's quite sad really. N'tabu was only able to see her once a year when he had his two weeks leave. Later he met Nellie and they lived together, but never told Hanna, whom he continued to visit annually. They had children but only two survived and Hanna, herself, died in childbirth. Petrus, as you know, is Nellie's child. After Hanna died N'tabu and Nellie got married but the children stayed on the farm with his mother until N'tabu was finally allocated a house and they brought all the children to Soweto to live.

I was worried about Petrus since N'tabu told me that he had joined the school children in their demonstration marches. They were peacefully protesting the government's education policy for blacks but some of the demonstrations turned violent after police fired on the students, shooting many in the back as they ran away.

I directed Petrus to a chair at the table, then prepared coffee and handed him the steaming mug. He warmed his hands around it while I cut thick slices of bread, spreading it with jam. His teeth sunk into the soft slices as hungry rumbles echoed from his empty stomach. I sat on the chair opposite.

"Why are you here? You are meant to be working on the farm, you know," I repeated, "But my brother told me you talked of going to Port Elizabeth to hear Biko.

He stopped chewing, swallowed and looked up with a frown as he began to speak. His pink tongue, shooting from the black cave of his mouth, spitting words, like a striking serpent, "The p'lice is no good, they jus' wan' trouble all the time. Ja, I go to Port Elizabeth but there's problems and Steve can't get there, the Security P'lice is everywhere so we hear he speaking in Queenstown instead, at the football field, so we going there and he speaking to the people. He is banned but he come there without the Security P'lice finding out. Biko is a good man y'know. He saying good things." He took another gulp of coffee, drops dribbling down his chin, his throat convulsing. He wiped his mouth with the back of his hand and the surface of his face was suddenly split with a smile, spreading slowly as he spoke in his own language, tongue clicking against teeth, giving me Biko's message.

"The government say Steve talking about revolution, but that is not so. Steve only saying the people must think good of themselves.

I replied in English. "That's wonderful and what Biko says is true but you should have stayed in school," I scolded, "if you don't finish your schooling what sort of job can you get? A cleaner? A gardener? You must do better than that. Remember when you were a little boy and how badly you wanted to go to school?"

It was the year Bobby was due to start kindergarten. He'd begged that Petrus be allowed to return home with us after the holidays and attend school with him.

"Petrus wants to go to the Mission School but his Grandma can't take him. She says she can't walk too far every day. So can he come to school with me?"

"Sorry, Bobby, he must stay on the farm."

"He can sleep in my room."

"They won't allow him to go to your school."

"Why can't he? He says he wants to go to school with me."

"Well, that's just not possible."

"Why? Who says so?"

"The government."

"Who's the government?" I attempted an explanation to the five year olds.

"I hate the government - I hate the government," he chanted, pushing clenched fists into his pockets while kicking at a stone. "C'mon Petrus, tell my Mom you hate the government; tell her you do want to go to school with me.

"Oew! *Inkosane*," was all Petrus would say, bending his head and lowering his eyes.

"That's enough, now Bobby. You're embarrassing Petrus. I'll speak to the Nuns at the Mission School in the village before we return home, they do take some boarders. I'll explain that Petrus' grandma can't get him to the school from the farm every day and arrange for him to become a weekly boarder. Would you like that?" looking at Petrus and handing them each a banana. A grin broadened his face as he bent his knees and cupped his two hands together to receive the fruit,

"Oew! Thank you, *Inkosazana*," was all he said then.

287

But he had much more to say now. He stopped eating, dropped the spoon on to the plate and stood up, leaning on the table and pushing his head forward as he switched to English, answering my accusations.

"The schools are no good. The government don' spend money for teachers or books an' when I finish going to school, there's no work. There not enough work on the farm because they got the tractors an' machines to do the jobs an' they even got machines to milk the cows. There's not jobs in the Homeland the people there got no money to pay wages. And I not finding work in Egoli either. I'm trying all the time. I'm speaking to the boss where my father working; he saying to me he don' need another boy to make the tea and clean and do messages. I'm asking him can't I learn to do the job like he does with the books and he laugh and say, 'You getting cheeky hey, you bleddy *kaffir*. You think you can do the white man's job - get outta here. That's against the law.' Then I'm asking the white man who building the houses. He telling me he already got boys to carry the bricks in the wheelbarrows so I'm saying can't I learn to build with the bricks. He get mad and telling me to *voetsak*. 'Why you wanna take the whiteman's job. You can't do that work, the government don' allow it.' Then I am trying at the Mines but they telling me I'm not big enough to work underground. Then I'm trying for work as cleaner, but too many people doing that job, and mos' times they wan' women to clean house an' cook an' be the nannies for the chil'ren." He shrugged in resignation and his words took me back in time as I recalled N'tabu; the same reasons for leaving the farm and the same difficulties finding work in the city.

His manner changed. He sat back on the chair and picked up the spoon, tapping it against the plate a smile breaking across his broad face. "But now I'm have got job in Egoli. I working for Biko's organisation in the Transvaal."

"Can you work in Jo'burg, have you got a pass to work here?" He brought out a thin square booklet from his hip pocket. I glanced through it, noting his faded picture stamped in the bottom corner. I turned the page. "This says you are a Xhosa. That you were born in Rustenburg, but it doesn't say you can work in Jo'burg?"

Shrugging my objections aside he answered, "No problem, they telling me where I mus' go to see a man who can fix my papers. I going there tomorrow. But now I mus' talk to Bobby. When's he coming home?"

"I've no idea," I lied, feeling badly about the deception. I abhorred the injustices inflicted upon black people and felt guilty at our prosperity in the face of their poverty. But the system prohibited my family experiencing the hardships suffered by N'tabu and Nellie and their family. I felt I was doing all I could within the law. I believed in the struggle but I didn't want my son involved. To put it bluntly, I was afraid for Bobby.

The kitchen clock recorded the passing minutes, like my nervous heartbeat pulsing in the silent room. I shivered then shrugged off the feeling of foreboding and spoke decisively, "I'll make some *mielie-pap*, but we'll have to talk seriously. You will bring trouble on yourself and your family," taking the packet of *mielie* meal out of the cupboard and preparing to mix the thick porridge. "You've heard how they treat prisoners in John Vorster Square?" I turned on the cooker and, putting the saucepan on the hotplate, began stirring.

He nodded, "Of course. I know that." His voice dropped. "My friend Spike, he taken in Soweto."

I continued, slowly stirring the porridge.

"People are put away without a trial, then the police produce mutilated bodies and say their prisoners committed suicide. The Security Police do as they like." My voice rose as I stirred more vigorously. The mixture in the saucepan bubbled and boiled. I recalled the disappearance of the young student who volunteered with me at the Party Office.

"We've made enquiries," his mother confided in me, "but were told that under the State of Emergency they can't tell us anything." I knew how she felt because I worried about Bobby's involvement even while supporting his opposition to apartheid. I felt split, torn in half. Petrus voice interrupted my thoughts,

"Ja, ja, I know that," he repeated, jutting his chin and clenching his fists, his voice brought my thoughts back to present and its problems. I was sure he did know, but wanted to make my point.

"My friend who taking me to the soccer field to hear Steve Biko, he asking me to help them. He saying 'can I take some pamphlets to some people in Alexandria Township?' I'm got the address here," patting his coat pocket. Then turning towards me, his face twitching he whispered, "Can you do me big favour?"

An icy hand gripped my throat, squeezing tightly and my voice squeaked past the constriction, stammering my assent while at the same time nodding my head, trying to imagine what favour he wanted - what message for Bobby?

"Is it O.K. if I'm leaving my suitcase here?"

I nodded again, relieved that was all he was asking.

He had discarded the blanket and the balaclava and his strong odour pervaded the warm kitchen. A combination of sweat and the herbal oils he rubbed on his body. He wore faded jeans, a white collarless dress shirt buttoned to the throat and navy-blue pin-strip jacket with matching vest. The handed-down business-man's suit, designed to cover a corporate corpulence, hung loosely on his thin frame. White shirt-tails showed below his jacket. On his feet a pair of sneakers that were too big. He took a folded paper from his pocket and handed it to me.

"This is where I'm taking the papers. Bobby say he can help me. Is he telling you when he coming home?"

"Well," I hesitated, thinking of what to say. "I'm not sure exactly when he will be back but I can help you? What is it you want Bobby to do? I can drive you wherever you want to go. Is it money you need?" I opened a cupboard and took out a purse with some notes and small change.

"Take this. You must be short of money if you haven't been working," pushing it into his hands. He rummaged in his suitcase, taking out a bundle of printed notices.

I stopped stirring and dropped the spoon, sending splutters of steaming grey, gluey globules in all directions, and ran over to the table, glancing at them in dismay, immediately realising they were "Black Consciousness" pamphlets. These were illegal and if discovered here, or in Bobby's or Petrus' possession, by the police, would mean a lot of trouble. My hand shook as I picked one up and read.

No strong call for violence... only strong words urging the people to believe in themselves. No strong call to rise up against white people... only strong words to rise above the feeling of inferiority white people instilled in them; to make decisions for themselves; to be conscious of being black and to be proud of it.

I put the pamphlet down and turned towards Petrus.

"I agree with Biko. African people SHOULD reclaim their sovereignty, they SHOULD make their own decisions about their lives. One would think that the government would support a leader advocating non-violence but instead, it does everything in its power to harass Biko and find a reason to arrest him and suppress his movement." We were both silent for a while, each with our own thoughts before I continued, "if the police catch you with these pamphlets you know what can happen."

He nodded.

"Well then you must NOT become involved, Petrus. What can YOU do against the power of the State?"

He frowned and shook his head at me then stood up, pushing his chair back and leaning forward; he put both hands firmly on the table like a rock resisting the wave's rage, while the wind waged.

"I MUS' DO THIS THING."

A sudden gust unhooked the kitchen window, blowing it out with the drapes. I ran towards it, putting my arm through the bars and pulling it shut and saw signs of an approaching storm.

"Summer storms are starting early," I observed, pointing to the darkening sky. The valley was shrouded in black clouds banked up on the horizon and severed by streaks of lightning, resembling exploding gunfire while thunder rumbled like a cannon, echoing from the distant hills. I saw the wild fig tree on the boundary, split by lightning in a storm last summer and hoped it would survive this one. Then the rain began to fall, huge drops - silver bullets - spiking the gravel driveway, splattering it outwards.

I savoured the smell of the wet earth until my attention was drawn to the smell of burning, rising with the steam over the saucepan. I ran back to the cooker to rescue the porridge boiling over and carefully scooped out a serving, leaving the burnt crust. My charm bracelet slipped down my wrist. Delicate charms each one eighteen-carat gold, my mother told me, when she gave it to me for my twenty-first birthday. Her mother had given it to her, she said and I recalled my Grandmother sitting at the grand piano in her drawing room with persian mats on polished floors, the charm bracelet fallen over her wrist, rows of cultured pearls hanging down over her full bosom.

I gave Petrus the dish, which he took with both hands before sitting down; while I put a pan of milk on the hot plate to warm for more coffee and took the mugs off the shelf. I remembered when Petrus' grandma gave me those clay mugs, it was after I arranged for him to attend the Mission School.

"Oew! Missis, Missis," she had said, clasping both hands together. "Oew! The Missis she pay for my boy to go to the Mission School." Leaning forward and taking my hand in both of hers, "Oew! Thank you Missis, thank you," her tongue darting between lips drawn inwards by sunken, toothless gums. Rows of beads hanging down over flattened breasts. Bracelets with charms made of bones fell over her wrists as she picked up the clay mugs with a giraffe drawn on the sides, and handed them to me. Her broad bare feet, stained grey with dirt, showed below her long cotton skirt. We stood in front of her thatched mud hut with grass mats on the dung floor.

"Are you sure no one saw you come here?" My question prompted by the sound of a car outside, heard above the storm. The police patrolled the suburbs regularly, looking for illegal workers; people without passes like Petrus: they raided private property, searching back-yard rooms of women domestic workers who might have husbands living with them. Petrus shifted a lump of porridge inside his mouth, circling his lips as he answered, "Nobody seeing me come here."

"Are you positive? How did you get here?"

"I'm taking the taxi from the railway station. The taxi driver dropping me by the shops and I'm walking here."

"Was anyone about?"

"No. No one. Well. . . maybe I see a car but it stopping at that other house down the street," frowning.

"Which house? Did anyone get out?"

We heard the bang of a car door.

"Police!" I whispered, before he could reply, my voice scraping hoarsely. I grabbed the pamphlets. We couldn't burn them - no fireplace. Besides, Petrus said they must be distributed. Where to put them? Where to put Petrus? I looked around the clinical kitchen. Nowhere here! Upstairs? The bedrooms? Under a bed? The trapdoor in the ceiling? Possibilities, but places police would look.

We heard footsteps on the driveway. The milk in the saucepan boiled over - I ignored it. My breath coming in gasps. My palms moist. My body began to shake while my mind tried to solve the problem of where to put the pamphlets? My knitting-bag? Innocent enough, but hardly big enough. The garbage can? Sure to look there. The dress-making patterns! Of course! The folded pamphlets would fit in the paper pattern envelopes.

Picking up the bundle from the table, I silently sped across the shiny tiled floor to my sewing room off the kitchen and pulled down the carton of dress-making patterns.

"Look out!" I screamed and Petrus sprang aside. Spiders had run out from under the box, scrambling sideways across the floor in all directions, then disappearing behind the cupboards, I gave an involuntary shudder while frantically opening the paper-pattern envelopes and pushing in the

292

pamphlets with Petrus helping. There weren't many and when the last was out of sight he returned the carton to the top shelf in the cupboard while I moved the saucepan of milk bubbling on the stove.

We heard the doorbell peal.

"Get upstairs," I whispered hoarsely, "lock yourself in the washroom. I'll tell them my mother is in there." They surely should have enough delicacy, I thought, to prevent them breaking down THAT door. Petrus disappeared up the staircase as the bell stopped ringing and footsteps approached along the side pathway; then a loud knock on the kitchen window. I jumped, shaking with fear, putting my hand to my mouth to suppress a scream. My head awash with wild thoughts. The dog barked, jumping up to the window.

"Anyone home?"

I collapsed against the kitchen cupboard, recognising the familiar voice, then collected myself and ran to open the back door, throwing my arms around Bobby in the doorway, dripping wet and silhouetted in the sunlight, shining through the rain.

"Sorry I had to ring the bell but I can't find my key."

"Bobby! I thought you were only coming home tomorrow. But oh, I'm so glad it's you. I'm so glad it's you," I repeated hysterically, crying and laughing at the same time.

"And look - a 'monkey's wedding!'" I pointed at the sky beyond the open doorway, the sun was shining through the rain. Bobby hugged me then, feeling my shaking body, looked alarmed. "Hey! Take it easy there, Mom. I'm O.K. Only soaking wet! What a thunderstorm. But what's up? Why are you in such a tizzy?

I explained.

"Well you're right, the Security Police are everywhere and usually in plain clothes so you never know who they are." He paused, then cursed under his breath, " Bloody 'rock-spiders'."

Petrus, hearing the noise, crept downstairs and entered the kitchen.

"Hoew! Bobby man, I'm been looking for you, hey"

"So, what you want? My Mom says you have some of Biko's pamphlets. But you have to be careful, man, you know the bloody Security Police don't play around. You betta watch out for those bloody 'rocks'..."

"That's EXACTLY what I've been trying to tell him," I interjected. Bobby put up his hand to silence me, then continued, "But you know

Mom, Petrus DOES have the right to make his own decisions about fighting for his freedom."

Petrus nodded, putting up his clenched right fist.

"Of course," I mumbled.

Bobby put his arm around me, "C'mon Ma, you worry too much. How about a cuppa tea," and turning to Petrus, threw his other arm across his shoulder, "and let's get those pamphlets out the paper pattern box and I'll take you where you have to go."

I stood at the window and waved as they drove off and saw the garden swept by the storm. The wild fig tree split in half and the tousled branches of the acacia hanging down, water dripping off the leaves like tears. I pushed my tousled hair off my face and wiped my eyes.

Chapter 50

Kate
Pretoria, c.1976.

I am torn, split with conflicting thoughts racing through my head, since Bobby and Petrus left this morning with those illegal pamphlets to deliver. I waved them off with a heavy heart, fearing for their safety. Of course apartheid is wrong and I support the fight against it. I also support Biko's movement, but I'm afraid of the security police. As I wait for Bobby and Petrus to return I look through an old family picture album and see Durban where I was born and raised and where the early British settlers were rooted in colonialism. I see crested white waves on white beaches for whites only and I remember peaceful picnics in the Valley of a Thousand Hills. Now terror triumphs there.

I see my mother, my extravagant, extroverted mother who was always there for us, along with Violet of course, our nursemaid as well as Rose, our cleaner and cook, and Freddy the gardener. I remember Violet. Poor Violet, who never had a proper home after she moved to town to find work, leaving her children to be raised by her mother on the farm. She had various men living with her but we never knew which one fathered her children. Sometimes my father gave permission for her children to stay during school holidays and I played with them under the banana trees at the bottom of the garden. My father planted those trees to hide the wood and iron hut where the servants lived. He called it "the eyesore," and made sure it was out of sight.

Oh look! A picture of my father, my bigotted although benevolent father. He believed that women and natives should know their proper place. I remember wanting to continue my schooling at university and his reply,

"You don't need higher education. What you do need, my girl, is a good man so you can become a good wife and raise a family." After he died, I remembered how I regretted knowing so little about him. He worked in government and although secure in his position I sensed his insecurity. He really believed black people were inferior and feared their rise to power. He was impatient and irritable, keeping his family at a distance yet, at the same time, supportive and kind. I remember once how he stayed at my bedside day and night and nursed me through a fever. I think if I were to plant a tree for him it would be the Cactus.

People say I take after my father in looks, black hair and black eyes, for which I now need glasses for reading. I hang my glasses around my neck on a string of small beads strung like a chain of daisies made for me by Petrus' grandma. Petrus' grandma... I remember her so well, and holidays on my Grandfather's farm and my friendship with N'tabu, Petrus' father. I never thought of them as being different in those carefree days on the farm. All the children played together, rode horses and swam in the river.

I put the picture album down and open my grandmother's grand piano and play a soothing sonata by Beethoven. I think of moonlight and warm beaches and waves lapping on the shore and a feeling of calm washes over me.

Glancing at my reflection in the oval framed, bevel mirror I see my calf-length skirt and ankle-strap shoes. Out of date now, but once called the "New Look." I prefer longer skirts and never wore a mini, even in my young days! My dark hair, styled in a fashionable bouffant, falls over my face as I glance at the side table covered with a fringed cloth and silver framed family photos.

I walk outside and see the acacia growing in the lawn. The pool by the patio; the wild fig tree on the boundary, split in half when struck by lightning last summer. I see the house I planned - white walls and high blue slate roof with dormer windows. If I were ever to build another, it would look the same, and then I think about Nellie and N'tabu's house in Soweto.

The clock strikes the hour, time to prepare dinner. Bobby and Petrus are still not home. I cook roast beef and yorkshires, my favourite, but I also favour *braaied Boerewors* - farmer's seasoned sausages cooked on the barbecue.

I see chintz-covered couches and bone-china bowls. Royal Doulton ornaments and silver candle-sticks on the Adam fireplace. I also see a wood carving of a Zulu man, sitting smoking a pipe on the stinkwood table by the window and a water-colour of the Drakensberg Mountains at sunrise, hanging on the wall.

I remember when the house next door caught fire. I worried that the fire would spread and feared the loss of these family treasures, reminders of my mother and my grandmother and of my grandfather's farm... and of Petrus' grandmother.

People think my possessions mean everything to me but that's not true. Some black people believe that liberal whites are patronising and cannot relate to their problems, living in comfortable homes with the best education for their children and never harassed by police. On the other hand there are whites who call us *"kaffir-boeties"* - nigger lovers. Sometimes I feel I have no place here, I don't fit. I am torn. I am split. I believe Bobby is doing what is right. I admire the concern he shares with his student friends, but I'm afraid for him.

Arthur supports Bobby's involvement in politics. He believes young people should be aware of injustices in society. He taught me that happiness does not depend upon possessions and position. He taught me to think in positively. But it is difficult to be positive.

I think about life in the suburbs. Peaceful barbecues beside a blue pool under purple Jacaranda trees in yellow sunlight, then I think about the townships where grey smog hangs on the hillside.

I recall holidays in Capetown at the foot of the Mountain which so often is covered with a cloth of cloud and Cape Point where the two oceans meet, surging and thrusting white spray upwards against black jutting rocks. Can I leave this place? I look again at the split fig tree at the bottom of the garden.

Chapter 51

Soweto
Circa 1976

Nellie rose wearily from her bed, glancing at the illuminated figures of the alarm clock on the wooden box beside her. Almost three-thirty. She shivered as her bare feet felt the cold linoleum.

N'tabu stirred. "Is it time to get up?"

"No, it's early."

"So why you wake me up?"

"I can't sleep. I'm worried about Philemon. Yesterday his friends are here and they are talking, talking all the time about trouble at the schools. They say they won't go to school, that to-day they are marching in the streets in protest," shaking her head, "first Petrus make us worry and now Philemon."

N'tabu sat up abruptly. "I wish Philemon won't lissen to all this talk. He mus' jus' go to school and get educatin."

"That's the problem. They don't believe they getting educatin. They say that the schools, teaching them in Afrikaans, keeps them back I also tell Philemon to keep away from trouble but he won' lissen to what I say." She sighed, winding a blanket about herself and shuffling across to the window.

Outside the sky was black. White frost crusted the ground, throttling tufted grass and strangling struggling shrubs. A draught of cold air brushed Nellie's cheek. She shivered again, as fear's icy fingers flayed out, touching her, sending shivers down her spine.

She continued talking as she lit the candle. "Samuel, he also telling Philemon he mus' stay out of trouble, but Philemon jus' laugh, he say he not frightened of the p'lice."

She walked through the cold house to the kitchen and knelt down to sweep the grate of the cooker before laying fresh kindling and lighting the wood. After filling the kettle, and placing it on top of the range, she took two mugs from hooks on the shelves above, placing them on the table covered with a blue plastic cloth. She lifted the curtain in front of a wooden box, serving as a grocery cupboard, took out a tin of condensed milk and pierced a hole. Her shivering abated, the warmth from the fire slowly spreading. While she waited for the kettle to boil, she measured the *mielie-meal* for the family's breakfast, then sliced bread and set the table.

N'tabu joined her in the kitchen and wrapped his two hands around the mug of steaming tea she gave him. They sat opposite each other across the wooden table, speaking in whispers, not to waken Philemon and Lettie and Lizzie.

"I wish you can stay at home today, N'tabu. I'm worried about these chil'ren," pointing towards the room where they slept. The two girls shared a double bed and Philemon lay on a mattress on the floor.

N'tabu shook his head. "That's impossible. I'm losing my job if I'm staying away. Can't you telephone your madam and tell here there is trouble here in Soweto today?" He threw back his head, drained his mug then pushed it across the table for a refill. She stood up and walked to the range, pouring boiling water from the kettle into the tea-pot then returning to the table to refill his cup before finally answering.

"It's no good. The madam, she work and I mus' look after the baby."

N'tabu banged his cup down, spilling tea and shouting, "So you have to leave your chil'ren to look after the white madam's chil'ren."

Nellie looked dismayed. "What mus' I'm doing, N'tabu?"

* * *

Moonlight filtered through the branches of the tall gum trees, casting strange shadows as wind rustled the leaves. Bobby parked his '58 Volkswagen and walked slowly over uneven ground towards the dis-used mine shaft visible against the sky. He'd had a message from Samuel. He'd returned from spending two months with Katrina but his future was still unresolved as he felt torn between his desire to be with her and his desire to live in his home country.

He heard a sudden movement in the bushes and spun around, breath suspended. Samuel's voice hissed in a whisper and Bobby let out a murmured sigh. The two clasped hands and walked towards a tin hut, door hanging half off hinges.

"So you got my message." Samuel's head was bowed. "It's bad news about my brother Philemon. He was shot by the police today." He looked up at Bobby as the latter stopped in his tracks. Bobby started to speak but Samuel put up his hand and continued talking.

300

"We think he's dead and the p'lice have got his body. At least that's what his friends are saying. They say they were marching peacefully with all the other school chil'ren when the police started firing and the chil'ren turned around and ran away from the guns but the police keep on shooting. The people are saying that the chil'ren are all shot in the back.

"Philemon's friend, he says he saw Philemon get shot and fall down and when he go back to look for Philemon after the p'lice have gone, he can't find Philemon anywhere so he think Philemon mus' be alright and got away and he come to my parent's house. They asking all his friends but nobody have seen him. My father is asking at the police station in Soweto. He also asking at the hospital at Baragwanath but he can't find Philemon. We think the police are taking away the bodies of some of the children."

Bobby let Samuel talk without interruption, although his brain buzzed with questions.

"My parents are very sore in their hearts because they told Philemon to keep out of trouble. They say the children can't do anything against guns. First Petrus give them worry and now Philemon."

They stepped inside the hut and saw blackened bricks and wood kindling. Collecting some old newspaper lying in a corner, Bobby set a fire, and with palms spread out over the low flame they both squatted before it.

"The situation gets worse every week." Bobby said, "I'm going to get out of this bloody place one of these days," resolving his indecision with one sentence. We can't trust anyone at the university; the police have planted informers everywhere, and it's impossible trying to report the truth in the press which is blocked by the state of emergency legislation." Bobby, now a reporter for a local newspaper. "Every story we write has to be scrutinized by lawyers and invariably has to be scrapped. Won't pass government censors." He clenched his fists in anger.

They sat in silence. Samuel scratching in the dirt with a dry twig. After a while Bobby continued, "They took a friend in the middle of the night . He was helping people cross the border into Botswana. You know we have an organization to help people get out?" He turned to Samuel, "What's the point in staying and getting caught, then sweating it out in John Vorster Square and being beaten up by some mindless cop? Maybe we can do more for the cause outside the country?" Bobby justified his sudden decision.

"That's why I want to see you. Because they killed my brother, now I must do something."

301

Bobby stood up, and began pacing, while Samuel continued. "I want to see you because I must get to Botswana. Can you help me?"

Silence again, broken by the noises of the night. A dog barking, frogs croaking in a nearby *vlei*.

"Ja, I can arrange that but what about your parents?"

Samuel stood and stamped on dying embers.

"My parents must understand. Once I believe, like them, that we will get freedom peacefully, that more white people will see that apartheid is not good. But not anymore. Petrus and Philemon were right, white people won't change. We mus' force them."

Bobby nodded. "Most white people are brainwashed by the government, burying their heads in the sand like a lot of ostriches, pretending everything is OK." He stood up, "Meet me here, same time tomorrow. I'll tell you then what to do. Don't talk to anyone," he advised, clasping Samuel's arm above the elbow and shaking his hand, speaking in his language. "*Sala kahle*, my friend." - go carefully.

Samuel nodded and repeated, "*Sala kahle*."

Chapter 52

The Volkswagen moved slowly over the dirt road. Bobby sat at the wheel, peering through the windscreen as wipers swished - swished, backwards and forwards, backwards and forwards, sending out droplets of rain like waving sparklers on Guy Fawkes night. Mud splashed on the wheels as he drove through a puddle, before coming to a halt beside the hut. He saw a figure in the shadows and hesitated before applying the brake, ready to accelerate if necessary, then recognised Samuel.

He waved then leant across, opening the passenger's door, letting in the beating rain. Samuel removed his hood and squeezed on to the front seat then turned to Bobby. "Thank you for coming. I'm worried in case you have trouble."

"Everything is O.K, but listen carefully to what I say. You must carry all names and addresses in your head." He handed Samuel a waterproof pouch containing money and a compass.

"Today you go to the milk depot in Melville but only after mid-day when Jeremiah M'lundi is in charge. He's on afternoon shift. Tell him your name is Albert, he is expecting you and will ask if it has been raining in your village. You reply that it has not, then ask him for a job with the milk delivery. He will give you overalls and tell you when to be back at the depot for the next day's delivery to Parktown.

"The driver of the delivery van is also one of our people. He will put you off at a certain address. You must knock on the back door, a white man will open it. Ask him how many bottles of milk he wants. Now listen carefully, this is important. If he says he forgot to put out coupons and says wait while he gets them, you can go inside. If he says he doesn't want milk, then you must leave, get back to the delivery truck as quickly as possible."

Samuel nodded.

Bobby continued. "He will take you to people travelling in a covered van with farming equipment and supplies to their farm on the border. If there's a problem and it doesn't work out this time you'll have to wait a few weeks before we can organise another ride."

The last quarter of a pale moon hung in the west like a slice of gouda. The delivery van drew to a halt. Samuel jumped off the back, then reached up to lift out two bottles of milk, noting the house number on the gate. He walked up the long tree-lined driveway his feet grinding gravel.

The house was in darkness except for a light from a window at the back, beaming a yellow stripe across the paved yard.

He walked up the steps but had a fleeting sense of alarm. Was it too peaceful, he thought. No dogs sniffing and snarling. Fear cloaked him. Most people kept dogs. He shivered, although beads of sweat gathered under his knitted wool cap. Then he remembered, many people like himself called at this address and there would not be a dog to sound an alarm. He relaxed, shaking himself, dislodging fear that sat like a *tokalash* on his back.

A gentle tap on the door. It opened a fraction, a white face appeared. Samuel's voice croaked. "How much milk you want today, master?" The yellow stripe broadened, the door opened wider.

The voice unnatural, pitched high, shaking a little. "I'm sorry I forgot to put out the coupons." Relief surged through Samuel, his sigh misting the air in front of his face. He stepped forward and then noticed an almost imperceptible shake of the head and hesitated but it was too late. He felt a hit from behind and fell forward, hard steel pressing his back.

Samuel lay on the floor of the empty cell in John Vorster Square. No food for two days and a few mouthfuls of water at intervals during interrogation. He continued claiming ignorance of the existence of any organization and insisted he just delivered milk.

The questions went on and on. A *sjambok* cracked across his back. "Stand up, you bloody *kaffir*." The procedure repeated until he fell unconscious. He was brought round and felt he was drowning, head immersed in a bath of water. He choked.

A voice through the open door. "You betta take it easy, man. This one has to be transferred to Pretoria Central. The Kommandant doesn't like his prisoners arriving too beaten up." Samuel lay still, faking. The owner of the voice walked into the room and kicked at Samuel with a heavy boot. "Viljoen says Special Branch suspect a contact with a group of students and ex-students from the university who get people across the border."

A van drove into the courtyard of Police Headquarters; Samuel bundled into the back, the doors banged closed. The engine revved, the vehicle lunged towards the petrol pumps. Vosloo, the driver, elbow resting on the open window, jerked his head out, shouting at the black attendant. "Hey! You there! You boy! Fill her up and check on oil and water and be quick about it!"

304

The black attendant jumped to attention. Samuel groaned, Vosloo and his partner, Sergeant Erasmus, ignored him, continuing their conversation.

"We gotta get back quick from Pretoria for the police dance to-night, hey man! Viljoen say we must wait to get a police escort car but I tell him we can be OK if we leave early enough. This kaffir's not important, man, not like Biko hey!"

Erasmus laughed. "Ja, *dis reg*! But if we want to get back early we betta get going now. Why's that bobbejaan taking so long to put in some petrol, what's he doing in the engine?"

Vosloo put his head out of the window again, shouting, "Hey, you there, get a move on, what's the matter with you boy, why you looking in the engine? I just said fill her up."

"Sorry, my *baas*, but you said I mus' check oil and water." Muffled voice from under the hood. "It's all OK. Everything fine baas. No problem, you won' have any trouble - engine very good my *baas*," he said, grinning broadly.

Vosloo muttered a curse, "You took long enough you bleddy *bobbejaan*, you people are all the same, lazy bastard," turning to Erasmus and laughing, "He says the engine's very good, I like that hey! What the hell does he know about engines anyway - he jus' come out the trees!" They both laughed. Vosloo released the brake, noisily changed gear and slammed his boot down on the accelerator.

Erasmus reached into the shelf under the dashboard, bringing out a half empty bottle of brandy. "A quick snort for the road, hey man, a drink to the blokes who caught this bugger we've got in the back. What about that, hey?"

Vosloo hesitated, "Maybe not man, not while I'm driving this bleddy thing. If we have a problem and they smell *brandewyn* then we get the chop, hey."

"Ag man, c'mon, jus' one for the road, there's not much left here anyway."

Erasmus put the bottle to his mouth, tipped his head, swallowing the golden liquid, then smacked thick lips together, handing the bottle to Vosloo who took it with his one hand, keeping the other on the wheel. They finished the bottle between them, then broke into song,

"My Sarie Marais is so ver van my haart... daar in die ou Transvaal...."

Samuel heard their voices as they sped through the deserted streets. Neon lights flashed through the barred windows, then blackness. The city was left behind.

Samuel stirred. His head dizzy as he tried to remember where he was. He blinked in the yellow beam that suddenly pierced the darkness, then pulled up on to his hands and knees, peering through the bars, and saw a black sedan following.

The van shuddered, engine spluttered, faltered, picked up momentarily, then died. Vosloo swore, opening the cab door, "I thought that *kaffir* said the engine was O.K. Stupid bastard, must've put the oil in the wrong place - they got no bleddy brains, man, that's why they'll never be anything - but they want to run this country, over my dead body I say."

"Ja, *jy's reg - hulle is heeltemal dom*, man." Erasmus, slurring words, followed Vosloo to the front of the van, then held a flashlight while his partner opened the hood to investigate the problem. The car behind stopped, headlights beaming. Samuel heard voices in Afrikaans, police escort, he thought, then a scuffle and muffled groans, the back door of the van was unlocked and opened. He was pulled out and helped to the waiting car.

Once again speeding northwards, this time in the back of the black sedan. The man at the wheel spoke, "This was an easy job, man, those policemen didn't think you important enough for an escort and one of our men fixed the engine." He put his head back, laughing loudly.

His companion joined in, then turned to face Samuel sitting in the back next to another of his rescuers. "That old man Solomon Mfumba he knows all about cars hey! He's working a long time in that garage at p'lice headquarters putting in the petrol, but when the white man is fixing the car Solomon mus' fetch the tools, then he mus' hold the tools and always he's watching the white man when they fixing the cars. He knows about engines that Solomon."

"Heow man! I'm wishing I can fix cars."

"We're taking you to a safe place on the border." The driver interrupted, expression now serious. "You must cross the river in the night, you'll find a small row boat tied up where we drop you. But you must watch out for crocodiles man, they can tip it over easily. We lost someone last week like that."

Samuel grinned, after his past experiences, crocodiles didn't even scare him.

"You must also watch out for patrols; the army and the police are all over the place up there," the driver continued.

Samuel's grin faded, nodding his head his fears returning as he realised his danger. His life had taken a dramatic turn. His intentions to work peacefully for change had been shattered by the bullet that took his brother's life.

Chapter 53

Soweto
Circa 1977

Winter comes early in Soweto. It moves freely over the barren veld, blighting dry grass and sleeting cracked windows. Nellie's heart was cold and heavy as she prepared the morning meal. It was ten months since the day Philemon and the other Soweto school children were killed and Samuel had left the country. They had no knowledge of his whereabouts nor of Petrus'. She feared that both had gone underground, working for the banned African National Congress.

Wind howled through gum trees, shaking down any remaining dead leaves, killed by the early frost. Nellie turned towards N'tabu as he walked into the kitchen,

"I'm thinking always about Philemon and what happened to him. And Petrus and Samuel. Maybe they also dead. What mus' I do?"

N'tabu slowly shook his head. "We can do nothing, but we mus' also think of Lizzie and Lettie. They can't always live in such sorrow."

"That is so. Tonight I'm making some good stew with chicken and spinach." It was Thursday, her day off.

Lizzie and Lettie pushed past each other, running into the kitchen, shouting greetings at their mother.

"A white madam came and talked to us at the school today," cried Lettie.

"She tell us she will be taking chil'ren from Soweto to dance in a competition in London with chil'ren from all over the world," continued Lizzie.

"She teaches white kids ballet but now she say she wants to teach the black kids ballet and the coloured kids as well." Lettie added.

Nellie looked up from the sink where she was cutting chicken for the stew.

"What you talking about? Ballet dancing? How can you learn to do ballet dancing? Where will you get the money for lessons, if you do get so lucky to get chosen, where will the money come, to go to London?"

Lizzie and Lettie replied in unison, "Money won't be a problem."

Nellie paused, the kitchen knife in her hand, "Oh! So money won't be a problem," she mimicked. Then changed her tone. "What you mean money won't be a problem?" placing the knife in the sink and wiping blood from the chicken's entrails off her hands. Reaching out she took the letter from Lizzie who cried out eagerly.

"Here, read what it says."

Nellie slowly read out aloud, her index finger with traces of fat and blood from the chicken, followed the type-written words across the page.

"A committee will be formed of white, black and coloured parents who will then raise money to pay for the trip and those black and coloured children whose parents can't afford the fees for ballet lessons will be allowed to attend the classes free of charge."

She folded the sheet over and pushed it into her apron pocket while commenting with a sniff, "They won' get much money here in Soweto."

When N'tabu arrived home later that night she showed him the notice from the white ballet teacher. He shook his head, "They only take the black and coloured chil'ren so the people overseas can't say they only for white people." Pausing to read the notice once more. "What's this ballet anyway? Ballet's not our people's dancing. We have our own dancing."

Lettie and Lizzie opened their mouths to protest but N'tabu held up his hand. "How can they ask the people of Soweto to give money for this dancing for a few of the chil'ren when so many of the chil'ren don't have enough food to eat or clothes to wear?"

* * *

N'tabu was right of course but the project went ahead anyway. Money was raised from the business community in affluent white Johannesburg.

"I'm very sorry, hey madam, but it's against the law to have mixed audiences." The clerk in the government office shouting at me in reply to my request for a permit, allowing the newly formed multi-racial ballet company to perform in towns across the Witwatersrand. Our Vicky was a member of the cast.

"But that's ridiculous. The cast is made up of all races," I shouted back.

"That's allowed, madam. It's O.K. on the stage but not in the hall, hey."

"But the parents want to watch their children perform. Most of them will have to travel a long way in buses from Soweto and other townships on the Reef with their children. Of course they must be allowed to see them dance. They can't be expected to wait outside in the bitter cold."

"I'm very sorry, ma'am, but that's the law. No mixed audiences and God forbid there ever will be in this country."

The following day I was at the Department of the Interior.

"It's going to take a few months to get these applications for passports processed for the young people who are black and for those of mixed race. The others will be no problem," the official told me, shuffling through the papers I handed him.

"What do you mean, months? We haven't got months, not more than two, anyway."

"These people can't just get passports you know. We have to examine each application carefully."

"But you said the passports for the whites will come through soon."

"That is correct, ma'am. But not for the others, hey." The official slowly shook his head, glancing at his watch. It was three-thirty five in the afternoon, time to pack up for the day, his mind was on other matters, like buying a copy of Die Volksblad to read on his commute home in the train to Voortrekkerhoogte

It took many interviews in high places for permission for the non-white children to be allowed passports to travel overseas. The tour was successful and the dancers finally returned home. After a year of close association friendships across the colour line were formed but, when it was all over, each went their separate ways. Apartheid was still the law. Nothing had changed. Would it ever change, I asked myself

Chapter 54

Pretoria
Circa 1977.

"We'll have to get the blazes out of this country, said Bobby, "times are bad here and getting worse. The Laws will never change. People are still being racially classified so Katrina and I will never be able to marry." Outside a thunder storm raged, lightning flashed against the steel grey sky and hail stones hammered on the window-panes like Bobby's words in my head. I wanted to argue with him, tell him he should stay and work for change but I knew it to be a forlorn hope. More people were banned and detained without trial and more were dying mysteriously in detention. Biko, an advocate of non-violence, had a violent death. Bobby, involved with helping political activists cross the borders to neighbouring African states was, himself, in danger.

* * *

We stood around nervously as Bobby lined up to have his baggage checked in at Jan Smuts International Airport. His ticket was for Canada. The intercom crackled. The voice of the airport official calling his name. I felt my stomach contract in fear. Arthur approached the counter, enquiring on Bobby's behalf. If the police were looking for him, Arthur could signal us and Bobby could slip into the crowd.

"Ooh! *Ja meneer*, you forgot your baggage ticket, hey." The tension eased.

The hands of the clock on the wall moved forward. Time to enter Passport Control and Bobby joined the line-up. The intercom crackled again. I held my breath, watching two policemen approaching the line. They reached Bobby, hesitated, then walked on, stopping in front of someone further down. My breath hissed out. Bobby looked up with a grin, put up his thumb and waved cheerily then filed out through the door to the waiting plane.

The jet rose, and for a moment seemed to hang there. Swirls of black smoke billowing out of the exhausts. Time suspended, then soared with the rising plane. Nothing could happen now. Bobby was safe.

* * *

Mother was ailing.   She missed Bobby, and like me, she hated the family being separated.

"Damn apartheid," I said, then thought, *Could we possibly leave as well?* But I didn't say it for fear of upsetting my Mother. Could she travel and settle in another country at her age? Emma had. My mind was on the future - Mother's on the past.

"How strange it is that the course of one's life at times, seems to hang on the slimmest thread.   Is it chance or some divine plan?"

Silence as I considered her words.

"That's the Determinists belief - all things are determined by factors outside our control."

"It appears like that sometimes," said Mother, "that would mean we have no free will. It was St. Augustine, who said we could do nothing 'except by free choice of the will'."

"It's all so confusing," I said.   "Milton claimed God 'made man just and right, sufficient to have stood though free to fall' yet his writings make man a victim of God's predestined plan and Satan's prearranged plot."

Mother nodded.   "Do we have free will or does everything happen because of past events?   If the white farmer hadn't raped Ruth... if Paul's mother hadn't intervened to prevent his marriage to Sara... if the German sniper hadn't killed Gerry..." a tear trickled down her cheek as her voice trailed.

"And if you had had that abortion," I added.

"Don't remind me of that."

"That's alright, you had no choice. Times were bad."

"I had few choices because I was a woman, but Ruth, Sara and Emma had even fewer."   She frowned, shaking her head.

We sat at the breakfast table, Bobby's latest letter from Canada lay open before us.   He was staying with Pieter until he could get his own apartment. He and Katrina were making wedding plans.

I read Bobby's letter to Mother,

"Fancy that!" I commented, "Emma's grand-daughter and your grandson. It's so sad Emma missed all this."

Hetty had written in a previous letter, about her mother's death.

"Ma passed away peacefully. It was so strange, you know, how Ma settled in here. Almost as if she had found peace at last."

I turned back to Bobby's letter, repeating my remark, "Emma's grand-daughter and your grandson. That should make you happy. I stared out the window looking past the summer scene to an imagined winter landscape in Vancouver.

"Perhaps we could all get over for the wedding." I said but Mother hadn't heard. Her face was grey and her hand clutched her chest. Her breath was coming in gasps. I cried out in fear, running to her side. But there was nothing I could do.

Mother was the last of her generation.

We left South Africa shortly afterwards. There seemed "no hope" for any "great hope" of change. Apartheid remained the law. We could stay, pretending to lead a normal life. We could stay and become involved in resisting apartheid, but to many black people, sympathetic whites were suspect. The system gave us all the advantages. The fight was theirs. We could leave...

I remembered Anna and Ruth and where it all began. They found new hope in the friendship they forged. I remembered Lisa and Sara who strengthened the bond of friendship and I remembered Emma who lost all hope and broke the friendship. I remembered Hetty and her struggle to come to terms with the legacy of her great-grandfather. And then I remembered her daughter Katrina and my son Bobby, great- great-grandchildren of Anna and Ruth, bringing the families together in spite of apartheid.

EPILOGUE

Johannesburg
Circa 1994.

It's Tuesday in the township. The Soweto streets are noisy. Cabs careen around corners, spraying stones and sand. The joyous sound of singing rises with the wind that wafts into windows, lifting with the laughter, as a long line of patient people, like a brightly coloured snake with undulating sides, moves slowly forward while children play outside corner stores, kicking soccer balls or old tin cans.

Nellie looks out on the familiar street, lined on each side with the square box houses. She sits with N'tabu at the kitchen table with the blue plastic cloth, mugs of strong tea in their hands. They had voted early. She takes a sip, her hands shaking then wipes her open palm across her mouth and chin, then down the side of her apron as they listen to the voices singing the national anthem of the new South Africa.

"Oew!" she exclaims, "How can I believe such a thing? I don't know how I can say 'thank you God' that the suffering of our people is over.'" She remembers the years after Hanna died when she and N'tabu married and were allocated a house in Soweto, she remembers the difficult days, raising her own family and Hanna's while commuting daily to her job in the suburb; she remembers the school children marching in peaceful protest and she remembers when Philemon is shot while running away from the police. Nellie remembers it all. And now, the struggle is over.

"Now we can get a better house. Oew! I never think I can ever live in a house like my madam."

"What you mean we can get a better house? Where we get the money to get a better house?"

"You can get better job now at your work. You don' have to make the tea and clean the place no more."

"What better job?"

"*Meneer* van der Merwe's job."

"I can't do his work. I never learn it.

"But they say we can bet better jobs and better houses now. Jus' like the white people."

"How can we, we never go to school like white people. The government never spend money on our schools. Where the money come from now? Dr. Verwoerd, he say they mustn't let black people get too smart then who the white people got for servants? It going to take a long time for all our people to get educatin' so they can get the good jobs and the nice houses."

"Oew! N'tabu. Why you talk like this. Madiba, he say we can get all the things same as the white people."

"Ja, the A.N.C. make plenty promises but where the money come from. Apartheid did too many bad things it can take a long, long time to fix all that."

"The white people mus' pay more taxes."

"You think they will do that? Pay so much so the government can buy back the land they took from blacks; so they can put money for educatin' and hospitals?" he said, shaking his head. "It goin' to take a long time, mos' people won' see change. Maybe only Petrus' chil'ren will see change."

They sit silently while Nellie twists her apron around her fingers and N'tabu also recalls the past. He remembers when Hannna was arrested and sent back to the Homeland and he remembers meeting Nellie and struggling with his guilt along with all his other struggles. But now, they say, the struggle is over.

Nellie is not to be cast down.

"I dunno why you talk like this." She picks up the newspaper and with her forefinger marks out the words as she reads from Mandela's speech. "Madiba, he say 'the election is a realisation of our hopes and dreams.' I got hope, the people got hope. Why you think they wait so long in the streets to vote today?"

"How can everything be alright jus' by voting? The people mus' stop robbing and killing but they do that because they got no money, because they got not jobs. White people won't put their money to make jobs when there is so much violence."

"I know there was too many years when the people don't have hope, but now, they can have hope." Nellie jumps up from the table, pulling N'tabu with her and stamps out some dance steps, arms waving and fingers snapping.

"O out of that no hope, what great hope have you?"
William Shakespeare: The Tempest.

FAMILY TREE 1:

Anna   m.   Frederick

Martha	Lisa	Anton
b. 1872	b.1874	b.1875
	m.	
	Jack Patrickson	

Jack	Meg	Harry	Danny
	b.1896		b.1903
	m.		m.
	Tom		Winnie

Davey	Johnny	Kate	
		b.1928	
		m.	
		Arthur	

Bobby	Alexa	Vicky
b.1952	b.1955	b.1958
m		

Katrina (Hetty's daughter)

FAMILY TREE 2:

Nkiwe (Ruth)   m.   Tembu

Joe

Raped by Frikkie (white farmer)

Sara
b. 1876
m.
Sol Meintjies

Emma   Jakob
b. 1896   b. 1903
m.   m.
Etienne Frobisher   Mtonya

Jan   Hetty   Many children   N'tabu
b.1918   b.1928   b. 1928
                  m.   m.

          Herman Kruger   (1)   Hanna
                                                         d.1960
Susie   Pieter   Katrina   Samuel   Elsie
b.1951   b.1952   b.1958   b.1952   b.1953
                            m.
                  Bobby (Kate's son)

                                                (2)   Nellie

                                        Petrus Philemon Lizzie Lettie
                                        b.1955   b.1957   b.1958 b.1959

WHAT HOPE HAVE YOU!

Glossary of South African Terms.

kopje	Small hill.
veld	Prairie
Karoo	Semi-desert area in South Africa
donga	Ravine
putu	Thick corn meal porridge
dung	Compacted cattle manure
nie	No
hulle is dom	They are stupid
doeks	Head scarves
mielie	Corn
lobola	Money paid by bridegroom to bride's father usually paid in cows
tula babba	Keep quiet, baby.
baie warm	Very hot.
kaffir	Derogatory term for a black person
kraal	Enclosure within which tribal huts are erected.
God in Hemel!	God in Heaven!
asseblief, baas.	Please, master
hou stil	Keep quiet
waarom is jy so laat?	Why are you so late?
cicadas	Crickets.
spoor	Trail or footprint.
maas	Sour or curdled milk.
baas	Boss or master
Dominee	Minister of Religion
biltong	Jerky
kind	Child
alles sal regkom.	Everything will turn out right.
middag	Good day
meneer	Mister
mevrou	Mrs.
tot siens	Goodbye
wag 'n bietjie	Wait a minute
baie dankie	Thank you very much
stoep	Porch or verandah
asseblief	Please
uitlanders	Foreigners

Boers	Farmers
Witwatersrand	Ridge of White Waters
koeksusters	Doughnut type of cake
dis nie probleem nie.	It is not a problem
braai	Barbecue
dorp	Small town
dit is baie sleg.	It is very bad
Oom Paul	Uncle Paul (affectionate term for President Paul Kruger)
melk tert	Milk tart
goeie more	Good morning
kappie	Bonnet
wat makeer?	What is the matter?
krantz	Steep sided valley
hou stil	Be quiet
Swartbooi	Black marked
kom nou	Come now
Rontbooi	Red marked
braai vleis	Barbecued meat
konfyt	Jam
meebos	Dried apricots
goei middag mevrou	Good afternoon madam
ek weet	I know
sy is baie pragtig.	She is very pretty
exkus	Excuse me
Pommie	Slang term for a British person
laager	Circle of wagons
asseblief	Please
here	Gentlemen
dames	Ladies
blankes alleen	Whites only
Suikerbosfontein	Sugarbush fountain
koop die "Cape Times"	Buy the "Cape Times"
kerel	Young man
wat makeer my liefde	What is the matter my love?
donga	dry river bed
Egoli	African's name for Johannesburg "city of gold"
bioscope	movie house
piccanins	small children
Vroue Federasie	Women's Institute
ouma	grandmother

jy weet?	do you know?
boet	brother
Uitlanders	foreigners
domkop	stupid
oupa	grandfather
braaivleis	barbecue
koeksusters	sweet cakes similar to doughnuts
Mevrou	Mrs.
stoep	verandah
I.D.B.	illicit diamong buying
Jy weet, groot geraas!	Big trouble!
knobkerrie	Knob-headed wooden stick
Khosa	A southern African tribe
mielie-pap	corn-meal porridge
Meneer	Mister
Khula	Big
Tsotsie	A bad street person.
Skelm	A naughty person
Bobbejaan	Monkey
Tokoloshe	Mythical beings supposed to live near certain rivers and used for purposes of witchcraft by witchdoctors.
Konfyt	Jam or jelly
Domkop	Stupid
Madiba	African name for Mandella

Piet-my-vrou   indigenous bird with distinctive call
(Afrikaans) sounding like its name - usually heard in the early mornings.
Knobkerrie   thick stick carved from wood with round
(Afrikaans) knob at top - carried by African men.

Hemel	Heaven
Kaffirs	derogatory term for black people
Jy weet	you know.
Veld	grassland or prairie

Khosana (Zulu) pronounced inkosana:eldest son or prince, son of respected person.Used deferentially
Khosazana, pronounced inkosazana: eldest daughter, or princess, daughter of respected person.

Homeland   Areas of S.A.designated by the govt. to be tribal homelands of Africans. 80% of the people allocated 13% of the land.

Egoli   African name for Johannesburg-city of Gold

Voetsak   get out!   (Afrikaans)

Xhosa   an African tribe.

Mielie-pap   porridge made from ground corn.(Afrikaans)

Mielie-meal   ground corn

John Vorster Sq.   Security police headquarters

Monkey's wedding   When the sun shines in the rain.

Rocks   short for "rock-spiders" (creatures who live under rocks. A derogatory term for Afrikaners used by English-speaking S.A. implying being dumb and devious. The majority of the government and police force were Afrikaners, referred to as "rock-spiders" or "rocks" for short.

BIBLIOGRAPHY

Bunting, Brian. The Rise of The South African Reich. England: Penguin, 1964.

de Villiers, Marq. White Tribe Dreaming.   Canada: MacMillan,   1987.

Farwell,   Byron.   The   Great   Anglo-Boer   War.   Canada: Fitzhenry &Whiteside,   1976.

Goodwin, June.   Cry Amandla!   New York: Africana, 1984.

Kruger, Rayne.   Good-Bye Dolly Gray.   London: Cassell, 1959.

Kuzwayo, Ellen.   Call Me Woman.   Ravan Press: Johannesburg, 1985.

Lapping, Brian.   Apartheid, A History.   England:Grafton,   1986.

Laurence, John.   The Seeds of Disaster.   England: Gollancz,   1968.

Mandela, Nelson.   Long Walk to Freedom.   United States, Little, Brown, 1994.

Mathabane, Mark.   Kaffir Boy.   New York: MacMillan,1986.

Wheatroff, Geoffrey.   The Randlords.   London: Weiderfeld,1985.

Printed in the United States
2337